THE APC

Deep in “
South Ara
correspond
beautiful Amira Shallai, an Egyptian research physician, come together at an out-post of the New Peace Corps. Neither is aware that the idealists and soldiers of fortune they encounter there are secretly intent on a mission that could change the world . . .

We are en route to the climax of Alfred Coppell’s enthralling new novel wherein:

Revolutionaries in Saudi Arabia overturn the government and hold more than a hundred Western diplomats hostage in the American Embassy. . .

The head of the CIA and his mistress, keeping a tryst on his yacht on the Potomac, are interrupted by a masked assassin. . .

A famous New York publisher leaps from a window of his East Side town house. . .

A billionaire philanthropist, famed for his constructive good works, funds in secret a mercenary army bent on destruction. . .

Are these random happenings, or are they part of a lethal, grand design?

Also by Alfred Coppel

THE HASTINGS CONSPIRACY

and published by Corgi Books

The Apocalypse Brigade

Alfred Coppel

CORGI BOOKS

A DIVISION OF TRANSWORLD PUBLISHERS LTD

THE APOCALYPSE BRIGADE

A CORGI BOOK 0 552 12078 2

Originally published in Great Britain
by Macmillan London Ltd.

PRINTING HISTORY
Macmillan edition published 1981
Corgi edition published 1982
Corgi edition reprinted 1982

This book is set in 9½/10 Paladium

Corgi Books are published by
Transworld Publishers Ltd.,
Century House, 61-63 Uxbridge Road,
Ealing, London W5 5SA

Made and printed in Great Britain
by Hunt Barnard Printing Ltd, Aylesbury, Bucks.

To Billy Abrahams, for enthusiasm
and dedication beyond the call of duty

Apocalypse: 1. the "revelation" of the future granted to St. John in the isle of Patmos. The book of the New Testament in which this is recorded.

– *Oxford English Dictionary*

And he that overcometh, and keepeth my works unto the end, to him will I give power over the nations . . . .

– *Revelation of St. John the Divine 2:26*

One
July 12, the first day

And whoso slays a believer willfully,
his recompense is Gehenna, therein
dwelling forever.

—Holy Qur'ân, fourth sura

1 Washington, D.C.

The waters of the Potomac felt like warm velvet as the girl swam slowly around the anchored sloop in the summer twilight. The heat of the day had raised a thin mist from the river: it haloed the lights that were coming on along the shore of Cobb Island and almost obscured the glow of Colonial Beach on the western shore. The wind, never strong at this time of year, had died completely, leaving the surface of the river dark and smooth as a mirror.

Candace Moran could see the tiny anchor light on the *Pandora's* spar reflecting a thin, yellow path on the water. The finger of light seemed to follow her as she swam. She noted that Cole had the cabin lamps on now. She guessed that he was still hunched over the chart table, working on those papers that demanded all of his attention since they dropped anchor a thousand yards from the shore of Cobb Island.

It had not been one of their more notable afternoons, the girl thought sulkily. She had been Cole Norris's mistress for almost a year, and she understood that a man of his age—and one with so much on his mind—could not always behave like a young lover. But recently Cole's moods had become impenetrable, and Candy was apprehensive about the future.

Their assignations aboard the *Pandora,* Cole's small sloop, were a reasonably well kept secret in the Central Intelligence Agency. This was remarkable in Washington, where gossip and loose talk are common coin. But if the Director of Central Intelligence couldn't have a clandestine relationship, she told herself, who in the world could.

She rolled onto her back and shivered sensually at the flow of the water over her body. She ran a hand over her large breasts, barely cupped by the string bikini top. She felt the water's heat penetrate her loins as she kicked

languorously in a wide circle around the anchored boat. Surely Cole must be finished with his work by now.

She turned back onto her stomach and began to swim toward the *Pandora*. Far upriver she could see the bluish brightness in the mist caused by the lights of the battery of huge purification plants near Alexandria. Completed in the mid-1980s, they had finally brought the great river back to life. Beyond lay the amber glow of Washington, fading rapidly at the zenith, where the river mist thinned to allow a few stars to be seen.

As she approached the *Pandora*'s black fiberglass hull, the lights of the far shore glinted in the mirror finish. Like all of Cole Norris's possessions, the *Pandora* was tidy, meticulously kept. She thought of herself at the same moment and smiled. Cole's taste couldn't be faulted. He liked pretty things. Like the *Pandora*. Like me, Candy thought. The idea made her feel better, more secure. Cole wouldn't give up something he enjoyed. And Candy Moran knew how to give a man like Cole pleasure. If he was moody and distracted these days, it wasn't his sex life that was troubling him. It was his job. These were terrible days to be DCI—Candy Moran had been around Washington long enough to know that. Troubles with the Congress, a President Cole couldn't be sure of, revolutions in Arabia and Central America. Cole had every right to be preoccupied. And it was her job, Candy thought, to take the great man's mind off his problems.

She caught the boarding ladder and hung weightless in the water for a moment, thinking about Cole. He was an older man, with one of the most sensitive and important jobs in the administration. Candy was not an overly brilliant girl, but she had a full understanding of what powerful men required of their women.

In a swift movement, she slipped off the tiny patch of her bikini bottom. Then she pulled the tie loose and removed her bra. It was delicious, she thought, how the removal of so little could make her feel so *naked*. She crumpled the minuscule swimming suit into a ball and tossed it up onto the deck.

Weight shifted aboard the sloop and set it to rocking slightly in the brackish tide.

Candy Moran smiled and climbed the ladder. The air felt almost as warm as the water. She glistened in the light

1 Washington, D.C.

The waters of the Potomac felt like warm velvet as the girl swam slowly around the anchored sloop in the summer twilight. The heat of the day had raised a thin mist from the river: it haloed the lights that were coming on along the shore of Cobb Island and almost obscured the glow of Colonial Beach on the western shore. The wind, never strong at this time of year, had died completely, leaving the surface of the river dark and smooth as a mirror.

Candace Moran could see the tiny anchor light on the *Pandora*'s spar reflecting a thin, yellow path on the water. The finger of light seemed to follow her as she swam. She noted that Cole had the cabin lamps on now. She guessed that he was still hunched over the chart table, working on those papers that demanded all of his attention since they dropped anchor a thousand yards from the shore of Cobb Island.

It had not been one of their more notable afternoons, the girl thought sulkily. She had been Cole Norris's mistress for almost a year, and she understood that a man of his age—and one with so much on his mind—could not always behave like a young lover. But recently Cole's moods had become impenetrable, and Candy was apprehensive about the future.

Their assignations aboard the *Pandora*, Cole's small sloop, were a reasonably well kept secret in the Central Intelligence Agency. This was remarkable in Washington, where gossip and loose talk are common coin. But if the Director of Central Intelligence couldn't have a clandestine relationship, she told herself, who in the world could.

She rolled onto her back and shivered sensually at the flow of the water over her body. She ran a hand over her large breasts, barely cupped by the string bikini top. She felt the water's heat penetrate her loins as she kicked

languorously in a wide circle around the anchored boat. Surely Cole must be finished with his work by now.

She turned back onto her stomach and began to swim toward the *Pandora*. Far upriver she could see the bluish brightness in the mist caused by the lights of the battery of huge purification plants near Alexandria. Completed in the mid-1980s, they had finally brought the great river back to life. Beyond lay the amber glow of Washington, fading rapidly at the zenith, where the river mist thinned to allow a few stars to be seen.

As she approached the *Pandora*'s black fiberglass hull, the lights of the far shore glinted in the mirror finish. Like all of Cole Norris's possessions, the *Pandora* was tidy, meticulously kept. She thought of herself at the same moment and smiled. Cole's taste couldn't be faulted. He liked pretty things. Like the *Pandora*. Like me, Candy thought. The idea made her feel better, more secure. Cole wouldn't give up something he enjoyed. And Candy Moran knew how to give a man like Cole pleasure. If he was moody and distracted these days, it wasn't his sex life that was troubling him. It was his job. These were terrible days to be DCI—Candy Moran had been around Washington long enough to know that. Troubles with the Congress, a President Cole couldn't be sure of, revolutions in Arabia and Central America. Cole had every right to be preoccupied. And it was her job, Candy thought, to take the great man's mind off his problems.

She caught the boarding ladder and hung weightless in the water for a moment, thinking about Cole. He was an older man, with one of the most sensitive and important jobs in the administration. Candy was not an overly brilliant girl, but she had a full understanding of what powerful men required of their women.

In a swift movement, she slipped off the tiny patch of her bikini bottom. Then she pulled the tie loose and removed her bra. It was delicious, she thought, how the removal of so little could make her feel so *naked*. She crumpled the minuscule swimming suit into a ball and tossed it up onto the deck.

Weight shifted aboard the sloop and set it to rocking slightly in the brackish tide.

Candy Moran smiled and climbed the ladder. The air felt almost as warm as the water. She glistened in the light

1 Washington, D.C.

The waters of the Potomac felt like warm velvet as the girl swam slowly around the anchored sloop in the summer twilight. The heat of the day had raised a thin mist from the river: it haloed the lights that were coming on along the shore of Cobb Island and almost obscured the glow of Colonial Beach on the western shore. The wind, never strong at this time of year, had died completely, leaving the surface of the river dark and smooth as a mirror.

Candace Moran could see the tiny anchor light on the *Pandora*'s spar reflecting a thin, yellow path on the water. The finger of light seemed to follow her as she swam. She noted that Cole had the cabin lamps on now. She guessed that he was still hunched over the chart table, working on those papers that demanded all of his attention since they dropped anchor a thousand yards from the shore of Cobb Island.

It had not been one of their more notable afternoons, the girl thought sulkily. She had been Cole Norris's mistress for almost a year, and she understood that a man of his age—and one with so much on his mind—could not always behave like a young lover. But recently Cole's moods had become impenetrable, and Candy was apprehensive about the future.

Their assignations aboard the *Pandora*, Cole's small sloop, were a reasonably well kept secret in the Central Intelligence Agency. This was remarkable in Washington, where gossip and loose talk are common coin. But if the Director of Central Intelligence couldn't have a clandestine relationship, she told herself, who in the world could.

She rolled onto her back and shivered sensually at the flow of the water over her body. She ran a hand over her large breasts, barely cupped by the string bikini top. She felt the water's heat penetrate her loins as she kicked

languorously in a wide circle around the anchored boat. Surely Cole must be finished with his work by now.

She turned back onto her stomach and began to swim toward the *Pandora*. Far upriver she could see the bluish brightness in the mist caused by the lights of the battery of huge purification plants near Alexandria. Completed in the mid-1980s, they had finally brought the great river back to life. Beyond lay the amber glow of Washington, fading rapidly at the zenith, where the river mist thinned to allow a few stars to be seen.

As she approached the *Pandora*'s black fiberglass hull, the lights of the far shore glinted in the mirror finish. Like all of Cole Norris's possessions, the *Pandora* was tidy, meticulously kept. She thought of herself at the same moment and smiled. Cole's taste couldn't be faulted. He liked pretty things. Like the *Pandora*. Like me, Candy thought. The idea made her feel better, more secure. Cole wouldn't give up something he enjoyed. And Candy Moran knew how to give a man like Cole pleasure. If he was moody and distracted these days, it wasn't his sex life that was troubling him. It was his job. These were terrible days to be DCI—Candy Moran had been around Washington long enough to know that. Troubles with the Congress, a President Cole couldn't be sure of, revolutions in Arabia and Central America. Cole had every right to be preoccupied. And it was her job, Candy thought, to take the great man's mind off his problems.

She caught the boarding ladder and hung weightless in the water for a moment, thinking about Cole. He was an older man, with one of the most sensitive and important jobs in the administration. Candy was not an overly brilliant girl, but she had a full understanding of what powerful men required of their women.

In a swift movement, she slipped off the tiny patch of her bikini bottom. Then she pulled the tie loose and removed her bra. It was delicious, she thought, how the removal of so little could make her feel so *naked*. She crumpled the minuscule swimming suit into a ball and tossed it up onto the deck.

Weight shifted aboard the sloop and set it to rocking slightly in the brackish tide.

Candy Moran smiled and climbed the ladder. The air felt almost as warm as the water. She glistened in the light

shining into the cockpit from the open companionway.

She stood for a moment, one hand on the furled mainsail. She stepped into the cockpit and posed near the helm so that Cole would get the full effect when he climbed the companionway ladder. We'll make love right here, she thought, here in the open. She called huskily: 'Cole. I'm back. Come on up and see.'

There was a movement below. Cole blotted out the light as he filled the companionway. He started to climb the ladder. He seemed larger than life. Too big, too broad. There was something strange about his face. She was startled. Her own nakedness that had so pleased her, just a moment ago, became vulnerability. The breath congealed in her throat. Her skin felt as though the air had turned icy. She felt the beginnings of cold terror, because the figure that had risen from the belly of the sloop was certainly not Cole Norris. It was immense. Its skin was black and shiny. It had a round, flat face that reflected lights, like tiny stars. She moved, and her own dark image shone there, in the flat, dark void.

For just an instant she caught a glimpse of a man lying faceup on the cabin sole. Oh, God, it was Cole and his eyes were open, unseeing.

She screamed.

The assassin in the dry suit slashed with a knife. Candy felt a searing pain, like the touch of a whip, across her breasts. She clutched at them and felt her fingers touch something hideous and unfamiliar.

She looked down, shocked, and would have screamed again, but a black-gloved hand caught her hair, expertly jerked her head back. Then the blade razored across her throat almost severing her head from her body.

The killer let her crumple onto the teak grating and coldly, dispassionately, set to work.

Tomas Vano, the harbormaster of the Colonial Beach Yacht Club anchorage, puffed alight an evil-smelling twisted rope of an Italian cigar and regarded with wicked amusement the young security man's attempt to slide his chair closer to the open door of the tiny dock office. Perched on shore close to the finger piers, the cluttered room was sheltered from any breeze that might blow over the river. The air reeked of bitter smoke and the garlicky bouquet of the remains of Vano's supper of spaghetti *alla vongole*. The harbormaster always made a point of having his meal sent in when the DCI was out on the *Pandora*.

John Rees, the security man, was a recent recruit to the Agency's CI Directorate. He had never before drawn the assignment old hands called 'the seat on *Pandora*'s box.' Generally it was more experienced counter-intelligence officers who guarded the DCI's back while he was on the boat with one of his women. But Rees was conscientious and able. It seemed to him that this particular procedure was a major flaw in the wall of security surrounding Director Norris. But the DCI was not a man one lectured on the subject of security. It he chose to sail alone with his mistress of the moment, he wouldn't hear any criticism about it from a very junior security officer named John Rees.

Still, Rees thought, there would be hell to pay if the DCI's minivacations on his boat ever became common knowledge. Other men as high in the administration could make free with the city's secretarial pools, but the DCI was supposed to be cleaner than Caesar's wife. It was one of the odd remnants of the Company's purgatory after Watergate.

Rees checked the time and unlocked the case of communications gear that came with this assignment. Norris was entitled to some privacy, but that didn't free him of the responsibility of answering a radio call each sixty minutes he was out of his bodyguard's sight. If that interrupted his screwing, Rees thought, that was just tough.

He opened the case and snapped on the power. When the built-in quartz-crystal chronometer-encoder came up exactly on 2105 hours, he keyed the transponder. The amber light showed that the duplicate equipment on board the *Pandora* was working properly. Rees lifted the microphone to his lips and said quietly: 'Twenty-six, check in please.'

A great cloud of acrid smoke from Captain Vano's cigar drifted toward the open door.

'Twenty-six. Check in now, please,' Rees said again.

The speaker in the case was silent. Rees frowned.

'Problem?' Vano was not a believer in all the fancy electronic gear he had seen on *Pandora*. Stuff like that, he often said, never worked properly in a marine environment.

'Twenty-six, this is twenty. You are thirty seconds overdue. Come in.'

Captain Vano stubbed the cigar in a littered ashtray. 'Let me try to raise him on channel twelve,' he said, suppressing a grin at his inadvertent pun. If that Moran piece and her beautiful tits couldn't raise Norris, nothing on the radio ever would.

He picked up the mike of the large marine UHF set mounted over his desk and said: '*Pandora,* this is the Colonial Beach harbormaster. Over.'

The speaker of the UHF hissed and whispered with the distant voices using the same ship-to-shore channel at the limit of the set's range, but there was nothing from the *Pandora*.

'*Pandora, Pandora,* this is Colonial Beach,' Vano said again. 'Come in. *Pandora*.'

Rees studied the chronometer. 'He's more than a minute late. Let's call the Coast Guard.'

'Easy does it, Mr. Rees,' Vano said skeptically. It offended his seaman's sense of the fitness of things to call the Coasties unless things were really unraveling. 'He's probably busy. Jesus, he isn't alone, you know.'

Rees hesitated. At the time of the last contact, *Pandora* had been at anchor off Cobb Island and snugged down for several hours' stay. It was possible that the DCI was not responding because he was busy with Candy Moran— But no. Rees made up his mind abruptly. 'Call the Coast Guard, Captain Vano. Do it now.'

On the foredeck of the *Pandora* the anchor light cast a dim illumination on a scene from hell. The assassin, his rubbery skin smeared with Candy Moran's blood, had just finished fastening a sixty-pound weightbelt around the corpse of Cole Norris. Candy's mutilated body lay in a congealing puddle in the boat's cockpit. Her blood, running through the cockpit drains, streaked the gleaming black transom and dripped, ever more slowly, into the dark water under the stern.

The killer inspected the foredeck critically. Satisfied, he hauled in the anchor rode, chain, and the light Danforth anchor. He stowed everything neatly in the foredeck locker.

The sluggish current began to drift the sloop toward the lights of the main channel. This section of the Potomac was called Kettle Bottom Shoals and the average depth of water here was no more than ten feet at low tide. But there was more depth in the ship channel—twenty to thirty feet.

The man in the dry suit was sweating in the heat. He moved aft, stepping carefully over the sticky cockpit grating, and he went below. He studied the cabin carefully for a time, then gathered the papers Norris had been working on at the chart table. The killer unzipped his suit and thrust the papers inside, against his chest. He zipped the suit closed again and snapped off the master switch, a red toggle on the boat's electrical panel. *Pandora* was now totally dark.

The assassin once again emerged into the cockpit. He did not give the savagely slashed body there a second glance. It was no longer of any interest to him.

A voice from below startled him and he froze in the act of stepping over the coaming.

Someone said distinctly: '*Twenty-six, check in please.*'

The killer's breath hissed through his teeth as he realized he was hearing the self-contained radio gear he had been told Norris always carried aboard the yacht.

'Twenty-six, this is twenty. You are thirty seconds overdue. Come in.' There was a note of anxiety in the voice. The assassin ignored it and stepped up onto the cabin top. He stood, judging the sloop's rate and direction of drift. In the near distance a pair of channel buoys flashed their lights at four-second intervals. The mist was thickening. The shore of Cobb Island was almost invisible.

He made his way forward now to where Cole Norris's body lay. He lifted it over the toe rail and under the lifelines and then released it. He stood for a time and looked at the water as the body disappeared beneath the surface.

All tasks completed, the assassin recovered his rebreather and strapped it across his chest. He preferred rebreathing gear for this kind of attack. In his SEAL days in Vietnam, he had used it often. Depth was limited with a rebreather, but this water was as shallow and murky as the Mekong. And the equipment left no telltale trail of bubbles as an aqualung would do.

He sat on the cabin top and pulled on his fins. Then he sealed his faceplate, took the rebreather mouthpiece in his teeth, and lowered himself into the water.

The *Pandora*, derelict and crewed only by the corpse of Candy Moran, onetime secretary in the McLean headquarters of the United States Central Intelligence Agency, drifted slowly through the deepwater channel. In the unlighted cabin a voice said, '*Twenty-six, this is twenty. We are on the way.*' But Candy Moran did not hear it, nor did Director Cole Norris, lying in the silt and mud of Kettle Bottom Shoals under four fathoms of blood-warm water.

TWO
July 13, the second day

The developing world . . . sees increasing the explicit politicization of the international economy as an opportunity to forge a new economic order more favorable to its interests. By contrast . . . Western governments see politicization as a threat to both economic prosperity and political harmony. The containment and reversal of the trend toward increasing politicization are among the most urgent international problems of the next decade.

—Fred Hirsch, *The 1980s Project:*
'Alternatives to Monetary Disorder'

2 Lugano, Swi rland

shington, July 8th

Michael:

After all this time you will be surprise receive a letter from me. Let me put your mind at rest. his is no olive branch. I still feel about you exactly as I d when you left the Company. And knowing you, I do no delude myself that you have changed your opinion of us.

I am offering you something that, as a journalist, I do not think you will ignore. It will appeal to your writer's sense of omnipotence. You may suspect that I am using you. Be assured that I am. It happens that we have, at this moment, a community of motives. As a newsman, with the breed's unbridled taste for meddling, you can do me—and possibly your country—a service.

I am compiling a special report for the President, and I am sending you a copy. It is, of course, highly classified, which means that I am putting my ass in your tender care. You know that I would not do a thing like this if I had any other option. This is serious business.

The main subject of the report is Calder Smith Davis and his most recent project: a kind of holy rota of sanctimonious capitalists and politicians known as the International Strategic Studies Group. You may have heard of it. It is not secret, though the members do not exactly seek public notice. I have spent some time investigating the ISSG and its ties to the New Peace Corps that the Davis and Smith trusts have been bankrolling for almost seven years.

Davis is seventy-six now, and there isn't a cannier man in America. He is, as you probably know, a Trilateralist and a member of the Club of Rome. He has been a Bilderberger since that group was formed. What you may not know is that Vincent Loomis dotes on him. I do not expect anyone at the White House to be delighted with my report.

Recently, speaking [illegible]meeting of the Commonwealth Club in San Francisco[illegible]is said that 'though there are no direct connections be[illegible]n the ISSG and the New Peace Corps' future selecti[illegible] NPC projects may be made after consultation betwee[illegible] two groups. As far as I have been able to learn direct[illegible]the NPC is still the global troop of do-gooders it has [illegible]ays been—despite the enlistment of a number of people [illegible] curious background. The report will dwell on that poi[illegible]at some length. What is peculiar is that since the formati[illegible] of the ISSG, the New Peace Corps has been growing at [illegible]prodigious rate and is said to be straining even the enorm[illegible]s resources of the Davis and Smith family trusts.

Knowing yo[illegible] tender regard for the brown races, you no doubt approv[illegible] of the NPC. Read my report with an open mind and *without* prejudice. Try, if you can, to forget that it was I who wrote it.

I have sent this letter directly to your not-so-secret bolt-hole in Switzerland. Yes, Michael, we do keep track of our former officers, and we are not the only ones. So exercise some care how you handle the material you receive from me. I am sending it to you in care of your publisher, Samuel Abbott. Drop what you are doing and come to New York to take charge of it. Sam will not want to hold it long. And don't give him a bad time about his connection with us. Remember you once had such a connection yourself.

I have never liked that self-righteousness in you that allowed you to pass judgment on what we did in Laos. You allowed yourself to become too personally involved with the Meo and the Montagnards. You expect right to prevail simply because it is right. Only a fool believes that, so take care. I bring this up not because I have any hope you will ever change, but because I want you to understand that there is a certain amount of danger in what I am putting in your hands. The Administration is stiff with ISSG people and they will not like what I am doing.

If this sounds paranoid, put it down to my having spent so many years inside the Company. You will hear from me again after I have spoken to the President.

Cole

For an hour, since ending his telephone conversation with

Isaac Holt, Michael Rivas had been watching the summer fog receding down the broad expanse of the Po Valley. Nearer at hand, the lake of Lugano and the town on the shore were still covered with mist, but the two mountains flanking the lake, Bre and Generoso, were bright green in the light of the morning sun. Soon it would begin to grow warmer, and by midday the tower apartment in the villa where Rivas lived would be suffocating. The lovely view would be hazed by the yellow industrial smog rising from the factories of Milan, one hundred kilometers to the south.

Rivas was hardly conscious of the morning coolness. Holt's news had numbed his senses. His brother was dead—killed, Ike Holt said, by some ragtag terrorist group who would probably be claiming the crime within days, or even hours. Rivas had asked if it was possible that the KGB had been responsible. Cole was a Cold Warrior. But Holt doubted that this had been a Soviet action.

Rivas understood the dangers of Cole's work, but he had made it into the upper echelons. He was a supergrade—the CIA equivalent of a general. He had been, in fact, *the* supergrade—the DCI. Generals shouldn't die like this. But apparently sometimes they did.

He touched Cole's letter on the worktable before him. He had found it waiting on his return from Afghanistan. A surprise, because Cole would have had to be desperate to turn to his wetback brother for help.

Yet the letter hadn't been written by a man afraid for his life. For his career, yes. For his reputation as the hard-bitten, good-Nazi superspy. The DCI. The man at the apex of the dark pyramid. Rivas knew his brother well enough to know that he hadn't been expecting violence when he wrote it. How surprised, how *indignant*, Cole must have been when the assassin struck.

Cole Norris and Michael Rivas had not met face-to-face since a distant afternoon on an airfield in Thailand almost a dozen years ago.

Yet there he is, Rivas thought, touching the letter again with his fingertips. The distilled Cole Norris, come back from the grave for a last shot at the younger brother.

Cole's personality came through the lines of the letter loud and clear. That crack about the brown races. So typical. He had never been able to make peace with the fact that his mother had married again after divorcing his father. And to someone outside the Anglo-Saxon Protestant pale that meant so much to the Norris clan. Rivas smiled mirthlessly. The elegant Spaniards of the Rivas family had been equally dismayed when their son gave their ancient name to a *gringa*, and worse—a divorced woman, a non-Catholic.

It all depended on the point of view, Rivas thought. The ancestors in morion and breastplate he remembered from the dark portraits on the adobe walls of the vast ranch house in Guerrero—to a small, light-skinned boy it had seemed that they were frowning their disapproval of *him*.

He ran a hand over his stubbled cheeks wearily. He had arrived only yesterday afternoon. The flight from Karachi had been long, rough, and grimy. The month he had spent in the high mountains of the Hindu Kush had worn him down. The Mujahadeen Afghans had their war to fight and their lives to protect. It had been left to him to keep up or not. The Russians in the patrolling gunships would not have cared that he carried only notebook and camera. Too many years of losing conscript soldiers in a guerrilla war made them even more tired and nervy than the Afghan resistance fighters they were doggedly trying to exterminate. They strafed and napalmed anything that moved in the cold, arid mountains. Rivas had begun to wonder if he had not grown too old, at forty-one, for the kind of work he did.

And yet, he thought, I am alive. It is Cole who is dead. How is that for irony, brother mine?

He turned and went into the tiny kitchen to put water to boil for *caffè filtro*. There was more than a nighttime bitterness in his mouth. There was the coppery flavor of death.

The kitchen was cold, as all the rooms were. This was, as Cole had written, a hiding place. A shelter where he could rest between assignments, or work when the mood struck him. He had been writing a novel for years. It would never be finished, but he came to it as to a lover, after a time in the moraine valleys of Afghanistan or the rain forests of Paraguay. He was a journalist who specialized in all the places in the world where man was being beastly to his fellow man. For a moment he wondered how Isaac Holt had found him so quickly, and then he didn't wonder at all. Naturally, the Company would know precisely where to find the dead DCI's half brother. He must have been *very* tired to think otherwise, even for a moment.

He poured the boiling water into the filter pot and carried it, with a cup, back to the worktable. He was thinking distractedly about the proud Mujahadeen he had been with only two days before. They were still sniping Soviet soldiers with their antiquated Enfields. And Rivas had wanted so very badly to find that they were being supplied with weapons and medical materiel by the Agency. He had wanted that to be true. But he had found no evidence of it at all. The grizzled old men and boys who were killing three hundred Russians a week were doing it with rifles and bullets they bought at exorbitant prices from the gunsmiths on the other side of the Pakistani border.

The Agency had brought in a few supplies in 1980, enough to make a campaigning President appear resolute. And then the Mujahadeen had been abandoned, just as the highland Meo had been, all those years ago in Southeast Asia.

Rivas drank some scalding *caffë* and wondered, How much did Cole have to do with *that* decision?

He sat down in an unsteady chair and rested his head on his arms. Fatigue swept through him in waves. So did the memories.

He thought about the girl on Cole's boat. Somehow it was a double insult to Cole that a mistress of his should be so treated. Cole used women the way other men used liquor. They were his anodyne for the pressures he lived with, for all the cruel, shitty things a man on the way to becoming an Agency supergrade had to do.

Cole had always regarded himself as one of the chosen, which made the insult of murder just that much worse. The strange thing about it was that Rivas felt it, too. Ironically, it was the *latino* part of his heritage that responded. Would Cole have laughed at that? Or had he been counting on it when he wrote?

Which brought Rivas back to the letter. He raised his head and read it still again. It had not been sent to his flat in San Francisco, which was the nearest thing to a home he had. Cole had sent it directly here to Switzerland. It had been mailed in Washington five days before. Had he had time to complete his report to the President? Was it in Sam Abbott's possession now? On its way to him? Or had it never been finished? Cole had left him no option. By getting himself killed he had given the whole matter a dark force that Rivas could not ignore.

He stared for a time at the dimly reflected self-image in the window behind the worktable. A lean, drawn man with dark shaggy hair turning gray. A deeply lined face with slightly Asiatic eyes, a cheek scarred by the tip of a North Vietnamese bayonet. Cole had inherited their handsome mother's good looks. Michael—Miguel on his American birth certificate—looked like his father. Like one of Cortez's captains, his mother used to say.

He held the letter thoughtfully. How like the man it was: Tinged with irony. Cold, distant. Sibling distaste in almost every line. But quixotic, very. It wasn't like Cole to tilt at windmills, and that is what investigating an American legend like Calder Smith Davis was—an act of foolish bravery. Or perhaps simply a foolish act.

Davis was a giant. Born early in the century to immense wealth, he was the survivor of four brothers. The older Davises, Stansfield, Courtney, and Bertram, had devoted their lives to patrician public service. They had been ambassadors, special envoys, Cabinet members. Stansfield had even made a try for the presidency. But he had failed because Americans no longer bestowed the presidency on patricians. Stansfield Davis had died a disappointed man.

Calder had taken a different road. He was a businessman and financier. He had never sought public office. He was known—no one of his wealth and power could be anonymous—but he was not, had never been, a public man.

Yet it was Calder Smith Davis who had removed the curse of public envy from the Davis billions. It was Calder who made the Davis name a synonym for dynamic, worldwide philanthropy.

Through the Davis and Smith family trusts and the huge Davis Foundation, enormous sums of money were channeled into projects all over the world. The foundation supported medical research, reclamation projects, study groups, and scholarships. The arts and sciences were heavily funded by the Davis Foundation. There was scarcely a philanthropic project anywhere in Europe, Africa, or South America that had not, at one time or another, received Davis money.

As chairman and chief executive officer of the huge New York and World Trust Company, Calder Davis controlled or influenced most of the world's largest multinational corporations. And from them he demanded a steady stream of substantial contributions to help support the myriad projects encouraged by the Davis Foundation. *Capitalism with a heart* was a phrase invented long ago by Davis Foundation publicity men, and no investigative reporter, no matter how hungry to find fault or corruption, had ever been able to suggest that the puerile slogan was less than the truth.

One of Davis's personal projects had been the re-creation of a new Peace Corps, funded by the Davis Foundation and by large contributions from the New York and World Trust—influenced by multinationals as well as by generous donations from Davis's own fortune.

Rivas had encountered these dedicated New Peace Corpsmen all over the world. They did hydraulic engineering and flood control in Bangladesh, provided medical services in black Africa, fought famine in shattered Cambodia. An international force, the NPC workers Rivas had met in the field were without exception more professional, better trained and equipped, and more soundly motivated than the originals. And all of their efforts were paid for, not by taxes and not exclusively by Americans, but by the international financial power of the Davis Foundation.

Rivas considered what Cole had said about the NPC's sudden spurt of growth since the establishment of the International Strategic Studies Group. For years Americans had been suspicious of organizations such as the Trilateral Commission and the Bilderbergers, tended to see dark plots in any such elitist groups. The ISSG would naturally come under that same blanket of suspicion. But Cole? Surely Cole had known better than to suspect nasty One World plots from the politicians, scientists, and academics who were forever forming these kinds of blue-sky think groups. It was simply out of character for a man as sophisticated as Cole Norris.

And there was another oblique statement in the letter that Rivas found perplexing. The remark about the NPC enlisting 'people of curious background.'

What, precisely, had Cole meant to imply by that? The NPC took on every sort of professional. That seemed to be the only requirement: that he or she be good at what needed to be done. There was no limit to the number of specialties and disciplines represented. There were doctors by the thousand, engineers, social workers, planners of every kind, construction workers, biologists, physicists, entomologists—the list was endless. And the NPC got the best. The pay was, unlike the stipends given in the original Peace Corps, generous. With the resources of perhaps a hundred of the largest corporations in the world to draw upon in addition to the vast Davis and Smith family trusts, it should be, Rivas thought.

So what, then, had troubled Cole about the NPC's taste in volunteers? Collingwood?

Before leaving the United States for his most recent assignment in Afghanistan, Rivas had read about the enlistment in the New Peace Corps of Brigadier General J. E. B. Collingwood. It had been an unusual enough event to attract some editorial comment from the *New York Times*.

Collingwood (whom Rivas had met long ago in Laos) had been the man chosen to command the so-called Rapid Deployment Force President Loomis's predecessor had stationed in Egypt.

Soon after Loomis's inauguration, he had decided to reduce the RDF to a cadre and bring it home to Fort Bragg, North Carolina, 'as an economy measure.'

Collingwood, a Special Forces soldier whom Rivas remembered as having a volcanic temper, had reacted predictably. He had appeared in public forums to issue some strong statements criticizing the administration's defense policies as penurious and shortsighted.

President Loomis had promptly instructed Andrew Traynor, the Secretary of Defense, to discipline General Collingwood, reducing him to the rank of colonel and separating him from his beloved RDF. For a time the dispute had been a cause célëbre in the States, and then the media had grown bored with it and public interest had flagged.

But Jeb Collingwood had resigned from the Army. Three months later he had suddenly joined the New Peace Corps. A press release from the European headquarters of the NPC had simply stated the fact and added that ex-general Collingwood was to be employed in building roads in Surinam.

'Perhaps,' the *Times* editorial writer had concluded, 'General Jeb Collingwood will now have the time and solitude to reflect upon the unwisdom of an American military man criticizing the decisions, however questionable, of his Commander in Chief.'

It had been a sad business, but there was nothing sinister about it that Rivas could see. The NPC hired every sort of man and woman in every conceivable specialty. Why not hire from the Army, if the man in question had ability and was useful—as Collingwood plainly was.

Rivas stood thoughtfully. What, he wondered, had happened to Cole to make him so suspicious? It was not likely that Cole had had any direct dealings with Calder Davis. Davis had always taken great care to see to it that there was never a suggestion that the NPC had any connection with Central Intelligence. In the Third World, where the NPC did most of its work, such a thing would be considered a taint.

Here was a man in his eighth decade, a legendary man, confidant and adviser to Presidents of both political parties and many political colors, an American original. Calder Smith Davis might well be the last great Yankee philanthropist. At a time when the world seemed intent on submerging itself in a turbid sea of terrorism, disorder, and war, Davis was a spokesman for reason, calm, and above all, for peace.

And yet Cole suspected him—of what? There was little specific accusation in the letter. That was like Cole. To imply without documentation had always been Cole's style. It must have made him a formidable DCI. It certainly had made him a slippery Case Officer at a time when no one in the government had been willing to accept direct responsibility for some very contemptible decisions.

Rivas stood, considering. As Cole had suggested, it was possible that the years spent in the house of mirrors that was the Central Intelligence Agency might have touched him with paranoia.

But someone had murdered Cole and that girl—someone had seen to it that no matter what the official version of the event turned out to be, Cole Norris would be forever under suspicion of being at least indiscreet and possibly even a killer. His reputation would always be suspect. That was a *fact*.

A Norris might be able to figure some subtle angle, some clever twist out of that box. A Rivas had no alternative but to take direct action and blunder ahead, fueled by instinct and anger.

'All right,' he said aloud. 'We shall see, *hermano*.' Even as he made the choice to involve himself, he realized that he was doing exactly what Cole would have expected him to do.

Rivas looked at his watch. By afternoon he could be at the Milan airport, Malpensa, and there was an Alitalia flight to Kennedy at six-thirty. With the time difference, he could be in New York by eight in the evening.

He went into the bed alcove, took a canvas bag from under the rumpled cot, and began swiftly to pack.

3 Lake Nasser

Amira Shallai stood beside her stacked belongings on the dock as the station workmen, dark-skinned *fellaheen* from the north, unloaded the little lake steamer's deck cargo. Lake Nasser shimmered and danced in the heat of the afternoon, and the members of the station staff who had come to see her off stood sweating under a merciless, brassy sun.

She was conscious of the soft, liquid sounds made by the waves lapping at the muddy shore. It was a thing she had lived with for almost two years: the life-sounds of the immense ugly lake. It was the voice of drowned villages and submerged desert, of the changes that had come to Upper Egypt over the years as the High Dam had slowly inundated the land from Aswan to Akasha East, across the Sudanese border.

Amira was tall for an Egyptian, with finely made features that some of the more romantic young men at Kalabishah Station (young Cecil Sawyer, for one) often compared with the famous head of Nefertiti. Amira's skin was the color of polished ivory, delicate in texture, but seemingly impervious to the savage desert sun. She wore her gleaming black hair pulled back in a severe style that was intended to defeminize her, but which succeeded only in accentuating the classic purity of her profile. Behind large sunglasses, her eyes were enormous, with clear whites and irises of such dark brown that there appeared to be no contrast between iris and pupil. The effect was so startling that observers might well have imagined that Akhnaton's queen had, indeed, been somehow reborn in the person of Dr. Amira Shallai.

Her figure, full by Western standards, had been refined by the harshness of the living conditions at the Kalabishah Research Station. She was dressed in the well-faded khaki trousers and bush jacket that were the working uniform of New Peace Corpsmen all over the underdeveloped world.

But even at a distance, no one would have mistaken Dr. Shallai for a man.

At twenty she had been simply beautiful in the voluptuous Egyptian style. At thirty-five she had become the sort of woman who, once encountered, was never forgotten.

Amira was a physician, trained in the United States at Johns Hopkins University, and a specialist in desert medicine. She had been a member of the research staff at Kalabishah for twenty months, an NPC member for nearly four years. She had been born into the relatively small Coptic Arab community of Alexandria. The family had been established in that city for generations, and it was a peculiarity of Egyptian society—even in the militant years under Nasser—that the persecution of *Nasrani*—Christians—was indolent and haphazard, subject to mitigation if enough money changed hands.

As the only daughter of a wealthy family, Amira might have completed her medical training and returned home to practice without incident, untouched in any real way by the violent politics of the times. But before Amira's departure for America, she had been betrothed, according to Arab custom, to a distant cousin—a young man she had known since childhood, and for whom she felt a warm and genuine affection.

André Rahal was a student at the American University in Beirut. A *Nasrani* like Amira, when the Lebanese civil war exploded into religious conflict, Rahal quickly joined Major Haddad's Israeli-supported Christian militia. Rahal was an indifferent soldier, and in the violent environment of battles with both the PLO and the Syrian regular army, had no time to improve his military skills. In the course of a spoiling raid on a PLO unit operating out of a Palestinian refugee camp in south Lebanon, he was captured. Before any attempt could be made to rescue him, he was tortured to death by Palestinian women demanding military information he did not possess.

The news reached Amira at Johns Hopkins in the last year of her medical schooling. A young woman given to making swift decisions, she let it be known among her many Jewish fellow students that she was now political. Within a month, she had been recruited by Mossad.

The tenuous Israeli-Egyptian amity spawned by the Camp David accords spared Amira the distasteful necessity of spying on the country of her birth. Instead, the target assigned her by the spymasters in Jerusalem was the organization which had built and maintained the research station at Kalabishah and hundreds like it throughout the Third World: the New Peace Corps.

Dr. Cecil Sawyer, the most junior member of the radiology team at Kalabishah (and the staff member most hopelessly in love with Amira Shallai), shifted miserably from foot to foot on the hot dock planking. His pallid English face was flushed equally by the heat of the day and his agitation at the thought that once the lovely Dr. Shallai stepped aboard the little steamer for Aswan he would probably never see her again.

He found himself talking—*babbling,* he thought desperately—about all the wrong things as the dreadful moment approached. He was engaged in a project using radioisotopes to trace the life cycle of the bilharzia-carrying freshwater snails infesting the lake, and he chattered about it with manic intensity. This, despite knowing that Amira was unlikely to be interested any longer in mollusc counts or the predation statistics on recent plantings of European warm-water pike. She was neither a parasitologist nor a radiologist and there was no reason on earth for her to care whether or not the nasty-tempered fish relished the beastly snails.

She was leaving Kalabishah in minutes now, and starting on the roundabout journey to Arabia—to another NPC station doing God only knew what in the Empty Quarter. There was always a standing request for medical personnel to serve in hardship posts in places like the desert of southern Arabia. Amira had volunteered, and in so doing brought the world crashing down around Cecil Sawyer.

Until joining the NPC, young Sawyer had never been out of England. He was still receiving one cultural shock after another even in a place as relatively civilized as Upper Egypt. The very idea of the beautiful Amira going off to serve in a country ripped by revolution and anarchy gave him cold chills. It hardly mattered to him that she would be separated from the mobs in the streets of Riyadh by a thousand kilometers of wasteland. It was, in fact, that very wasteland that terrified young Dr. Sawyer.

When he had heard the news of Amira's transfer, he had

pulled everything possible out of the station library to learn about the Empty Quarter. What he discovered was not calculated to ease his mind.

The Arabs called it Ar Rub' al Khali. It covered approximately the bottom third of the entire Arabian Peninsula. It was one of the most forbidding and desolate regions remaining on earth: a million and a half square kilometers of blowing sand, pebbled desert, alkali sinks, and blistering sun. He had heard rumors that the NPC team there, at what was called EQ Station, was trying to locate deep aquifers by using ground injections of radioactive isotopes. Other stories suggested that the NPC had taken over the abandoned air base at Ibrahimah with the approval of the old Saudi government as a site for a new and experimental liquid-metal nuclear power reactor, one that would serve the electrical needs of Arabia in that future time when the thirsty industries of the developed world had, at last, drunk the vast Arabian oil reserves dry.

But whatever the NPC scientists were doing in the Rub' al Khali was not Cecil Sawyer's concern. Amira Shallai was. For whatever reason, she was going into a place that was still populated only by a handful of *bedu* tribesmen, savage nomads eking out a living by stealing and raiding for camels. It was like something out of the annals of the nineteenth century, when British Arabists by the dozens immolated themselves trying to live like the inhabitants in that moon-barren waste.

That was where Amira would be, and soon. It was almost more than Cecil Sawyer could bear. And yet all he could do now was chatter about fish and snails and bilharzic *fellaheen* with mud between their toes. What he wanted to say was that he would miss her terribly, that without her this dull place on the shore of the ugly lake would become unbearable, and that he would regret until the end of time that they had not become lovers.

☢

Dr. Emilio Sforza-Barzani, the Director of Kalabishah Station, interrupted Dr. Sawyer with scarcely a thought that he had done it.

The plump little Milanese shoved his way through the group of senior staff members gathered to say their good-byes as the porters began to carry Amira's luggage aboard the rickety boat.

'We shall all miss you, *cara dottoressa,*' Sforza-Barzani said with florid gallantry. 'We shall all miss you very much. You have lightened our tasks simply by being here among us.' The statement was perhaps a bit overripe, but it was actually not far from the truth. Kalabishah Station was staffed, as all NPC stations were, by international teams. Dr. Sforza-Barzani did not have a high opinion of Egyptian science or scientists, but Dr. Shallai was not a run-of-the-mill Egyptian physician. She was intelligent, alert, and resourceful. She was, Sforza-Barzani believed, almost as good as a man.

And then, of course, she was beautiful. As she turned to speak with another of the staff members on the dock, Sforza Barzani looked surreptitiously at the swell of her breasts partially exposed by the open collar of her jacket. He repressed a sigh. Losing Dr. Shallai to EQ Station, the Director of Kalabishah thought sadly, was going to depress the morale of the male staff of the lakeside station for some considerable time to come.

It was time. The farewells were almost all said. Amira was embracing the last of her co-workers.

I'll tell her now, Cecil Sawyer thought desperately. I will say Dr. Shallai—Amira—I am in love with you. Don't go.

The luggage was on board. The black-skinned captain was waving from his tiny wheelhouse. The lines were being made ready to take aboard.

Cecil Sawyer said, 'I hope you have a very pleasant journey, Dr. Shallai. The very best of luck to you at EQ Station.'

Her dazzling smile struck him like a blow to the heart. She said, 'Thank you, Cecil. Good luck to you.'

He watched her step onto the steamer's deck holding flowers the botanists had grown in the hydroponics tank.

The steamer moved away from the dock slowly, the screw churning mud from the shallow bank. Cecil watched the ribbon of water between the ship and the dock grow wider. Amira stood at the rail waving to the men and women on the shore.

Its speed increasing, the fusty little boat turned toward the north. The staff members began to disperse, walking back toward the concrete block buildings of the station. But Cecil

Sawyer, his blue eyes filled with tears, stood on the pier until the steamer vanished in the sunglare of the distant horizon.

By eight in the evening the lake steamer was moving slowly along the northwestern shore near El Sibu. The sun was touching the horizon and the first stars were beginning to show in the powdery desert sky.

At Amada, Suleiman Dayir, an Egyptian maintenance engineer from the crew at the High Dam, had come aboard. He was on the last leg of his monthly journey around the lake checking the pumping stations of the irrigation network that was the Aswan High Dam's reason for being. It was a boring, tedious job and one Dayir thought beneath him. But it carried with it a fair stipend and an impressive title; Dayir's wife, Fatima, was able to queen it over their poorer relatives because of it. A government sinecure was not a thing to be lightly regarded in Egypt these difficult days.

Dayir was a swarthy man with a too-ready smile and a body already running to fat. He wore a rumpled white suit of European cut and a large zircon ring on the little finger of his left hand. He had introduced himself to Amira as 'Engineer Suleiman Dayir' almost immediately after he had come aboard. Amira sensed at once that he was considering how best to ingratiate himself with this obviously liberated countrywoman of his. To most Egyptian men, 'liberated' meant 'available.'

He had remarked on how fortunate it was to have company on this dreary boat's overnight run to Aswan, and without encouragement had gone on to explain to her the importance of his position and the absolute necessity for keeping the various pumping stations around the lake running at top efficiency.

Amira, who had chosen to travel at least partway by slow boat for the express purpose of spending some time alone to organize her plans and consider her new assignment, had not been communicative. She had, in fact, excused herself and walked around to the far side of the steamer to stand alone and look at the slow panorama of the shore.

The steamer was old, of Russian manufacture: a riverboat, actually, left behind when the Soviet builders completed the High Dam. It had a small deckhouse with three tiny cabins, broad fore- and afterdecks where the cargo was carried, and a tall, narrow wheelhouse atop the house. The boat's noisy machinery filled the space inside the shallow, beamy hull and the entire vessel smelled of oil and soot and moved in a haze of stack gas from the high, pipelike funnel.

There were no feeding accommodations aboard, and passengers were expected to embark prepared to fend for themselves. Amira had been given a hamper of sandwiches and a thermos bottle of sweet cold tea by the cooks at Kalabishah. It was too hot to eat, and would be for several hours yet. She hoped the fat engineer would not make it necessary for her to seclude herself in her cabin, which was like a furnace from both the heat of the engine and the lingering heat of the day.

Standing at the rail, she could see the last of the sunglow reflected in the water as the boat labored slowly past the ruins at El Sibu. In the dark lee of the sand dunes there were tiny lights, the working lanterns of a party of archeologists camped between the diggings and the shore. Since Davis Foundation money had begun to pour into Egypt in ever larger amounts, a dozen or more digs were being conducted along the edge of the drowned valley that had become Lake Nasser.

Amira watched idly and considered her immediate future. At Aswan she would board the airplane to Cairo. Perhaps there would be time for a short visit to Alexandria, but she doubted it. Her parents never missed an opportunity to complain of her choice of career. She often wondered what they would think if they knew that in addition to her NPC career, she had another, more dangerous, one. It was possible, she told herself, that it was this need to deceive that somehow always made it impossible to find the time to visit Alexandria.

No, she thought, no Alex this time. From Cairo she would take the Egypt Air flight to Salalah in Oman. For months, ever since the Muslim radicals occupied the American embassy, it had not been possible to fly directly from Egypt to Riyadh. Egypt, the revolutionaries had declared, was now a lackey of the West and in particular of Satan America, so Egyptian aircraft were not welcome on the holy soil of the Islamic People's Republic of Pan-Arabia. Her sources reported that near-anarchy reigned in the oil fields of the Gulf coast, and there were rumors of increasing numbers of

Russian technicians appearing at the pipeline terminals of Ras Tanura. Oil production was falling rapidly and tankers from Europe and Japan were waiting for periods of up to thirty days to be loaded, and then were forced to sail with partial loads.

Travel inside Arabia was difficult for Middle Easterners and nearly impossible for people from the West. The Sultanate of Oman was the last country on the Arabian Peninsula friendly to the West, and it was through the port of Salalah that EQ Station was being supplied with personnel and materiel.

How long this would continue, Amira's Mossad contact warned, was impossible to say.

During the twenty months Amira had been at Kalabishah, she had worked with a number of Controls. The most recent was a man with the improbable name of Mohammed Py, a tour guide making his living by leading foreigners around the monuments of Abu Simbel, the Nineteenth Dynasty temples of Rameses II which had been relocated (by a huge expenditure of largely American money) on the sandstone cliffs overlooking the rising waters of Lake Nasser.

Py, a lean and leathery delta *fellah* with an entrepreneurial talent for intrigue, was a shrewd and cautious man, but one with a seemingly bottomless purse of unsuspected abilities. He had first appeared at the lake during the brief and hopeful flurry of petroleum explorations in the Aswan basin by an Egyptian-British-American consortium of energy companies.

The test wells had been a disappointment and had been abandoned, but Mohammed Py had remained at Abu Simbel guiding tourists (a great many of them young and fit Israelis) through the temples.

It had been through Py that Amira had received orders to seek a transfer to EQ Station and discover what, exactly, the scientists of the NPC were doing there. Mossad's interest in the isolated station had recently been aroused by the announcement in the *NPC Journal* (and on the back pages of some British and American newspapers) of the assignment to EQ of Dr. Nicholas Kristof, a Nobel laureate for his work in nuclear medicine, and Dr. Helen Clevenger, an expert in the latest techniques for the disposal of waste products resulting from the reprocessing of spent fuel rods from nuclear power plants.

Though Py had been circumspect as always about suggesting Israeli motives, he was, after all, a Middle Easterner, and as such unable to resist the impulse to pass on rumors. He had heard—not officially, of course, he hastened to assure her—that the men in Jerusalem were growing desperate for oil and were considering the feasibility of a military strike into the Gulf states to secure a steady supply. They were being restrained by the possibility, unlikely but always present, that the work being done by the NPC in the Rub' al Khali was a front for nuclear weapons development by the Pan-Arabian revolutionaries. Mossad considered it strange, Py said, that the NPC was still allowed to work in undisturbed isolation in a country that was engaged in a violent rejection of the West and Western values.

Amira's experience of the New Peace Corps ethic made her very doubtful of such a scenario. But in the Middle East in the last half of the twentieth century no one could ever be certain of anything without firsthand knowledge.

The last sliver of sun had vanished below the horizon, leaving a blood-colored sky reflecting in the swiftly darkening mirror of the lake.

The lights on shore were fewer now, as the steamer sailed slowly north. Amira watched the passing desert thoughtfully. This lake was an anomaly in the arid landscape, a vast watery blot the priests of ancient Egypt would have feared and cursed. The High Dam had made it possible to irrigate huge tracts of desert, but it had also stopped the yearly flooding of the Nile Delta. It was that flood that, time out of mind, had enriched the soil of Lower Egypt. Now the salts leached from the ground and made it necessary for the government in Cairo to spend millions in foreign exchange for chemical fertilizers. Until recently, the Saudis had supplied the money needed for purchases from the West. But the Saudis were in exile now, their kingdom in the hands of fundamentalist radicals and Communist-trained militants. There would be no more subsidies for Egypt.

The United States was willing to supply weapons, but foreign-aid programs were met with hostility in the United States Congress. The Americans were wracked by indecision and a growing taste for isolationism. They simply could not be relied on to support their allies. The Shah of Iran had discovered that, and so had the Saudi princes, to their sorrow.

The uncertain peace between Egypt and Israel held, but meanwhile the Egyptian population continued to grow, the High Dam destroyed the ancient ecosystem, and famine threatened.

The law of unforeseen consequences, Amira thought. One could never be certain of what would result, over time, from actions that seemed so right and proper at the time.

Her gentle cousin's baptism in the faith of Jesus Christ—known as the Prince of Peace—had led him by whatever twisting trail into the forces of Major Haddad and finally to a horrid death at the hands of the Palestinians.

She was still surprised, when she allowed herself to be, by the rage and hatred that filled her when she thought of the way of André's dying. Perhaps, she often told herself, she was veneered with Christianity, but Arab to the depths of her being.

Most Arab women, Christian or Muslim, still clung to the Arabic traditions of seclusion and *chador*. But many had taken up the gun. It surprised her how easily she had done so. Her parents would not believe it, had someone been so cruel as to let them know. They were cultured, civilized people. They had sought to release her from the old, repressive ways. They had set her intellect free and shared her pride in achievement. But André Rahal's murder (and that was what it was, because there had been no profit in killing him) had jolted Amira onto another, very different track. It had convinced her that the only important work was political, and that nothing lasting could be accomplished in Egypt or anywhere in the Arab world until the terrorist grip on the Arab soul was broken. Evil old men like Habash and Arafat had to die. Not to pay for André, or the athletes killed at Munich, or the children slaughtered at Ma'lot, or for the corpses they had scattered across the world—there was not enough blood in their old bodies for that. But for what they had done to their own people, making them outlaws among civilized folk everywhere with their hot-eyed calls for the *jihad*.

The terrorists no longer fought for the Palestinians. That issue could have been solved a generation ago, Amira thought, by resettling the displaced on the millions of hectares lying empty in a dozen Arab countries. The

Palestinians' cleverness and the billions of dollars of Arab oil revenues could have made the desert bloom. No, the terrorists fought for chaos, for hatred, for the same terrible joy the refugee women must have felt as they slowly hacked André Rahal to death.

Suleiman Dayir lounged in the bow, smoking a cigarette and watching the NPC woman. His gaze, now that it was disguised by the deepening dark, was frankly appraising.

To Dayir, whose gender preferences were nonspecific, Dr. Shallai's masculine dress was highly erotic. Women of his class simply did not dress in this casual and provocative way. He closed his eyes and allowed his imagination free rein. In this dreamlike state he slipped his hands under the faded khaki, fondled the soft, full breasts, thumbed the nipples (dark, he was certain, with well-defined areolas) erect. He allowed himself another slit-eyed glance at the way the tightly belted jacket accentuated the smallness of her waist, the roundness of her hips and thighs and buttocks. She almost certainly was wearing no undergarments, he thought. It was too hot and in any case it was an article of faith among his common associates that Westernized women went naked under their outer clothing. He imagined the texture of her skin. Like velvet, he was certain, damp with perspiration and perhaps even a bit downy. Suleiman did not hold with the American practice of trying to make the human body hairless. There would be, he thought, a dark line of fine hair from pubis to navel and the belly would be soft and rounded. It was a wonderful body, like a dancer's, perhaps even like a strong young boy's. He felt his loins aching.

Suleiman believed that Egyptian women who adopted Western ways could be had by any man with a determined approach. He had no actual experience to support this notion, but the *mullahs* who had dominated most of his early education believed it, and the *mullahs* were invariably wise. Plainly, this woman had abandoned modest seclusion. She was obviously upper-class, and women of her social caste did not encumber themselves with sexual restrictions. When he had introduced himself to her he had seen quite plainly the interest in her manner. True, she had not immediately sought further contact, but one could hardly expect that on such short notice.

The steamer would not dock at Aswan until morning. He and she were the only passengers. The crewmen were already dozing amid the crates on the foredeck and the captain was unlikely to leave his wheelhouse.

In his travels through the villages on the lakeshore, Suleiman Dayir had found very little in the way of sexual diversion. The women were Muslim peasants, veiled, secluded, and dangerous to approach. The boys were too thin and smelled bad. These trials had not made a complete celibate of him, but it had been some time now. He found himself sweating with anticipation.

A crewman had told him Dr. Shallai was a physician from Kalabishah Station. Though he disliked women whose accomplishments exceeded his own, the fact that the woman was a medical doctor meant that she was accustomed to the sight of the unclothed male body. That increased her erotic appeal as his active imagination worried the notion like a pi-dog chewing at a bone.

Presently he could check himself no longer and he strolled aft to where Dr. Shallai stood looking toward the passing shore. He produced a box of cigarettes and offered one.

'Thank you, no,' she said, without turning. She was as tall as Suleiman. Their heads were on a level. He thought of her as a large woman, which she was not, but it was easier than thinking of himself as a small man.

'You don't smoke.' Dayir sighed self-deprecatingly and lit a cigarette for himself. 'How very commendable. It does not become women to smoke. It is unfeminine.'

When she did not immediately respond to this sally, he added, 'Of course, I have often considered giving up tobacco myself.' He leaned on the rail so that his arm touched hers lightly. He showed her his best, white smile. 'But it is, after all, a very small vice. Don't you agree, doctor?'

She glanced at him briefly with what could have been—but surely was not—an expression of exasperated dismissal. Her eyes, enormous in the dim glow of the single yellowish deck light, seemed focused elsewhere.

'I see that you are with the NPC,' he said. 'At Kalabishah, I believe I was told.'

'Yes,' she said, and moved to increase the distance between them.

'The Davis Foundation is everywhere,' he said in badly

pronounced English. It was well to let her know at the outset that he, too, was an educated person.

She made no reply, and he permitted himself to move closer. The scent in her hair was like jasmine. It was well known that women who wore perfume did so to attract the attention of men. He felt the beginnings of an erection.

She had moved into an angle of the railing and he followed, letting his thigh brush hers.

She said calmly, 'Don't do that.'

Dayir suppressed the impulse to suck his teeth in annoyance. But then, he thought more tolerantly, the amenities must, after all, be observed. He backed away a step. He could feel the perspiration running down his cheek from his pomaded hair. Darkness had diminished the heat only slightly. The air was moist and smelled of the water hyacinths that had begun to grow in thick rafts near the lake's shores.

'How fortunate we are,' Dayir said, 'to have pleasant company on this dull little voyage.'

Without answering him, Dr. Shallai stepped past him and walked down the deck to the aftmost of the tiny cabins. The heat inside must be searing, he realized, but she stepped through the door without a backward glance.

For a moment he was angry, nonplussed. Then he noticed that she had left the narrow louvered door slightly ajar, hooked by the catch in that position.

For several minutes he remained where he was, wondering if this could be construed as an invitation. She had seemed distracted. Perhaps even unfriendly. But simply because she did not wish to strike up an acquaintanceship on deck where they could be seen and overheard by the *fellaheen* crewmen did not necessarily indicate a lack of interest. Quite the reverse, in fact.

For the better part of a half-hour he leaned against the railing, arguing the merits of the case with himself. The door *was* open, after all. And in this heat she would hardly stay in her tiny sleeping cabin unless she was waiting for him to make the next logical move.

He strolled past the cabin. There was no light inside. It was far too early to think of sleep, so she must therefore be waiting to see what he would do.

Perhaps she was watching him. Perhaps—and the thought revitalized his sagging erection—she was waiting for him nude on the bed, those breasts unconfined, her thighs spread and moist.

His breathing quickened as he turned back and stood for a moment in front of the door. Carefully he reached for the latch. He lifted it quietly. He trousers felt tight and confining. Moving delicately on his small feet, Dayir stepped into the dark cabin.

'Dr. Shallai?'

The world exploded into a star-shot burst of pain as the heel of a small, hard hand drove into his nose. He felt someone take a firm grip on his wrist and swing him, off-balance, hard into the steel doorframe. His shoulder struck the edge painfully, but he could manage only a squeak of terror because it seemed that his nose had suddenly swollen to three times its normal size, blocking his breathing. In the next instant he found himself lying facedown on the deck between the cabin door and the railing, his arm twisted behind him and a knee planted firmly in the small of his back. His crotch was hot and wet. In his fright, he had voided his bladder.

A hand reached into his coat pocket and his pocketbook was expertly extracted. It was searched swiftly and then discarded on the deck beside him.

Amira Shallai said, 'You stupid, foolish little man.'

Suleiman Dayir heard himself babbling in a thick, nasal garble. His throat was filled with phlegm and blood from his savaged nose. His face reverberated with a throbbing agony. His nose, he thought, was surely broken.

Amira released his arm and said, 'Get up.'

Suleiman crawled to the railing, using it to pull himself to his knees. He gathered his papers and pocketbook with shaking hands. When he lifted his face, blood from his nose ran over his chin and soiled his white coat. He gasped and gagged. 'Mistake,' he said indistinctly. 'Mistake—I thought—my own cabin—I thought—' He was having great difficulty remembering what he had thought at the moment of lifting the latch to the woman's door.

The captain's voice came from above. Suleiman heard him shout, 'Is everything all right down there?'

The last thing Engineer Dayir of the Aswan Dam Company wanted was to have the black captain of the lake steamer he used every month see him like this, blood-spattered, on his knees, brought to this humiliating position by a madwoman in trousers. 'Nothing—' Suleiman gabbled thickly. 'All right—quite all right—'

Amira Shallai studied him coldly and then extended a hand to help him to his feet. He shied away from her as from a cobra. He hauled himself more or less erect, covering his urine-stained trousers with both hands. He stumbled away in that crouching position, his swollen nose dripping red onto the deck. When he reached his own cabin he flung himself inside and slammed the door behind him. In the hot dark he found the light switch and ran rusty, tepid water into the basin fixed to the bulkhead. He bathed his face tenderly, sobbing with pain. He had begun to wonder what possible explanation he could give Fatima or his co-workers for his condition. The face in the mirror showed a bulbous, swollen nose and the beginnings of two very black eyes. His fouled trousers clung clammily to his thighs as he hobbled to the narrow bunk and lay down with a moan.

One thing was certain. He would not emerge from the safety of his cabin until the boat docked at Aswan and that woman was gone. He shuddered with mingled fear, humiliation, and pain.

He thought about Dr. Shallai with hatred clogging his throat. He would find a way to be revenged on her. He had friends, important friends. He was a man respected by the PLO. Let her look to herself, the Westernized bitch. Suleiman Dayir was not a man to be trifled with.

In his quarters at Kalabishah Station, Dr. Cecil Sawyer sat at his desk disconsolately watching the moths batter themselves against the light.

He had come to a decision. He would apply for a transfer to EQ Station.

He had heard that the higher-ups (he thought of the NPC managers in those terms) were encouraging medical personnel to apply for positions in the Empty Quarter. They were working on nuclear power there and they could surely use a certified radiologist.

Resolved, he drew a pad of paper from the desk drawer and began to write. As he did so, his bruised spirits began to rise.

He was *doing* it. He was actually doing it. The thought of the Rub' al Khali filled him with apprehension, but he was suddenly resolved: he would take leave and carry his request to Cairo tomorrow.

Sforza-Barzani wouldn't be pleased, he thought. The tracer work on the lake snails was actually useful, important work and it would suffer somewhat by having to wait until a new radiologist was brought into Kalabishah Station. But none of that mattered somehow, he thought, feeling the beginnings of unexpected joy. He would see her, be with her, again. She would be surprised when he turned up. 'Here's your bad penny, Amira,' he would say in an offhand way. And she would smile with pleasure at seeing him again so soon.

He told himself, as he wrote his request for transfer, that he was doing it because she needed him. She needed him to protect her from all the formless dangers with which his imagination had populated the terrible place to which she—and now he—had chosen to go. She was, he decided with loving and naive condescension, really only a woman, after all.

4 Washington, D.C.

The men gathered in the Treaty Room of the White House had all been awakened by urgent telephone calls in the early morning, but the meeting had not convened until nearly noon.

Charlie McKay, the President's Chief of Staff, had chosen the Treaty Room as a place for their meeting rather than the more customary Crisis Room in the Executive wing, hoping to dodge the White House press corps.

Carl Shepherd, the Director of the Federal Bureau of Investigation, had little hope that Charlie's gambit would succeed. White House reporters had an instinct for recognizing a developing crisis, and what the administration had on hand was nothing less. Cole Norris, the country's number-one spy, had been scooped from the bottom of the Potomac by a dredge and his yacht had been found aground with a mutilated woman's corpse aboard. No one was going to keep that kind of story unreported for very long.

Shepherd, a stout, midwestern lawyer in his early fifties, felt rumpled and out of place in these surroundings. Provincial in heritage, education, and outlook, he had never really felt at home in Washington. He knew next to nothing about police work; he held his present post because he had raised a million and a half dollars for President Vincent Loomis's campaign. He did his best to run the Bureau well, but what he hoped for was a federal judgeship sometime in Vinnie Loomis's second term. Until then, he told his wife, Dolly, he would do his best with the Bureau.

Shepherd accepted with grateful pleasure a cup of hot coffee from the white-coated steward who was circulating with a silver pot. He unconsciously avoided looking across the table at Isaac Holt, the dead man's deputy and a man who made Shepherd decidedly uncomfortable. No one,

Shepherd thought, could look into those eyes and feel any warmth.

Holt was moving swiftly to take over the investigation of the double killing and it troubled the FBI Director. The Bureau had gone through some bad times in the past, but it was on the mend, and Shepherd could not see how it would benefit the administration to allow the Central Intelligence Agency to take over a task that was—by law, as Shepherd understood it—outside its legal purview.

But it had been Holt, as Deputy Director of Central Intelligence, who had telephoned the key men in the administration to arrange this meeting with the President. He was plainly intending to assume command of the investigation and Carl Shepherd was uncertain as to what he should do, and how far he should go, to prevent it.

Despite the air conditioning, Shepherd felt himself sweating. Through the tall Georgian windows of the handsome room he could see the Ellipse and the sere, littered grass around the base of the Washington Monument. A dozen special agents had to be on hand there every day just to watch the demonstrators who had turned the place into a kind of radicals' shantytown. Many of the demonstrators had been there for weeks, chanting and marching and smoking pot to show their support of the Arabian revolution. Some were Arab students who until recently had been supported by the Saudi government, attending universities and postgraduate schools across the United States. Now they had transformed themselves into Islamic fundamentalist revolutionaries, screaming imprecations at the United States and committing every sort of vandalism to show their approval of the revolutionary committees in Riyadh.

To Shepherd, the whole business had a terribly familiar ring. There were demands for the return of the Saudi royals who had taken refuge in the United States, and for indemnification by the 'imperialist aggressor'—meaning the United States. There were even one hundred diplomats held hostage in the American embassy in Riyadh—men and women from a half-dozen Western nations who would be held, the Pan-Arabian revolutionaries declared, until Satan America came to her senses and returned the Saudi princes and all their worldly goods. The administration had been unable to resolve the crisis and now, Shepherd understood (though he had not been present when the decision was made), an attempt to negotiate with Riyadh was going to be made by Calder Davis, friend of Presidents and creator of the New Peace Corps.

Shepherd did not know whether he approved of this or not. It seemed somehow improper to turn such a negotiation over to a banker in his seventies rather than to the Department of State. But fortunately it was not a decision Carl Shepherd had to make.

Helping the police keep order in Washington, though, *was* his responsibility and he had his hands full. The demonstrators were well aware of their civil rights and they used them to burn American flags, build cooking fires on the grass, harass park policemen, and overturn the chemical toilets that the rangers forlornly hoped would prevent them from fouling the grounds.

Even at this distance Shepherd could see that the flags on the staffs surrounding the great obelisk were gone, replaced with Marxist banners or signs extolling Allah the Compassionate and demanding 'Death for Loomis.'

With a sigh, Shepherd turned his attention to the other men in the Treaty Room.

Charlie McKay, overweight and overworked, his sparse hair carefully arranged to cover an expanse of waxy scalp, was in close and worried consultation with Elmer Harper, the gaunt, pallid ex-*Washington Post* reporter who now held the thankless post of Press Secretary.

Everyone in the room seemed on edge and secretive, except for Ray Turner, the Secretary of State. He sat alone and composed near the head of the conference table, his thoughts—as usual—private and unreadable.

The mind of Secretary of State Raymond Scofield Turner was not, at this moment, focused on the death of the Director of Central Intelligence. Turner was an old man, and death, no matter how violent or unexpected, was something he regarded as a part of life: an event to be faced with as much courage and as much dignity as fortune might allow. Cole Norris had not been permitted much dignity in his dying, and that was a great pity—as was the death of a young and pretty woman whose misfortune had been to be with Norris at the moment his death found him. But Secretary Turner was reasonably certain that the deaths would eventually be explained and that the killer would face retribution—in this world or the next. The Secretary was a quietly religious man.

What troubled Turner most was that yesterday the President had informed him that there was no genuine consensus among the American people, and failing that, the government could not take action against the revolutionaries who presently held a hundred Western diplomats hostage in the American embassy in the former Saudi capital. The allies whose nationals were involved were equally paralyzed.

Therefore, the President had said, he would rely on the good offices of Calder Smith Davis to negotiate the freedom of the captive diplomats.

Davis, as a man who had channeled literally billions into humanitarian work within the Third World through the NPC, was to be given the task that Raymond Turner believed belonged by right and tradition to the United States Department of State—and if need be, to the United States Department of Defense.

It was totally in character that immediately upon being told that the vital and delicate processes of negotiating for the hostages was being handed to a banker, an industrialist, a director of multinationals and a doctrinaire internationalist—all in the person of Calder Davis—Raymond Turner had tendered his resignation.

The resignation had been immediately refused.

The Secretary was aware that a very good case could be made for the President's decision to use Calder Davis as a quasi-diplomat in these troubled times, when showing the American flag was unpopular in the Third World. But it pained him deeply and offended his strong sense of American history. He found himself wondering how it was that a Calder Davis had come to command greater respect abroad than an American Secretary of State—or even an American President.

Moodily, the Secretary sat under the large chandelier of sparkling crystals and studied the inscribed plaque set into the Treaty Room's white chimneypiece. Among other things, it read: *Here the treaty of peace with Spain was signed.*

What a tragedy it is, Turner thought, that the same nation that once had believed utterly in its own Manifest Destiny is now reduced to having bankers sue for its diplomats—and allows its chief intelligence officer to be murdered like some Mafia hoodlum and cast into the river.

The President of the United States, closely followed by Peter Gilmartin, his National Security Adviser, swept into the room.

Vincent Todd Loomis (Vinnie to his close associates) was a heavily muscled man of medium height with the large hands and feet and sloping shoulders of a manual laborer. Expensive tailoring softened the grossness of his figure, but the jowly cheeks and the small eyes set in padded sockets and the heavy, sensual lips gave him the look of a Tiberius in twentieth-century dress.

These physical characteristics, when seen on a home television screen, conveyed an impression of strength and solidity. It was this quality of being enhanced by the electronic image that had carried Vincent Loomis from the Arizona state legislature to the House of Representatives and finally into the White House. He, even better than his critics, realized that election was not always a mandate to lead. He was a man of the House, one accustomed to the need for biennial approval, and he knew how swiftly public opinion could change among electors who received most of their information from three-minute spots on the evening news telecasts. In his inaugural address he had promised the people that he 'would lead you only where you wish to go.' To Vincent Loomis the sine qua non of politics was not vision but consensus.

Peter Gilmartin, a handsome man with features stronger than his convictions, opened a folder and looked cautiously around the room as if expecting someone other than himself to call the group to order. Since this was, in effect, an ad hoc committee of the National Security Council, which Gilmartin chaired, no one did.

'Well, then,' he said. 'Will you begin, Ike?'

Holt took command easily. Seldom referring to his notes, he summarized for the group all that was presently known about how the Director of Central Intelligence and his current mistress had died on the *Pandora*. This took some five minutes and the President fidgeted impatiently through all the recital. Carl Shepherd guessed that he had heard it all before, from Holt on the telephone.

When he had done with his recitation, Holt took several eight-by-ten glossy prints from his case and handed them to Gilmartin. The National Security Adviser paled slightly and handed the pictures quickly to the President.

Holt said, 'That is what Rees and the Coast Guardsmen who boarded the yacht found in the cockpit. The boat was found grounded, by the way, off Kingscopsico Point. About eight nautical miles from Cobb Island. Rees radioed McLean and we immediately sent a helicopter. No one but Rees, the Coast Guardsman, and the Colonial Beach harbormaster have seen what you see there. Rees took the pictures himself.'

The President blinked his eyes as he looked at the gruesome photographs. He touched his mouth with his handkerchief and passed the prints to Raymond Turner.

'That poor young woman,' Turner said quietly. 'What a horrible way to die.'

'Cole came up in a dredge bucket of mud,' Holt said coldly. 'His body is in the Alexandria morgue. When all the necessary pathology is done, we propose to bury him in Arlington. Quietly.'

Carl Shepherd looked across the table at Holt and suppressed a shudder.

When the pictures of the abbatoir on the *Pandora* had made the complete circuit of the conference table, Holt retrieved them and put them away in his case.

'Who did this thing?' the President asked.

'If you are considering a public statement, sir—and I do not recommend one at this time—I believe we must attribute the killing to a terrorist or terrorist group, presently unknown,' Holt said.

'We will have to issue something to the press as soon as possible, Mr. President,' Elmer Harper said. 'There is no way we can keep this quiet.'

'It would be best if we don't have the media badgering us with questions every ten minutes, Mr. President,' said Holt.

Harper raised the level of his protest, conscious of the potential for trouble if the press became really hostile. 'Be straight with the reporters, Mr. President. Otherwise we'll have nothing but heartburn.'

'Raymond?' the President asked. 'What do you think?'

'Unless Isaac can say for certain that the national security is involved, Mr. President, I think the public should be told whatever we know whenever we know it. Someone has committed a vicious crime. Let Carl's people get on with the business of finding the guilty party.'

Holt frowned, but remained silent.

Loomis sat for a moment, his mouth compressed into a thin line. 'All right,' he said, looking around the table. 'Tell me this now. Is there any possibility—any possibility at all—that this is what it could appear to be? That Cole went crazy and killed the girl and then killed himself?'

Peter Gilmartin said, 'Something like this happened before, you know. A few years back. A former Agency man named Paisley. It went into the book as suicide—' He broke off when he saw the skeptical expressions. 'No,' he said. 'I suppose not Cole—'

'Carl?' the President asked.

'I don't think so, Mr. President. There is a superficial similarity between this and the Paisley case, but I can't see Cole Norris as a man likely to commit suicide. And then the *way* the girl was killed—I could be dead wrong, of course, but it almost seems to me that whoever did it wants us to concentrate on *how* it was done rather than *why*. Do terrorists work this way? I don't know.'

'Well, Raymond?'

'I think Carl is probably right, Mr. President. It has all the earmarks of something intended to tie everyone up in scandal and publicity. Perhaps while something is done elsewhere. Quite possibly in Riyadh.'

'We come back to that, Raymond?' the President said disapprovingly.

'Forgive me, Mr. President. I didn't mean to reopen a closed subject. But you asked my opinion.'

'And I value it, Raymond,' the President said frigidly. 'But Calder will handle the hostage problem. That was settled yesterday.'

Holt said woodenly, 'May I proceed, Mr. President?'

Loomis nodded silently.

'The Coast Guardsman who boarded the *Pandora* is being debriefed at McLean. With your permission I will speak to Treasury and arrange a transfer out of Washington. I hope that meets with your approval, Mr. President?'

'Yes.'

'I really feel that this is an internal CIA matter,' Holt said, looking at Carl Shepherd.

Shepherd looked at the President.

'*Is* national security involved, Ike?' Loomis asked.

'Anything involving the Director of CIA is likely to involve the national security.'

'I'm not prepared to give you a blank check,' Loomis said.

'I don't ask for one. But at least let us do the preliminary investigating without outside interference,' Holt said. 'Cole had been acting oddly for some time. Secretive, short-tempered, dealing with people outside the Agency. I don't mean to suggest that Cole was turned or anything like that, though we can't totally ignore the possibility. He may just have been under great strain. If there are outside connections, I would like the opportunity to track them down.'

The President sat in thought for a moment and then made up his mind. 'All right. For the time being it is the Agency's business. But Elmer and I will prepare a statement for the media and release it tonight or tomorrow.'

He looked at Raymond Turner and Turner did his best silently to convey his disapproval of the decision to exclude, even temporarily, the FBI. But Loomis chose to ignore the wordless protest. Instead, he said, 'Now what about Cole's family? They must be told.'

'Cole has an ex-wife in Santa Barbara and another in Maui. I will notify them,' Holt said. 'There are no children by either marriage.'

The President asked. 'Isn't there a brother?'

'A half brother, Mr. President. Cole's mother remarried after her divorce from Cole's father. A Mexican rancher named Rivas. The half brother's name is Michael. He's a free-lance journalist.'

'I place him now,' the President said. 'You had better speak to him personally as well.'

'I have already done that, sir,' Holt said. 'He's in Switzerland, just returned from Afghanistan. The Agency always keeps track of its former employees, sir.'

'How did he take it?'

'With Rivas it is hard to tell, Mr. President. Well enough, I suppose. He and Cole were not close.'

'I don't want him hostile,' Loomis said. 'This administration has enough trouble with the press.'

Press Secretary Harper said, 'He's never written anything about us that wasn't salted with ground glass. Handle him with care, Ike.'

'Oh, I shall, never fear.'

The President pushed back his chair and stood. Everyone in the room did the same. He said, 'I want it understood that there will be no leaks about any of this. Elmer and I will prepare the statement for the media people. No one else is to comment. And I mean *no* one.' He turned to the Secretary of State and spoke in a far warmer tone. 'Ray, would you join Peter and me in the Oval Office? I shall be speaking to Calder soon and I want the benefit of your thinking on the Riyadh situation.'

As far as the President of the United States was concerned the question of who killed Cole Norris and why was now the responsibility of others.

5 New York

To Rivas, who had grown accustomed to the high, cold air of the Hindu Kush, the heat of the New York July was like being enveloped in a warm, soggy blanket. The sun was down and the evening air under the thin overcast smelled of too many cars, too many people, and too little open space. The plastic seats of the shabby Checker taxicab felt slippery to the touch and Rivas's denim shirt clung to his sweat-damp skin.

The Van Wyck Expressway's city-bound lanes were clogged with traffic. For as far ahead as Rivas could see, there was a chain of tail lamps brightening and dimming as the traffic moved at a slow, uneven pace toward Manhattan. From time to time the three lanes of traffic would come to a complete stop as other traffic on the inbound ramps tried to force its way onto the expressway. Behind the dirty windows of the brick apartment blocks facing the road, Rivas could see lights burning and the bluish glow of television sets.

'You want I should take the Midtown Tunnel or the Triborough Bridge?' The driver, a long-haired young Puerto Rican (Juan Milpero, according to the Transport Authority license fixed to the open partition between front and back seats), spoke without turning.

'Take the Triborough,' Rivas said. Sam Abbott lived in the East Seventies and was waiting for him now. Rivas had called from Kennedy. Sam had heard about Cole. But if he had heard *from* Cole recently, he had not been willing to say so on the telephone.

With the rusting armillary sphere and globe at Flushing Meadows just coming into view in the twilight, the traffic bogged down once again. The driver, his arm draped over the open window in a futile attempt to catch a breeze, half turned and asked, 'You Mexican?' Then, perhaps thinking that the question might offend and reduce the size of his tip, he added: 'I see your name on the bag, that's all.'

Rivas grinned silently and then said, *'No, Soy yanqui, como usted.'*

'Ah. Just thought you might be Chicano.'

It was peculiar, Rivas thought, that most of the Hispanics one encountered in the United States and spoke to in their own language would almost invariably reply in English. It was as though they refused any ethnic contact with persons not demonstrably of their own particular group or class. Was it the Cole Syndrome in reverse? Rivas wondered. In Europe or Asia, when one used a particular language, the reply was offered in the same language. But that didn't happen in the United States. Perhaps that said something about the way the unassimilated regarded America these days. They seemed to sense the undercurrent of anger Americans were feeling toward all 'foreigners.' It had always been present, but the Arab oil embargoes, the Iranian calamities, and now the troubles in Arabia had brought it much closer to the surface. It seemed that Americans hated all dark-skinned people now, and native ethnics were growing wary.

Rivas knew a great deal about ethnic prejudice. He had lived with it for most of his forty-one years. The Norris family had despised and resented him, despite his American birth, as a 'Mexican.' And his aristocratic father's relations had disliked his mother's Celtic ancestry, his blue eyes, and his fair skin. Americans were prejudiced, but no one could suggest to Rivas that Hispanics were less so. He knew better.

In school at Menlo and Stanford, he had managed to miss the militant toleration of the 1960s. He had escaped the condescension of affirmative-action programs and lowered standards for minorities, so at least his education was genuine. He had never developed a taste for indiscriminate egalitarianism. That, he often told himself, was a characteristic shared with his Norris connections.

Michael Rivas had always had a well-developed sense of who and what he was. He did not regret his experience. A certain amount of rejection tended to temper the personality.

A trio of motorcyclists roared past the stalled cars, weaving between the lanes. Reluctantly, the traffic began to inch forward again. Rivas drew a deep breath of the sodden air and contained his impatience. It took time, he realized, to become accustomed once again to the irritations of a totally mechanized society. But it did seem to him, fresh as he was from a simpler place, that America was determined to choke itself on machines.

As the line of cars began to move again, a fourth cyclist pulled abreast of the Checker and rolled there, opposite the open rear window. The rider's dark face shield presented a blank and somehow threatening image. Rivas could have reached out and touched the man—if man it was. There was certainly no way of knowing who or even what wore the black leathers, the black plastic helmet, the shiny face without features. There was something very sinister about the clothes one wore for certain sports, Rivas thought. Cyclists, sky divers, scuba divers all tended to look like commandos in some futuristic battle. Or perhaps twentieth-century devils working their own particular asphalt strip of hell.

The rider slowed and fell in behind the Checker. Rivas looked away, his attention elsewhere.

When he heard the rising exhaust note again, he twisted in the seat to look back. He felt a familiar prickle of warning: long experience had sensitized him to the presence of danger.

Through the rear window he saw that the cyclist was moving forward again, veering out onto the shoulder of the road.

Within seconds the motorcycle was once more beside the open window. With great clarity, Rivas saw the black-clad rider reach back into the plastic saddle packs on the rear fender and pull out a short shotgun. The barrel had been cut off and the stock reduced to a pistol grip.

Rivas gave a warning shout and started for the floor of the cab. The weapon discharged with a flat, echoless boom. Rivas felt a blow on the head; the partition between himself and the driver dissolved into diamond dust. The heavy shot smashed the framed license bearing Milpero's likeness and passed through the inside of the taxicab, carrying away half the young man's head.

The Checker swerved into the car in the lane beside it with a crumpling noise. Rivas felt a second impact as the car behind slammed hard into the taxicab's trunk. Brakes screeched and there was a third, more gentle thump as the tangled cars came to rest against the link fence on the divider strip. From down the line of traffic there came more squealing of tires and the sounds of damaged metal as the cars behind the Checker stacked into an accordion of bent bodywork, punctured radiators, and blowing horns.

Rivas opened the car door and flung himself out onto the rubble-strewn ground of the divider, looking for the motorcycle and its rider, but there was no sign of either.

For just a moment he knelt on the ground thinking dazedly that he had just returned from reporting a guerrilla war in a place where the gunships shot at everything that moved, and yet it was here a dozen miles from downtown Manhattan that he was nearly a casualty. He felt something warm and sticky running down the side of his face and he brushed it away and staggered to his feet, turning toward the cab jammed between the fence and the first car to rear-end it.

The taxi driver sat slumped against the door. Half of his head and face was gone. Blood and brains ran horribly out of the cavity.

He became aware that people were shoving and pulling at him and shouting questions. Others were running up the road from the stalled cars behind. He heard someone gasp and vomit, making terrible gagging sounds. A girl began to shriek hysterically until someone pulled her away from the Checker.

A man's voice in his ear said to Rivas, 'Man, you're bleeding! You better sit down.'

Rivas touched his head and his hand came away bloody. Suddenly his skull began to ache and throb.

He pushed his way through the crowd to the cab and opened the front righthand door. People shrank away from what was inside. Rivas sat down on the seat and reached for the radio. The smell of blood and sweat filled the confined space. The driver's dead hand twitched eerily.

Rivas pressed the microphone button and said, 'Can anyone hear me?'

A bored voice came from the speaker. 'Who's calling Ajax Checker?'

'Can anyone hear me?' Rivas asked again.

'Give us a number, Ajax,' said the voice. 'A number, can't ya?'

Rivas read the number on the strip of Dymo tape on the face of the radio. Then he said, 'There's been a shooting. On the Van Wyck just west of Flushing Meadows. Call for a police helicopter.'

'*What* did you say? Is that you, Milpero?'

Rivas said, 'The driver is dead. Send the police.' He replaced the microphone in its clip and ignored the agitated questions coming from the speaker. From far down the expressway came the noise of automobile horns being blown in angry frustration.

Rivas walked through the crowd until he reached the dry grass of the road verge. The glare of headlights hurt his eyes. People backed away from him, frightened by his bloody appearance. He heard someone telling him to sit down, that he was hurt.

He thought, Yes, that's a good idea, and sat down abruptly, as though his legs had collapsed. He closed his eyes and suddenly and very clearly recalled a dead Afghan civilian, a young boy, sprawled among a squad of slaughtered Russian conscripts in a ditch beside the road to Kandahār. What the boy had been doing traveling with Russian soldiers, no one knew. The grizzled old Mujahad who had set the ambush had simply looked, shrugged, and walked away. Who could tell? Perhaps the boy had been a collaborator, a Communist. What did it matter? God, he said, is great. What is, is. The Will of Allah.

I have the answer, Rivas thought with fevered insight. The boy had been a bystander, a noncombatant in the wrong place at the wrong time. Like young Juan Milpero—who should have selected a safer fare from the crowd of passengers at Kennedy.

He lowered his aching head onto his arms and settled down to wait for the police to arrive.

The wall clock in the duty physician's office stood at ten twenty before the NYPD detective gave any sign that his interrogation of Michael Rivas was coming to an end. He made it plain that he was not satisfied with the answers he had been getting. But his weary gloominess suggested he had expected no less.

From time to time the young black doctor in charge of the emergency room would look in past the uniformed patrolman at the door to ask how much longer they intended to occupy his office. He had warned the detective sergeant that this was not the time to be badgering an injured man, but the policeman was dogged.

It had only been the timely arrival of Sam Abbott, and Abbott's threat to call one of Abbott Press's attorneys, that had dissuaded the sergeant from taking Rivas in as a material witness.

'Let's go over it one more time, Mr. Rivas,' he said heavily.

Rivas, sitting in the doctor's chair, his bandaged head aching and stinging from the pull of a half-dozen sutures in his scalp, looked exasperatedly at Sam Abbott.

The publisher, a short, excitable man with bright, probing eyes and an electrified aureole of longish gray hair, said, 'It seems to me, Sergeant, that Mr. Rivas has already answered your questions—a number of times.' Abbott, as Rivas had cause to know, could assume a headmaster's severity on demand. He was quite capable of intimidating anyone who made the mistake of equating his bookish manner with gentility.

'Just one more time, Mr. Abbott,' the policeman said. 'Just to make sure I have everything straight.'

Outside the cubicle, through the glass partitions, Rivas could watch the grisly night routine of Booth Memorial's emergency room: accident cases, drug overdoses, victims of crime and happenstance. Somewhere in another part of the hospital lay the body of Juan Milpero, murdered by mistake. That was the worst kind of death, Rivas thought, because it combined malice and chance to create meaninglessness.

The policeman was watching him with dark, tired eyes. 'You are sure the weapon was a shotgun,' he said.

'Yes.'

'Cut down, you say.'

'Yes,' Rivas said again.

'Gauge?'

'How the hell would I know?' Rivas snapped, his irritation breaking through. 'Sixteen. Twelve. Whatever.'

The large-bore shotgun, stock and barrel shortened, was the classic tool of the contract killer untroubled by any need for neatness. An ugly, brain-spattering weapon with a wide, devastating pattern. Rivas knew that he was fantastically lucky to be alive. If the assassin had not been firing from an unsteady gun platform, Rivas would be with Milpero in the hospital cold room.

Sam Abbott said, 'I think we should end this now, Sergeant. Mr. Rivas is obviously not well.'

The policeman turned the pages of his notebook carefully, rereading what he had written there in the course of the lengthy interrogation. He heaved himself to his feet with what seemed to be a great and weary effort and said, 'We may want to talk to Mr. Rivas again.'

'Yes, yes,' Abbott said testily. 'You have my address and number.'

Rivas stood unsteadily. His head throbbed. 'We're finished now?'

'I guess so,' the sergeant said. 'We don't have much to go on.' He opened the door into the emergency room and signaled to the uniformed policeman to go bring their car. He turned back to Rivas. 'You are free to go, Mr. Rivas.'

The poor bastard thought he had a Mafia assassination attempt on his hands, Rivas thought. If it were only that simple.

Abbott said solicitously, 'Are you all right, Michael?'

'I'll make it,' Rivas said. Standing so suddenly had brought a wave of dizziness and he steadied himself on the doctor's desk. 'Let's get the hell out of here.'

The emergency-room physician, his dark face glossy with sweat, came in. He examined Rivas critically. 'How are you feeling now?'

'Better,' Rivas lied.

'I doubt that,' the doctor said. 'You can expect quite a bit of pain for a day or so.' He wrote hurriedly on a prescription pad and handed the paper to Abbott. 'This is for codeine. See that he takes it strictly according to instructions or he'll be on cloud nine.' He gave Sam a small envelope. 'This will get him through tonight until you can get the prescription filled in the morning. See he gets some rest. In three days he can come back here or get some other physician in Manhattan to take out the sutures.' He turned back to Rivas and said disapprovingly, 'You had a near one. You were damned lucky.' He went back into the emergency room without another word. Rivas guessed that duty like this tended to produce sharp-edged personalities.

Sam Abbott said to the detective sergeant, 'If there is nothing more?'

The policeman pocketed his pad. He gave Rivas a sad-eyed look. 'Let me know if you plan to leave town, that's all.'

In the back seat of the leased limousine that was one of Abbott's few corporate extravagances, Rivas leaned against the soft leather cushions and said wearily, 'Thanks for helping, Sam.'

'It is the least I could do for one of my authors who's just been shot at,' Abbott said, looking out of the window at the Manhattan skyline. The air conditioning made a soft, sibilant whisper. For the first time in hours, Rivas felt cool. He rubbed the scar on his face and said, 'No questions?'

'Of course, questions,' Sam Abbott said. 'Are you up to more interrogation?'

Rivas turned to look at the older man. 'Don't you mean debriefing?'

Abbott made no direct response to the thrust.

'How much do you know about what happened to my brother?'

'I was told what you were told, I suppose. It was a terrible thing, Michael.'

'Why hasn't there been anything about it in the newspapers?'

'There will be tomorrow. The White House will make a statement.'

Rivas said pointedly, 'Then they told you a bit more than they did me.'

Abbott drew a deep sighing breath and closed the glass partition between the front and back seats. 'All right, Michael. Let's have it.'

'How long have you been a Company asset, Sam?' Rivas asked.

Ordinarily Rivas could read his friend's expression easily, but not now. Abbott's face was masked, wary.

'My God, Sam,' Rivas said bitterly. 'After all these years can't we trust each other?'

'Michael, be careful who you trust.'

'Goddamnit, do *we* have to play these games? Just answer my question. How long have you been tied to the Agency?'

'A long time,' Abbott said. 'A very long time.'

'Give me one or two facts,' Rivas said. 'My head hurts too much to be clever.'

'All right. I trained Cole. During the war.'

'Good God. I had no idea.'

'There was no reason for you to know. When Cole and I

were at Camp X, you were in nursery school.'

'I knew Cole was in the OSS. I never had any idea that you were,' Rivas said. It was like being given a glimpse of ancient history. When Rivas himself had served the Agency in Southeast Asia, most of the former OSS people had been supergrades—station chiefs or planners in McLean, Virginia. Many had already retired. Rivas realized suddenly that his brother could not have been more than twenty-one or -two and fresh from Princeton at Camp X, the fabled and supersecret Canadian training site set up to produce spies by Sir William Stephenson's British Security Coordination. And Sam must have been a very young man himself, one of the bright young intellectuals recruited to create the cadre that would, over time, become the Central Intelligence Agency.

Sam said, 'I ran Cole as one of my agents. You knew that he did two missions in Occupied France?'

Rivas shook his head. 'No, I didn't. I used to wonder what Cole actually did during the big war, but we never spoke of it. Or of anything else, when he could avoid it. We weren't close, Cole and I.'

'He tried to change that, you know.'

'By recruiting me?' Rivas asked sardonically.

Abbott shrugged. 'That was probably as large a gesture as your brother was capable of making, Michael. Intelligence work was all Cole's life. Maybe by sharing it with you he was trying to say something.'

Rivas stared for a time at the city they were approaching. Presently he said, 'Well, it doesn't matter now, does it?'

'I can't answer that. You'll have to.'

'I guess I will at that,' Rivas said thoughtfully. He looked at the man sitting beside him and wondered how much more there was here that he, Rivas, had never suspected. He said, 'And you, Sam. What about you?'

'I was active until Kim Philby ran. When he went east, I retired. A number of us had to. We had known him and worked with him. He knew everything there was to know about our operations. He rolled up networks by the dozen. The damage he did was enormous.' Again he lifted his shoulders in a shrug. 'I was ready to retire, though. I was working here in New York. Never mind what I was doing. It is a fantasy to imagine that an intelligence service can stay out of domestic operations. But since what I was doing wasn't strictly legal, I was glad to turn in my ticket.'

'So the Agency set you up in publishing.'

'Is that an observation or an accusation? Abbott Press is a legitimate publishing venture. A damned good one. I am the only Agency asset in the house and I've never done anything for the Company I'm ashamed of. You can believe that or not. It's the truth.'

Rivas studied the other man for a moment before replying. Then he said, 'Did Cole send you something to deliver to me? Something outside of channels?'

Abbott shook his head. 'No, Michael.'

'Is *that* the truth? Cole was working on something he wanted me to see. It was something the Agency might prefer I *didn't* see. But I'm asking you as a friend. Did you get something from my brother?'

'No, Michael, I did not. You'll just have to decide whether or not you want to believe me.'

'I have a letter written by Cole before he was killed. He was working on a report he wanted me to know about. He said he was going to send it to you to hold until I could collect it.'

'I know he was working on something he thought was important,' Abbott said. 'He told me that much the last time I spoke with him. But that was more than a month ago. He called to ask me to do some research for him. You know how the Old Boy network functions. You do what you are asked, and you don't ask inconvenient questions. But that is all, Michael. If he ever finished whatever he was working on, it never came to me.'

'What sort of thing did he want from you?'

'He wanted to locate some former associates.'

'Damn it, Sam, stop hedging. If Cole wanted any old associates located, the Agency could do it far more easily than you could.'

'I know that. Cole didn't want to do it that way. One doesn't ask why, Michael. You know that. One simply assumes there are good reasons. That's what it means to be an *asset*.'

'All right, Sam. At the moment you are the only asset *I* have. Who did Cole want to locate?'

'A man named Ian Wyndham. Does that name mean anything to you?'

It did, Rivas realized with a shock. Wyndham was a shadowy figure in the world of international intrigue. One of the Wild Geese, an almost legendary mercenary captain, now retired into the English countryside.

'And did you locate him?'

'Oh, yes,' Abbott said, half smiling. 'He is living in the south of England. On a boat—it's called the *Wild Goose*, for old times' sake, I suppose.'

'Who else did Cole ask about?'

'A Dr. Nicholas Kristof. A Dr. Helen Clevenger. Not actually associates of Cole's, but interesting people.'

'Kristof the Nobel laureate?'

Abbott nodded. 'The same. And Dr. Clevenger is a woman who has recently patented a technique for removing some dangerous wastes from nuclear fuel rods as they are reprocessed. They are both, by strange coincidence, members of the New Peace Corps.'

Rivas thought about the odd statements Cole had put in his letter about the NPC. He asked, 'Anyone else?'

'Some synfuels hotshots on the Secretary of Energy's staff. Also some of the Pentagon specialists on Andrew Traynor's procurement analysis teams. Cole worried a good bit about staffers. He used to say that they had altogether too much influence on policy. I don't know if that's true generally, but it certainly is true of the people who work for Defense and Energy. Cole wanted particularly to know if any of the folks he asked about had ever worked for any of the companies Calder Davis controls.'

'Surely the FBI investigated all of them before they were hired?'

'Maybe so. But there were some damned interesting coincidences.'

Rivas looked at the lights on the river as the limousine moved onto the Triborough Bridge. He suffered an unpleasant flashback to that moment on the Van Wyck Expressway when the young Puerto Rican Milpero asked: 'Midtown Tunnel or Triborough?' just minutes before having his head blown away. The driver had died because someone had tried to kill Michael Rivas, and someone had tried to kill Rivas because he was Cole Norris's brother and knew—what, exactly? That his brother had become paranoid about Davis? How much sense could be made of that?

He asked, 'Did Cole ever ask you for specific information on Calder Davis himself?'

'Nothing specific—no. But he was interested, I can tell you that.'

'All right, Sam,' Rivas said, reaching into his pocket. 'You had better read this now.' He handed him Cole's letter.

Abbott turned on the overhead light and read carefully. When he had finished, he folded the letter neatly and handed it back, using his fingertips, as though it were too warm to touch comfortably.

'I'm not really surprised, Michael,' he said.

'Is that all you have to say about it?' Rivas realized that Abbott would speak only with great reluctance. It seemed that the men who had trained at Camp X all those years ago were a special, old-fashioned breed. They had been conditioned by the time, the circumstances, and the kind of war they fought. It made them very different from so many who came after them: men sworn to keep silent, but willing to dishonor their pledges—for money, or to soothe some late-blooming sense of self-important righteousness.

'What more do you expect me to say?' Abbott asked. 'Cole was obviously disturbed when he wrote that letter.'

'Disturbed, yes. But not crazy.'

'Cole wasn't the kind of man who goes crazy.'

'I'm glad to hear you say that much, at least,' Rivas said shortly. 'Ike Holt as much as said that Cole had been approaching a breakdown.'

'Remember that part of Holt's job was to protect the DCI.'

'Holt's job? Since when, Sam?'

'Since the Loomis administration cut back on personnel. It wasn't Ike's job directly, but the new table of organization puts Internal Security under the Deputy DCI's supervision.'

Rivas frowned. 'This is beginning to have a bad smell, Sam.'

'Now don't jump to conclusions, Michael.'

'Conclusions, hell,' Rivas said angrily. 'Someone tried to blow me away tonight. That gives me the right to do some complaining, I think.' He stared hard at Abbott. 'Or was it the Agency who tried to kill me, Sam?'

'I don't think so.'

'We were set up by someone, Cole and I,' Rivas said.

'The Agency doesn't murder its DCIs,' Abbott said. 'It isn't the KGB, Michael.'

'Don't give me homilies about the lovable Company, Sam.

Quit fencing with me. If you know anything at all that can help make sense of all this, I want to know it.' The discussion was turning oblique and unpleasant. Sam Abbott was beginning to sound more and more like a man delivering only selected bits of information.

'I don't have much, Michael,' Abbott said. 'That's the truth. I can tell you that when I talked to Cole, he told me he wished he could discredit Calder Davis with the President. Maybe it was just an unguarded remark, but Cole seldom made unguarded statements of any kind. I think he meant what he said. He told me Davis was so deep into the administration that it was as though the banks and multinationals had a Cabinet department of their own. Cole didn't believe that private individuals and foundations supported by multinationals should be doing things that were the proper function of government. He had too many doubts about their loyalties.'

'What else did he tell you?' Rivas felt the need to rediscover his brother; to reconstruct the man from these fragments of talk was almost impossible, but it was Rivas's only option now that Cole was dead.

'It sounds, Sam, as though Cole's whole focus was shifting. Whatever happened to the great Cold Warrior? Wasn't he worried about the Soviets anymore? Good God, everyone knows—or thinks he knows—that the KGB is at least partially behind what's happening in Arabia.'

'Cole didn't discount that. But I don't think that's what he was working on when he died,' Abbott said. 'If he was really working on a personal report for the President, I haven't any hope that you or I will ever see it.' He stared at the still-heavy traffic surrounding them, slowing their speed along the parkway.

'Could Ike Holt have known what Cole was up to?'

'It's possible. But your brother was a careful man, Michael. That's why he did his private work on the *Pandora*.'

'He wasn't careful enough, Sam,' Rivas said wearily. 'Did he ever say to you that the President was expecting a private report from him?'

'Never. I don't think Vincent Loomis would welcome any report from a subordinate criticizing Calder Smith Davis. The old man is a legend.'

Rivas said thoughtfully, 'I would like to have the information you gathered for Cole, Sam.'

'Michael, why don't you just drop this? Stay out of it.'

'I don't really have that choice, do I? What do you suggest, that I put an ad in *The Times* telling all future hit men that nobody had to worry about me, that I'm opting out?'

'This is no joking matter,' Abbott said.

'I hardly need to be told that.'

Abbott sighed. 'I suppose you're right. Unless you would be willing to drop out of sight for a while. I could help you arrange that.'

'Just give me what you have on Ian Wyndham and the others. And arrange a meeting for me with Holt.'

'I can understand you wanting to talk to Isaac Holt,' Abbott said. 'But you intend to go to England to see Wyndham?'

'I'll go farther than that if I have to.'

'You're thinking about what Cole wrote about the NPC recruiting "people of curious background." '

'Well, it can't be a pure coincidence, can it?' Rivas looked hard at Abbott. There was something about the way he made the last statement that spurred Rivas on. 'You know something more, Sam. Damn it, let's hear what it is.'

'May be nothing at all.'

'Let me judge.'

'Cole thought the NPC was recruiting mercenaries. That's why he wanted to talk to Wyndham. If mercs are being hired anywhere in the world, Wyndham would know.'

Rivas maintained a tight silence as the limousine turned into the warren of Manhattan's East Side.

Sam Abbott said, 'I know how unlikely it sounds. It's rather like accusing the Salvation Army of secretly buying tanks. But Cole believed it.'

Rivas now realized how much Cole's hint had been gnawing at his mind. At first it had unsettled his convictions about Cole's state of mind. The notion was preposterous. But was it, really? In a chaotic world one had to consider *all* the possibilities. Sovereign governments appeared unable to accomplish even the most straightforward tasks. Once that became an axiom, one could begin to consider all that a covert paramilitary branch of an organization such as the NPC could accomplish. The NPC was already established in half a hundred countries across the world. It was lavishly funded. There were NPC research teams in every sensitive area of the Third World. The great multinationals which supported the NPC with tax-free millions also controlled plenty of transport, communications, and manufacturing. Half the oceangoing ships in the world and three-quarters of the world's air transport were owned, or at least controlled, by the same people who, under the guidance of Calder Smith Davis, backed the NPC. Most of the Western world's most sophisticated weaponry was built by companies having corporate connections with the banks and multinationals. If such a force existed, it could be used anywhere. They would kill to protect the secret. . . .

'You aren't laughing, Michael,' Abbott said.

'Are you?'

'No, I'm not. When you think about it, and about how badly the world needs some kind of police force . . .' Abbott shrugged.

'But Cole apparently looked at the possibility in a different way,' Rivas said.

'Your brother was a traditionalist. He hated the One-Worlders.'

'Hold it, Sam. It's too easy to slip into paranoia. If Cole was onto something like this, why didn't he follow through with an Agency investigation? Why should he have gone off on his own, with a report for the President outside the regular channels of the government?'

'Why, indeed? If he was right, of course, then the reason is fairly obvious. How did he put it to you? "The Administration is stiff with ISSG people." '

'But the government has always been thick with members of organizations like the ISSG. The Bilderbergers, the Trilateralists, the Club of Rome group . . .'

'Those groups never had the field army the ISSG has in the New Peace Corps,' Abbott said. 'They never recruited people like General Collingwood, for example.'

Rivas shook his head unwillingly. 'I don't like what I'm thinking, Sam. I've always laughed at people who worried about *Them* taking over the world. I don't believe in monstrous international conspiracies run by the gnomes of Zurich or the wicked oilmen or the money changers. It's just not a reasonable idea.'

'It never has been.'

'My God. You really think it's happening.'

'I'm not sure,' Abbott said. 'What I am sure of is that

things are changing. Governments used to have the will and the strength to maintain some kind of order in the world. That isn't so any longer. There is a power vacuum in the Third World—and that's where most of the industrialized countries get their raw materials. When there's a vacuum, something fills it. The Soviets have been trying, but they can't seem to cut it. They can destroy governments, but their economic system is so bankrupt they can't replace what they destroy. Look at Cuba, Michael. Thirty years of Castro and communism and the Russians still have to pour billions into the island each year just to keep the regime going. So maybe, just maybe, Davis and his friends have decided enough is enough.'

'Where is Jeb Collingwood now?' Rivas asked.

'According to the *NPC Journal*, he's building roads in Surinam.'

'You don't believe that.'

'It isn't the sort of job that would interest the best irregular soldier in the Army for very long.'

The limousine drew up in front of Abbott's brownstone on East Seventy-first, and the driver opened the door and stood silently. Rivas realized that the man was probably Sam Abbott's bodyguard. He looked competent.

Abbott said, 'We won't need the car again tonight, Martin.' He glanced at Rivas and half smiled, reading his thoughts. 'Yes, Michael,' he said. 'The Company pays Martin. He sees to my comfort and safety. It is that kind of world, isn't it, Martin?'

'I'm afraid so, Mr. Abbott,' the chauffeur said.

Rivas followed Abbott up the stairs and through the grilled doorway. His head was still pounding and he felt he might drop at any moment. His discussion with Sam Abbott was like a bad dream.

When Abbott led the way into a book-lined study, he said, 'Let me get you some water. You'll take one of the good doctor's happy pills and get some sleep. We can talk some more in the morning.'

Rivas sat down in a deep leather chair and gripped the arms as though he feared falling. He wanted to rest, but he couldn't leave it alone yet. 'Did Ike Holt know what Cole was going to do?'

'Go direct to the President? I don't think so. But there's no way to be certain.

'I had better see Holt tomorrow.'

'You're in no shape to travel, Michael.'

'Tomorrow,' Rivas said stubbornly.

Abbott spread his hands in a gesture of defeat. 'All right. I will try to reach him in the morning. You can take the shuttle to Washington.' He poured water from a carafe and handed Rivas one of the pills from the envelope the doctor had entrusted to him. 'Now take this and we'll bed you down for the night.'

Rivas did as he was told and then asked, 'Where's Martin?'

'Nearby,' Abbott said almost sadly. 'He is always nearby.'

When Sam Abbott left him in the guest room, Rivas lay down on the bed and closed his eyes. The vivid images burned in his mind. Cole—his features blurred by murky water. A murdered girl. The dead Puerto Rican. The silent Martin. Sam. He felt he should be approaching some kind of revealed truth, but the pattern refused to coalesce and the pieces went spinning off into a vast emptiness as Rivas slipped into a heavy, drugged sleep troubled by dark dreams.

6 Washington, D.C.

'Mr. President,' Calder Smith Davis said, 'I want to thank you for arranging to have Mr. Holt brief me on the situation in the Riyadh embassy. The information should be most helpful.'

Vincent Loomis regarded his visitor respectfully. The old man sat erect on one of the two yellow sofas flanking the white-columned fireplace that was the dominating feature of the yellow Oval Office of the White House. The bronze doré chandelier with its chains and drops of rock crystal shed a soft light on Davis's silver hair and unlined face. The banker was in his late seventies, fragile and delicate as a Dresden figurine. The eyes were arresting, pallid and knowing. He had seen and experienced a very great deal.

'I hope, Calder,' the President said, 'that you will be able to interest those people over there in some sort of negotiations. So far the government hasn't even been able to get them to talk to us. Frankly, I am being very heavily pressured by the Joint Chiefs. They want to take direct military action.'

'There was a time, Mr. President,' said Davis, 'when I would have agreed with the Joint Chiefs of Staff. But I am older and wiser now. There are better ways than unilateral action by the United States.'

Though he would never have said so to Calder Davis, Vincent Loomis had no intention of following the recommendations of his military advisers on the Arabian crisis. At least not so long as oil continued to leave Ras Tanura for the West. He remembered only too well the fiasco of President Carter's attempted commando rescue in a similar situation. Vinnie Loomis was far too clever a politician to make any similar misjudgment now in the Arabian Peninsula.

The very day that the militants had overrun and captured the American embassy in Riyadh, Loomis had decided to ask for help from Calder Davis. He represented the international financial community, and that community had vital interests at stake in Arabia. Loomis had concluded that Calder's friends and associates could take initiatives with the Pan-Arabian radicals that the United States government could not. And if their efforts failed, Loomis thought, the responsibility for that failure could not fall on the government or the Loomis administration.

'I thank God for men like yourself, Calder,' the President said. 'I understand pragmatists and value them.'

'I will accept that as a compliment, Mr. President,' Davis said dryly. 'Though I am not so sure it really is one. My brothers were the idealists in the family. Perhaps that is why they were such failures as politicians.'

'Not failures, surely,' Loomis said, filling balloon glasses from the decanter of Armagnac on the low table between himself and Calder Davis.

'Oh, they did well enough, one supposes,' Davis said. 'But they failed in the end. Stansfield wanted more than anything in the world to stand where you are standing, Mr. President. He never really had a chance.' He lifted the glass and inhaled the bouquet of the liquor but did not drink any. 'Very wealthy men do not belong in government. They lack the common touch and they make themselves ridiculous when they attempt to acquire it. Somehow there is something absurd about a man with millions safely invested in tax-free securities and trust funds pretending to be a populist when he knows that the taxes that will pay for all the social programs he advocates will come out of someone else's money.' He favored Vincent Loomis with a thin smile. 'I have never done that, Mr. President. If I am proud of anything it is that. I have never pretended to be anything except what I am. A simple businessman.'

The President laughed and shook his head. 'That is a *slight* understatement, Calder.'

'Well, yes, of course it is. I was indulging myself in a very small joke. What I meant was that I am happy that I have been able to serve my country simply by being what I am. I wish Raymond could forgive me for that.' He touched the rim of his glass with a delicate fingertip and made it ring softly. 'He is a great man, Mr. President. What a pity it is that this is no longer the age of great men.'

Loomis, standing beneath the Rembrandt Peale painting

of George Washington, let his eyes rest on the stand of presidential colors flanking the door opposite the fireplace. Before formal dinners, it was traditional for visiting heads of state to congregate in this handsome room directly above the original Oval Office. And when the President of the United States led his guests down the grand staircase to the State Dining Room, the colors were taken from their stands and carried ahead while the Marine band played ruffles and flourishes. The grandness of the procedure never failed to thrill Vincent Loomis—and, secretly, to awe him a little. The President was a man of many uncertainties, but he had schooled himself never to let them show. Though the responsibilities of the office often threatened to overwhelm him, he *enjoyed* being President. And he could, he thought, by virtue of his great office, always call on men such as Calder for the exercise of an expertise he himself did not possess, and of powers that the presidency itself did not command in this egalitarian age.

Vincent Todd Loomis was not a sensitive man. He knew that his relationships were governed by a native shrewdness rather than any innate ability to evaluate the true worth of others. He also knew that this was a failing in a man, and a potentially tragic flaw in a President.

But such wistful, private speculations were fruitless. He was what he was, no more and no less. It was a pity that he was a politician rather than a statesman, that he was not more or better than he was. But he *was* the President of the United States. Many greater men had accomplished far less.

With a sigh he thought how much more agreeable it would have been to be President of the United States in some less turbulent time.

Calder Davis said, 'You seem depressed, Mr. President. I hope it is not the company.'

'Nothing like that, Calder. It is just that this has been a particularly difficult day.'

'The Chinese have a saying—a malediction, actually: "May you live in interesting times." Our age qualifies. Most emphatically it does.'

'This business about Cole Norris is very upsetting. We will be making a statement to the media people early tomorrow morning, but no matter what we say it is bound to become a circus,' Loomis said gloomily.

'Is there any indication yet of what actually happened?'

'Ike Holt thinks it was a terrorist action. I have some doubts about that, but I have nothing to put in its place. Holt could well be right.'

Davis said neutrally, 'I am confident the matter is in good hands. Mr. Holt is a clever man.'

Loomis allowed himself a single flare of petulance. 'Norris was a fool to put himself in so vulnerable a position. He should have known better.'

'That was Isaac Holt's opinion as well,' Calder Davis said. 'I know very little about such things.' His tone changed almost imperceptibly, became tinged with sadness. 'I am sorry for that Moran woman. It is a terrible thing to die like that, and so very young.'

'Yes.' Loomis suppressed the urge to shudder as he remembered the gruesome pictures taken aboard the *Pandora*.

'Perhaps we should speak of other things, Mr. President.'

'Yes, by all means, Calder. Have you considered yet how you will approach those lunatics in Riyadh? We must get Ambassador Kleinerman and the others out of there, and soon. The administration's job-approval rating has dropped twenty points since the militants challenged us.'

'Do not, Mr. President, make the error of thinking of the Muslim militants as lunatics. They are anything but. They know that they have their hands on the throat of the developed world and they intend to keep them there. Whatever we do to obtain the release of Mr. Kleinerman and the rest must be very carefully organized with that fact in mind.'

Loomis stood and paced for a short time before settling down again, this time in one of the Louis XVI chairs flanking the yellow sofas. He did not wish to risk offending Calder Davis with gratuitous cautions, but it was well to remind him of the extent of the danger in the task he was assuming.

'They have threatened to kill the hostages several times,' he said. 'Of course, I don't think there is any real possibility of their doing that as long as they think they can extract concessions from us.' He finished his Armagnac and refilled his glass from the decanter. 'Frankly, we don't yet have any really clear notion of what they want from us. Oh, there is the expected thing, naturally, imitating the Iranians. They want us to return the Saudi royal princes who have come here, and all their money. There are plenty of our people who would like to see us hand the Saudis over. The academics and the intellectuals who encouraged the revolution from the beginning. And the Left, of course. The Left is always for handing over anti-Communists. But the voters, Calder, they say hell, no. They are frustrated and angry. If I were to deport the Saudi princes and their families, I really believe I would be impeached. Americans may not want to risk fighting, or even pay taxes for defense, but they won't be dictated to by a bunch of raghead radicals.' He frowned heavily. 'Meanwhile the Soviets sit in Afghanistan and half of Iran ready to take over the entire Gulf and its oil if we make a wrong move. You are taking on a very delicate situation, Calder.'

'I am very aware of that, Mr. President,' Calder Davis said quietly.

'I just hope the problems are clear to you.'

'I think we have a good chance of success,' Davis said. 'The revolution in Arabia may turn out to be a blessing in disguise. I know that sounds sanguine, but trust me, Mr. President. Let your mind be at ease.'

Loomis regarded Davis for a time and then decided that the mood was right to broach a subject that had been troubling him and that he had been reluctant to discuss directly with Davis until now. 'Calder, may I ask you something that has bothered me for quite some while?'

'Please do,' Davis said politely.

'Why did the NPC take on Jeb Collingwood? It didn't look very good, you know, after the way he attacked administration policy.'

'General Collingwood has talents and training the NPC needs, Mr. President. He is a splendid administrator. Many ex-military men find their way into industry. It happens the general found a place in the New Peace Corps.'

Loomis swallowed hard and said, 'You are not exactly being responsive to my question, Calder.'

'Forgive me, Mr. President. I thought I was. Are you asking why the NPC enlisted a former soldier? Or are you asking why the NPC welcomed someone who publicly objected to your decision to reduce the size of the Rapid Deployment Force and bring it home to Fort Bragg?'

When the President did not reply immediately, Calder Davis smiled slightly and said, 'Let me elaborate, then, sir. You and the general had a disagreement and you fired him.'

He raised a hand to forestall protest. 'Very well, you *retired* him. That was your right as Commander in Chief, naturally. But the NPC is growing, Mr. President. We now have more than eighty thousand Corpsmen in some fifteen hundred locations across the world. We need good, competent men of proven ability. General Collingwood is such a man, as I am certain even you will agree.

'There is another consideration, though it was not a factor when Collingwood offered to join us. That is his military judgment. It will plainly be necessary for me to evaluate the military situation in Arabia before making the opening moves in negotiation with the Pan-Arabian revolutionaries. Ordinarily, such an evaluation would be made here in Washington, by the Department of Defense. But please bear in mind that if I am to negotiate with the Arabians, I shall have to do it as a member of the international community, *not* as a citizen or even as a representative of the United States. I therefore need an independent adviser. General Collingwood will be able to function in that capacity. If you object to this arrangement, Mr. President, please say so now, so that I can withdraw promptly and allow you to make other, more congenial, arrangements.'

The threat, though politely stated, was nonetheless a threat. Loomis realized that he must either give Calder Davis carte blanche or look elsewhere for help in resolving a crisis that seemed to everyone in the administration to be irresolvable. Presidents, Loomis knew, should not be given ultimata by private citizens. But the parameters of the Arabian problem made surrender both inevitable and intensely attractive.

By allowing Calder Davis to handle the crisis as he thought best, the President was invoking the resources of a vast combination of commercial and political interests and powers. The responsibility was thereby diluted, allowing Vincent Loomis—if it came to that—to delegate the blame. And if there was to be credit, Calder's reticence would allow Vincent Loomis to be the public hero.

'Calder,' the President said, 'I asked for your help and I would not, under any circumstances, interfere. You must handle this problem in the manner that seems best to you.'

Calder Davis got to his feet. 'Thank you, Mr. President,' he said, 'And now, if you do not mind, I will take myself off to my bed. It is late, and an old man needs his rest.'

At the head of the grand staircase, Davis paused and said, 'I have asked my administrative assistant to bring something over to you in the morning, Mr. President. You may find it interesting. It is a report by a group of Intercontinental Energy engineers on a new process for extracting petroleum from coal. At the moment the cost per barrel is still thirty dollars higher than the price of Arabian crude, but just think, Mr. President—if there were no Arabian production, or if it should fall by as much as forty percent, this country could become the world's largest oil producer. The bank's economists have appended an estimate of the percentage of the market we would need to bring the price within reason. I think you will find it fascinating, Mr. President. George Rossmore will be flying back to New York with me tomorrow night. I'll see to it that he receives a copy as well. Good-night, Mr. President.'

Vincent Loomis watched the old man going down the wide, curving staircase, his small feet silent on the deep carpet. The oblique and offhand mention of the Secretary of Energy was slightly unsettling. George Rossmore was close to Calder, perhaps closer to him than to anyone in the administration. Not for the first time Vincent Loomis wondered if he had not allowed Calder's direct influence to grow too strong in the Loomis administraton. Yet what could be wrong with that, really? There had never been a doubt in Loomis's mind, or in the mind of anyone else in the government, about where Calder Smith Davis's loyalty lay. It was always with the United States. And for the next six years, the President thought, that meant with Vincent Todd Loomis.

Three

July 14, the third day

The days of inexpensive oil are behind us, and the basic issue is how to organize the transition from conventional oil to new sources of energy, such as synthetic fuel.

—Øystein Noreng, *Oil Politics in the 1980s: Patterns of International Cooperation*

7 Washington, D.C.

Michael Rivas stood on the lower steps of the Lincoln Memorial letting the massive stream of chattering, sweating tourists flow around him. Some paused for a time to snap pictures of the immense statue in the shaded colonnade, others shouted after their children, still others climbed the broad flight of stairs with expressions of almost superstitious awe, like savage acolytes approaching an Olympian presence.

The sun burned down on the vast expanse of granite with a shattering intensity that made Rivas's bandaged head throb painfully. The humid air was like damp cotton in his lungs.

He had ridden the morning shuttle flight to Washington National, much against Sam Abbott's advice, and now it was nearly noon as he waited for Ike Holt to appear amid the crowds visiting the memorial.

Holt had offered to meet him in his office at McLean, but Rivas had balked at that. He wanted people around him, and when Abbott had given Holt the story of yesterday evening's attack on the Van Wyck, Holt had agreed to meet Rivas in a public place 'if it would make him feel more secure.'

The morning news telecasts had carried the White House statement on the death of Cole Norris. Rivas wondered which particular terrorist group was being blamed for the killing. Press Secretary Harper had simply read the statement to the cameras and had refused either to speculate or to answer questions shouted at him by members of the White House press corps. The death of Candace Moran had been mentioned, but the statement had implied death by drowning. There had been no elaboration or details.

Rivas slowly climbed the stone stairs until he stood in the shadow of the colonnade. It was, he thought, a moving and impressive memorial to the martyred President. It had been a number of years since he had visited the place and he stood for a time looking up at the sad, brooding face towering over the milling mass of tourists.

Despite the heat and the carnival atmosphere of Washington in mid-July, the great, somber building and the immense statue of the man who saved the Union had a quieting effect on the throng. Even children who, moments before, had been running and shouting, seemed at least momentarily overpowered by the elegance of the shrine. Whole families stood, faces uplifted, as though touched by some dimly understood emotion. For an instant they seemed to be experiencing a bonding with all the others standing at the feet of the seated giant.

They would come to stand for a time and then move on, out into the blistering sunlight, gradually resuming the unruly attitudes they had abandoned under the influence of the memorial's mystery.

These, Rivas reminded himself, were the real Americans, with their sunburned faces, ugly sandaled feet, flowered shirts, dark glasses, snapping their Instamatic cameras, eating their hot dogs and plastic-wrapped sandwiches, complaining to their wives and husbands, herding their children. Floridian pensioners in shiny leisure suits, Californians in cutoff jeans and long hair, midwesterners in the wrinkled wash-and-wear trousers and tacky white shoes—this was *their* city, the capital of *their* republic. When one thought or spoke or wrote of The Americans, these were the people who gave flesh-and-blood reality to the abstraction. One tended to forget this, and it was a mistake. The United States was not the politically sophisticated land one might assume it to be, watching a PBS television show about the dangers of nuclear power or a network discussion about the advantages and disadvantages of SALT or the latest welfare program. The United States was what *these* people wanted it to be, and if they made their decisions fecklessly and in ignorance, one could despair, but one could not deny that it was their country. These were The People of the Constitution's preamble.

Clever politicians understood this. Great ones felt it in their bones. Journalists, Rivas thought self-critically, too often forgot it.

He turned to look to the north, across the browning grass

and the Reflecting Pool to the Washington Monument, where a throng of demonstrators milled around the base of the obelisk, waving hand-lettered banners and listening to speakers haranguing them through portable bullhorns. Since the 1960s, Washington had become a city of demonstrations, and these expressions of 'the right of the people peaceably to assemble' reached a seasonal peak during the hot and humid District of Columbia summer.

A gray government motor-pool sedan approached the circle around the monument from the direction of Twenty-third Street. It slowed and came to a stop at the curb and a thin, balding man got out of the rear seat, spoke briefly to the driver, and then began to scan the crowd.

Rivas recognized Isaac Holt. He had not seen the Deputy DCI for more than four years. He had interviewed him in New York on the occasion of Holt's assumption of the Deputy's post at Central Intelligence.

Rivas stood in the shadows and watched while the gray sedan moved away, leaving Holt peering up at the monument. It was characteristic of the man, Rivas thought, that he would use so nondescript a vehicle rather than the black limousine to which his rank entitled him. Holt seemed to have spent all of his government career cultivating the colorless anonymity of the perfect spook. Yet Rivas was aware of the fact that behind the bland, unremarkable façade of the man there was a sharply honed and totally ruthless mind. It would only have been a matter of time, Rivas thought, before Holt would have taken over Cole's job of DCI. For all of Cole's brilliance, Isaac Holt was better suited to the task of running a secret army of eighteen thousand people. Now, Rivas had no doubt, Holt would soon step into the post of DCI with scarcely a ripple.

He wished that he were better equipped to deal with Holt, wished that he knew exactly what Cole had thought of his deputy. He suspected that there had been no great affection between the two men. The cold and detailed way in which Ike Holt had described Cole's death on the telephone seemed to indicate that it had not been a traumatic event for the Deputy DCI. But then, it was difficult to be certain. Isaac Holt was not a man who showed his feelings. One could make a mistake by recklessly assuming that he had none.

Rivas watched Holt begin to walk slowly up the stone stairs. He was dressed in a gray summer suit and yet he seemed to meld with the more garishly garbed crowd of tourists around the monument. Rivas had the odd feeling that if he allowed himself to lose sight of Holt for a moment, he would vanish in the throng. Rivas rubbed at the scar on his face and wished that his head would stop throbbing under the bandage. The sutures felt like bits of wire embedded in his scalp and he had to resist the impulse to claw at them with his fingernails.

'Hello, Rivas,' Isaac Holt said. 'Welcome to Washington.'

'Let's walk,' Rivas said.

They moved through the tourists around the colonnade toward the side of the monument. The sun, as Rivas stepped out of the shadows, seemed to scour his eyes. He put on a pair of dark glasses.

'Are you all right?' Holt asked. 'We didn't have to meet here, you know.'

'I'm fine,' Rivas said. 'And I like this place.'

A faint smile hovered over Holt's thin, bloodless lips. 'Lincoln doesn't deserve to be the patron saint of liberals, you know. He's the only President ever to suspend *habeas corpus*. Think what the ACLU would have made of that.'

'I can see you are really broken up over what happened to Cole,' Rivas said.

'More than you know. But then, you've been away from us for so long you've probably forgotten the drill.'

' "Carry on. Keep smiling," ' Rivas said bitterly. 'I remember, all right.' He sat down on a stone balustrade because his legs had begun to tremble. The heat of the sun trapped in the stone burned his loins and thighs, but he needed to rest.

'You look terrible,' Holt said. 'How bad was it?'

'It gave me a headache. But it killed the boy driving the cab. I want to know why, that's all.'

Isaac Holt stared at him, his narrow eyes colorless in the blazing sunlight. 'The Agency didn't set you up, Rivas, if that's what you're thinking.'

Rivas said, as evenly as he could manage, 'I hope that's the truth, Holt. Because the next time I'm going to be ready.'

'Don't talk nonsense. The Company doesn't do things like that anymore. We haven't for years. Besides, there is no reason the Agency would want you hit.'

Rivas looked away, across the summer-burned parkland to the flat, still water of the Potomac. 'Did Cole talk to you about a special project he was working on for the President?'

'What sort of special project?'

'A confidential report for Loomis.'

'I know of no such confidential report,' Holt said. 'If Cole was working on something for the President, I would have known about it.'

'He wrote me a letter,' Rivas said.

Holt waited, gray lips compressed. Presently he said, 'I don't suppose you'd show it to me.'

'I destroyed it,' Rivas said.

'I see. And what did Cole have to say in this letter you destroyed?'

'Only that he was working on a report for Loomis.'

'Did he say Loomis ordered it?'

'No. It was Cole's own project.'

'I see,' Holt said again. 'I find it strange that he would tell you anything about what he was working on, Rivas. He did not hold you in particularly high regard, you know.'

'I know it better than you do,' Rivas said. 'But I think Cole was desperate. Or as desperate as Cole was capable of being. And somebody knew what he was doing and worried about it enough to kill him—and try to kill me.'

'And you think I am that somebody?'

'Are you?'

Holt shook his head in disbelief. 'I'm thinking that paranoia runs in your family, Rivas.'

'Maybe,' Rivas said. 'But someone came aboard the *Pandora* and tried to make it appear Cole had flipped out and cut up that girl and then killed himself. Who would do a thing like that without a good reason?'

'I can think of a number of possibilities,' Holt said quietly. 'Moscow Center must have at least a dozen men in it who would like to see Cole dead and discredited. He was a good DCI, you know. One of the best we have ever had.'

'The statement the White House released—about "some terrorist group"—was that your idea?' Rivas asked.

'Yes. But I would have preferred no statement of any kind.'

'Stonewall,' Rivas said.

'There is a limit to the public's right to know. I would have buried the whole business.'

'That, I can believe with no trouble at all,' Rivas said. It was growing difficult for him to contain his dislike of the Deputy DCI.

Holt said coldly, 'What are you after? A story?'

'I want to know who killed my brother and his girl and a Puerto Rican cab driver and damned near killed me. I want to know why. Then I'll know whether or not there is a story I can write.'

'You press people make me sick to my stomach,' Holt said. 'You'd sell your country for a four-minute spot on network news.'

Rivas felt a surging of anger in his belly. 'What have you done recently to make the world safe for democracy?'

Holt looked at Rivas with eyes that were hard and expressionless. 'Look out for yourself, Rivas,' he said, and started to walk away. He stopped and turned back, looking like a pillar of gray salt in the white sunlight. 'Stay out of this business. You don't know what you're playing with, Rivas. The Company takes care of its own dirty laundry.'

'Does it, now,' Rivas said. 'This is FBI country. Has someone issued a special hunting license?'

Holt's voice was as cold as breaking ice. 'Be careful, wetback. Next time you may not be so lucky.'

It struck Rivas with the force of a blow that Holt had lied when he said he didn't know what Cole was working on. He had a hundred ways of finding out and Rivas was certain that he had done just that.

Holt turned and walked away without another word. Rivas sat on the stone balustrade and watched him go stiffly, almost primly, down the granite steps to the street. In spite of the wet riverbottom heat of the day, Rivas felt as though he had been brushed by a chill north wind. Holt was a genuine, old-style spy: cold-blooded, colorless, dangerous as a cobra. A man like that would never doubt that the end justified the means, even if the means were murder.

8 Riyadh

David Kleinerman, onetime United States Ambassador to the Kingdom of Saudi Arabia, sat on the narrow iron cot in the dusty darkness of a storage room in the embassy's sub-basement and listened to the muffled sound of chanting in the street.

Kleinerman's hands were bound, his feet were bare, and his clothing consisted exclusively of a pair of Marine fatigue trousers. There was a two-week stubble of gray whiskers on his face. He was a fastidious man; his unwashed state and the smell of the toilet bucket in the corner of the storeroom distressed him almost as much as the fact that he had not seen the sunlight since the militants had burst into the embassy some one hundred and ninety days ago.

Isolation and worry over the state of his own people and the other Westerners who had taken refuge in the embassy had reduced Kleinerman from a robust two hundred pounds to less than one hundred and seventy. His six-foot frame seemed draped with flesh and there was a bitter-tasting metallic film in his mouth and throat that made him wonder if his food was being drugged.

A less angry man might be collapsing now, but David Kleinerman was sustained by his sense of outrage and the fury he felt toward his own government and its lack of action.

Remembering the chain of stupidities that had led to the occupation of the American embassy in Teheran a decade ago, he had watched developments in the Saudi capital with increasing apprehension. He had sent repeated cables to Washington warning that the Saudi monarchy was tottering and recommending active and forceful support for the faltering princes. When it had become obvious that the Loomis administration was no more competent to deal with the situation than the Carter administration had been in Iran, David Kleinerman had—on his own authority—begun to send all but the most vital personnel out of the country. He had succeeded in reducing the staff of the embassy to fewer than fifty when the blow had fallen.

In three days, the Saudi armed forces had disintegrated and the mob had assumed control of Riyadh. Pitched battles had been fought—were still being fought, though Kleinerman had no direct knowledge of the encounters—between the remnants of the Saudi authority and the Pan-Arabian revolutionaries, between Sunni and Shi'ite demonstrators, and between the foreign workers (mostly Palestinians and Iranians) and the new Revolutionary Action Committees.The *mullahs* had attempted to establish some sort of order by conducting Islamic courts of justice and enforcing draconian verdicts, but the executions had merely served to whet the rioters' taste for more violence.

Many of the foreign embassies had been closed in time, but some had not. There were half a dozen Canadians, thirty Italians, ten Frenchmen, six West Germans, and a pair of Spaniards somewhere in the embassy, though Kleinerman did not know where they were being held. The French and the Italians were the survivors of what was believed to be more than two hundred diplomatic personnel from those embassies—neither of which had been closed in time. All the Westerners had sought refuge in the American embassy because it had been thought to be the most physically secure and because they had been convinced that after the experience of Iran the Americans would never again permit themselves to be humiliated by rampaging militants of any sort. They had been wrong and were now prisoners along with the Americans.

David Kleinerman was a Wall Street lawyer by trade and he had been, for most of his life, a devotedly nonviolent man. But at this moment none of his former associates would have recognized him. He spent much of his time imagining that President Vincent Loomis sat in this dark cubicle with him, and that Loomis had to absorb in silence the vituperation and contempt his ambassador heaped on him. At other times, Kleinerman allowed himself the delicious luxury of imagining American fighter planes flushing the streets of Riyadh with cannon fire. He realized these were not the daydreams of a totally sane man, but for the first time in his life David Kleinerman knew the full meaning of what it was to hate.

At irregular intervals the Ambassador was visited by a militant he had come to suppose was the leader of the three hundred or so revolutionaries who had occupied the building. This young man (Kleinerman estimated his age at something more than twenty-five but under thirty) operated under the nom de guerre of Abou Moussa, the name of one of the legendary Arab irregulars of the Israeli war of independence.

The militant displayed considerable education, and Kleinerman was certain that he had been one of the privileged Arabs sent, in far different times, to the United States by the Saudi government.

The Ambassador was uncertain as to exactly why Abou Moussa chose to interrogate him repeatedly. He suspected that it was a personal choice, since the man was obviously and virulently anti-Semitic and seemed convinced that David Kleinerman was Jewish, which he was not. In fact, Kleinerman thought, his grimly German-Lutheran father would probably have been more offended by that accusation than by his distinguished son's illegal detention in the basement of his own embassy.

The chanting of the mob surrounding the embassy compound never ceased. It went on, nerve-wrackingly, day and night. Kleinerman knew that it was being orchestrated in the same way the demonstrations in Teheran had been. He wondered if the Western media people were allowing themselves to be manipulated again. In Iran, the American television networks, fascinated by the surging crowds, the hate banners, and the threatening vocalizations, had in effect become instruments of the militants' propaganda planners, many of whom had been trained by the Soviet KGB. Kleinerman was torn between a desire to know that he and his people were not being forgotten, and that Riyadh was being covered constantly by the press, and the realization that so long as it was, chances for rescue were almost nil.

He tried to swallow the tinny taste in his throat and wished for a cigarette. He had been told by others that two weeks of abstinence would remove all traces of tobacco hunger. It wasn't so. He thought he would do almost anything for a smoke. *And a bath.* God, he thought, how degrading it is to stink. He scratched at the gray hair on his chest with his bound hands. He was actually becoming almost proficient in doing simple things with his wrists bound. And there was damned little to be done in this closet, he thought, that wasn't simple. One ate—not well, because the embassy food supplies had been distributed to the street mob on the first day of the occupation. One defecated—with difficulty, because there was only that reeking bucket. One slept—a little only, because the dim single light was never extinguished and the street crowds never shut up: *Death to Loomis! Death to the Western spies! Death to Satan America!* These people were in love with death, Kleinerman thought. Or one would certainly imagine they were, if one were to take them at their chanted word.

Kleinerman, who had taken his appointment seriously enough to try to learn something of the Arab culture, smiled mirthlessly and quoted a line he remembered from the fourth sura of the Qur'ân: *God loveth not the speaking ill of anyone in public.* He wondered how the *mullahs* got around *that* dictum straight from their holy book.

He closed his eyes and tried to remember more. It was an exercise he found strangely soothing. But all that he could recall was a verse of the thirty-fifth sura. *If God should punish men according to what they deserve, he would not leave on the back of the earth so much as a beast.*

In Ambassador Kleinerman's situation, it was not a particularly comforting thought.

Mohammed Musayid ibn Sulayil, who was once pleased to claim blood ties to the family Saud, but who now preferred to be known by his chosen name of Abou Moussa, hurried down the steel stairway leading into the sub-basement of the American embassy.

Over his soiled tiger-striped military fatigues he wore an open *thobe,* the white robe of the devout Saudi Arabian male, and his thick, dark hair was covered by a *ghutra,* the traditional corded headcloth.

Mohammed Musayid had taken the name of Abou Moussa when he entered the training camp established in the late 1970s by Colonel Muammar el-Qaddafi for the purpose of training the revolutionaries who would eventually overthrow the Saudi monarchy. As a member of a cadet branch of the ruling family of Saudi Arabia, Mohammed Musayid had been something of a prize for the Libyan recruiters and their KGB advisers. He had been educated at the University of Southern California, where he had learned to speak flawless American English, to surf, to drink, and where he had developed a surpassing passion for the daughter of a wealthy southern California Jewish family. His liaison had alienated his family and reduced his circumstances, but being a young man of headlong enthusiasms, he had not allowed his family's disciplinary measures to dissuade him from the regular bedding of this co-ed mistress.

It had been a not-too-inexplicable coincidence that the girl's family had regarded their relationship with a lack of enthusiasm that matched that of Mohammed's Arabian parents. But they had found themselves in a stronger position to put an end to it. The girl, too young and immature to sacrifice all for love, was removed from school and sent off to a *kibbutz* in Israel where, her father told her severely, she might have an opportunity to reflect on the proper behavior for a nice Jewish girl. Being a proper Jewish liberal was one thing, he declared, but running the risk of becoming the father-in-law of an Arab, even one so aristocratically connected as Mohammed Musayid ibn Sulayil, was carrying liberality too far.

Young Mohammed might have survived the destruction of his dangerous romance had not the strictures placed on him by his own family included a savage cut in his allowance and orders to return home immediately at the end of the school year.

Mohammed did not wait. Raging against his family, and succumbing once again to his lifelong anti-Jewish conditioning (that had only just been held at bay by his enjoyment of Judith Ackerman's nubile and suntanned body), he had sold his Ferrari and left the United States for Paris. There, in the expatriate Arab community, he had been easily recruited by the headhunters of Al Fatah, the most active group within the Palestine Liberation Organization.

But Mohammed had been too valuable to waste on border raids into Israel—an occupation with a distressingly high rate of violent fatalities. As a Saudi, he was much more useful to the revolutionary movement in his homeland. He was already growing ashamed of his broken love affair with a Jew—most particularly with a Jew who had, in effect, rejected him. He found it easy to blame much that had happened to him on the vulgar and godless environment of the United States. And he spent much of his time dreaming that one day he would be revenged on the members of his family who had treated him so cavalierly.

In Paris he acquired a smattering of Marxist dialectic. There he was introduced to that arm of the PLO that was soon to begin calling itself the Pan-Arabian People's Islamic Revolutionary Army. He was taught by an uncomfortable but efficient cadre consisting of fundamentalist *mullahs*, French KGB agents, and Palestinian terrorists. When his indoctrination was complete, he was sent to Libya for final training in weapons, strategy, and tactics.

Now Mohammed Musayid ibn Sulayil had come home in the person of Abou Moussa, commander of the Revolutionary Action Committee occupying the embassy of Satan America in Riyadh.

David Kleinerman had almost managed to doze off when he heard the militant at his door exchange greetings with Abou Moussa and then the turning of the key in the lock.

Abou Moussa was armed, as always, with two heavy Russian military automatics tucked into the belt of his tiger fatigues. He was carrying a large Japanese tape recorder, and his white teeth showed in an exultant smile under his drooping Emiliano Zapata—style mustache.

'Good afternoon, Ambassador Jew,' Abou Moussa said. It was his customary greeting, and David Kleinerman had, after some protest, learned to ignore it.

'Good afternoon, Captain,' Kleinerman said hoarsely, his throat dry. 'Or is it general? I can never tell with you people.'

'I am a major of the Pan-Arabian People's Islamic Revolutionary Army. You know that. You have been told.'

Kleinerman felt a twinge of happiness at having tweaked the suddenly glowering young man's *amour propre*. But it was a small triumph. It was Kleinerman who sat with his hands tied and his feet bare.

Abou Moussa sniffed at the air and then called in the militant standing in the hallway. The young Arab entered with his Russian AK-47 at the ready. Kleinerman had hoped that by now the militants would have stopped making so much threatening play with their weapons, but he realized that they did it as much to maintain their own courage as to frighten their hostages. Still, the Ambassador thought, it must terrify the women captives each time one of these savages prodded or gestured with a loaded automatic rifle.

'You,' Abou Moussa said, gesturing at the toilet bucket. 'Take that out of here.'

The young militant slung his rifle and took the urine-and-feces-filled bucket out of the storage room with an expression of distaste on his dark face.

'I want you to hear something,' Moussa said, snapping on the tape recorder. 'We knew this place was a nest of spies.'

A voice began to come from the speakers. Kleinerman had some initial difficulty, but soon identified it as the voice of one of the Marine guards, a nineteen-year-old Kansan named Billy Earle Saugus.

The Marine detachment, under strict orders from Washington (orders that Kleinerman knew had been strongly protested by Secretary of State Turner) not to use 'deadly force' to protect the embassy compound, had been swiftly overrun by the hundreds of armed militants who had come over the wall and through the gate. He remembered seeing at least two of the Marines being beaten and mistreated after surrendering their arms. One of them had been Private Billy Earle Saugus.

The private's voice, sounding thin and strained, and using words he had never learned in Kansas or at Marine boot camp, was saying: 'We have been under the direct command of Mr. Haines Lofton, who is purported to be the trade attaché, but who is really the CIA man here. We know this is wrong and that we have committed crimes against the Arabian people. . .' There was more of the same, spoken haltingly, with many pauses and mispronunciations and a total lack of any semblance of conviction.

When the taped voice stopped, Moussa turned off the player. 'Well, Ambassador Jew? What do you have to say about that?'

'What am I supposed to say about it? It's a joke.'

'No joke. No fake. A confession.'

Kleinerman strove to keep the anger out of his voice. 'You intimidate a nineteen-year-old farm boy and that's supposed to impress anyone? Private Saugus never used a word like "purported" in his life, you foolish man. What do you think you accomplish with this sort of thing?'

'This is only a beginning, Ambassador Jew.'

Kleinerman regarded the younger man from beneath raised eyebrows. 'Did you know that you are a Semite, you anti-Semitic bastard?'

'Watch your mouth.'

'Even assuming I could do such a thing, what if I refuse? What will you do, shoot me? I really don't think so.'

'Not you, Ambassador Jew. We shall start with some of the others. We could shoot one a day for nearly two months.'

Kleinerman shook his head. 'You won't do that.'

'Why shouldn't we? We are not afraid. We are fighting to reclaim our country from the CIA.'

'Do you really *believe* that?' Kleinerman had spent so much of his life dealing with rational people that he found this sort of discussion difficult to maintain.

'Before we have done,' Moussa said in deadly earnest, '*you* will believe it.'

'I think not, young man,' Kleinerman said. 'And if you shoot so much as one hostage, you'll have a division of Marines in Riyadh in twenty-four hours.' He wished that he believed *that*, he told himself, but he did not. There was no conceivable set of circumstances that the Ambassador could imagine that would bring that kind of reaction from the Loomis administration. It was tragic, but it was true. Nor was any military rescue likely from Europe, certainly not from the Italians or the French. And even the West Germans had long ago decided that it was necessary to 'tilt' toward all Arab revolutionaries in order to keep their oil-fired industries humming and their Mercedes and Volkswagens speeding along their *Autobahnen*.

For a moment Kleinerman remembered a discussion he had had with Calder Davis in New York before accepting the appointment to Riyadh from Loomis.

'I know you feel that international law is crumbling,' Calder had said, 'and so it is. But we must uphold what structure can be saved, David, preserving it against the time when civilized people are ready to establish some sensible world order.'

What must Calder be thinking now? Kleinerman wondered. Was he watching the final decline of the West with aristocratic disapproval and discussing it with his fellow patricians in some quiet and comfortable meeting room reserved for the ISSG, the Trilateral Commission, or the Council on Foreign Relations? Davis was a man of action, but there were forces loose in the world that were beyond redemption. At least it seemed that way to David Kleinerman, viewing the world from the sub-basement of the American embassy in Riyadh.

When he abandoned his grim reverie, Kleinerman was rather surprised to find that his visitor had gone without another word.

He leaned back against the concrete block wall and sighed. Then he noticed that the bucket had not been returned to its corner, and all of his world-ranging concerns refocused themselves on the fact that he needed to relieve himself and if the glowering militant standing guard outside his door chose to be uncooperative, he, David Kleinerman, United States Ambassador to the Kingdom of Saudi Arabia, would have to urinate against a wall.

9 Cairo

The man known in Cairo as Helmuth Reich pushed his ample frame away from the table and allowed himself the gratifying privilege of a rolling belch. He had eaten well, drunk well—far better than one could do at home—and now he was prepared to interrogate his visitor with all the thoroughness expected of a field agent of the KGB.

Reich was well pleased. He was enjoying a remarkable run of good luck. On the very day he had received instructions from Moscow Center to investigate any leads that would disclose the nature of the activities of the New Peace Corps in Arabia, his PLO contact had appeared with a piece of news that would surely interest the men of Moscow Center.

Reich, an independent, deep-cover agent operating outside the local KGB *rezident's* authority, had begun his career in intelligence as an agent of the East German Security Service. But his talent for undercover work and his devotion to Marxist Leninism had won him a coveted post inside the KGB itself, as well as secret Soviet citizenship. Of course, the East Germans still believed he worked for them, and in a manner of speaking, he did. His reports to Leipzig were models of correctness and a source of vast quantities of useful information on the Egyptian military. But his politically sensitive material went not to East Germany but to the heartland of the Revolution, the USSR.

The difficulty of implementing the riskier provisions of the last Camp David accords between Egypt and Israel had created a certain air of petulance in Cairo, and this in turn had opened the doors to the establishment there of an East German trade mission. The Americans had been characteristically sluggish in providing Egypt with credits and aid in sufficient quantities to sustain Egyptian agriculture, and the East Germans had lost no time in filling the obvious need. The East German chemical industry was only too happy to supply the phosphates and nitrates needed to revive the lands left chemically anemic by the flood control of the Aswan High Dam.

Reich's cover was a post as the head of the sales department of the chemicals division of the East German trade mission. He performed very well, and in the last two years had become known in Cairo as a 'friendly' Communist and one of the more jolly hosts among the foreigners resident in the capital.

His trade-mission job allowed him to travel freely everywhere in Egypt, and to deal directly with *fellaheen,* small farmers and government bureaucrats alike. It was triply delicious to Reich when he considered that he was helping East Germany sell off the chemical by-products of a huge and busy industry whose main task was the production of vast quantities of chemical warfare weapons, and at the same time procuring significant amounts of military intelligence for his native land and even more valuable political intelligence for his adoptive country, the Soviet Union.

In the time he had spent in Egypt he had managed to establish a huge and complex network of spies and informers inside the Egyptian government, among the foreign diplomats in Cairo, and within the many radical groups that made up the Palestine Liberation Organization.

His money came from Libya, from the seemingly bottomless coffers of Muammar el-Qaddafi, who was by now tightly under the control of the planners in Moscow Center. This allowed Helmuth Reich to do very good business (in the ancient and approved way of dispensing *baksheesh)* among Egyptians and other Arabs, and at the same time to live luxuriously in a suite atop that pyramid of Western decadence, the Cairo Hilton.

Now, late on a summer evening in July, he had finished his meal on the terrace overlooking the city and the River Nile, lighted his excellent Havana, and settled back to hear the report of one of his PLO contacts, a black-skinned desert Arab known only as Achmed, a thin and somewhat sinister figure in shiny black suit and red-checked Palestinian *kaffiyeh.*

'I would offer you something to drink, but I have no wish to offend,' Reich said, helping himself to schnapps.

Achmed gestured swiftly, as though putting aside some satanic temptation. He was not, as Reich well knew, one of the new-style liberated Arabs. He was a desert man, uncomfortable in his city clothes, in this soft set of rooms bright with polyester fabrics and chromium trim; and genuinely revolted by the sight of even a European drinking alcohol. He was a *bedu* from the Arabian Peninsula, and a Sunni Muslim of the Wahhabi persuasion, which made him grim, puritanical, an excellent executioner and torturer, and very bad company, Reich thought amusedly.

'Allah is compassionate. Allah is merciful. May Allah forgive you,' the desert man said, regarding his host with eyes as cold as black agate.

'But you will not, eh, Achmed?' Reich, who had a talent for languages, replied in fluent Arabic. 'Well, we won't worry about that. Tell me more about Py.'

'The cell at Abu Simbel is Black September,' Achmed said, 'as you know.'

'I should. I have supplied them with weapons often enough,' Reich said.

The Arab ignored the thrust, he even agreed that it was justified. The tiny remnant of the once powerful Black September group used up weapons and explosives at a prodigal rate, yet they seemed able to accomplish little in the way of sabotage against the increasingly efficient Egyptian secret police forces. But they remained close to the people and they paid for their weapons with information Achmed doubted Reich could obtain from any other segment of his Egyptian network.

'They have been watching this Py creature for several months. He has been suspected of Zionism ever since he came to Abu Simbel.'

'And did you prove Zionist sympathy? Did he confess?'

'Unfortunately he died while being questioned. But his wife was more forthcoming,' Achmed said.

'When, exactly, did they take them?' Reich asked.

'Last night. He had spent the day guiding some French tourists through the temples, and the Septembrists were waiting for him at home.'

Reich rose and walked to the balcony's edge. From where he stood he could look across the Nile to Giza and beyond; in the distance, he could see the floodlighted Pyramids. Unlike many of his northern countrymen, Helmuth Reich loved Cairo.

He turned back to Achmed. 'There is no need to give me

details of how he died. You people tend to be unnecessarily brutal. Just tell me what his wife volunteered.'

'Many harsh things are necessary in the service of Allah,' Achmed said grimly.

'The Merciful, the Compassionate. Yes, I do understand all about that. Py's wife?'

'She was jealous of him. She believed he had other women.' Achmed's manner showed exactly what he thought of any Muslim woman jealous of her man. 'There were unexplained absences and it disturbed her mind. So she followed him. Several times. She found that he was meeting with one of the women from the NPC Station at Kalabishah. When she saw the woman, she knew that it was not an ordinary assignation. So she made inquiries. It was a woman physician named Amira Shallai, a woman of Alexandria. A *Nasrani.*'

And that, Reich thought, would be enough to condemn the unfortuate Py, whom they already suspected of being a Zionist spy.

As it happened, Helmuth Reich knew quite a good deal about Dr. Amira Shallai. He knew that she had been educated in the United States, that her family were rich Alexandrian bourgeois, and that her betrothed was killed in the fighting in Lebanon. It was Helmuth Reich's job to know such things. He had, in fact, considered the oddity of a well-born Christian Arab woman serving as a doctor at a place like Kalabishah—not one of the region's most attractive places. But there were many rich bourgeois in the New Peace Corps, which was, after all, one of the most active agencies of imperialism left in the path of the World Revolution.

What Reich had sometimes wondered about the handsome Dr. Shallai was: where were her loyalties? Apparently Achmed and his Black September thugs had no difficulty answering that question—to their own satisfaction, at least.

'The woman is plainly a Zionist,' Achmed said. 'She works with Jews. The NPC is rotten with Jews and Zionists.'

'I believe my information is that she is Egyptian,' Reich said. 'Of course that is no assurance that she isn't a great deal more than that.' Actually, he had wondered if it were not possible that Dr. Shallai might have CIA connections.

'She is on her way to Arabia,' Achmed said.

'Now that *is* interesting. To the NPC station in the Rub' al Khali?'

'Yes. By now she is probably on the way to Oman. The station is supplied from there.'

'I am aware of that,' Reich said quietly. 'May I know how you know so much about her travel arrangements?'

'An informer.'

'I see. One you can trust?'

'No. A man of no consequence. But one anxious to impress us.'

Reich waited, eyebrows raised.

'A man named Suleiman Dayir. A functionary of the government crew at the High Dam. He was on the lake steamer with her.'

'And she told him where she was going?'

Achmed frowned. 'Of course not. He learned it from the steamer crew. Her belongings were marked for air shipment to Salalah. That means the Jew station in the Empty Quarter. Black September knows all about that.'

In point of fact, Reich thought, Black September knew next to nothing about the NPC Station in the south Arabian wasteland. His own controllers at 2 Dzerzhinsky Square in Moscow had almost no hard facts about the station, so it was improbable that a ragtag remnant of Black September terrorists knew more. It was typical Arab hyperbole. These people, Reich thought wearily, lived in a self-induced trance of fantastic happenings and nonexistent successes. Now that they had murdered the unfortunate Py—who may or may not have been an Israeli spy (how would anyone ever know now?), they imagined they had uncovered some great and mysterious plot against the true religion, the legitimate rights of the Palestinian brothers, and Allah the Compassionate knew what else.

One of the less—until now—significant bits of information Reich had gathered about Dr. Amira Shallai was that she had a young admirer at Kalabishah, one Dr. Cecil Sawyer, who must now be desolated by her transfer to Arabia. Reich had some sources within the local NPC administration. He began to consider how these bits and pieces might be combined to produce something useful to Moscow Center.

'What, exactly, did Dayir have to say about the lady doctor?' Reich asked.

Achmed's expression showed his disgust. 'He volunteered

only the information that he thought she might be an American agent, since she works for the New Peace Corps.' His black eyes regarded Reich steadily. 'And we have it on your authority that the NPC is an agency of American imperialism.'

Reich corrected him carefully. 'Of *international* imperialism. You really must learn to be more precise, Achmed. Otherwise your usefulness to me will diminish swiftly.'

Achmed looked at Reich with hatred—the hatred of the fanatic for the known atheist. 'We learned from the crewmen that Dayir attempted to enter her cabin on the steamer. She disabled him. Bare-handed.'

Reich suppressed an impulse to smile. 'Did she, now,' he murmured. 'Poor Mr. Dayir.'

'I told you he was a man of no consequence. But that she was able to hurt him so easily suggests that she has been well trained by someone.'

'Quite possibly so,' Reich said thoughtfully.

'Is my information of value?'

'Of some value,' Reich said.

'Then I am instructed to ask for more weapons. Explosives and time pencils.'

Reich walked to the door of the suite to indicate that the interview was over. 'I will consider it,' he said. He knew that he would produce the desired items, of course. The remnant at Abu Simbel was unimportant, but they might be useful at some time in the future. It was worth it to keep them supplied with what they desired. But one did wonder what tourist bus would be blown up or which three-thousand-year-old statue would be defaced by the angry, defeated men and women of the Black September cell. They were becoming anachronisms, Reich thought. It might be well to discuss their liquidation with Moscow Center.

When the Arab had gone, Reich returned to the balcony and poured himself another glass of schnapps and stood for a time looking down at the dark ribbon of the Nile.

He, like most of the members of the world's intelligence communities, had heard of the death of Cole Norris, the American spymaster. The murder had sent a shockwave through every intelligence service in the world, followed by aftershocks of suspicion.

To Reich it seemed impossible that any organization in the

Arab world could be responsible. They simply had not the power or the expertise to track and murder an American DCI. It was inconceivable to Reich that any group that could produce an Achmed or a Black September commando could muster the force to penetrate even so flimsy a shield as American security. No, blowing up airline terminals and machine-gunning day schools was the PLO style.

But the feeling that something peculiar had happened within the strange brotherhood of spies and saboteurs was disturbing. It made everyone in the profession feel vulnerable. But, Reich told himself with a sigh, those were the risks of spying as a profession.

Considering now his talk with the Black September man, he felt once again that he was having a streak of luck. And one should always ride with good fortune.

Recently Moscow Center had been harassing him for not producing any usable information about the NPC in the Rub' al Khali. Anything remotely connected with oil and the problem of how to get more and more of the stuff had begun to obsess Moscow. And the Soviet planners, provincial as only Russians could be, seemed to be unaware, or at least unconcerned, that Reich was separated from the old air base the NPC used in Arabia by nearly two thousand kilometers of mostly trackless nothing.

But Reich did know somewhat about the NPC station at Kalabishah, and that might be parlayed into something more useful to the computers at Dzerzhinsky Square. Thanks to the Septembrist thug, Reich now knew that Dr. Amira Shallai was on her way into the Rub' al Khali, leaving behind a lovesick young Briton.

Reich congratulated himself on having taken the time and effort to cultivate one of the bored bureaucrats in the personnel section of the NPC's office in Cairo. Surely a clever man could build himself a tidy operation out of resources such as these.

Suppose, he told himself, just suppose it were possible to recruit the romantic Dr. Sawyer and entice him to go into the Rub' al Khali and fetch out the lovely Shallai and bring her here, to Cairo? The lady, who seemed suspiciously adept in the ancillary arts of espionage, might prove a golden seam of information.

Even if the operation produced nothing of great value to the Soviets, it would serve to remind the bureaucrats at

Moscow Center that Helmuth Reich was a tireless worker in the cause of World Revolution. And anything that might remotely concern Arabian oil was certain to interest the Kremlin.

He finished his schnapps, permitted himself another thunderous belch, and went inside to telephone his tame NPC clerk.

10 Washington, D.C.

'It is Mr. Shepherd, sir,' the houseman said decorously, his long gray face touched with an expression that showed his disapproval of anyone choosing to make a social call at eleven o'clock at night.

Secretary of State Turner, already half prepared to retire and dressed in pajamas, silk dressing gown, and patent-leather slippers, looked up from his book and said, 'Show him in here, Hemmings.'

Presently, Carl Shepherd, attaché case in hand, appeared in the warmly lit library. He looked about curiously. This was the first time the FBI Director had ever entered Raymond Turner's Georgetown town house. The two men were not friends; except professionally, they seldom encountered one another in the Washington social circuit.

Shepherd took note of the wall-to-ceiling collection of fine books, the lovingly cared-for antique furniture, the deep Persian carpet. The room had the smell of leather bindings and furniture polish overlaid with the rich odor of good tobacco. It was a man's room, a place that might once have known a woman's touch but now had acquired the atmosphere of an old, exclusive, gentleman's club.

The FBI Director had never known Elvira Turner, but he recognized the portrait above the dark fireplace from photographs he had seen of the Secretary's dead wife. The painting showed a handsome woman of perhaps thirty-five, formally dressed in the fashion of the war years.

Turner gave his servant an order with a barely perceptible gesture and the man retired silently. Then the Secretary said, 'Please. Sit.'

Shepherd dropped obediently into one of the least comfortable chairs, his briefcase held on his lap. For all the world, he thought, discomfited, like a man applying for a job in a law firm too obviously elitist to hire him.

'I'm very sorry to appear like this, Raymond. But I'm troubled and I didn't know where else to turn.'

The houseman silently reappeared with a silver tray, a decanter of brandy, glasses, and a siphon of soda.

'Thank you, Hemmings,' the Secretary said. 'We won't require anything more.'

When Turner and Shepherd were alone, he asked, 'How can I help you, Carl?'

Shepherd shifted his weight in the overfirm chair. 'Well, that's just it, Raymond. I'm not really certain. But I desperately need to talk to someone I'm sure can be trusted.' He realized, even as he said the words, what an indictment he was leveling at all the other men who served at the top level of the Vincent Loomis administration.

A thin smile softened the severe lines of the Secretary of State's long, lined face. 'As bad as that.' He poured brandy, added soda, and handed the glass to his guest.

'I had a call from Peter Gilmartin this afternoon,' Shepherd said. 'He's been getting heat from Ike Holt, I think. I was told that the Bureau should stay far away from the Norris business. A question of national security, Peter said.'

'I see,' Turner said thoughtfully. 'Was Peter speaking for the President?'

'He didn't say so, but of course, he is. He wouldn't take so much responsibility on his own. I half expected it after what Ike Holt said at yesterday's meeting. But frankly I don't know what line to take.' Shepherd swallowed some of the brandy and soda and put the glass down on the shining surface of a Queen Anne end table. 'You've seen the papers, of course. And the television newscasts. The media are winding up to fall into one of their feeding frenzies. They smell a cover-up.'

Turner ignored the reference to the press. It was true, as Shepherd said, that the sparseness of the White House statement on the death of Norris and the Moran girl was providing the media people with exactly the sort of adversary situation they relished. But Secretary Turner, of all the adminstration men, believed that no government could function on the basis of remaining totally open to whatever delving the media felt like doing. There were times when 'silence' did not necessarily mean 'cover-up.'

'Ike Holt intends to conduct the investigation,' Shepherd went on unhappily. 'But that's not the worst of it. Did you watch the late news?' He drank some of his brandy and soda to ease the dryness in his throat. 'Someone took a shot at Michael Rivas yesterday on the Van Wyck Expressway. It didn't make last night's telecasts because no one remembered Rivas was Cole's halfbrother. They did today, though, and they are supposing all sorts of connections.'

'Supposing?'

'Well, of course they would. They'd be damned fools to ignore the relationship. I put the New York field office on it right away. Maybe I shouldn't have done that. There is no federal crime involved. But I did it anyway. So far they've turned up a fat zero. Do you know Cole's brother, Raymond?'

'No. I have read his reportage. He's good. Sharp mind—if a bit quixotic. Was he injured?'

'Slightly. The driver of his taxicab was killed. The New York police are handling the investigation. A thing like that, some assassin using a shotgun on a journalist on a public road, makes them look bad. They don't like it. What they like even less is that Rivas stayed one night in New York with his publisher and then left—without telling them. I understand they're trying to get a judge to issue a warrant claiming that he is a material witness. Nothing has happened on that yet.'

'And is Ike Holt right? Is national security involved in the case?'

'That's what's so frustrating, Raymond. I don't know. And I should. But you were at the meeting. You heard the President agree with Ike that the Bureau should keep hands off.'

'I think you must regard what the President said only as a suggestion, Carl. Unless you receive a direct order from him you cannot vacate the field to the Central Intelligence Agency. Congress has stated plainly and without any equivocation that the CIA's writ does not run inside the United States. They may find that crippling—we may even agree with them—but it's the law.'

'I know that, of course,' Carl Shepherd said. 'I suppose I just needed to hear it again.' He essayed a weak and mirthless smile. 'And you are the only man in the administration I'm likely to hear it from.'

'You may run into a severe problem,' Turner said. 'I doubt that it will happen, but if the President gives you a direct order—you may be faced with a crisis of conscience.'

'You mean I may have to resign.'

'Yes.'

'I know that, too,' Shepherd said unhappily.

The FBI Director looked so hunted that Raymond Turner felt a twinge of pity for him.

'I have come asking for moral support,' Shepherd said, 'but I haven't been entirely spineless, Raymond. I was so disturbed yesterday by some of the things Ike Holt said that I've ordered him put under surveillance.'

Turners eyebrows arched in surprise. He had not expected anything quite so direct from Carl Shepherd. But then, he reminded himself, even uncertain men take positive actions when they are closely pressed.

'I know,' Shepherd said. 'I've had a whole bunch of second thoughts about it, but I didn't know what else to do. And it paid off, in an odd sort of way.' He felt thirsty and finished his brandy and soda in a single draft. 'Ike met Rivas today. At the Lincoln Memorial. I don't know whether that means they are working together secretly, or perhaps Rivas simply doesn't trust Holt. Unfortunately, my people were not close enough to know what they discussed. But they parted on what appeared to be bad terms.'

'Cole's brother is here in Washington?'

'That's just it, Raymond. He went directly from his meeting with Holt to Dulles.'

'To Dulles?'

'He didn't go back to New York. He took a Concorde flight to London,' Shepherd said. 'Something else, too. My people think someone was following him. A government sedan trailed him out to Dulles and then whoever was in the car saw the FBI agents and took off. My people had to follow Rivas, and so they couldn't stay with the driver of the government car. By the time they had some backup, of course, whoever it was had long since disappeared.'

Turner regarded Shepherd speculatively. 'And by this time Michael Rivas is in England.'

'That's right. And, of course, I couldn't have told my people to stay with him. Once Rivas is out of the country he is in Agency territory.'

'Yes. The law works both ways. A pity, perhaps, but that was what Congress intended.'

'That's as may be,' Shepherd said, 'but I couldn't very well just leave it at that, could I? After all, its becoming nearly certain that there is some sort of conspiracy working here. So I telephoned Sir Allan Sawkins at Scotland Yard and asked for help. I would imagine Special Branch now has Michael Rivas under observation.'

For the first time a full-blown, if wintry, smile appeared on the Secretary of State's face. 'So you are not quite so uncertain as you say you are, Carl,' he said.

'No, I suppose not,' Shepherd said nervously. 'I had to take some action, after all, even if Rivas is now playing—or doing whatever he is doing—in Isaac Holt's ball park.' He paused and studied Turner for a moment. 'The President is going to appoint Ike Holt DCI, isn't he?'

'I believe so.'

'Well, maybe it *is* a good choice. I don't know. I'm uneasy about it, though. I can't quite tell you why, except that it seems to me that Ike is terribly quick to cut corners. I don't think the country should have to go through another time like the mid-seventies.'

'I agree,' Turner said.

Carl Shepherd drew a deep sighing breath. 'I'm glad I came here tonight. I know what's right, Raymond. It's just that sometimes I need a corroborating opinion. I thank you for it. I think I'll go home and get some sleep now. Dolly will be wondering what I'm up to.'

When the FBI Director had gone, Raymond Turner sat thoughtfully in his silent study. It was strange, but sometimes the least likely men had a gratifying way of surprising one with an unexpected show of integrity.

But what Carl Shepherd might now expect at the hands of an irritated President was cause for some concern. It would be a pity if Shepherd were to fall from grace because for the first time he had acted with the alertness and conviction that his post demanded.

11 Washington National to Kennedy

In the handsomely appointed lounge area of Calder Davis's TriStar, Secretary of Energy George Rossmore relaxed with a drink and a fine cigar. Calder Davis came into the lounge looking frail and pallid. Rossmore knew that the financier disliked flying. He often told his associates that he was a product of a slower, more measured age: a time of private trains and ocean liners. The Secretary found this wryly amusing and incongruous, since Davis's many enterprises made it necessary for him to fly hundreds of thousands of miles each year.

Davis was followed by one of his staff of male secretaries burdened with a number of briefing books and files, which he placed on the conference table before retiring. Rossmore was struck by the similarities in the life-styles of Davis and old Raymond Turner. Both men were widowers, both were served by a male staff of servants who seemed to perform their functions in absolute silence, as though they were guided by telepathy. But then, he thought, that shouldn't surprise anyone. Both men instinctively surrounded themselves with subordinates trained to care for their needs with an assurance that lesser men would have found intimidating. Rossmore's own manner of dealing with servants was tumultuous, with a constantly changing roster of slovenly maids and incompetent butlers and chauffeurs.

Davis settled into the chair at the head of the table with a deep sigh. 'I always like to have a word or two with the boys on the flight deck,' he said with a thin smile. 'I shall probably always need reassurance that all this actually works as it should.' He glanced about him at the luxuriously fitted interior of the aircraft. 'Well, no matter. To work, George.' He opened the first of the briefing books. 'Let's begin with the status of the synfuel program.'

Rossmore unzipped his own briefcase and extracted a

red-banded file. 'On the government side, everything is on schedule, Calder. The Committee on Energy has approved the ongoing subsidy program. There has been some opposition from environmentalist groups, but nothing that cannot be handled. A problem may arise when the plants move into volume production. The water-consumption projections DOE has received from ConEn's engineers are still very high. The farmers and ranchers in the Wyoming basin are likely to start raising hell once the press gets hold of the numbers.'

'I appreciate that, George. We have a full team working on a method of reducing the water consumption and I think they are getting somewhere. But for the time being, you will simply have to see to it that the press does not get the figures.' He gestured delicately with a thin, blue-veined hand. 'I rather think that the media will have its hands full in the next few days.'

'Is ConEn ready in Europe?' Rossmore asked. 'I understood the Germans were having second thoughts about making the change so swiftly.'

'There have been some discussions,' Davis said, 'but the decision is really out of the hands of the Bonn government. The plant is in place, the Ruhr mines are open.'

'That eases my mind somewhat.' Rossmore turned several pages of the file before him. 'The strategic reserve is within eight percent of capacity. And there is still oil in the tanker fleet en route here. Eighteen and a third million barrels. In fact, we are still loading small amounts at Ras Tanura. The rebels in Riyadh haven't got their act together yet. Satan America and her European satellites are still getting a little oil out of the peninsula. When does Collingwood move?'

'That depends on the weather. He needs reasonable weather to fly his helicopters.'

'Has he asked about EQ Station?'

'As far as the general and his men are concerned, the station is simply a communications and radar warning base. I see no reason to burden him with more information than that.'

'Andy Traynor is rather badly worried about the last helicopter transfer,' the Secretary of Energy said. 'Our Secretary of Defense is rather a weak reed, I'm afraid.'

'The inspectors were shown some defective parts,' Calder said. 'Rotor gears, I believe. They were told the faulty components were installed on eighty of the new machines and that they would all have to be retrofitted. The helicopters were flown to Tokar ten days ago.'

Rossmore was struck by the command of detail. But then, one did not build financial empires by being careless or poorly informed.

'The Kfirs we bought in Israel and the Panavia Tornados are also at Tokar. The last guard personnel for EQ Station are due tomorrow in Salalah. The transport aircraft are still in Johannesburg and they will fly to EQ Station as soon as the weather permits. All that remains to consider is the unexpected. There is always the unexpected, George.'

Four
July 15, the fourth day

These, in the day when heaven was falling,
The hour when earth's foundations fled,
Followed their mercenary calling
And took their wages and are dead.

—A.E. Housman, 'Epitaph
on an Army of Mercenaries'

12 Salalah

To Amira Shallai, who was seeing the Arabian seacoast of Oman's Dhofar province for the first time, the terrain and weather were pleasant surprises.

This most favored bit of the Arabian Peninsula was not, as she had expected, simply the seaward edge of the great deserts of the interior. By a happy climatological chance, the province was just brushed by the yearly monsoon that dominated the weather of the Indian Ocean. The result was a narrow coastal plain rich with semitropical growth: groves of coconut palm, rustling fields of sugarcane, plantains, wheat, millet, indigo, and cotton. To the south lay the sparkling blue of the Arabian Sea, to the north the slender littoral was protected from the fierce heat and sandstorms of the Rub' al Khali by the rugged barrier of the Qara Mountains, the southern slopes of which were, even in midsummer, laced with sparkling streams and watercourses. It must have been this narrow edge of land between sea and mountains, Amira thought as she looked down past the Boeing's wingtip, that the ancient Romans had called Arabia Felix.

Salalah, as the aircraft circled to land, looked like a city of sandcastles: the Old Town dominated by the massive, crenelated fort that the British of the Raj had dubbed 'Oman's Balmoral' in the days when it had been the fortress-palace of the Sultan of Muscat and Oman. But even here, a thousand miles from the major oil fields of the Gulf coast, the new oil money was changing the landscape. Oman's petro-revenues were infinitesimal compared to Arabia's, but there was still enough to account for a forest of new steel-and-glass skyscrapers, an expansion of the old RAF—Imperial Airways base into a large, modern airport, and the inevitable complex of seaside resort hotels.

The port facilities looked extensive to the Egyptian

woman, though she had only an imperfect understanding of the complex of cranes and derricks forming the heart of the kingdom's primary port for the handling of containerized cargo. There were a dozen ships in the harbor, only two of them tankers loading crude from the pipeline terminal. The pipeline, a fellow passenger was only too glad to explain to her, was a masterpiece of Japanese engineering bringing oil through the Qara Mountains from the small, but high-quality fields at Hajmah, 450 kilometers from Salalah.

Amira's informant was a Mr. Haramaki, a garrulous pipeline engineer, one of a group of Japanese nationals under contract to the government of the kingdom.

The airplane had made the journey from Cairo half empty. In addition to the Japanese group, there had been a half-dozen Omani civil servants returning from a conference in Amsterdam, a silent and noncommunicative group of ten South Africans who kept strictly to themselves, and a number of Ethiopian merchants who had joined the flight at the stop at Assab, on the African coast.

This stop had been made necessary because extra fuel was needed to give a wide berth to both the hostile air patrols of the South Yemenite air force and the sandstorms sweeping the whole of the Rub' al Khali.

The flight had been long and tiring and Amira did not sleep comfortably on airplanes. But as she looked down at the green land in the sparkling morning sunlight, she felt oddly refreshed. Such was the effect on an Arab, she thought, of growing plants and a well-watered countryside. It was as though the blood of her nomadic desert ancestors stirred in response to the glistening streams and the green fields below. With such a land to sustain them, she mused, it was sad that the history of the Omani Arabs was notable mainly for constant warfare and tribal feuding, palace coups and dynastic murder. Until the mid-1950s, even slavery had been countenanced on this lovely coast. The thought chilled her and dampened her spirits.

The airplane approached the new airport from the sea, and as it passed low over the port, Amira could see steel containers bearing the NPC bands of green-and-white standing on the docks and being loaded into sand-colored trucks. Mr. Haramaki, who had been politely curious about the woman doctor in the uniform of the New Peace Corps, commented on the activity below. 'Your organization must be doing interesting work in the Empty Quarter, doctor. I understand the living conditions are very severe?'

'So I have been told,' Amira replied distractedly. The Japanese had been solicitous throughout the long flight and she had no wish to be rude to him, but for these last few moments of the journey, she preferred to be alone with her thoughts.

'It is a wonderful thing that men and women of goodwill from all over the civilized world do, this NPC,' Haramaki declared. 'Many Japanese have joined, you know. I would have done so myself, but unfortunately I have a large family to support in Kyoto.'

A further exchange was prevented by the stewards moving down the aisle admonishing passengers to fasten their seat belts and bring their seat backs to the upright position.

She was met at Omani customs by a heavyset, gray-haired man who introduced himself as Colin Hadfield—*Colonel* Hadfield, that was—who had been detailed to meet her and transport her to the new chain-owned Hotel Oasis in the New Town. Amira was wryly amused at the insistence on his military title and the soldierly appearance he had managed to establish by adding a red beret and a swagger stick to his NPC desert clothing.

Colonel Hadfield was in his sixties, Amira estimated. He had a strong face, burned to the color of mahogany by the Arabian sun. His eyes were a clear, innocent blue that Amira associated with English country folk. Though how long it might have been since the colonel had seen his native England, Amira did not care to guess. He was one of a once familiar breed in the Middle East, the British soldier—Arabist, men captured completely and early in life by the desert and the people who lived in it.

On the short journey into the New Town in the colonel's NPC jeep, her estimate of Colin Hadfield was confirmed. He had served, he told her with some pride, as a regimental commander of the Oman Trucial Scouts, one of the many native military units the British had organized wherever the necessities of Empire had required law and order, Western-style.

'They were a fine unit, Dr. Shallai,' Hadfield said, wheeling the jeep precipitously by a line of lorries heading for the Qara passes. 'I served with them from 1946 until they were incorporated into the Sultan's Northwest Frontier Force in 1962.' He favored her with a weathered smile. 'In all, I have lived here—on the coast and in the desert—for more than thirty-five years.'

Amira listened with interest and studied the countryside around her. It was a kaleidoscopic jumble of the new and the ancient. The road ran through irrigated fields of sugarcane. Ahead of the jeep, traffic clogged the narrow asphalt road that led to what Colonel Hadfield called 'New Town' with an unmistakable note of distaste in his British speech. The brilliant sun struck spearshafts of light from the glassy cliffs of the modern towers dominating the skyline. Yet farther inland and at a number of places along the shore behind them, Amira could see the tall, narrow buildings of mud brick that seemed to shoulder one another in an effort to thrust their rectangular tops up into the harsh daylight. On the bluff overlooking the harbor stood the old fort, dominated by its central barrel-shaped tower with crenelated walls. A veritable Beau Geste of a fort, Amira thought, that looked as though it had been built by some gigantic child playing on some gargantuan, sandy strand.

With pleasure, she let the wind tangle her dark hair. The sun was bright, but far from uncomfortably warm.

'We would ordinarily fly on into EQS,' Colonel Hadfield said. 'But it will have to be a lorry convoy, I'm afraid. It is difficult to credit, but there are sandstorms on the other side of the Qara.' He waved a hand in the direction of the mountains, purpled by distance, but green in the foothills.

'How soon, Colonel?' Amira asked.

'Tomorrow, doctor. It will take us most of the day just to reach the Qara passes. It won't be a pleasant journey, I'm afraid.'

'I am accustomed to discomfort.'

'I'll deposit you at the Oasis,' Colonel Hadfield said. 'It is a bloody awful tinsel palace, I'm afraid. But it is the best in New Town. For "best," doctor, read "newest." Nothing Western lasts very long here. The people want to accept it, and they try very hard. But it isn't in them. Thank God,' he added.

She regarded him quizzically.

'It's the bloody oil, you see,' he said with deep feeling. 'It has ruined Arabia. It's burying these people under a mountain of flashy, unsuitable new trash. You can't blame them for not being able to handle it. *We* invented it all and we can barely manage.'

'We, Colonel?'

'Well, I didn't mean Eygpt, of course. Egypt has a history to keep it on an even keel. And oil has never been a problem in your country.'

'We would not exactly call it a problem, Colonel,' Amira said, thinking of what oil revenues could do for the poor in the slums of Cairo and Alexandria.

'It has been in Arabia, doctor,' Hadfield said, his voice harsh. 'You should have known this country before. Oh, yes, you should have, doctor.'

There spoke the Arabist, Amira thought. Colin Hadfield was indeed one of the British romantics, very possibly one of the last, who thought of the Arabian desert as a bitter paradise.

'If you wish,' Hadfield said, 'we can meet for dinner later. I would like very much to show you the Old Town—the real Salalah. Would that suit?'

'Yes, thank you, Colonel. I would like that.' Amira was growing curious about this old Peace Corpsman who carried himself like a serving officer in a British regiment, and who hated oil and what it had done to his beloved Arabia. What, she wondered, would such a man be doing in so pacific an organization as the NPC?

The Oasis Hotel was what Colonel Hadfield had warned it would be. The lobby was a labyrinth of plaster-and-chrome arches—vaguely Arabic in style—vinyl and miracle-fabric furniture, and plastic tiles molded to resemble the real thing. The rooms, and there were four hundred of them, were sterile cubicles with glass walls and windows that could not be opened. The air conditioning was hardly needed in the temperate climate of the coast, but it still supplied a hurricane of frigid air from the vents that set the polyester drapes to swaying.

Already the furnishings were beginning to show wear and were marked with the stains left behind by previous guests, most of whom, Amira concluded, were foreigners—salesmen and concession seekers—who appeared to be everywhere.

The hotel was staffed almost entirely by Palestinians,

Indians, Lebanese, and Egyptians. The few native Omanis in the place seemed riveted to the half-dozen or so large television sets in the public rooms, all of them engrossed in Arabic-dubbed reruns of old American and British television shows.

Through the glass wall of her tenth-floor room, Amira could look across the jumbled confusion of the New Town to the reddish towers of old Salalah. There the buildings jammed against one another, not quite square and level, so that they appeared to be leaning against one another for support. Here and there could be seen the spires of mosques, from which, in other days, the *muezzins* called the faithful to prayer. Now, apparently, that task was performed by tape or record player amplified and broadcast from the mosques by immense loudspeakers, the shape of which marred the ancient symmetry of the holy buildings. It was plain to see, Amira thought, what it was that Colonel Hadfield complained of.

She bathed and rested in the chilly room until midafternoon, then she went down to the restaurant and ate a light lunch on the terrace overlooking the port. In the benign air she found it difficult to believe that beyond the mountains the weather was so severe that flying was impossible. But she had been warned that southern Arabia was a land of violent contrasts.

After lunch she returned to her room and slept until almost dusk, when she awoke and dressed, then went down to the lobby to await the arrival of Colonel Hadfield.

Through the Moorish arch that separated the bar from the main lobby she could see a number of the young South Africans who had been on the aircraft with her. They were sitting stolidly apart, drinking imported beer. It surprised her to see several men in Arab dress drinking as well. Apparently the Sunni prohibition against alcohol was not taken seriously in this part of the Kingdom of Oman.

'Yes, doctor.' Colonel Hadfield had appeared, quite silently for so large a man, beside her. He wore his NPC uniform still and, in Amira's honor, two rows of service ribbons. But instead of his customary beret, he wore the checked *kaffiyeh* of the Trucial Scouts. He nodded in the direction of the Arabs in the bar. 'It shakes one a bit to see that,' he said, 'particularly if one remembers other days.' He switched to fluent Arabic and quoted: ' "What, do they not ponder the Qur'ân? Or is it that there are locks upon their hearts?" ' For a moment he looked to Amira like an Old Testament figure, burnished face framed by the Arab headdress, eys hard with fanatic faith.

She stood and for a moment she, too, seemed out of time, anachronistic. She had dressed in a loose gown of green chiffon with a cowl at her throat. Her hair was pulled tightly back from her face, accenting her pale skin and exotic features.

'You know the Book very well, Colonel,' she said.

'One can't live here as long as I have and not know it. It doesn't disturb you, doctor, to hear an unbeliever quote the Prophet?'

'I am *Nasrani*, Colonel,' Amira said. 'A Christian like yourself.'

'Your pardon, doctor. I should have known that.'

'There is no reason why you should.' She raised the green cowl so that it covered her head and the lower part of her face like a *chador*. 'I am looking forward to seeing the Old Town, Colonel.'

In English, and with a sudden change to British military formality, Colonel Hadfield said, 'It will be my pleasure, Dr. Shallai.'

The restaurant, in a sandstone building deep inside the maze of streets that formed the oldest part of Salalah, was dark and filled with Arabs. The British colonel was obviously a known and favored customer. They ate in an alcove, separated from the main room by a beaded curtain. The air was heavy with the smell of savory cooking and Arab music was being played.

The colonel had fallen oddly silent in this place and Amira wondered if in his mind he were not reliving some memory of a time when he had been a young officer in a place similar to this one, but in a land and time very different.

'In the old days, Colonel,' Amira said, 'we could not have shared a meal this way. The twentieth century has some advantages, after all.'

'You are right, of course. I thank you for reminding me,' he said. 'I hope you'll forgive an old soldier for pretending the past was all music and sunshine.'

'Forgive *me* for saying so, but it seems odd that a man

such as yourself should end up in the New Peace Corps, Colonel.'

'There is work for all. One contributes what one can.' The pale, English eyes regarded her soberly from under the corded headdress. 'You will see when we reach EQS, doctor.'

'Can you tell me about it?'

'It would be better if you waited to see for yourself. I am not a scientist. Besides, I have been away on temporary posting. In the Sudan.'

'And before that?'

'South Africa.' It was immediately plain to Amira that Hadfield did not wish to discuss his own itinerary further.

Aware that he had been abrupt, he added: 'Dr. Clevenger will brief all newcomers when we arrive at the station.'

'All newcomers? Are there to be others?'

'Why, yes. Those young men who arrived on the aircraft with you are going to EQS.'

'I see,' Amira said, but she was not certain that she did see. The standoffish South Africans had not looked like scientists to her.

To cover her momentary discomfiture, she said, 'What was it like here in Oman when you first arrived, Colonel?'

'That was a long time ago, doctor. The old Sultan, Said bin Taimur—the one who was dethroned by his son, Qaboos, the present ruler—was king in Oman then.' Hadfield's manner changed, grew younger and less guarded as he spoke of his early days. 'I am from Somerset, doctor. Do you know that country at all?'

'I have traveled through it. But I do not know it well.'

'Somerset,' Hadfield said, almost dreamily. 'It is one of the most beautiful parts of England. I grew up near the market town of Taunton. Yes, quite beautiful. The autumns there are remarkable.' He fell silent for a moment. 'There is a small museum in Taunton, doctor. Really quite small. But it is a treasure-house to a Somerset man. It has artifacts dating back to the time of the Lake People, who lived in that part of Britain long before even the Saxons or the Romans came. It is the continuity, you see? The feeling that one is part of a long line of Somerset men who have gone out of the county to the ends of the earth. The honors of the Somerset Yeomanry—my own regiment, doctor—are all there in that tiny museum. Twelve Victoria Crosses. Twelve of them, doctor. And the Mahdi's prayerbook—taken by a Somerset soldier when Kitchener defeated the Mahdi after the relief of

Khartoum. A lovely place, doctor. It says so much about how the world used to be and what part in it we British once played.'

A silent waiter appeared to remove their dishes and bring coffee, dark and bitter and pungent. Amira filled their tiny cups from the brass carafe.

'They disbanded the Somerset Yeomanry in 1958, Dr. Shallai,' Colonel Hadfield said. 'The nation could no longer afford a military tradition and so the Labourites closed the book on regiments that were old when William and Mary ruled England.' His face seemed carved from volcanic rock, etched with deep lines of an ancient grief. 'By that time, of course, those of us who were willing to stay abroad were finding places in old Empire units, like the Trucial Scouts. Believe me, doctor, I was grateful to be needed. Soldiers are not popular once a great war has been won. We make people uncomfortable. We remind them of things they want very much to forget.'

'The people once ruled by you British are not ever likely to forget you. Or forgive you, for that matter,' Amira said evenly. She could sympathize with the ex-soldier. It had to be painful to be bypassed by history. But she was an Egyptian, and all Egyptians had unpleasant memories of the British. To have been a member of a subject race in the Great Raj was an injury not easily forgotten. She said so frankly. If she was to work with Hadfield, she must be honest.

'Please forgive my tactlessness, doctor,' Hadfield said. 'But since we *are* being frank, let me remind you that for three hundred years we kept half the world from slaughtering the the other half in tribal squabbles. I was here in the fifties, when the Saudis decided that the oasis of Buraimi belonged to them. And the Sheik of Abu Dhabi decided that *he* had a claim. It was not a great dispute—most of the world never heard of it. But it was real enough to the Arabs who would have died in the fighting if the British agent in Abu Dhabi and the Trucial Scouts had not turned the Saudis out of the place. As late as that, Dr. Shallai, what remained of the Raj was still keeping the peace.'

'I do not deny it, Colonel. But as one of the benighted people once protected by Britain, I sometimes feel that there is much to be said for independence.'

'I am making a hash of this evening, Dr. Shallai,' Hadfield said contritely. 'I am not so Blimpish as I sound, believe me.'

Amira favored him with a flashing smile. 'Our war is over, Colonel. We shouldn't fight another battle now.'

Hadfield sipped thoughtfully at his coffee. 'Let me say only this, dear Dr. Shallai. Lord Curzon said it better than I could ever do. He was speaking to the tribal chiefs of this very coast and he said, "We have saved you from extinction at the hands of your neighbors. We have opened the seas to the ships of all nations and enabled their flags to fly in peace. We have not destroyed your independence, but preserved it." There was a good deal more about the accomplishments of the British Empire in this part of the world. Of course, that was in 1902, and two great wars have finished England as a great power. But on balance I think you will have to agree that the world isn't much improved. Who is there now to keep Arabia from grabbing Oman, Oman from stealing a bit of Yemen, the Russians from taking the whole lot?' He sighed heavily. 'It is the oil, you see, that makes it so terrible now. Not only is it ruining the people, it is tempting outsiders to take what they want—what they *need*.' He held out his cup for Amira to pour again. 'Thank you, doctor. Have I rambled on too long? Old soldiers tend to do that, I'm afraid.'

'Of course not, Colonel. One thing we Egyptians learned from you British was the habit of polite disputation,' she said with a smile. 'But you shouldn't worry so, Colonel. Surely the Americans will protect us?'

'You don't believe that, doctor. Nor do I. Once it seemed reasonable. When timidity and exhaustion overcame us British, I suppose we did expect the rich, eager Yanks to shoulder the burden—'

'The white man's burden, Colonel?' Amira asked dryly.

'*Touché*, doctor. But what I really meant was the burden of keeping the world running straight into the future without too many people killing each other and without the Reds snatching whatever takes their bloody fancy. The Yanks had the means. They still do. But they don't have the will—the nerve, if you like. It may have been having that damned war in Southeast Asia playing every night in their living rooms. War should never come home like that in any case. One shouldn't see the honored dead until they are safely tucked away in flag-draped coffins with volleys being fired and last post being played. Only soldiers should see other soldiers being killed. Death is the military's trade and they understand it. Civilians never do. But all that hardly matters now. It won't be the Americans who save the sum of things. They can't even retrieve their own people—and ours—from a rabble of confused Marxist fanatics. Someone else is going to have to take a hand.' He fell silent, looking drained and every one of his sixty-odd years. He gave Amira a thin smile. 'So you see, doctor? Damn the oil men fight for, and damn the weak men who have let matters come to this pretty pass.' He put his cup down on the brass tray and said, 'Now it is late, Dr. Shallai. I have enjoyed this evening but I think I had better return you to your plastic palace. Tomorrow will be a long, tiring day.'

13 Dartmouth

In the stillness of early summer, the River Dart and the oak woods on the steeply sloping banks resembled a Constable landscape. Michael Rivas switched off the engine of the hired car and sat for a time, scanning the peaceful scene before him.

The narrow macadam road that passed for a main highway from Paignton had brought him through some of the loveliest countryside he had ever seen. The hills in this part of Devon were rich with apple orchards and plunging meadows, accented with stands of English oaks and rhododendron. In these surroundings it was difficult to remember the bleak mountains of Afghanistan or the searing heat of Washington. It was even more difficult to think of this countryside as part of a world in which spies were murdered and continent-spanning conspiracies were being hatched.

The road came down out of the hills to the river and ended at the water's edge, where a cable-tug ferry ran across the anchorage to connect with the road once again on the western shore.

Rivas had parked on the outskirts of the village of Kingswear, and across the water he could see the roofs of Dartmouth.

The river was well populated with anchored pleasure boats, small launches and sailboats, and an occasional fishing craft. At some distance from the rest, he could see Ian Wyndham's boat, just as Sam Abbott had described it, a long-hulled and powerful-looking Benetti that resembled a motor torpedo boat far more than it did a pleasure yacht. The foredeck was protected by weather cloths on the rails; Rivas could see that there were people moving there, hidden from the shore. The sun reflected from the water onto the white topsides in a rippling pattern. The boat's name, *Wild*

Goose, was boldly displayed in gold letters across the broad teak transom.

Rivas studied the vessel for a time. It rode to its own anchor, rather than to one of the many mooring buoys in the roadstead. It was an opulent craft of eighteen or more meters and had to be worth a half-million pounds. For a retired mercenary, Ian Wyndham seemed to be doing very well for himself.

Sam Abbott had told him that Wyndham lived aboard the *Wild Goose* at Torquay. But inquiries in that center of British yachting had elicited the information that Captain Wyndham was presently in the roads at the mouth of the Dart. 'The captain,' the dockmaster of the Royal Torbay Yacht Club at Torquay had informed Rivas rather loftily, 'likes to spend time near his alma mater.'

The alma mater in question was the Britannia Royal Naval College, the buildings of which could be seen on the rise of the hills overlooking the river. Wyndham was a graduate of the naval college, though some unspecified trouble about a ship's fund had led to his resignation from the Royal Navy many years ago. From the navy he had drifted into the French Foreign Legion and the fighting in Chad. Abbott had not been certain, but it was generally supposed that Wyndham had deserted the Legion to join the Wild Geese—that is, to join the mercenaries under Colonel Hoare and others when they were carving fiefs out of the bloody shambles left behind by the departing colonial French and Belgians.

Twenty years as a mercenary had made Wyndham into a wealthy man, but nothing he could have done in Africa would account for the kind of affluence represented by the great motor yacht now anchored in the Dart. Captain—or Colonel (he used the titles interchangeably)—Wyndham had surely found another, more generous, source of income. Rivas, now following his journalist's instinct freely, was beginning to suspect what that source was.

Rivas started the car again and drove slowly down to the riverside in Kingswear village. He alighted and walked along the pebbled shoreline toward a dock showing a Boats for Hire sign. A boy, ruddy and freckled, stopped scraping paint on an overturned skiff's bottom and looked up at Rivas's approach.

'I need a boat,' Rivas said.

'One pound seventy-five an hour,' the boy said. Devon was marked in his speech. 'How long for?'

'I want to visit that boat.' Rivas indicated the *Wild Goose*.

The boy's eyes widened. 'You friends with Captain Wyndham?'

Evidently the mercenary was something remarkable in Kingswear. There was awe in the boy's voice.

Rivas pointed at the boats moored to the dock. 'Which one?'

The boy stood and wiped his hands on a piece of waste. He regarded Rivas critically. 'You American?'

'That's right.'

'Can you row, then?'

Rivas managed a thin smile. 'Some of us are clever,' he said. 'I can row.'

'One hour's hire in advance. And a pound for deposit.' The young face was stern and unsmiling. Running a hire-dock was a serious business.

Rivas produced the money, and the boy walked to a shack and returned with a pair of oars. 'Captain Wyndham doesn't take to visitors,' he said darkly. He laid the oars in the last boat in the line and said, squinting at the westerning sun, 'We close at seven, mind.'

He stood on the dock watching critically as Rivas clambered into the boat and cast off. He hoped the American had sense enough to secure the painter when he reached the yacht. He had no desire to row all over the river himself trying to retrieve a drifting boat.

When the American hailed the yacht, there was a reply to come aboard, which surprised the boy. The locals were almost always warned to stay clear.

He narrowed his eyes against the glare of sunlight on the water. The American was climbing up the accommodations ladder to the deck of the yacht.

'Is that Wyndham's boat?'

The speaker had appeared silently on the dock. The boy turned to face a very tall, very large man. The dark face was indistinct against the sun's glare.

'Yes, sir.' The boy's manner was very different with the newcomer. He had no desire at all to challenge this ominous figure.

'Who was that just went aboard?'

'An American gentleman, sir.' The boy did not want to

look directly into the large man's face. The eyes were too dark and cold, the lips too thin and bloodless. All of this he felt on an instinctive level, as though the mere near presence of the newcomer were somehow menacing. He swallowed hard and said, 'You want to hire a boat, sir?'

'No,' the man said, and turned to walk away, with the same weightless silence with which he had appeared.

The boy watched him step into a dark green Jaguar and back around to drive slowly away in the direction of the town.

☢

Rivas followed a black crewman off the fantail. He was a short and muscular man, young, with the purple-black skin of a Central African. Evidently Wyndham recruited his boatmen in the continent he knew best. The black spoke English with a French or Belgian accent. 'Go forward. Colonel Wyndham is expecting you.'

Rivas stepped past the crewman and made his way toward the foredeck. When he reached the top of the companionway ladder, he could see a stark-naked man lying on a canvas lounger. His brown skin was being rubbed with oil by an equally naked black woman.

Rivas had once met Wyndham and he remembered him as the sort of man who would do something like this. It had a certain shock value, and it was an amusement Rivas remembered as common among the mercenaries he had known in Africa. Other pastimes tended to revolve around games played with loaded automatic weapons, but Rivas guessed that Colonel Ian Wyndham was too much the gentleman of quality now to indulge in physically dangerous games.

Rivas waited until Wyndham sat up and wrapped a towel around his thickly muscled torso. The girl, a tall and thin African with breasts like small, unripe melons, made no move to cover herself. Her face, framed by corn-rowed hair that gleamed in the hot sunlight, was fine-featured and quite beautiful. She regarded Rivas with interest and spoke to Wyndham in some African dialect. Wyndham grinned, showing great horsey teeth in his weathered and creased face. He replied in the same dialect and the girl laughed.

She stood and walked into the pilothouse, squeezing by Rivas to do so. She smelled of cinnamon and scented oil.

'She likes you, Rivas,' Wyndham said. 'She's gone to tell her sister about you.'

Rivas ignored the remark and said, 'You got my message.'

'I had an RT call from Abbott.' He poured liquor into a glass standing on a table beside his lounger. 'He said you'd get here. He didn't say why.' He extended the glass and Rivas took it but did not drink.

Wyndham's eyes were gray, almost colorless. Set deep in that face the color of burnished wood, they seemed metallic. He hooked a deck chair with a bare foot and pulled it toward Rivas.

'Sit,' he said. 'Then tell me why you're here. I don't have many guests, you know.'

As Rivas lowered himself into the chair he caught a glimpse of a Fabrique d'Armes Belgique F-19 machine pistol on the deck under Wyndham's lounger. Obviously, any *unwanted* visitors to the *Wild Goose* would receive a harsh welcome. Wyndham caught the direction of his glance and showed that toothy smile again. It was not particularly warming. 'A man in my business has to take precautions,' he said.

Rivas wondered what other lethal bits of military hardware could be found aboard the *Wild Goose*. Enough to start a small war, he imagined.

'There's been a lot of recruiting going on lately,' he said. 'I thought you might be able to tell me about it.'

'There's always recruiting going on,' Wyndham said.

'This is special. Very high quality. Recent experience. The best.'

'Is this for a story?' Wyndham asked. Rivas had once done a piece on the mercenary for *Harper's*. Wyndham, who unlike most of his colleagues enjoyed personal publicity, had written Rivas a letter of appreciation after the article appeared.

Rivas essayed a smile. 'If there's a story to be written—yes.'

'Money in it?' Ian Wyndham, even among professionals known for their love of money, was outstandingly avaricious. He had once looted the national treasury of a faltering African state to pay his commando, though rumor had it that he had kept most of the hard currency in the vaults for himself.

'Quite a good deal of money, if there's a real story,' Rivas said.

Wyndham made a vulgar sucking noise and rubbed thumb and forefinger together in the immemorial sign. Under the hot sun, the sweat ran down his brutally muscled, oiled body. 'Give me some idea, Rivas. I want to know if you and I mean the same thing when we talk about "a good deal of money." '

'If I can get a book out of it, two hundred thousand.'

'Pounds?'

Rivas shook his head. 'Dollars.'

Wyndham leaned back and shrugged. 'Ah, well. Any front money?'

'I might manage a few thousand.'

'How few?'

'Five? But only if you have something I can follow up on right away,' Rivas said, thinking that $5,000 to Wyndham (who probably had a million or more in a Swiss bank) would leave his own bank account nearly drained.

Wyndham considered. 'That's not much,' he said finally.

'I'll go fifty-fifty with you on the book earnings.'

Wyndham's crooked-toothed smile reappeared. 'I always fancied myself a writer *wallah.*'

'You've been recruiting mercs for the NPC.'

'I don't know anything about the NPC. Why would that gang of holy rollers want soldiers?'

'All right. For General Collingwood, then,' Rivas said.

'You *do* hear things, don't you, old man.'

'I'm more interested in what you hear, Wyndham.'

The mercenary regarded Rivas with those metallic, cold eyes. 'I heard that your brother was killed.'

'You heard right,' Rivas said.

'Any connection between that and this—' Wyndham paused '—this book you want to write?'

'I don't know. If there is a connection, I haven't found it yet.'

'Did Abbott tell you I could help?'

'Sam told me to ask you if anyone was recruiting. I'd have come here anyway, in time.'

'I'm sorry about your brother. He was a good soldier,' Wyndham said. 'He just had the wrong employer.'

'I'm more interested in your employer, Colonel.'

'You won't get anything about who hired me, Rivas. I don't work that way.'

Rivas felt a rising tide of angry frustration. Was this a dead end, then? he wondered. God knew, Wyndham didn't need money—and if a promise of $100,000 wouldn't move him, it was difficult to guess what might.

'But I'll tell you this much,' Wyndham said. 'I have been recruiting. So have a half-dozen or so other old Geese. Only you are very late, Rivas. My last shipment went out two days ago.'

'Where?'

'To Oman. Salalah.'

'Americans?'

'South Africans, as a matter of fact.'

'How many have you sent altogether?' Rivas asked.

'Three thousand—give or take a few.'

Three *thousand*, Rivas thought. And Wyndham was not the only old mercenary dealing in military talent.

'Collingwood?'

'I didn't say that. As a matter of fact, I was never told about a commander. Everything has been handled blind. It works better that way. You probably know how it goes. Someone needs so many, with such-and-such skills. So much a head. There it is.'

'And you sent three thousand men to Salalah?'

'Salalah and a few other places.'

Rivas stared long and hard at the hulking figure sweating in the sunlight. Presently he said, 'Send me.'

'Be serious,' Wyndham said. 'Why should I do that?'

'One hundred thousand dollars.'

'That's maybe money. *If* you write a book. If you *live* to write a book.'

'And five thousand now.'

'Do I look as though I need money?'

'You look as though you want money.'

Again, the uneven smile appeared under the cold eyes. 'You are quite a judge of character.'

'Send me,' Rivas said.

Wyndham studied him in silence. 'How much do you remember from Laos days?'

'Enough.'

Wyndham pursed his heavy lips. Rivas waited, reining his impatience.

Suddenly Wyndham shouted something in dialect, and the façe of his crewman appeared in the wheelhouse window. The mercenary gave instructions, then turned to Rivas and said, 'Let's just see, shall we?'

Rivas drew a deep breath, feeling that he had crossed a secret threshold. He said, 'I'm not an Agency plant, in case that should be worrying you.'

'It doesn't worry me a bit,' Wyndham said. 'The Agency and I have worked together before. Both parties satisfied.' He held up his glass. 'You aren't drinking.'

'Let's see if there's anything to drink to.'

'All right. Let's.'

The crewman appeared carrying a thin folder. He surrendered it to Rivas and returned aft. Wyndham said, 'Go on. Have a look.'

The material consisted of a number of pages copied from a U.S. Army officer's 201 File. The subject was one Captain John Emerson Hayden, a 1965 graduate of the Military Academy. Hayden's career lay displayed on the neatly typed pages. Rivas leafed through to the last sheet. After being passed over for major by a promotion board for the third time, he had been retired four years ago 'for the good of the Service.'

Rivas turned the pages back and read the laconic entries. Hayden had served in Special Forces in Vietnam. He had won a Silver Star at Dak To. Then he had fallen under suspicion of having committed 'war crimes' in some minor highlands skirmish. A village headman suspected of harboring Viet Cong had died under questioning by members of Hayden's Montagnard Mike Force. A board of inquiry had cleared him, but the stigma had blighted the rest of his military career. After he left Vietnam his assignments had been low-level and in hardship posts. He had briefly recouped his fortunes by wrangling a posting to the Rapid Deployment Force in Egypt. But the timing had been bad. A month after his arrival in the Sinai, the RDF had been drawn back to the continental United States and reduced to a headquarters and a cadre. At Fort Bragg, Hayden had gone off the tracks badly. Reprimands for insubordination appeared in his record. He was again passed over for promotion to major. There were arrests for drunkenness. His wife had filed charges of assault against him and then divorced him. There were problems with the civilian authorities: arrests for drunken driving, an assault on a North Carolina state trooper. Finally, under threat of a general court-martial, Captain Hayden had retired from the Army.

It was a sad chronicle of a potentially good officer gone wrong. The badly reproduced photograph in the file showed a dark, angry man. The captain was five pounds heavier than Rivas and a half-inch shorter. But it was just possible Rivas might pass for Hayden if the record were not studied too carefully.

'Where is he?' Rivas asked.

'He didn't make his rendezvous with the others. Drunk, maybe. Or dead. He seems a good case for a mouthful of revolver to me.'

'Where was he supposed to report? And to whom?'

'Salalah. To an old Trucial Scout *wallah* named Hadfield.'

'When?'

'He was scheduled out with that last batch of South Africans who arrive sometime today. You can't always tell with raghead airlines,' Wyndham said. 'But if you want to risk it, you can have Hayden for five thousand dollars in advance and a hundred thousand if you live to write a book.'

'All right,' Rivas said. 'I'll take him.'

'How you get there is your affair. But you better take the Concorde as far as Bahrain, or you might just get there too late,' Wyndham said. 'I don't know for certain, but I think the force is close to going into action.' He stood up, a stocky, gnarled figure in a wrinkled towel. 'Have we something to drink to now?'

Rivas nodded and stood. The sunlight sparkling on the water dazzled him and the wound in his scalp itched and burned where the medic at Heathrow had been persuaded to remove the sutures. Suddenly he felt incredibly weary. The liquor—it was thick Cuban rum, he realized—burned its way into his belly.

'You look as though you could use a rest,' Wyndham said. The black girl, dressed now in a short, flowered shift, had appeared the moment her man stood to indicate the need for privacy was finished. Wyndham put an arm around her slender waist and looked challengingly at Rivas. 'There's another like this below, writer. Interested?'

'No time,' Rivas said wanly.

Wyndham shrugged. 'Leave a check with the black *fellah* inside. He will give you my Swiss account number.' The old mercenary sank back down on the lounger and drew the girl onto his lap. His interest in Michael Rivas was at an end.

14 Washington, D.C.

The safe house stood in the black ghetto of the capital, a district of boarded-up storefronts and moldering residences, frame houses many of which had been standing since the turn of the century. Black children played in the street, older blacks sat on the splintery steps of front stoops, drinking Cokes and Dr Peppers and fanning themselves in the heat. The asphalt in the street softened under the noon sun and a smell of cooking mingled with the pungent odor of marijuana in the motionless air.

The CIA house was a two-story wooden building with a small weedy patch of brown grass in front; the windows facing the street had been, like many others in the neighborhood, painted over on the inside. The only furniture in the house was some steel cots, but the interior walls and the door and window frames had been reinforced with heavy metal panels and expensive locks. The terminals and contact devices of a high-quality security system guarded the interior perimeter.

In the dim and airless living room, John Washington, a black CIA agent assigned as driver and bodyguard to the Deputy Director, lounged on a cot reading a tattered copy of *Time* magazine. His coat lay on the cot beside him. His broad chest strained the damp fabric of his shirt. There was a Police Special in the holster under his arm. The sounds from the street came faintly into the darkened room as Washington turned the pages of his magazine, waiting for the Deputy Director to reappear.

At the rear of the house, in a room at the end of a long, dark hall, Isaac Holt was speaking into a single-station scrambler telephone.

The reply from Kingswear had the flat, expressionlessness of computer-reconstituted speech.

'He has been on the yacht for forty minutes. He is coming ashore now. Shall I take him?'

'No.' Holt's own voice was strained with barely reined anger. The time to kill the meddling bastard had been missed. He had talked to too many people now, and that eliminated a simple assassination as a solution. 'No,' he said again. 'Stay with him. Don't let him lose you again the way he did here.'

'What about Wyndham?'

'Wyndham will be taken care of in due course,' Holt said. The mercenary was marked for it. All the recruiters were. But that could wait for the cleanup. 'Rivas will probably be heading for Heathrow.'

'I could take him on the road.'

'I said no, goddamnit. Just stay with him, but not too close. I don't want the damned Cousins messing into this. There will be time to take Rivas later. Wyndham will send him either to Oman or Tokar. You check Tokar first. If he isn't there you'll know where to look.'

Rivas had offered the mercenary money, of course, and Wyndham had not refused. He was not the sort of man who could resist a bribe, which was what made him first useful, then dangerous, and finally doomed.

'Before you leave London, contact Carmody in the office there. He will tell you how to reach me next. I don't want this link used again. Understood?'

'Understood.'

'You'll have your chance to earn your pay. Tell London to arrange your passage through Bahrain. There is an airplane loading last-minute items there. You should get to EQ about the same time Rivas does. And remember, no more misses. I don't want him coming back here with a story for the fucking media. Ever. That's all.' He broke the connection and replaced the scrambler phone in a scabby, paint-peeling cabinet.

Holt sat for a time on the cot feeling weary. Once it began, the killing never seemed to end. Rivas, above all others, had to go. Wyndham, too. And Abbott? Possibly. He would have to go to New York and pump Sam dry first. Then how many others?

Ike Holt had a sudden unbidden and chilling thought. Was Calder Davis sitting in his damned palace—Atalanta, he called it—ticking off names, too? And if he were, was Isaac Holt on the list?

Shivering, the Deputy Director of Central Intelligence left the secret room, carefully closing the steel-reinforced door behind him.

15 Tokar, Sudan

Waves storm-driven by the howling *khamseen* rolled up the shelving white beach—almost to the wheels of the desert-camouflaged command car parked at the high-tide mark. The sky, sea, and even the sunlight were stained brown by the sand blowing across the narrow sea from Arabia. The temperature stood at one hundred fourteen degrees Fahrenheit, making the metal surfaces of the vehicle and the weapons the men carried painful to the touch.

The compact officer wearing the red beret with a United States Army brigadier general's star on it stood on the highest bit of sand near the track, looking out at the mud-colored sea.

At forty-six, J. E. B. Collingwood, onetime general officer commanding the RDF and presently commander of the freebooting force known to its members simply as 'the Brigade,' was in his military prime. Collingwood had spent two decades on active duty with the American Army, always with elite troops in the field. He was recognized everywhere in the world among military men of all nations as one of the brightest—and hardest—commanders of light infantry ever to wear uniform.

His features were regular, cheekbones broad and high enough to hint at some distant American Indian ancestor, lips thin and firm. His eyes, hidden now behind large sand goggles, were clear blue and almost innocent in their unblinking, direct regard for whatever held his attention. His hair was cropped close to his skull, black-turning-to-gray and dusted now with the tawny sand that covered everything under the hot *khamseen* blowing out of the barren heart of Arabia across the angry sea.

Jeb Collingwood had that quality, rare in any time but essential to great commanders, of evoking fanatical loyalty among his subordinates. He understood instinctively that professional soldiers needed to give loyalty. His experience told him that there were almost no commanders now who could accept it, use it, and return it. He set about making himself into such a commander, and he succeeded totally. His officers said, 'Give Jeb a squad for a day and they'll storm hell for him tomorrow.' The comment was military hyperbole, but far from being untrue.

Like many soldiers, Collingwood modeled himself after Alexander. Unlike most, he approached the reality.

But twentieth-century America was not fourth-century B.C. Macedonia. The very qualities that made him a great soldier had made him into a political liability for President Vincent Todd Loomis. For political reasons the President had made certain decisions that weakened the military posture of the United States. It would have been impossible for Jeb Collingwood to remain silent. He spoke, and his career was shattered.

As a result, a certain bitterness now leavened his military genius, and this bitterness tempered both Collingwood and the force that Calder Davis and his associates had put at his disposal.

Only its size limited the capabilities of the Brigade. It was lavishly equipped, manned by the best professional soldiers a vast recruiting organization could provide, and commanded by possibly the best man alive for the particular job. Under Collingwood, the weapon that was the Brigade had developed a fine cutting edge. And it was swiftly outgrowing its parent, the NPC.

Peter Stuart, ex-major of the British Army's Special Air Service Regiment and General Collingwood's executive officer, stood at his commander's side, regarding the angry sea. He felt the impatience that had begun to permeate the entire Brigade as the time for action approached, and the unexpected bad weather rasped his nerves.

Collingwood said, 'I wish I were Moses, Peter. But since I'm not even Jewish, it appears we will have to wait on the weather.'

Stuart had the errant thought that his commander was far more like Joshua than Moses. Stuart was a man who knew his Bible well. The last survivor of a family with a long military tradition, he had come to the Brigade after the newly elected Labour government in Britain had disbanded the SAS.

Stuart turned away from the sea to look back at the soldiers waiting at the parked command car. There were four of them, two South Africans, an American, and a South Korean. It was Collingwood's habit to pick men at random from the other ranks of the Brigade to accompany him on these excursions outside the base-camp perimeter. In this way, there were many men scattered through the Brigade's formations who had had close personal contact with the commander. It was an archaic, and extremely effective, way of developing the close rapport with the troops that Collingwood believed in.

Stuart, who was something of a military historian, often compared the Brigade to the *condottieri* of fourteenth-century Italy. A band of mercenaries under strong leadership was probably the most effective military force civilization's darker powers had produced. A force that knew exactly what they intended to do, were prepared to do it, and were totally indifferent to the effect in the world outside the band of brothers had not been seen in the world for six hundred years. The mercenary bands that had prowled black Africa after the departure of the colonial powers were only shadowy precursors of the Brigade. They had neither the doctrine, the weapons, the numbers, nor the leadership of this new power. It was true enough that the Brigade, now eleven thousand strong, owed its existence to the New Peace Corps (Stuart appreciated the irony of this) and to the shadowy men of great wealth and power who had called the NPC and the Brigade into being. But once created, the Brigade had taken on a life of its own, permeated by the personality of its commander. It happened that the Brigade was to be used to free the hostages now being held by the Muslim radicals in Riyadh. But the Brigade would have followed Collingwood in an assault on London or Washington, if he had ordered it. Perhaps, Stuart thought wryly, that was why the men in the boardrooms had equipped it only to operate in the Third World.

'We aren't doing any good here, Peter,' Collingwood said. 'Let's get back to camp.'

'There will be a weathercast we can pick up at 1300 hours, sir,' Stuart said. Brigade meteorologists were equipped to receive transmissions from the Eurosat weather satellite 25,000 miles above the Mediterranean.

The two men walked back to the command car, leaning

against the force of the southwesterly gale. The soldiers stood as their commander and his executive approached.

'Let's go back, Gossage,' the general said. Stuart knew that once he learned a man's name, he never forgot it. It was one of the many small things that combined to make him the troop commander he was.

The men mounted the command car and started inland along the sandy track. The camp at Tokar, where the main force of the Brigade had staged, was thirty miles from the coast at the base of the Kassala mountain range. The site had been chosen for two reasons. It was within troop-carrying helicopter range of Riyadh and it was in a narrow strip of Africa that was not customarily scanned by the recce satellites of either the United States or the Soviet Union. The first formations of the Brigade had arrived in the Sudan five months ago, and the buildup had been steady since then. Collingwood and his staff had arrived four weeks later and since then the training and equipping schedule had been nonstop.

Peter Stuart had once remarked to the general that it was peculiar that the idea of the Brigade, and the actual establishment of its components, had begun long before the Pan-Arabian radicals had overturned the Saudi monarchy and seized the Western hostages. Collingwood had replied only that the Brigade was an idea whose time was long overdue. Much that had happened in the world since the Iranian revolution would not have happened if the Brigade, or some unit like it, had existed to protect the interests of Western civilization. 'That might sound grand, Peter,' the general had said, 'but it is the simple truth.' And Stuart, whose beliefs were formed by his years in the Special Air Service Regiment, a similar but smaller unit, was inclined to agree. If Western governments abdicated their duty to suppress disorder, other means were justified.

Occasionally it troubled Stuart's English sense of the fitness of things that the Brigade was, in effect, an immensely potent Committee of Vigilance. But vigilantism was the natural result of a failure of law. No officer or soldier of the Brigade held doubts about that.

The command car was a new one of West German manufacture. The materiel supplied to the Brigade was the pick of the arsenals and industries of many nations. French missiles, Japanese communications gear. British, Belgian, and Israeli small arms were supplemented by American helicopters. The providers had been generous, Stuart thought, and seemed determined that the Brigade should not want for the best equipment available. Within the last two weeks sections of Israeli Kfir fighters and the Panavias had arrived at the Tokar airstrip. When the Brigade went into action there would be ample air cover to protect the airborne troops. Intelligence briefings had indicated that the former Saudi air force was largely grounded, its American aircraft immobilized by a lack of spares and proper maintenance. The staff, which consisted of a New Zealander, two Swedes, a half-dozen British-trained Omanis, a West German, and three Britons, as well as four Americans who had resigned their commissions in the RDF to stay with General Collingwood, were confident and ready for battle.

The men, officers and other ranks alike, wore the ordinary twill trousers and bush jacket of the NPC. The Brigade was far from being a smart parade-ground unit. In all the months of training, the men had never marched together. Their only flag was the rainbow flash of the NPC. Collingwood had frequently toured the outlying bases around Tokar, addressing the men and supervising their training. It was his habit to mingle freely with the troops and he seemed always able to infuse them with his own confidence and enthusiasm. By now every man in the Brigade understood the mission and was ready to carry it out. Stuart was conscious of being a part of something new in military history. A new force in the world had come into being and he was proud to be part of it.

The two officers seated in the rear of the command car rode in silence, the sandy wind plucking at their clothes and stinging their faces.

Jeb Collingwood's mind was fixed on the last details of the coming mission. He was well pleased with the troops. All were skilled professionals and he was certain they would have no trouble overwhelming the rabble of Pan-Arabian radicals holding the embassy. The plan of attack was simple and direct, as all good battle plans were.

He suspected that many of the anonymous industrialists who backed the Brigade had some naïve notion that the mission could be accomplished without serious bloodshed. But war was not like that. Combat, even on a small scale, always exacted a blood price. There would be casualties.

Most of them would be suffered by the people holding the embassy, and the remnants of the Saudi military. It would have reduced the price somewhat if he had been allowed to penetrate the disorganized Saudi units and promise them a return of the princes, but Calder Davis had vetoed that possibility. Calder had other plans for the oil-rich peninsula—that was plain. But as a soldier Collingwood was accustomed to political decisions. He disliked having to accept them, but there was no choice. So some of the old Saudi troops would fight. So be it, he thought. The Brigade could handle them.

Time was desperately short for the West, Collingwood believed. His concern had led him into the defiance of presidential authority that had wrecked his military career. He was thankful to Calder for giving him this second chance to serve the cause he deeply believed in—the defense of a faltering, timid Western civilization. He thanked God that there had been a man with the wealth and will of Calder Davis to call the Brigade into being. He regarded it as destiny that he, J. E. B. Collingwood, was available at the right time and was in the right place to command it.

The wind blew with slightly less force among the low foothills of the Kassala range where the Brigade was encamped. As the command car made its way along the sandy track between the sere hills, both Collingwood and Stuart were pleased to see almost no sign of human habitation. The outlying posts on the perimeter of the Tokar camp were so heavily camouflaged as to be almost invisible. But both officers knew that they were being observed as they approached by soldiers dug into the rust-brown slopes. The company commander whose men protected this particular approach to the camp was an Afghan Muslim commanding a mixed platoon of Baluchis and Pathans. No one in the force save Peter Stuart, who had an eye for the ironies of politics, found it odd that there should be a few Muslims in a brigade consecrated to protecting Western values and interests. Muslims, of course, had a long history of slaughtering one another and the Briton had no doubt at all that this particular platoon would respond as well as any other in the Brigade when it came time to fire on Muslim fanatics. For the few southwest Asians in the force it would be enough that the Pan-Arabian radicals were generally thought to be mostly Marxists.

Once within the perimeter, the command car approached what would have appeared to a casual observer to be a Sudanese village. The habitations were newer than those in Tokar proper, and considerably cleaner. But the distribution of buildings, seen from above, would have displayed no military characteristics whatever. There were rather more vehicle tracks on the hard earth than would be expected in this desolate part of the Sudan, and to the immediate west of the new village lay a broad, level, apparently empty field. The dimensions of this dusty plain were sufficient to allow for the landing and takeoff of medium-sized aircraft designed for use in less-than-civilized conditions. At the southern end of the field, placed to face the prevailing wind, five unmarked Kfir fighters stood under camouflage netting. Around the field perimeter stood odd mounds of what seemed to be packed earth but was earth-colored plastic over more netting. In each such mound was parked a helicopter.

But it was the inhabitants of this primitive city that marked it for what it was: the main base camp and headquarters of the Brigade. The population was totally male, and they were unmistakably soldiers—soldiers of a very special sort, who carried themselves with arrogance, whose weapons were always to hand and in perfect condition, soldiers who were ready to fight.

At the entrance to the mud-brick building serving as Brigade headquarters, Collingwood and Stuart alighted from the command car and were greeted by the sentry on duty. All military units—particularly elite ones—tend to develop instant traditions. In the Brigade it had already become traditional for all to address one another by name, never mentioning rank, in the manner of the early Israeli Army. The single exception was the form of address used in speaking to the commander, who was always either 'General,' or simply 'sir.'

It was assumed (and Collingwood's training methods confirmed it) that every man in the Brigade knew his officers by sight, making badges of rank unnecessary. The only badge in the entire force was the single tarnished star worn on Collingwood's beret.

The man on duty at the door to the headquarters, a young former ranger of the U.S. Army, came briefly to attention as a gesture of respect and suppressed the saluting instinct. That, too, was not done in the Brigade. This was a new, free-form sort of army. 'How was it on the coast, Mr. Stuart?' Eight years of military service in the old kind of army made the 'Mr.' impossible to omit.

'Worse than here, Davey,' Stuart said in passing. He knew that the soldier was voicing the impatience felt by everyone in the unit. The Brigade was finely honed, ready for the assault. If the weather didn't improve soon, some of the edge would begin to go.

Inside, Cory Conant, a former major of the RDF who had resigned to follow Collingwood into exile, stood and said, 'We've received the personnel list for the last shipment to Oman, General.'

Collingwood stepped around the large sand-table model of Riyadh that dominated the room and sat down at his desk. He removed his beret and goggles and tossed them to the young soldier serving as his orderly that day. 'See if you can organize some cold beer, Charlie, to wash the sand down.'

'Yes, *sir.*' The young ranger moved as though on a vital mission.

Collingwood took a message form from Conant. On it was typed a decrypted dispatch from the NPC office in London. 'These are the last for Oman, Cory?'

'Yes, General.'

On the form, the Brigade cypher clerk had written the names of the recruits together with a digest of their military records.

'From Wyndham?'

'Yes, sir,' Conant said.

Collingwood held Wyndham and people like him in low regard, but he appreciated the fact that the old mercenary produced results. Most of the men he had supplied to the Brigade were experienced, excellent soldiers. He glanced down the list of names. South Africans, all of them, with experience in the Namibia fighting and in the border battles with Zimbabwe. The last name, however, was of an American. An ex-captain with Vietnam experience.

'Hayden,' he said. 'John Emerson.'

'Know him, General?' Peter Stuart asked.

'There were five hundred thousand of us in Nam, Peter.'

'He was in the RDF.'

'So were fifteen thousand others,' Collingwood said. 'But I see he has a Silver Star and some commendations.' He frowned at the further notations. 'He has had liquor trouble since then.' He looked up at Conant and grinned suddenly. 'But we'll fix that, won't we, Cory?'

'We will that, sir. It's a dry, dry country.'

'Anything else?'

Conant handed him a second message form. It, too, had been sent from London, but the symbols on it indicated to Collingwood that it had originated in Washington, with Isaac Holt.

Collingwood disliked Ike Holt. It troubled him that Holt was using the instrumentalities of the United States Central Intelligence Agency to support the Brigade. It was true that the Brigade had been called into existence to protect American interests the government of the United States no longer seemed capable or willing to protect, but that did not absolve Holt of a peculiar sort of duplicity. In addition to that, Collingwood had the feeling that Holt was serving himself more fervently than he served either the NPC or the government of the United States. And now that Cole Norris was dead, Holt was very near to being appointed Director of Central Intelligence. Collingwood foresaw problems that were far outside his purely military purview. But Calder and his friends would have to see to those. . . .

He read the message, scowling at what he saw there.

'Holt is adding another man to the commo staff at EQ Station,' he said. 'A communications specialist—but Holt takes the trouble to say he is a former Navy SEAL and that he's been used in Cuba by the Agency.'

He crumpled the form and dropped it into the waste-basket. 'Another one of Holt's hoods, most likely. EQ is stiff with them.' What he didn't say to his staff was that he didn't like Isaac Holt's way of loading every enterprise with spies and gorillas. 'Well, I'm afraid this one will be poor Colin Hadfield's problem, not ours.'

Almost every troublemaker who had found his way through the mercenary pipeline to the Brigade had turned out to be one of the Deputy DCI's hoods, Collingwood thought. He had sent a message to Holt demanding that he stop trying to place spies inside the Brigade.

The young ranger reappeared from the mess with a musette bag filled with cold cans of German beer. The officers helped themselves and Collingwood tossed a can to the orderly.

The general disliked beer, but he opened a can for himself and drank deeply with every evidence of pleasure. When he had finished, he crumpled the can, dropped it in the basket, and said to his deputy, 'All right, Peter. Let's forget Ike Holt now and go see what the rainmakers have to say about when we can expect the damned wind to stop blowing.'

16 London

From a corner office in the glass-and-concrete tower housing New Scotland Yard, Sir Allan Sawkins could look down on the city of London's lights glowing in the summer evening. Sir Allan was a career policeman and in the course of thirty years at the Yard he had seen many changes in the city. He had served Labour governments and Conservative governments with equal skill and dedication. He was, he liked to think, an apolitical professional—a man dedicated to the nation rather than to the particular group of politicians who might, at any one given moment, occupy the seats of power in Whitehall and Parliament.

For years Sir Allan had dreamed of retirement in northern Canada (a dream his city-bred wife, Innelda, secretly did not share). But a recent spate of currency restrictions ruling it illegal to send pension payments outside the United Kingdom now made it certain that Sir Allan's golden years would be spent no farther away from London than Lyme Regis or Charmouth.

He was brooding on this latest disappointment in a life lately given to many such reverses, when his desk communicator ping-ed and the voice of the constable minding the communications center came from the speaker: 'We have Washington now, sir. Line one.'

Sir Allan picked up the telephone and said, 'Sawkins here. Is that you, Mr. Shepherd?' He did not know the Director of the FBI personally, as he should—Home Office estimates had drastically cut funds for travel by police officials.

'This is Carl Shepherd, Sir Allan.' The connection, routed via an American satellite, was excellent. As though Shepherd were in Chelsea or nearer, Sawkins thought.

'About your request for surveillance of the journalist Michael Rivas,' Sawkins said, opening a new file that lay on the desk before him. 'We may have something for you.'

'Is this line secure, Sir Allan?'

'Of course, sir.' Sawkins felt mildly affronted by the question, the more because in point of fact he was not completely certain that the link was, indeed, secure. 'Perhaps you would rather I put my information in a written report and send it by diplomatic pouch.'

'No, no, of course not, Sir Allan,' Shepherd replied hastily. 'Please go on.'

'Very well. I must preface this by reminding you that we are very short of staff. Special Branch has been severely curtailed. You do understand this.'

'Of course, sir,' Shepherd said, and Sawkins imagined he heard a note of sympathy from a fellow policeman faced with many of the same problems. 'I do understand.'

'Yes. Well, then,' Sawkins said. 'Mr. Rivas arrived here by Concorde last night. He hired a car and left London early, driving toward the West Country. We kept him under surveillance continuously as you requested. He went first to Torquay and made inquiries about a certain Ian Wyndham—about whom more later, by the way. From Torquay, he was directed to Dartmouth, where he went aboard Wyndham's yacht lying in the river there. I'm afraid we cannot help you with what was discussed between Rivas and Wyndham. Our man was not equipped for such surveillance. But Rivas only spent a short time aboard the yacht. He came ashore and immediately returned to Heathrow, where he bought passage to Salalah, Kingdom of Oman, via Bahrain. Concorde again, as far as Bahrain. His flight departed at three, local time, so—' Sawkins glanced at the bank of world time clocks on the wall of his office '—he should have changed planes by now and he will probably be in Salalah late tonight. I hope this is helpful?'

'Frankly, Sir Allan, I don't know yet if it is. But I deeply appreciate your assistance.'

'There is a bit more,' Sawkins said. 'Just as you suspected. Rivas was followed. Down to Kingswear and back to Heathrow. The tail was very professional and we had some trouble staying with him. We spooked him, I'm afraid. We did distract him from Rivas. But after leading us around the maypole a few times, he ended up at Hearthrow, too, and took a later flight to Bahrain. U.S. passport, name of Harry Grant. We had no legal cause to detain him, so—'

'I understand that, Sir Allan,' Shepherd said.

'If he had made any attempt to interfere with Rivas, naturally, we could have detained them both. But under the circumstances, we simply observed them for the time—and bloody short time it was—that they were in the United Kingdom.'

'Of course, Sir Allan,' Shepherd said.

'There is something else that might possibly be of interest, Director,' Sawkins said. 'Wyndham, the man Rivas visited, is someone we have been watching, more or less closely, for some time. He is a notorious ex-mercenary soldier whom we suspect—though we have not been able to prove it—of recruiting. An activity that is illegal in this country, of course.' He waited for a comment from the FBI Director and when none was forthcoming, he went on. 'The Inland Revenue is very interested in Mr. Wyndham. They are reasonably certain that he is engaged in massive tax evasion. However, so far no one has found any proof of that, either. He is a very slippery operator, our Mr. Wyndham.'

'*Massive* tax evasion you say, Sir Allan?'

'The suspicion is that he has funneled at least a million pounds into a Swiss account. Possibly more.'

Shepherd's voice sounded slightly strained. 'Have you any idea of the source of all this money, sir?'

'Not yet. It comes from abroad, of course. There are very few opportunities to earn that sort of money in Britain these days, legally or illegally.'

'I see. Thank you very much for your information, Sir Allan. If I can reciprocate, you have only to ask,' the FBI Director said.

'I can add this, though I have no idea whether or not it will help,' Sawkins said. 'The Inland Revenue will be paying a visit to Mr. Wyndham soon. Possibly within twenty-four hours. If they find anything relating to his meeting with your Mr. Rivas I will let you hear of it immediately.'

'Yes. Thank you very much, Sir Allan.'

'Happy to help, old man,' Sawkins said and broke the connection. He sat back in his chair and considered. He *did* rather feel good, all things considered. Like a policeman again. It was a pleasure that came to Sir Allan seldom these permissive days.

In a small chamber filled with heating ducts and electrical conduits well below street level, Giles Norcross, a personal assistant too seldom seen by Sir Allen Sawkins, hunched over a small recorder.

As the connection was broken, the reels on the machine stopped turning. Norcross removed the headset he had been wearing and stared thoughtfully at the damp concrete walls. Then he removed the used reel from the recorder, closed the case, and replaced the set in a deep space between the wall and a conduit.

He deposited the tape reel in a plastic bag, sealed it, and dropped it into the inside pocket of his coat.

As he stepped from the lift at ground level, the constable guarding the reception desk in the lobby said, 'Mr. Norcross, sir. Sir Allan was asking for you.'

'Yes,' Norcross said airily. 'I know. All taken care of, Constable.'

He walked quickly out the door and down the broad concrete steps into the street. He paused for a moment by the rotating steel-and-enamel New Scotland Yard sign that stood before the building until a taxicab appeared at the head of the street. He flagged it and stepped to the curb. When the cab stopped, he gave the driver an address in Oxford Street. He settled down in the rear seat. The driver, a Spaniard by his accent (there were almost no proper British cab drivers any longer, Norcross thought with annoyance), turned to ask: 'Is that the address of the NPC, *señor*, if you please?'

'Yes,' Norcross said testily. Of course it is, you bloody man. He seldom risked appearing openly at the shabby London headquarters of the NPC, but this time he had a bit of information that could not wait.

17 Naziat-as-Samman, Egypt

Helmuth Reich lifted the frosty tankard and said in his best attempt at a British accent, 'Cheers. And good luck to us both.' He tasted the Pimm's Cup and sighed with satisfaction. Across the table, in the crowded intimacy of the tourist bar of the new hotel at Naziat, sat the young man who was going to earn credit for Reich in both the Abteilung's offices in Leipzig and the glass tower of the KGB in Dzerzhinsky Square.

The Khufu Hotel was throbbing with activity. Through the panoramic windows of the bar Reich could see the brilliantly floodlighted forms of the Great Pyramid and its smaller companions. In the foreground, even at this hour of night, there was activity in the sterilized and regimented 'bazaar' that the government of Egypt had allowed the Khufu's Lebanese promoters to build into a dazzling factory for the extraction of foreign exchange from Western tourists and petro-dollars from fellow Arabs.

It was all perfectly dreadful, Reich thought, with its garish imitations of Egyptian life, the new and tasteless buildings and the pulsating activity that never ceased. And he loved every bit of it. There was almost nothing that could not be had for a price now in Naziat. All the vice that once had made the *souk* of Cairo famous had now moved across the river to this carnival setting at the base of the Giza megaliths. If a man wanted liquor, he had only to order it. If he wanted a woman or even a plump boy, those could be provided as easily. Everything from postcards to hashish was ready at hand in Naziat. It was, Helmuth Reich thought, the perfect setting for his meeting with young Dr. Cecil Sawyer.

'Did you know, doctor,' he said, setting down his cold tankard, 'that they are planning to restore the Sphinx? I am quite serious about it. The government is letting a contract to a firm of Italian monument sculptors to renovate the old girl from tip to tail.'

Sawyer, surprised even to find himself here in Naziat with this strange and *gemütlich* German, could think of no sensible reply.

He had traveled to Cairo personally to present his request for transfer from Kalabishah Station to Arabia, anticipating trouble about it despite the fact that the NPC higher-ups were asking for medics to make just such a change. (Cecil Sawyer expected problems everywhere and from every source; during his short life every request he made had almost always been greeted with foot dragging and procrastinations.)

Instead, the Cairo personnel officer, a swarthy Palestinian who smelled terribly of *arak*, had promised to give the request his prompt attention. He had then suggested that Cecil speak with Helmuth Reich, an East German with strong government connections. Herr Reich, it appeared, was head of the sales department of the chemicals division of the East German trade mission which had appeared in Cairo when the Camp David talks with Israel had gone into limbo. He was a man, the Palestinian said, who was secretly in sympathy with the charitable doings of the New Peace Corps. He was interested (in the cause of East-West détente, of course) in establishing good relations with the Director of EQ Station. It was a delicate matter politically, and Reich was hoping to find a suitable envoy who could speak with Dr. Clevenger and her staff unofficially and in that way learn how the East German chemical industry might contribute to the work of the NPC. 'Later,' the Palestinian explained, 'the contacts can be made through regular channels.'

Sawyer, naive and provincial, was not *so* ingenuous as to believe that there was no ulterior motive in the suggested contact. But the personnel officer left no doubt that establishing a rapport with the jovial Herr Reich would go a long way toward expediting the immediate transfer Dr. Sawyer was seeking.

So it was that Cecil Sawyer now found himself in the crowded bar of the Khufu in Naziat-as-Samman at a late hour, drinking a great many cool and refreshing Pimm's Cups and listening to the German's jolly talk of international détente, the marvelous work of the NPC and the secret admiration for it that existed in East Germany, and the daunting possibility of a Sphinx with a face as Italian as Sophia Loren's

'Mr. Reich,' Sawyer said, 'it is very kind of you, I'm sure, to interest yourself in my case. But frankly, I'm a bit confused. I don't really see how I can help you.'

The German pursed his lips thoughtfully. His small eyes, bright and intelligent, were fixed on the younger man. Sawyer felt uncomfortable under the scrutiny. He realized that what he was playing at here was a case of what the Yanks called 'influence peddling.' The Palestinian personnel officer had made that very clear. This German was engaged in a bit of free enterprise—in the only form acceptable to his Marxist superiors. It was an attempt to 'feel out' Dr. Clevenger at EQ Station and see if some commercial advantage might be developed between the NPC and the East German chemicals trust. But Cecil Sawyer had no illusions about how much influence he, Sawyer, could exert on anyone at EQ Station, let alone the chief of that place. Apparently neither the Palestinian in Cairo nor this smiling Marxist entrepreneur seemed to realize what a very unimportant fellow they were dealing with here. That was odd, to say the least.

Cecil Sawyer was one of those relatively few individuals possessed of total recall. This mental quirk had helped him get through his medical studies and had made up for what he realized was a very ordinary intelligence. Even now, as he sat in the softly lighted bar of the Khufu, the bits of information were clicking into place in his brain like the inputs lodging in a computer's memory. The tiny scars of early and severe varicella on Reich's cheeks, the fleshy folds around the small, mobile mouth, the guttural and glottic clicks and rolls in his German-accented English and a hundred other small characteristics of the man were being filed away in Sawyer's encyclopedic memory. But none of these fragments of information served the most necessary purpose: that of trying to understand what kind of a bargain was being offered here, and who would profit by it.

'I am not a very important man in the NPC, Mr. Reich,' Sawyer said. 'I wouldn't want you to be under any misapprehension that I am. I don't even know Dr. Clevenger or any of the people working in the Rub' al Khali.'

'You are an honest man, Dr. Sawyer,' Reich said. 'I like

that. You are a man who can be trusted.'

'I hope so,' Sawyer said. 'Still . . .'

'I see you are too perceptive for anything but very plain talk, doctor.' Reich glanced about the crowded room and said, 'Perhaps it would be best if we took a stroll outside. I don't think it wise to speak here.'

Mystified, Cecil Sawyer waited while Reich signaled a waiter and settled the bill. 'Shall we?' Reich said, rising.

Outside the Khufu lay a broad area of sandy paving dotted with light-standards. The hotel, designed to resemble the general shape of the Saqqārah Step Pyramid, glittered dazzlingly in the desert night. The air was dry and warm, smelling of sand, the Nile, and of the foodstuffs being cooked and sold in the vast, artificial *souk* between the Sphinx and the Great Pyramid, whose floodlighted mass blotted out a huge portion of the starry desert sky.

Reich guided Sawyer away from the lights and in the direction of the river. In the near distance, the city lights of Giza blended into the lights of Cairo to form a carpet of brilliance against the eastern skyline.

'Doctor,' Reich said quietly, 'I am going to confide in you. I am a good judge of character. I know you can be trusted to be absolutely discreet.'

He paused, withdrew from an inside pocket a small leather folder, and handed it to Sawyer. In the uncertain light, Sawyer opened it.

'Let me help you,' Reich said. He shone a penlight on the plastic card within the folder.

Sawyer studied the card, feeling his heartbeat quicken. It was an I.D. in Helmuth Reich's name that carried the seal of the United States Central Intelligence Agency.

'I surprise you, doctor?' Reich asked, retrieving the folder and returning it to his pocket.

Cecil Sawyer felt a rush of unsettling and unfamiliar concerns. His first instinct was to turn and hurry away from the German. It was somehow improper that he, Sawyer, as a member of an international organization dedicated to purely nonpolitical activities, should even be seen in the company of a member of the CIA. Then he succumbed to a sense of total astonishment that this man, obviously not an American by birth, and known to be a functionary of the East German government, should be something so totally different from what he seemed to be. He realized, of course, that all intelligence services penetrated foreign governments—that was the job of intelligence services. But he had never personally known anyone involved in spying, and he had imagined that if he ever should meet such a person he would instinctively know. That was absurd, of course. Spies didn't carry signs on their backs. Not if they planned to remain spies for long.

It made sense, naturally, that there should be a substantial CIA presence in Egypt. And, when he considered it, there was no reason on earth why a CIA agent should not take on the persona of a member of an Iron Curtain country's trade mission.

'Have I shocked you, Dr. Sawyer?' Reich asked.

'No—yes. Yes, of course you have, Mr. Reich. That is your name? I don't know what to say,' Cecil said, agitated and confused.

'Reich *is* my name, doctor. I'm being straightforward with you. Completely. In fact, I am putting myself in your hands. The Egyptian government would expel me, at the very least, if my occupation should become known.'

'Yes. I can see that,' Sawyer said. 'What I don't understand is why you have told me this.'

Reich laid a confidential hand on Sawyer's shoulder. 'Let me make matters clear, doctor.'

'Good God, yes. Please.'

'Very well. You have asked for a transfer from Kalabishah to EQ Station, have you not?'

'Yes. I submitted the request today.'

'All right, doctor. Under normal circumstances that request would be forwarded to London, then possibly even to New York. The transfer you seek could take weeks.'

'The personnel office in Cairo suggested it might be handled more quickly.'

'Because I involved myself on your behalf, doctor.'

Sawyer stared at the stocky German. Or American. Whatever he was, could it be that the CIA had that much influence in the New Peace Corps?

'I assure you that is so, doctor.'

'Why?'

Reich favored Cecil Sawyer with a thin smile. 'You are an intelligent man, doctor. Of course there is a quid pro quo.'

'Of course,' Sawyer said faintly. He could hardly credit it, but he was going to be asked to *spy*. The question was: on whom? And why?

'My government is curious about the work going on in the Rub' al Khali, Dr. Sawyer.'

The statement struck Sawyer with the force of a blow. It had simply never occurred to him that the United States government might be unaware of whatever work was being done in south Arabia. But when he considered it, there was no real reason to assume that the powers in Washington did know. The New Peace Corps was the creature of an American's enterprise and dedication. But Calder Davis had taken great pains to form an organization that was truly international rather than American. He had known from the start that only in that way could the NPC function as it must among the people of the Third World, who, rightly or wrongly, were suspicious of American handouts.

'We know that there is some nuclear power research being done there,' Reich said. 'We assume that there are medical implications because recently a large number of physicians have been moved to EQ Station. We assume other things, as well, but we don't *know*.' He paused significantly. 'That is why we have assigned a penetration agent to the station, Dr. Sawyer.'

Sawyer felt the prickle of a dreadful premonition. He feared to hear what Reich would say next.

'I believe you are acquainted with a Dr. Shallai, doctor,' Reich said.

Amira. Oh my God, Sawyer thought. Amira was a CIA agent. The thought sprang into being whole and terrifying.

'You know her, of course,' Reich said.

'Yes,' Cecil Sawyer said thickly.

'Well, here is the problem, doctor. Her Control here in Egypt was a tour guide named Py at Abu Simbel . . .'

Sawyer remembered now the times Amira had absented herself from Kalabishah, departing on a lake steamer in the morning and returning to the station late at night. So she had been going to Abu Simbel, to get her orders from her Yank masters. God, it all seemed so impossible. And yet, not really so. Amira was a silent, private woman. Cecil had always both admired and feared her quickness of mind, so devastating in a woman as beautiful as she. The men at the station had compared her to Nefertiti. They had been more right than they knew. He was only now beginning to understand how complex a woman he had allowed himself to fall in love with—a lady as dark and secret as the fabled ancient Queen of Amarna. But Reich was going on, and what he was saying brought a chill of terror into the young doctor's belly. . . .

'Py was murdered by Black Septembrists. I am very much afraid he talked before he died. Talked about Dr. Shallai. They know who she works for now, I'm sorry to say.'

'By *God*, Reich,' Sawyer said in a surge of fear and anger. 'How could you do it? How could you involve a woman like that in something as dangerous as spying?' His emotions gave him a forcefulness that was quite uncharacteristic. He could not remember ever in his life having spoken to anyone this angrily.

Reich shrugged. 'Dr. Shallai knew the risks when she decided to help us. Washington felt we had to know at first hand what was going on in the Rub' al Khali. The NPC refused to cooperate, so we had to investigate on our own.'

'But now the Septembrists know about Amira,'

Reich noted the use of the given name, the anger of the badly frightened lover—or wishful lover, he corrected himself. Good. The interview was going even better than he had hoped.

'If the Septembrists know she works for you, then the Pan-Arabian radicals will know, too. Why . . .' The thought in Cecil Sawyer's mind was almost too horrible to contemplate. He knew how the remnants of the Arab terrorist gangs dealt with women prisoners—particularly those they believed were spies. 'They might kill her,' he finished lamely.

'They will kill her,' Reich said. 'Unless . . .'

'Unless what? Good God, Reich. Unless *what*?'

'Unless you help us, doctor.'

'I? What can I do? I'm a physician, not a spy. . . .' Sawyer felt the urgings of despair, of panic.

'I can expedite your transfer,' Reich said. 'I have that much influence, doctor. We can have you on a flight to Arabia in the morning. Will you help me save Dr. Shallai? You see, there is no other way I can reach her. We have no resources at EQ Station and we have no way of knowing if the extremists have penetrated the place. But we can get you in, and you can warn Dr. Shallai.'

'*I?* What can I do?'

'You can do what I tell you,' Reich said in a voice grown quite suddenly more steely, less probing. The fish had bitten, the hook was well set. 'We can arrange through our friends in the NPC for you to carry an emergency travel priority. All that you need do is find Dr. Shallai, convince her that she is in danger, and escort her back here to Cairo. To me, in fact. A relatively simple task, Dr. Sawyer, but a vital one. We can't afford to lose agents as skillful and dedicated as Amira Shallai.'

Cecil Sawyer's conventional mind was reeling with all this talk of spies and secret dangers. What Reich was suggesting *sounded* simple, but it was not simple at all.

'Mr. Reich,' he said in an agitated tone, 'there is nothing in the world I would not do for Dr. Shallai, but frankly, I must tell you that I have very little influence with her—I mean, I believe she values my friendship, but . . .'

'Really, Dr. Sawyer? I was given to understand that your relationship was closer than that,' Reich said. 'Forgive me, but I was under the impression that you were lovers. If I have been mistaken about your willingness to take the risk . . .' He let the sentence hang in the air.

'There is nothing I would not do for Amira,' Sawyer said intensely. He did not deny that he was her lover, although the omission shamed him. Yet if he did as Reich asked, if he could manage it—how far might Amira's gratitude not extend? He would never take advantage of it, of course, but wasn't it possible that she might look upon him as a man worthy of love?

Cecil Sawyer's voice was dry and frightened, but his words were brave enough. 'Tell me what you want me to do, Mr. Reich.'

When the Palestinian NPC clerk at the other end of the line hung up, Reich returned his false CIA credentials to the wall safe in his sitting room, went to the bar, and poured himself a glass of schnapps. Then he stepped out onto the terrace to look down at the city lights on the black surface of the Nile while he considered this night's work.

He was well pleased with himself, and he rather thought that his superiors in Moscow would be, too. Considering how little solid evidence he had to work with, he had constructed quite a lovely Potemkin Village, he thought. If it was mostly façade and supposition—still it had interesting possibilities.

He was almost certain that Dr. Shallai was an intelligence agent. Py had almost surely been a Control. The pity was that those stupid butchers who killed him had not had the foresight to milk him dry of information before allowing their natural *Schrecklichkeit* to overcome them. But still, he was as certain as could be—under the circumstances—that the Egyptian woman was a spy.

Now if the naïve Dr. Sawyer could pull himself together well enough to use the credentials Reich's NPC resource could provide and reach the woman and convince her that she must return at once with him to Cairo, all would work out nicely. Reich could have her across the Libyan border in two hours and in the hands of a KGB interrogation team in Moscow in twelve.

Not a great coup, Reich thought modestly, but better than most of the intelligence coming out of Egypt these days.

18 Salalah

Amira Shallai lay nude on the bed, sleepless in the breathless heat. The air-conditioning plant in the Oasis Hotel had inexplicably ceased to function. Either it had failed, which was likely, or it had simply been turned off for no discernible reason. The air in the room was stifling because the hotel had been built in the Western manner, with windows that could not be opened.

Since returning to the Oasis, Amira had devoted much thought to the elderly British soldier with whom she had spent the evening. Colonel Hadfield represented both the best and the worst of the old British Raj. There could be no doubt that the former Trucial Scout officer loved Arabia and things Arab. That was evident in everything he said and did. But his affection for the desert lands had locked him, it seemed to Amira, in the past. Hadfield was a Briton in the almost extinct Lawrence of Arabia mold, a man who would have been far happier to have ridden with Feisal to Damascus than he was now, acting as factotum for the New Peace Corps in Salalah.

But there was something about the way in which he regarded his present position that Amira found both perplexing and somehow disturbing. It seemed to her that the man was anticipating some profound change in both his own situation and in the character of the Arab lands he so obviously loved. His hatred of the oil companies—in fact, of oil generally—was obvious. He made no effort whatever to hide it. It had been the discovery of oil in the desert that had brought about all the changes he so plainly despised. Amira was certain that if he could have called on some occult power to turn back the calendar to the time when the *bedu* princes lived in the sand sea with their flocks and raiders, he would have done so in an instant, without regard for any of the advantages that had come to Arabia with the flood of petro-dollars.

The Egyptian woman shrugged aside the puzzle of Colonel Colin Hadfield and lay in the dimness considering her mission. It was an uncertain mandate she had been given. She had heard from her Mossad contacts a number of rumors concerning the worry in Jerusalem about the political upheavals in Arabia.

Py had told her some weeks ago that the people in Mossad were growing concerned over the possibility of a new alliance forming between the Pan-Arabians and the Soviet Union. She was not an expert on the subject of world oil, but it was becoming increasingly obvious that the radicals in Riyadh might soon seek to direct the flow of Arabian oil into Russia rather than westward. Even before the seizure of the diplomatic hostages in the Arabian capital, it had been only too apparent that the United States and its tepid allies were in a state of disarray and uncertainty over this possibility. No one in Jerusalem any longer believed that the United States intended to protect its own vital interests in the Gulf, let alone protect the interests of Israel.

This had all given rise to much speculation about what the Israelis might do to protect their own security. It had never been the Israelis' way to wait until they were overrun by events. They tended to consider, prepare, and strike—all at their own time and place. Preemptive war was an acceptable doctrine in Jerusalem.

Amira had heard a number of speculative rumors about something called Plan Aluf, which was nothing less than a swift strike across the width of the Arabian Peninsula to occupy the formerly Saudi oil fields and petroleum refineries. She had also heard much threatening talk from her fellow Arabs about the impossibility of such a move succeeding. It had been an article of faith for at least twenty years in the Arab world that the oil fields would be sabotaged long before any invader could occupy them. She often wondered if this were true.

What concerned her now was her own assignment from Mossad. It seemed a far distance from the kind of work she had signed on to undertake after the death of her cousin André. Still, one could not become too squeamish after taking on the task of being an agent of a foreign power. She might question, but silently. She had, after all, made her commitment.

What, then, did Mossad suspect was taking place at EQ Station that required the dispatch of a penetration agent? Were they simply probing? Or did they have definite suspicions? She had been given no information by Mohammed Py that would serve to answer that one most profound question.

She stirred restlessly, uncomfortably, in the heat. She could feel the dampness of her own sweat between her breasts, on her belly, on the soft inner flesh of her thighs. The heat was palpable, somehow erotic.

She closed her eyes, wishing for sleep. Vague memories troubled her. Her Arab heritage had been sufficient to prevent her having any sexual adventures while she was in America. With her cousin André Kahal, of course, there had been nothing at all. One did not disregard cultural prohibitions in the homeland.

She knew that she was a beautiful woman. Only a fool or a hypocrite would have indulged in self-delusion on that point. She knew that men were struck by her beauty, and that they were often aroused by it. She thought about that absurd and unpleasant man, Dayir, on the lake steamer. And about Dr. Sforza-Barzani, his Italianate passions barely held in check by his own sense of the dignity required of a station director. And Cecil Sawyer—the eager and touching way he found excuses to be near her, never finding the courage to speak about things other than the work they shared. She sighed heavily. There were always men—and yet there was no one man. That was a great pity, she thought. Some might be intimidated by her appearance and by her obviously superior mind. But one would imagine that after thirty-odd years of life she would have encountered one who could love her and whom she could love.

She wished for sleep and yet the thoughts tumbled through her mind in a disorderly, troubling stream-of-consciousness. Was it because she was afraid? she wondered. Had she somehow allowed herself to become entrapped in a profession for which she had no real aptitude, despite certain successes? Was she fearful of what she would find in the desolation of the Rub' al Khali?

There was a sound at the door, like something caused by the wind. But there was no way at all for the wind to penetrate this hermetically sealed tower of glass and plastic. She sat up swiftly.

It came again. Someone was scratching at the door to her room. She looked at her watch. It was just midnight.

She stood and put on a light robe. The soft scratching continued.

She walked across the dim room to the door and said, 'Yes, who is it?' in Arabic. There was no reply and she repeated the question in English.

This time there was a response. 'It is Mr. Haramaki, doctor. Please forgive me.'

Amira turned on a light and opened the door a crack. The small Japanese who had been her seatmate on the flight down the African coast smiled at her politely. 'Many pardons, Dr. Shallai. But I have just returned to the hotel and I understood you were departing tomorrow.' He was holding a carefully wrapped package. 'You remember me, Dr. Shallai? On the airplane from Cairo?'

'Yes,' Amira said. 'I remember you, Mr. Haramaki.'

'This package was delivered to me by mistake, if you please. It is yours. The book you were reading on the airplane. I knew I must return it to you immediately.' He thrust the wrapped package at her.

Amira was about to say that she had not left a book on the airplane, and that even if she had it would have been unlikely that the lax ground staff of the Royal Omani Airline would have taken the trouble to return it. But a sudden intuition prevented her. She said, 'Thank you for your kindness, Mr. Haramaki.'

The little Japanese sucked his breath and bowed formally. 'Yes. Very well. I am sorry to have disturbed you at this hour.' He retreated down the hall and Amira closed the door and latched it.

She went to a table near the draped window, weighing the parcel in her hands as she went. In a time when the use of letter bombs and other nasty devices was common, opening a strange package took some courage. But Mohammed Py had told her to expect a contact in Salalah, and Mr. Haramaki fit the requirements neatly. He was free to travel, a foreigner—and therefore not quite so subject to harsh treatment by the police of Arab states. It was almost a certainty that Haramaki was the expected courier. For a moment Amira let herself be mildly astonished at the extent and complexity of Mossad's networks. And then, too, one had to consider all the other intelligence networks spread across the world—the American, the Russian, the British, the Egyptian, the Arab. Net upon net until it seemed the planet must be strangled by the skeins of spies.

She shook off the depressing thought and opened the parcel. It was, as Haramaki said, a book. A travel guide she remembered him reading aboard the aircraft.

She leafed through the small volume and found what she'd known must be there. A single sheet of flash paper on which had been penciled seven number-groups.

The message was written in a simple substitution code that Amira had memorized long ago. This code was intended for quick messages rather than for heavily encrypted ones.

Amira found a pencil and substituted the proper letters for the numbers in the message. The result was simple, direct, and stunning.

ALUF IMMINENT REPORT FINDINGS SOONEST PY DEAD

For a moment Amira sat very quietly. Poor Mohammed Py, she thought, shivering slightly.

This was really a killing business. People died. Suddenly and mostly unpleasantly.

What could there be, she asked herself, up there in the sands of the high desert that demanded such risks?

But there was only a slight tremor of her hand as she found a match, struck it, and watched the flash paper vanish in a burst of flame and a curl of ash.

Then she turned off the light, removed her robe, and lay down on the rumpled bed. She pulled the sheet over her naked body and shivered slightly. Somehow, the stifling air no longer seemed so warm as it had ten minutes earlier.

Five
July 16, the fifth day

We cannot depend on an alliance of angels to defend the free world. . . .

—David Rockefeller, in an article in
The Wall Street Journal, Wednesday,
April 30, 1980

19 Oman

Travel-weary, dusty, unshaven, and wary, Michael Rivas sat in the rear of the covered truck as it climbed the steep, winding dirt road into the Qara Mountains. His companions (South Africans, whose speech was laced with Afrikaans) were all fit, youngish men whose common characteristics included a hard-eyed indifference to the discomforts of the mountain journey in the rear of the military six-by-eight truck.

The convoy consisted of four vehicles. In the van went a jeep occupied by four Omani soldiers. It was closely followed by a British-made command car and another six-by-eight truck laden with crates marked SCIENTIFIC INSTRUMENTS, but which to Rivas's experienced eye looked very like cases of light weapons. The vehicle in which Rivas rode with the Afrikaaners brought up the rear. In the cab of the truck rode the driver and a companion, both of them Europeans with the unmistakable bearing of long-term non-commissioned officers. Nothing was being done, Rivas noted, to disguise the essentially military nature of the convoy, despite the New Peace Corps markings on the vehicles.

This, Rivas thought, was at least part of what Cole had somehow discovered. In Washington the discovery had been a killing matter. But here, in this remote part of the Arabian Peninsula, very little effort was being expended to diss-emble. That could only mean that the need for secrecy was nearly ended. The Afrikaaners were taciturn, hard men. They regarded Rivas without curiosity and without friendliness.

In the early morning, less than an hour after his arrival at Salalah, Rivas had presented himself to Colonel Hadfield in the Old Town. He had immediately been given a tongue-lashing in the Briton's best Trucial Scout manner for having arrived independently and very nearly too late to join the convoy to EQ Station. If it were not for the delay caused by the weather, Hadfield said, ex-Captain John Emerson Hayden would now be adrift and alone without resources in the *souk* of Old Salalah.

Rivas had absorbed the criticism without comment and pitched his single canvas bag into the rear of the truck, but not before he noticed the second passenger in Hadfield's command car. One of the less laconic South Africans had sucked his teeth in what was intended to be a suggestive manner and volunteered the information that she was a medic destined for the staff of the desert station. Rivas thought she was one of the most beautiful women he had ever seen. He had not been introduced. It was obvious that Colonel Hadfield meant for the male recruits to keep their distance. Yank officers retired because of drinking and disciplinary problems, Rivas concluded, did not rank high on Hadfield's list.

☢

As the convoy climbed higher into the mountains, the sun grew hazy behind an overcast of dun-colored dust blowing over the ridges. Hadfield had brusquely told the recruits that there would be a general briefing immediately the convoy reached its destination. Rivas judged that from the condition of the roads and the rising wind flapping the truck's canvas cover as they approached the Qara summit, it might be some time before arrival.

He closed his eyes and let the motion of the truck lull him. He thought about the woman riding with Hadfield. Even in the heat and dust, dressed as she was in the field uniform of a New Peace Corpsman, she was stunning. Rivas guessed that she was Middle Eastern: she had the fine features, smooth skin, and gleaming dark hair of an Arab aristocrat. Rivas had seen such women in Beirut and Damascus, but he had not expected to encounter anyone similar in this remote place. Her manner and self-possession suggested a Western education.

One of the South Africans interrupted his reverie with a question. Rivas said, 'I'm sorry?'

The Afrikaaner indicated the barely healing wound on Rivas's head. 'Where did you get it?' The man was lean, burned dark by the sun. His sand-colored hair was cropped close to his skull.

'New York,' Rivas said. Then, because he could see that the answer aroused the interest of the others and needed further explanation, he added: 'I was mugged.'

The questioner showed short, gray teeth in a smile. 'Ah,' he said. 'Kaffir.' He spoke to the others in Afrikaans.

A burly young man seated near the tailgate said, 'Dangerous place, New York,' and grinned.

The man with the cropped hair said, 'I'm Hans Hendriks.' He made no effort to introduce the others. 'You?'

'Hayden,' Rivas said.

'Where did you serve last?'

'Nam,' Rivas said.

'Nothing since then? That was a long time ago.'

'Just Egypt. And Fort Bragg,' Rivas said. He didn't like the way this conversation was going. There were too many holes in his story, his cover was weak. He wondered what these men, experienced mercenaries, would say or do if they were to learn that he was a journalist. It wasn't a thing he would like to face at the moment.

'You missed the briefing. Old Hadfield was ready to leave without you,' Hendriks said.

'So brief me,' Rivas said shortly.

'Colonel Wyndham sent you?'

'That's right.'

'Then you don't need briefing.' Hendriks took a pack of Players from his bush-jacket pocket and lit one. He did not offer the pack around.

The burly man spoke quietly. 'We won't be joining the Brigade straightaway. I guess you were told that much by Wyndham.'

Rivas shook his head. 'The colonel was too busy with his Kaffir lady to tell me much.'

Both Hendriks and the burly man laughed. 'That's Wyndham, right enough,' Hendriks said.

'I'm Jan Marck,' the burly man said. 'We all served with Tyson's commando in the Zimbabwe war.'

There had been a sharp escalation in the Zimbabwean civil war a year ago. But this was the first time Rivas had encountered evidence that the rumors were true, and that Mugabe had been hiring white mercenaries to stiffen his collapsing, strife-ridden army. The battles had been many and the results had been like all the other military engagements in black Africa since the 1970s. Inconclusive.

Plainly these men were happy to be out of it. And *into* what? Rivas wondered. These didn't seem men who devoted themselves to lost causes. Morale was high.

Marck said, 'We're lumbered with filling out the guard force at EQ. Later, according to the colonel, we'll join the Brigade.'

There was something unsettling about the way Marck pronounced 'the Brigade.' There was too much Rivas did not know, and his ignorance could be dangerous. These were hard men. And 'the Brigade' sounded far more impressive and organized than some ragtaggle mercenary commando.

'Wyndham didn't tell you about the Brigade?' Hendriks asked suspiciously.

'Not much,' Rivas said.

'The general is one of your people,' one of the other men said. 'How come you weren't briefed?'

'I came in too late,' Rivas said. 'No time.'

Marck said, 'You signed on blind? Jesus, you must have been in the deep shit.'

'I was,' Rivas said laconically. Maybe I *am*, he thought.

'Christ, Wyndham will do anything for a bounty,' Hendriks said, laughing suddenly.

'You know ragheads?'

'Only Egyptians,' Rivas said.

'We have to stay loose. The Raschid don't care much for Europeans.'

'Raschid?'

'Camel-shit eaters who live in these mountains. Mean bastards. They hang around EQ Station, I hear. That's why we're saddled with this duty,' Marck said.

Hendriks said, 'They won't attack a convoy. But they are so dirt-poor they'll kill a single man for his boots. Colonel Hadfield loves the bastards. But even he doesn't travel alone in the Empty Quarter.'

'I thought no one lived out there,' Rivas said.

'No one does. Even the Raschid can't survive there for very long. When they travel they actually have to kill their beloved camels just to stay alive. They drink the blood. The colonel says they're the toughest people on earth. He ought to know. He was in the Trucial Scouts for thirty years. The old man's a soldier.' There was a hard respect in the use of the word. 'Soldier' meant something special in this company. 'He says the Pan-Arabian Reds have sent *mullahs* down here to stir up the Raschid and they've been messing around the perimeter at EQ Station ever since.'

'Maybe we can get in some hunting,' one of the other men said.

Marck asked, 'Who is the cunt with Colonel Hadfield?'

'He didn't introduce me,' Rivas said neutrally.

'She's an NPC medic,' Hendriks said. 'I heard in Salalah that they've been sending in three or four every time a cattle car arrives. Maybe they're expecting a lot of casualties.'

'I'll take my chances with *that* one anytime,' Marck said suggestively.

One of the other men laughed and said, 'That's not for grunts, Jan. You'll just have to keep on with the camels until we get to Riyadh. *If* we get to Riyadh.'

A trickle of sweat ran down Rivas's back.

'We'll get there,' Marck said. 'The colonel says we'll join the Brigade before it's over.'

Rivas swallowed some of the dust in his throat. So that part of Calder Smith Davis's New Peace Corps that carried arms was going to Riyadh to rescue the hostages in the United States embassy there. To men sitting in Washington and London and Moscow that would seem preposterous, Rivas thought. But to someone sitting in the rear of a military truck on the dusty track for the Qara passes it made cold, clear, hard sense. Calder Davis and his associates were going to do what the United States and all the nations of Western Europe were afraid to do. It was as simple as that.

And as complicated, Rivas thought. The political fallout from such an action would be enormous. As knowledgeable as he thought himself to be about the interplay of forces between nations and political factions, Rivas realized that he could not begin to imagine the upheavals a rescue attempt by a paramilitary force might cause.

But the South African mercenary's offhand remark made it all very real. Calder Davis and the NPC and all his secret colleagues of the International Strategic Studies Group were actually going to do it. Somewhere within striking distance of Riyadh at this moment the Brigade—Calder Davis's private army—was making ready to move. Davis was bringing back the fourteenth century. That was what Cole had believed and that was why he had been murdered: to protect the secret of Calder Davis's new *condottieri*.

20 The English Channel

On the bridge of the *Sudan Enterprise*, a rust-stained tanker of twenty thousand tons, Captain Florio Guindani dispatched the watch below. A thin, swarthy man with lank, greasy hair and black eyes nested in a deeply lined face, Guindani stood at the wheel and searched the dark sea ahead for the flashing light he had been instructed to expect.

The *Sudan Enterprise* sailed under Liberian registry and her ownership was listed as Greek. It would have taken a team of experienced investigators to follow her lineage through a half-dozen shipping and charter companies. But eventually it would have been discovered that the *Sudan Enterprise* was owned by an obscure subsidiary of the giant Continental Energy Group. Her crew was mainly Cypriot and Berber, her officers were Greek and Italian. Captain Guindani himself was a man who would have had great difficulty obtaining any other command. Five years before, he had lost a supertanker on the Minches, spilling millions in black crude into the sea and fouling miles of beaches. The accident had cost the charterers a fortune in lost contracts, indemnities, and higher insurance premiums.

Captain Guindani was one of a number of ship captains handpicked for use in certain contingencies by Isaac Holt. One of those contingencies was now in force, and Captain Guindani had dismissed the bridge watch so that none of the ship's officers would witness his rendezvous with the *Wild Goose*.

The sky to the east was brightening as the sun's early glow etched the French coast. The *Sudan Enterprise* was a full six miles west of the normal channel for entering these waters and there was a real danger of shoal water. But the vessel was lightly laden and moving slowly. Nonetheless, Florio Guindani felt a certain griping apprehension. He had good reason to fear the tricky navigation required in this turbulent and heavily traveled strait between England and France.

The searching beam of the radar, probing the predawn twilight, showed a half-dozen ships in the two traffic lanes of the channel approaches. But the track Guindani had chosen for the *Sudan Enterprise* was free of nearby vessels.

Guindani's ship had been en route from Rotterdam to the Gulf when Isaac Holt's message had been received through the company's radio station in Spain. Guindani did not know why his instructions had been what they were. He did not care. He knew only that in order to continue in command he must carry them out exactly. Guindani was not a man who troubled himself about moral choices. Without the *Sudan Enterprise*, there were only the slums of Genoa for Guindani. And Guindani was a man who knew about slums and starvation. He had been a boy on the streets of Genoa in the terrible years during and after the war. He did not intend to finish his life as he had begun it.

He had been concerned about the difficulty of finding a small vessel in these waters under conditions of radio silence. But he understood that there was a man aboard the *Wild Goose* who expected to be picked up by the *Sudan Enterprise*. He would be searching for the lights she carried high on her superstructure, as diligently as Guindani was now searching for the recognition signal on the power cruiser. With the tanker's weary engines turning at one-quarter ahead, Guindani suppressed his impatience with difficulty. In another half-hour it would be light and what needed to be done required the cover of darkness.

On the flying bridge of the *Wild Goose* Ian Wyndham scanned the sea to the north with a pair of powerful night glasses. The boat rolled slowly in the calm seaway, its diesels silent, all running lights dark except for the single flasher on the Benetti's stubby signal mast.

His crewman Jacques, the Congolese who had been with Wyndham since Africa, appeared out of the shadows and said in French, 'Your duffel is on the foredeck, Colonel. Ready to go.'

Wyndham's smile was white in the darkness. 'Is Liana still sulking?'

'Yes,' the Congolese said. He shrugged. 'Women.'

The girl had been furious when she had learned that she

was to stay with the *Wild Goose* instead of accompanying Wyndham on the tanker. She was a pushy bitch, Wyndham thought, but worth the trouble she caused. Better by far than her sister.

'When I've gone, give her this,' he said, taking a folded thousand-franc note from his pocket. 'Tell her to buy herself something in Calais. Make sure she's back aboard before you leave for Tangiers.'

The Congolese pocketed the note and nodded obediently. Wyndham regarded him for a moment, wondering if he intended to make personal use of the woman himself on the voyage to Tangiers. Probably. The journey would be a holiday for Jacques and the other crewmen. Two weeks of unrestrained license, sweating in the master cabin, fornicating themselves into insensibility. But at least he could count on Jacques to get the *Wild Goose* safely to port. Wyndham was undecided about what to do with the boat once it—and he—were safely in Tangiers. It wouldn't be too difficult to find a buyer in such a place. The *Wild Goose* was made to order for the drug-smuggling trade.

He returned to his search of the sea to the north. He was feeling pleased with himself. Of course he had known that sooner or later the British authorities would move against him. He had made too much money too fast for them to ignore him. He drew a deep sighing breath. He would miss the Dart and the green land of south England. He supposed that once an Englishman, always one. But it would be some time before he could return. The trick was to remain at least one, and possibly several, jumps ahead of the authorities. Having sure and secure sources of information made that easy.

Twelve hours ago he had received a message from the best and most reliable of his sources. A voice on the RT, identified by time and radio frequency only, had warned him of an imminent visit from—of all people—the agents of the Inland Revenue. It had informed him that Plan One was now to be implemented. Plainly his benefactors hadn't wanted him in the hands of the revenue people.

Plan One was noted on the charts Wyndham kept locked in the *Wild Goose*'s safe. It was only an X-mark and a time, but long ago it had been explained to Wyndham that at that place and time he would be picked up by a ship and delivered safely to Tangiers.

He had often considered the implications of Plan One and had been impressed by the resources commanded by the plan's originator. To make it function would require that at least once in every twenty-four hours a ship owned by, or at least controlled by, his employers would be within reach of the position noted on the chart. When he examined that conclusion he realized that the number of ships needed was large. Thirty or more. That meant more than one company or charterer, surely. The number involved could be substantial.

He had never doubted that his employers were enormously wealthy. The payments he had received for the mercenaries he had sent to Africa and Oman had made him rich. Wyndham was not a stupid man. That kind of money could come only from Arab oil or from the multinational corporations. The nature of the force he—and quite likely others of his own sort—had assembled over the last year tended to favor the latter conclusion. The really rich Arabs were almost all in the West now, run out of their homelands by the Islamic revolts that had spread from Iran to the other Gulf states. It was possible that his activities had been engaged by these people to build some sort of counterrevolutionary force. But the rumors that had drifted back to him pointed in another direction. The American Collingwood would be an unlikely choice to command a mercenary army for expatriate Arab sheiks. He would be the perfect choice, however, to command one for the great companies whose interests were being gored on the horns of an Islamic revival.

Wyndham decided to investigate further when he reached Tangiers. Suspicions were one thing, but certain knowledge was even more valuable than the fortune he had locked away in the Banque de Suisse.

Jacques, standing beside him, spoke suddenly. 'There. A ship.'

Wyndham, cursing his failing eyesight, said, 'Where?'

'There. To the northeast. Listen. You can hear her.'

Wyndham used the night glasses. 'I see it,' he said.

'Shall I start the engines?'

'Wait until she heaves to. Then we'll come alongside.' Now Wyndham could make out the tanker's shape against the light beginning to limn the eastern horizon.

For a time he watched the approaching ship. The sound of it came down on the wind: the rumble of machinery and the soughing of the now distinguishable white bone in her teeth. The tanker had altered course slightly, so that from the flying bridge of the yacht she looked fore shortened, a broad dark shape in the graying twilight of dawn.

'I'll go below and say good-bye to the cunts,' Wyndham said roughly. Actually, he was fond of the black girl and her sister. Their unrestrained sexuality had given him considerable pleasure and revived his aging powers. He was grateful for that and didn't wish to be on bad terms with either of the women. There was, after all, Tangiers to anticipate.

He clambered down the ladder and into the dark cabin. At the companionway to the master's quarters he bent over and said, 'I've come to say good-bye.'

'Go to hell,' Liana said from the darkness. 'Rot in hell.'

'Black bitch,' Wyndham said, grinning. 'I'll see you in Tangiers.'

'Why can't we go with you?'

'*We* is it now? I explained all that. You stay with Jacques and the boat and I'll see you in two weeks.'

'I hope your white cock rots,' the girl said. In French the imprecation sounded even more disgusting than it would have in English. Wyndham closed the companionway door and latched it. The bitches were capable of rushing the ladder onto the tanker, and the last thing one needed was two black whores as extra baggage. Whoever the master of the tanker was, he would report back to his bosses and it wouldn't do to let it be said that Colonel Ian Wyndham couldn't control his women.

When he stepped out on deck, the tanker was much closer. Its speed seemed undiminished. If anything, it appeared to have increased. Wyndham went onto the foredeck and strained to make out the details of the approaching vessel. He could actually read her name in the dawnlight. *Sudan Enterprise*. There was no one visible on her forward decks, and the bridge, far aft, was dark. He lifted his head and shouted to Jacques. 'What the hell are they doing?'

His crewman did not reply, but Wyndham suddenly heard him at the flying-bridge controls, engaging the starters. Cool, the diesels failed to catch immediately.

'What's happening, Jacques?' Wyndham called again.

'*They are not stopping!*' The Congolese's voice was shrill against the increasing rumble of the oncoming tanker's machinery.

The *Sudan Enterprise*'s bulb bow was plainly visible now. Her decks towered into the lightening sky. The rush of water as she approached was like the sound of a swiftly flowing river. The sound of her engine grew louder still. Wyndham became aware of the stink of oil and stack gases.

He turned and screamed at Jacques, *'Get the engines started! Get them started, goddamn you!'*

The beat of the tanker's engine was like a great drum. The black hull was like a rust-stained wall falling. Wyndham felt the *Wild Goose* come tremblingly to life and he struggled to keep his balance as Jacques slammed the throttles forward. White water frothed at the yacht's stern as the screws fought to put twelve tons of boat in motion.

Wyndham watched in horror as the dark band of water between the yacht and the onrushing steel mountain narrowed. Just before the *Sudan Enterprise* smashed the *Wild Goose* down into the black water, Wyndham heard himself scream in fury at his employers—his benefactors. The scream was wordless, helpless, and it ended as the great bulk of the tanker drove on over the disintegrating yacht. There were other screams, from the flying bridge and from the latched cabin below, but no one heard them.

Presently some flotsam appeared in the churning wake of the tanker: a few life vests, some seat cushions, a few bits of wood and paper. On one scrap of a chart was penciled an X and a rendezvous time, but this soon disintegrated in the oil-stained sea as the *Sudan Enterprise* swung east to the ship channel and continued on her interrupted journey to the Gulf.

21 Ar Rub' al Khali

As the convoy approached the summit of the Qara, Amira Shallai took note of the changing character of the land. Gone now were the watersheds of the Qara's southern slopes, and gone too was the green of growing things nurtured by the seasonal monsoon rains. Here, and to the north, Colonel Hadfield explained, the annual rainfall was not twenty inches as in the southern littoral, but twenty-one hundredths of an inch. The spine of the mountains was a broken, rocky plateau. The road had deteriorated to a rutted track scratched into the iron-hard soil. From her place in the command car, Amira could look east and west to the spiny ridges defining a series of barren passes, beyond which the ground fell away into a dusty, indistinct plain swept by sand-laden wind.

'The Omanis will be turning back soon,' Hadfield said. 'They will see us through the last of the Wahhabi country. They've pretty much subdued the Wahhabi and the Duru, but they don't like to mix it with the Raschid. They'll leave us on our own for that.'

'I had no idea there were still hostile *bedu* here,' Amira said. 'It all seems like something out of the last century.'

Hadfield put away the field glasses with which he had been studying the empty slopes that were gradually closing in on the convoy to form the first of the Qara passes. 'They don't amount to much militarily,' he said. 'But they can't be ignored. They are a brave and savage people.'

He spoke of the natives, Amira noted, with the dour admiration of the confirmed British Arabist.

'A warrior people. When the bloody oil is gone, they will still be here, scratching a living from these borderlands.'

'They actually live in the Empty Quarter?' Amira asked.

'No one *lives* in the Rub' al Khali, doctor. Just as no one lives on the Southern Ocean. The environment won't sustain human life. But the Raschid travel on the sand sea, and they still think of it as theirs.' He turned to look back at the trucks behind the command car. 'We'll break out the weapons as soon as the Omanis turn back.'

'Weapons, Colonel?'

'A precaution, that's all. I get on reasonably well with the Raschid, but one can't ever be sure what they will do. It depends on how badly they want the supplies we are carrying. That is why EQ Station is usually resupplied by air.'

Amira thoughtfully digested this information. The closer the convoy came to the sand sea of the Rub' al Khali, the more it resembled a military operation. She rode in silence, suppressing questions and considering the implications of the message she had received through Mr. Haramaki at Oasis Hotel. *Aluf imminent*. Well, it was logical enough. There was a certain terrible reasonableness about the decision that had apparently been taken in Jerusalem. The oil from the Gulf was inevitably drying to a trickle as the Pan-Islamic radicals gradually strangled production or diverted it to the Communist world to punish the West. With the supply dwindling, Western governments dithered—but of one thing the Israelis were certain: the West had no intention of sharing what it had with the Jews. The Jews, Amira thought, were a pragmatic people. Result: *Aluf*. The question was, *when*? A secondary question, and one of equal importance, was what is the NPC doing at EQ Station and can it threaten a preemptive Israeli move into the Arabian Peninsula?

'Tell me about the station, Colonel,' she said.

Hadfield looked at her guardedly. He was not a man who could mask his inner feeling easily. 'We will be there tomorrow, doctor.'

'But can you tell me what to expect, Colonel? A woman's curiosity, that's all.'

'There was once a Saudi air base there. It was called Ibrahimah. No one uses the old name now. It is just EQ Station.'

'An air base, Colonel? I had no idea.'

'It was a training facility, I believe. It was abandoned by the Royal Saudi Air Force and their American advisers during the Iranian-Iraqi war. All the aircraft and support units were moved to the north, to the Iranian border. The Saudis were afraid the Iranians would try to strike at the oil fields. So the place went back to desert until the NPC took it over.'

'Then it is a large place?'

'Large enough,' Colonel Hadfield said noncommittally.

'And what, exactly, are we doing there?' Amira asked bluntly. 'Everyone at Kalabishah talked about EQ Station, but no one ever seemed to know exactly what sort of work was going on there. There was talk of nuclear power experiments and oil exploration. But no one seemed to have any hard facts.'

Colonel Hadfield's pale blue eyes grew veiled. 'You will have your facts soon enough, Dr. Shallai.'

And I am obviously to be satisfied with that, Amira thought, and fell silent.

Despite the four-thousand-foot elevation and the increasing wind, the temperature was rising as the vehicles followed the road deeper into the passes. Amira felt the sweat run between her breasts. She helped herself to the water in one of the canteens strapped with webbing to the car's door panels.

'Try to ration yourself, doctor,' Colonel Hadfield said. 'We have plenty, but you never know in this country.'

Amira savored the metallic-tasting mouthful she had taken and returned the canteen to its sling.

'The Omanis will quit us at Ash Shisar,' Hadfield said. 'There is an old fort there that dates back to the time of the first Sultan of Muscat. It is a ruin, of course, but sometimes the Raschid use it to stable their camels. Camels are wealth here. They mean survival.'

'I am an Arab, Colonel. I know something about the way Bedouin must live,' Amira said.

'Forgive me, doctor, but the Raschid aren't your ordinary Egyptian Bedouin. They are people on the edge of extinction in a country that has earned billions in oil revenues. It tends to make them unpredictable.'

Amira opened the top button of her bush jacket and let the hot breeze evaporate the moisture on her skin. 'You say that with admiration, Colonel.'

Hadfield allowed himself a brief smile. 'I suppose I do. I admire any people who know how to survive in a land like this.' He raised his field glasses again and searched the barren ground ahead. 'That does not mean I trust them, doctor.'

Amira considered that statement for a time and then said, 'The men in the lorry back there. They are soldiers, aren't they.'

'Quite,' Hadfield said shortly.

'I didn't realize the NPC had any use for soldiers, Colonel. Forgive me if that seems rude.'

'No offense taken, Dr. Shallai. It simply happens that you are wrong. We do, indeed, need soldiers. Good ones and quite a few of them, as you will learn at your first briefing at EQ Station.'

'Will I also learn why, Colonel?'

'Yes,' Hadfield said bluntly. 'You will.'

'What is happening here, Colonel? Can't you tell me? I am not exactly in a position to oppose it even if I should disapprove.'

'I'm sorry, doctor. That's not my job. I am supposed to get you and those men to EQ Station together with the supplies we are carrying. I regret that you are being forced to travel this way, but the sandstorms have made it unavoidable.'

'I am not complaining, Colonel. I came from Kalabishah so I know something about uncomfortable conditions. But I seem suddenly to have joined some sort of militia. I would simply like to know why.'

'At the briefing, Dr. Shallai,' Colonel Hadfield said. 'There will be no more mystery after we arrive at the station, I promise you.'

The convoy veered slightly to the east around a rocky line of hillocks and Amira saw the settlement of Ash Shisar. It consisted of a group of rock huts roofed with corrugated iron. On the slope rising to the ridge behind the huts stood the ruin of a fort made of mud brick. It was the color of a camel's back, dusty brown, and it blended into the sere landscape so completely that it seemed to have grown there out of the earth. The jeep carrying the Omani soldiers had stopped and an officer laden with bandoliers of ammunition and carrying an American M-16 was signaling the convoy to halt. In a stone corral built against the crumbling wall of the fort, Amira could see a half-dozen camels guarded by as many men, all armed. They carried an assortment of weapons ranging from ancient jezails to Belgian FN automatic rifles.

The driver of the command car braked to a stop and Colonel Hadfield dismounted to speak with the Omani officer. The soldier, a thin, bearded man with nearly black skin, was gesturing in Amira's direction and speaking in Arabic so heavily accented with the local dialect that the Egyptian woman could understand only an occasional word.

Colonel Hadfield spoke to the officer and returned to the command car. 'He says he and his men will leave us here,' the Briton explained.

'He also says that if you have a *chador* or a veil, you should wear it. He says that it will offend the Raschid if you do not.'

'And will it, Colonel?' Amira asked.

'Yes. Very likely. There have been Pan-Islamic agitators down here from the north. Most of them haven't survived, but those who have have managed to stir up the Raschid.'

'I will see what I have in my baggage.' Amira dismounted and walked around to the rear of the command car, where her canvas bag rode strapped to the metal rack behind the spare wheels. She noticed that the men who had been riding in the truck behind the command car had also dismounted and were standing in the road staring at her.

She found a long scarf of white silk in her bag and wrapped it around her head, hiding her hair and veiling herself like a Bedouin woman. Without a word she climbed back into the vehicle and took her place, looking evenly at the Omani officer.

The man spoke again and Colonel Hadfield turned to Amira. There was the suggestion of a smile on his craggy face. 'Lieutenant Habooz says that the veil should be black and not white, but that if that is the best you can do it must suffice.'

In purest, classical Arabic she said, 'This woman thanks the sheik for his courtesy and advice. He should know that in my country men do not trouble themselves over matters of women's fashion. This woman is honored by his interest and promises that when she is next a guest in his country she will be more suitably attired.'

The Omani had difficulty following her speech and frowned darkly when Hadfield translated. He climbed back into the jeep and gave an angry order. The vehicle headed back toward the passes, leaving a plume of dust behind it. Amira watched it go, despising the prejudices of her people. Under his bourgeois pretensions, the fat and sweaty dandy on the lake steamer was like the Omani officer. And so were the PLO animals who had captured André and watched him die. Their Marxist theorizing made no real changes in them. This was the burden that her people bore, this weight of primitive prejudice that kept their minds in the thirteenth century. The Raschid, at least, had the excuse of poverty. But so many of the other Arabs, rich with oil money, had no excuse at all.

Colonel Hadfield walked down the road and gave an order. The men unloaded a wooden case and opened it. When Amira turned and looked again, they were all armed with M-16s. Hadfield and one of the men from the truck returned.

'This is Hayden, Dr. Shallai.'

The man nodded in acknowledgment. Amira noticed that he had a half-healed head injury. Hadfield signaled for him to climb into the rear seat. He took his place with the M-16 held familiarly in one hand. Amira was struck by the blue color of his eyes and the contrast they made with his sunburned complexion.

'All right,' Colonel Hadfield said. 'Let's move out. Slowly.'

The convoy, now without its Omani military escort, rolled forward. As the vehicles moved past the ruined fort, Hadfield raised his hand in salute to the Raschid tribesmen standing near the stone corral. There was no response. Amira felt a chill as she watched the silent Raschid regarding them with eyes as stony as their land.

22 Washington, D.C.

The President of the United States awoke from a restless sleep to the insistent tone of the telephone on the console near his bed. Automatically he looked at the glowing digital clock and saw that it was not yet five in the morning. Immediately the familiar knot began to form in the pit of his stomach. It was a thing to which Vincent Loomis had never become accustomed: this dread that any untimely telephone message might be a harbinger of some disaster, some tragedy which he, as President of the United States, might be called upon to avert.

He snapped on the bedside light and sat on the edge of the bed. The door to his wife's room stood open and it was a moment before his sleep-dulled mind remembered that Marie was not in Washington, but at Camp David, where she had taken the children to escape the wet heat of summer.

He rang for a houseman before picking up the handset. He needed coffee. The console panel flashed remorselessly, and Loomis sighed heavily and lifted the receiver. 'Yes?'

'It's Peter, Mr. President.' The voice of his National Security Adviser sounded thinner and more strained than usual. The man was less than a rock of strength in a storm, but he had always been loyal, Loomis told himself.

'We have a warning on the hot-line teleprinter, Mr. President,' Gilmartin said. 'We are to stand by for a two-parter from President Suslov, sir.'

Loomis suppressed a groan. The Soviet President was an old man, given to old men's quarrels and testiness. He was entirely in the hands of the only slightly younger men who now dominated the Politburo, hardliners like Batrayev of the KGB, who sensed that the Soviet empire was unraveling in a chaotic world and who were therefore savaged with fear and anger. A message from Suslov clearly meant trouble.

A black houseman, accustomed to President Loomis's

habits, appeared with a silver pot of strong, black coffee and a jigger of Irish whiskey. He prepared the decoction and departed as silently as he had come. Loomis lifted the cup and let the aroma clear the cobwebs from his mind. 'All right, Peter. I'll meet you in the Situation Room right away. Who is with you?'

'The Secretary of Defense has been notified. Shall I get General Lescher over here?'

Lescher was the new Chairman of the Joint Chiefs, a man favored by the military but regarded by the White House staffers as a political liability because of his right-wing views.

'Leave Lescher out of it for the moment. Have you contacted Ike Holt?'

'Holt flew to New York late last night, Mr. President.'

Vincent Loomis hunched his heavy shoulders in annoyance. 'What the hell for?'

'I don't know, sir.' Gilmartin said distractedly.

'Well, have him located and told to stand by. We may need him and we may not. It depends on what kind of trouble Suslov wants to make. It is Suslov, isn't it?'

'Oh, yes, sir. The warning is in the Olympus code.'

Olympus, Loomis thought. The code for gods and heads of state. Nothing good ever came couched in the language of Olympus. 'All right,' he said. 'I'll come right away.' He broke the connection and drank the whiskey-laced coffee down. He wondered briefly what his political opponents would say if they knew how he began his days. Better than prayer breakfasts or jelly beans, he thought sourly. But the sick anxiety in his gut was not warmed by the pungent beverage. It would take more than that to ease the tensions of this terrible—and wonderful—job. If only I were a better man than I am, he thought, momentarily surrendering to the doubts he lived with day and night. But good or bad, he had no choice but to carry on in the post he had spent half of his life seeking. He walked into the dressing room, shuffling like a man twenty years older than he actually was, a lumpish, almost pitiful figure oddly at variance with his harsh and blustery public image.

☢

The duty officer in the Situation Room, a major of the Army Signal Corps, said, 'The first part is coming in now, Mr.

Gilmartin.' The teleprinter was silently producing line after line of coded symbols.

Peter Gilmartin, his pale eyes still puffy with interrupted sleep, stood behind the officer and stared at the printout anxiously.

Gilmartin had met President Suslov on a number of occasions. The Soviet leader was nearly eighty, and though he had been a brilliant and ruthless manipulator of events for half a century, he was less than that now. Gilmartin was certain that he could deal with the old man. Therefore the Olympus message promised to be both a challenge and an opportunity. The United States and the Soviet Union had been quarreling actively since the Iranian-Iraqi war. Since then there had been at least a dozen crises of greater or lesser proportion as the forces of the two superpowers maneuvered along the sea-lanes of the oil routes and in the cockpit of Central Europe.

The removal of the Rapid Deployment Force had been the result of a suggestion by Peter Gilmartin, but it had not had the effect he had promised the President. The Egyptians had objected strenuously; the Israelis had taken the move as still another example of American perfidy and refusal to meet obligations; the Europeans had taken the withdrawal as an indication of American lack of resolve. The Soviets, who should have been delighted and grateful enough to renew the SALT negotiations Gilmartin desired, had shown themselves decidedly *un*grateful, taking the view that what they had was theirs (now including all of Afghanistan and parts of Iran) and what the Americans had remained negotiable. They had absolutely refused to remove their SS-20 missiles from Eastern Europe and had declined with equal self-righteousness to agree that their Backfire bombers (of which they now had nearly a thousand) were intercontinental weapons. This, despite a brazen display of virtuosity by a squadron of the beastly airplanes flying around the world nonstop, using aerial tankers for refueling.

These decisions, Gilmartin was sure, had been taken by the hard men surrounding Ivan Kirilovich Suslov. But the silent urgency of a hot-line communication suggested to Peter Gilmartin that Ivan Suslov and his grim colleagues of the Politburo had found some exploitable gambit in the constant chess game they played with the United States. They seldom used the hot line for anything else, and they never spoke to Washington without showing nuclear teeth these days.

Gilmartin looked away from the teleprinter to see the President walking heavily through the door.

'Well, Peter?' the President asked.

'Part one is in the translator, Mr. President,' Gilmartin said. Messages received on the hot-line teleprinter were immediately put through the electronic translator, a computer programmed by experts on Soviet political language. It had been discovered, somewhere in the warrens of the National Security Agency, that translation by human translators—men who spoke Russian but who were not, after all, confirmed Marxists—could miss nuances and shades of meaning. The results were specifically *Soviet* as opposed to merely Russian language rendered into English.

Vincent Loomis glanced at the bank of digital chronometers that gave the time in every time zone across the world. Gloomily he thought about the Americans and Europeans who were now approaching their two hundredth day as hostages in the embassy in Riyadh. A dozen times in each one of those one hundred and ninety-two days he had asked himself if he was doing the right thing by doing, essentially, nothing. But public opinion had never coalesced into a single, straightforward imperative. Without that Loomis feared to move. Now all of his hopes were concentrated in the frail person of Calder Davis. How the financier proposed to move, Loomis did not know—and did not wish to know. He prayed for success, suffering the secret self-accusation of inadequacy. But in the final analysis, he asked himself, and given the realities of today, what President could have done more?

He clung to the notion that he was acting as a man of peace. He had withdrawn the Rapid Deployment Force. He had cut the American presence in the Gulf to a minimum. He had done all that a prudent man could do to entice the Soviets to return to détente. What more could any man—any ordinary man—do? Yet he was troubled and frustrated by the tumbling confusion of events. What President had ever had to face the loss of his DCI by an act of murder? All that he had worked for and achieved now seemed suddenly to be diminished and cheapened. Events, never firmly under control, now seemed to have slipped through his fingers like grains of sand.

A Signal Corps warrant officer appeared with a sheaf of computer printouts carrying the blue-banded Olympus imprint. He handed them to the President and withdrew. Loomis sank down in a leather chair facing the electronic displays and began to read.

Presently, he said, 'Russian *bastard*.'

Gilmartin, startled by the exclamation, asked, 'Bad, sir?'

'See for yourself.' To the duty officer he said, 'Hurry up with the second part of this.'

'Going into the translator now, Mr. President.'

To Gilmartin, Loomis said furiously, 'Why hasn't NORAD reported to the NSC that the Soviets have repositioned a Cosmos?'

Gilmartin looked up from the printout, nonplussed. 'They may have, Mr. President. I don't recall it, but such things are pretty much routine.'

'Read on and see how "routine" it was for them, Peter,' the President said grimly.

Gilmartin returned to his reading of the message. It was not reassuring.

> CLEARING WEATHER UNDER THE FLIGHT PATH OF OUR COSMOS 9321 RECENTLY REPOSITIONED TO EXAMINE THE SOUTH ARABIAN PENINSULA DISCLOSES IMPERMISSIBLE ACTIVITY AT THE FORMER SAUDI-AMERICAN AIR BASE OF IBRAHIMAH IN THE EMPTY QUARTER. I REMIND YOU OF THE BREZHNEV DOCTRINE STATED BY US AT HELSINKI IN 1975 WHICH CLEARLY ESTABLISHES THAT THE USSR HAS THE RIGHT TO ASSIST EMERGING SOCIALIST NATIONS IN THEIR STRUGGLE AGAINST IMPERIALIST COUNTERREVOLUTIONARY AGGRESSION.

Gilmartin stopped reading long enough to exclaim, 'What in hell is he talking about, Vinnie? What is all this about "impermissible activity"? Does he mean Calder's NPC Station?'

'I can't read it any other way,' the President said.

Gilmartin's stomach knotted in a cramp. He wondered if he were getting an ulcer. God knew, ulcers went with this job, he thought. He read on.

> UNLESS IMMEDIATE STEPS ARE TAKEN TO CORRECT THIS NAKED EXERCISE OF MILITARY POWER TO THREATEN THE PAN-ARABIAN PEOPLE'S REVOLUTIONARY GOVERNMENT THE USSR WILL BE OBLIGED TO TAKE ACTION.

'I can't believe this,' Gilmartin said. 'I think they've gone crazy in Moscow. The NPC Station is nothing but a bunch of do-gooders screwing around in the desert. Even the ragheads in Riyadh don't worry about them.'

'We can ask for hard evidence,' the President said. 'If they've moved a Cosmos they must be getting photographs.' He turned to shout at the duty officer to hurry and bring the second part of the message.

Suddenly Peter Gilmartin was shaken by the memory of a piece of information he had possessed for more than two weeks and that he had forgotten in the recent rush of events. Loomis regarded him closely. 'What is it? You look a little green, Peter.'

Gilmartin stood in silence for a time, groping for exactly the right words. Presently he said, 'I'm sorry, Vinnie—but—' He found it very difficult to go on because linkages were forming in his mind that he would give much to be able to ignore. But his sense of duty drove him on. 'Two weeks before Cole was murdered, Mr. President, he put through a request that *we* reprogram a satellite to take a look at what the New Peace Corps is doing in the south Arabian desert.'

The President stared at his National Security Adviser. 'You mean we don't *know*?'

'We have Calder Davis's word that it's a research station, sir. But that is all we have, actually.'

'No one has a higher regard for Calder than I do,' Loomis said. 'But for Christ's sweet sake, Peter, we shouldn't have to rely only on that. Norris wanted satellite surveillance and the NSC refused him? I don't even remember such an item on the agenda.'

'It never got on the agenda, Mr. President. I'm sorry, I simply didn't think it was important.' The pain in his belly grew sharper. He could now imagine his hypothetical ulcer bleeding like an angry fountain.

'Did you speak to the Air Force?' the President demanded. 'Did they give you trouble?'

The temptation to pass the blame to the military was strong, but for all of his failings, Peter Gilmartin was not a dishonest man. He said, 'No. On my recommendation, Andy Traynor has ordered a cutback on shuttle launches. The costs were getting astronomical and we *have* promised to reduce the defense budget.'

Recent polls had shown that the electors believed the

Pentagon was growing wasteful again. The President was aware of this. He had, in fact, ordered many of the cuts in the Air Force operating budget himself.

The President's eyes were opaque, unfriendly. Peter Gilmartin knew how he disliked criticism, even by implication.

'Well,' he said icily. 'I think we had better do something about it right now, Peter. Tell Traynor to get a satellite in position or order some SR-71 overflights immediately—' His tone grew even harsher. 'Where the hell *is* Traynor? I thought you had him called.'

'I did, sir. Andy doesn't move too well in the early morning.'

'Maybe he'd move faster if he knew how close he is to getting his ass fired,' Loomis said. Gilmartin realized that this was an oblique way for Loomis to express loyalty to his National Security Adviser even though he was plainly angry. Gilmartin had refused to pass along the blame for a failure to act, so the President was doing it for him. From this moment on, the refusal of the National Security Council to consider Cole Norris's request would be the Secretary of Defense's fault. The decision troubled Gilmartin, but he knew better than to press the President. He had offered himself as scapegoat and the President had chosen Traynor instead. It was a common happening in the administration. There was a scale of loyalty against which all were measured. Those closest to Vincent Loomis were safest. Gilmartin allowed himself to wonder where on this scale Calder Davis could be found. He suspected that the President would go to extremes to believe the very best of a man he respected, admired, and, Gilmartin suspected, even feared.

The warrant officer appeared again with the second part of President Suslov's message. Loomis read it and handed the printouts to Gilmartin without comment.

> AS SOON AS WEATHER PERMITS AIRCRAFT FROM THE SOVIET CARRIER NOVGOROD WILL BEGIN MAKING OVERFLIGHTS OF THE IBRAHIMAH BASE AND SURROUNDINGS AND YOU ARE BEING NOTIFIED SO THAT NO INCIDENTS SHALL OCCUR. MESSAGE ENDS.

The message was curt, rude, threatening. 'He knows we

have nothing in the Gulf, Mr. President. Nothing any nearer than Diego Garcia,' Gilmartin said. 'I don't understand this.'

'It's plain enough if you know the old bastard,' Loomis said grimly. 'He's looking for an excuse to intervene in the Arabian Peninsula.'

'Mr. President,' Gilmartin said cautiously, 'with respect. What exactly is the NPC doing at EQ Station?'

Vincent Loomis regarded Gilmartin bleakly. 'I think we had better find out.'

'Davis is leaving for Geneva this morning, sir, to meet with the Jordanians, who think they can put him in touch with the Pan-Arabians in Riyadh. This wouldn't be a good time to delay him.'

'I have no intention of delaying him, Peter. I shall do nothing that might endanger his initiative about the hostages. But I want some digging done. I want a full NSC meeting today at noon.'

'That will be tough, Mr. President. I doubt we can convene one until tonight.'

Loomis's expression grew even grimmer. 'No later than two, then. I can keep Suslov waiting that long, but no longer. And if you can't locate Holt, have the Director of Operations here in his place.'

'Yes, Mr. President. I'll get on it now.'

The President picked up a telephone and said, 'Get me Charlie McKay.' He looked briefly at Gilmartin in dismissal.

As the National Security Adviser left the Situation Room he heard the President say to his Chief of Staff: 'Charlie, I want you to get some feelers out on the double. I need to know how the voters feel about Calder Davis and the New Peace Corps.'

23 New York

In his apartment in the East Seventies Sam Abbott awoke with a start. He was suddenly aware that there was someone in the bedroom with him, a dim figure outlined against the drawn shades that kept the early-morning light at bay.

'Martin?' Abbott lay tensely, waiting for a reply. The publisher was a man who had once been familiar with danger, and though he liked to imagine he led a different sort of life now, the memory was still fresh, ever ready to be recalled.

'It's Ike Holt, Sam.'

Abbott sat up in the bed, his heart thudding in his chest. Isaac Holt moved closer to stand at the foot of the bed. A gray man, Abbott thought, gray as the morning shadows. He had forgotten the menace that lack of color and definition could project.

'Martin let me in, Sam,' Holt said softly. 'I hope you don't mind.'

Abbott shivered, even though the summer heat was already in the air of the apartment. 'Why not,' he said, 'he works for you, after all.' He hoped he had managed some touch of bravado. For old times' sake.

Holt's shadowed eyes roamed the room, taking in the antique wardrobe, the chairs, the faded drapes framing the shaded window, and finally the worktable piled with the manuscripts on which Abbott had been fitfully working late into the night.

Abbott snapped on a light and looked at the clock on his nightstand. It was nearly six. He walked to the wardrobe and took out a dressing gown, using the time to order his thoughts and bring his anxiety under control. He took a seat in a winged chair. It was important to control this meeting, to play at being the host, no matter how unwilling. 'All right, Ike. Why are you here?'

Holt did not take a seat. He stood. Like a pillar of salt, Abbott thought. 'We need to talk,' Holt said.

'Let me tell Martin to bring us some coffee.'

'None for me.'

'I can't think without morning coffee. Sorry,' Abbott said. He walked to the door, opened it, and saw Martin standing in the living room. A burly black man was with him. Holt's man. No, they were *both* Holt's men, he reminded himself. 'Some coffee, Martin?'

'Yes, sir,' Martin said. He walked into the small kitchen. The black man stayed near the door. Abbott turned back into the bedroom and sat down again. Holt had not moved.

Abbott felt a flicker of anger beginning to burn in the pit of his stomach. That was good, he thought. A touch of temper helped to control the fear that was thickening in his chest.

'You saw Cole's brother,' Holt said. 'He was here.'

'I make no secret of it. Why should I?'

'Don't be hostile,' Holt said softly. 'We're both on the same side.'

'I don't know what side you're talking about, Ike,' Abbott said. 'I don't like this—you crowding in on me like this. Are we talking Company business or is this about something else?'

Holt ignored the question. 'Michael Rivas is meddling in things he shouldn't.'

'I think he knows that. Someone tried to make the point on the Van Wyck a few days ago,' Abbott said dryly.

'I tried to make him see reason when he came to see me in Washington,' Holt said. 'He wasn't cooperative.'

'Surely that doesn't surprise you.'

Holt's voice was thin as the cutting edge of a knife. 'It doesn't surprise *you*, does it, Sam?'

Abbott felt the chill the remark was intended to evoke. He concentrated on keeping the bead of anger in his belly alive. One needed that to keep at bay the fear men like Holt engendered. 'Michael Rivas doesn't frighten easily, Ike. And he is a persistent man.'

'Cole despised him,' Holt said.

'Wrong. Cole resented him. That went back to the time they were younger. But he never despised him. Rivas isn't the sort one despises.'

'I'm going to give you some information, Sam,' Holt said.

'It may not be news to you. Cole Norris was close to a nervous breakdown when he was killed. He had begun imagining all sorts of peculiar things. But maybe you know all about what he was imagining.'

'There was nothing wrong with Cole when I saw him last,' Abbott said. Immediately he saw the pitfall, but it was too late.

'When was that, Sam?'

'Months ago,' Abbott said quickly.

'If it was months ago, then you don't know anything about his mental state in the last weeks of his life, do you. But I don't think it was months ago, Sam. I think you were one of the last people Cole talked to outside the Agency.'

Abbott suppressed an impulse to run his fingers through his aureole of gray hair. It was a gesture that would betray his inner agitation and he desperately wanted to hide from Holt how deeply he had been shaken. This was *not* Company business. It was something far worse. Cole's suspicions had been right, and Holt was deeply involved, using his powers as effective head of the Central Intelligence Agency in the interests of others.

'Cole told me nothing of interest,' Abbott said, almost certain that Holt would know he was lying.

'Cole always had interesting things to say, Sam. I think he asked you to do some research for him. I think you did it. I think Rivas has been acting on that information you found for Cole.'

'I can't help what you think, Ike,' Abbott said. He was grateful for the interruption as Martin appeared with coffee. He poured a cup from the porcelain pot and drank it. It was scalding hot, the way he liked it, strong and bitter. When Martin withdrew, he said, 'Cole was my friend. We went way back. Whoever had him killed was a Judas.' His anger had spoken, perhaps unwisely, but he felt better for having said it.

'Rivas went straight from Washington to England to a man named Wyndham,' Holt said. 'But that won't be a surprise to you. It was you who told him about Wyndham, wasn't it, Sam?'

'I may have,' Abbott said. The coffee had left a strong, wry aftertaste in his mouth. He felt an odd fluttering in the muscles of his eyes. He was beginning to regard his own familiar room strangely, as though the dimensions were suddenly not what they had always been.

'And what else did you tell Rivas, Sam?'

The question seemed somehow insidious, engaging, to Abbott. He felt strangely less inhibited, less frightened.

'Tell me what you told Rivas, Sam. That's really all I want to know,' Holt said softly.

'I told him what I told Cole.' Abbott felt a thickness in his throat and a clumsiness in his speech.

'And what was that?'

'All that I could find out about the ISSG people in the government.' The walls of the room were moving away from him, leaving him in a great, dimly lit cavern.

'Cole spoke to you about Calder Davis, didn't he, Sam?'

Abbott spoke slowly, with an effort. He was horrified by his own willingness to share all that he knew with Isaac Holt, a man he feared and hated. 'Cole was afraid the NPC was recruiting soldiers. He said that if it were so, it was an act of treason.'

'And so you told him he was mistaken, naturally.'

Abbott shook his head. 'He wasn't mistaken. He was right.' With difficulty he focused his eyes on the gray man. 'And—so—you—had—him—killed.'

'It was necessary. You can see that it was necessary, Sam.' Holt spoke as gently as a lover, studying the older man's darkly dilated eyes.

'Rivas—will put it together eventually,' Abbott said laboriously.

'Rivas will never get out of Arabia alive, Sam.'

'Assassin,' Abbott said thickly.

Holt shook his head. 'It's a different war, that's all. Nothing works. It's all falling apart. We have to do something about it. Cole should have understood that.'

Abbott's chest felt constricted. The room had grown unbearable—hot, filled with viscous air. 'I can't breathe,' he said, pushing himself erect. Holt watched him curiously.

Abbott reached for the shades covering the window. They came down with a tearing clatter. The dregs of the coffee spilled on the tabletop. A stain spread across the blue-penciled typed pages there.

'Let me help,' Holt said.

'Stay away—*Judas*—' With a distant, increasingly isolated part of his mind, Abbott realized that he had been drugged with one of the hundreds of compounds found on the shelves of the pharmacies of every intelligence service in the world. Drugs to destroy the will to resist, to distort perception, to change friends into enemies and enemies into friends. In another few moments there would be nothing he could withhold from Isaac Holt. There would be no reality his interrogator could not take apart and reassemble. The clever chemists of the black world of espionage could perform wonders, Abbott thought. They could dissolve fear of treachery, of betrayal, even of death.

His emotions were almost entirely disconnected. He was humiliated that he had allowed himself to be compromised by so simple a bit of tradecraft as drugged coffee. An old spy should have never allowed himself to be caught that way.

But he was capable of tradecraft himself. Even with his mind half scrambled he felt the satisfaction in that.

He closed his hand protectively around the small metal object in his dressing-gown pocket. Then he ran two short steps to the window and crashed through. As he fell in a sun-bright shower of glass to the sidewalk three stories below, the drug performed a final mercy and convinced him that he was flying toward infinity through a sky filled with diamonds.

24 Ar Rub' al Khali

The *khamseen* was dying and a strange, eerie blue dusk was rising out of the darkness of the sand sea. The convoy had paused at the edge of a vast plateau of rocky hardpan dotted with spare, cruel thornbushes, all that could grow in this place where the great dunes touched the shore of the stone-littered plain.

The NPC party had made a steady thirty miles an hour since leaving the ruined fort of Ash Shisar, traveling north and east through the long afternoon. Toward evening the wind had fallen enough so that the sun had actually been visible through the sky filled with blowing sand: a bloated orange-red pool of fire settling toward the empty western horizon. The convoy had not encountered a single living thing.

Rivas struggled to stay awake and alert in the lead vehicle. His eyes felt grainy and his injured head had begun to throb once again. The air was so dry that his skin felt stretched and painful to the touch.

Colonel Hadfield, standing in the command car beside the driver, swept the sandy waste ahead with his field glasses. The light was going fast and somehow, Rivas guessed, he was checking landmarks. It was difficult to know what the man could see out there. To Rivas all that was apparent was a wasteland of frozen waves of sand stretching to the indistinct horizon. But it was obvious that the man knew this country as well as it was possible for any man to know it. It was equally obvious that he intended to navigate the sand sea in darkness.

Hadfield lowered the glasses and turned to Rivas. 'You can stand easy now, Hayden,' he said. 'The Raschid don't travel at night.'

Rivas lowered himself from his position on the back of the seat and began to dismount from the vehicle, intending to return to his place in the truck with the Afrikaaners.

'Stay where you are. You'll ride with us,' Hadfield said.

Rivas relaxed gratefully against the hard webbing of the seat. He propped the M-16 between his knees and closed his eyes.

'You don't look well,' the woman said. 'Drink some water.' She held out a canteen and managed a glance of defiance at Colonel Hadfield. Rivas guessed the colonel had lectured her about water discipline in the desert.

Rivas looked at the eyes above the white veil. They were enormous.

'Drink,' the woman commanded. 'Then let me have a look at that injury. I am a physician,' she added, as though to reassure him.

'Thank you,' Rivas said, and took the canteen. He wet his lips, took a small slow swallow, and handed the canteen back to Dr. Shallai.

'You are exhausted,' she said. 'How long had you been traveling before you joined us?'

Rivas said, 'Days, I think.' It felt like months, even years. Had that morning in Lugano when he read Cole's letter really been only three days ago?

'I need some light,' Amira said to the driver. The man was an Arab, dark-skinned and thin to the point of emaciation. 'Light,' she said again, her voice sharpened by medical impatience.

Colonel Hadfield spoke to the driver in the local dialect, and the man handed him a pocket flashlight from his webbing. Hadfield passed it to Amira. 'He can't speak, doctor. He was a slave of the Wahhabi. They cut out his tongue.'

Amira suppressed a shudder.

'The Wahhabi are gone,' Hadfield said shortly. 'The tribes the Trucial Scouts didn't kill have gone north long ago.' He dismounted from the vehicle and walked through the gathering dusk to the trucks in the rear.

'Fascinating people,' Rivas said laconically.

Ignoring his comment, Amira said, 'Let me see that injury.'

He inclined his head and felt her fingers on his skull, firm and searching but remarkably gentle.

Amira said, 'How did this happen?'

'An accident,' Rivas said.

'It looks like a gunshot wound,' she said.

Rivas did not reply.

She shone the flashlight into his eyes and moved it slowly right and left. 'You probably have a mild concussion as well,' she said. 'How long ago did this—accident—take place?'

'A week,' Rivas said, pulling away from the light. 'Maybe a bit less.'

Colonel Hadfield reappeared and stood looking up into the high vehicle curiously. 'What's the problem, Dr. Shallai?'

Rivas met Amira's eyes directly. The scarf had fallen away from her face. He felt an odd sense of complicity developing between the woman and himself.

'It is nothing, Colonel,' Amira said. 'Will we be going on now? Can we find our way across the dunes at night?'

Hadfield climbed back into the car next to the silent driver. 'We will be at EQ Station by dawn,' he said. He spoke to his man and the convoy started into the deepening darkness of the sand sea.

Amira Shallai rode thoughtfully, considering the quiet American beside her. He was different from the others, different from Colonel Hadfield. The colonel and the Afrikaaners in the truck behind all had the mark of professional soldiers about them. They reminded her of the Israeli paratroopers who had guarded the camp at Arod where she had undergone her field training. Rough men, even those few who were obviously gently bred and well educated. They had an openness about them that suggested their lives were governed by simple, easily understood rules.

The presence of such men on this journey already told her a great deal about the reality of EQ Station. An important part of her training had been devoted to developing an ability to recognize the capabilities of the persons with whom she came in contact. It was part of the Mossad tradecraft she had acquired easily. Her instructor, a former Nazi-hunter worknamed Shimon Gur, had said that she had a talent which was almost as good as being lucky.

But her talent foundered on the man sitting so wearily beside her. She guessed that his name was not really Hayden and she felt instinctively that he was not, like the others, a soldier.

But guessing what he was not did not tell her what he was. She wondered if his task in this place were the same as her own. On the surface, at least, it appeared that Colonel Hadfield accepted him at face value. But that could easily be because Hadfield was not troubling to think very deeply about any of the men in the convoy. As they left Salalah farther and farther behind, Hadfield's attitude and bearing became more and more that of a serving officer dealing with troops.

In the several years Amira had spent in the New Peace Corps she had frequently allowed herself the luxury of speculating on the reason for the Corps' quasi-military organization. She had suspected herself of regarding it from a skewed point of view. She was, after all, a secret member of a quasi-military organization herself. This had made her judgments less than unbiased and accordingly she had weighted her conclusions in favor of NPC innocence.

Those conclusions were now almost certainly proving to be false. The NPC might be the peaceful organization it seemed to be—its good works in the Third World were part of the historical record. But it was not *exclusively* peaceful: the last twenty-four hours had convinced her of that. Colin Hadfield and the men in the truck lumbering along behind the command car were plainly and unmistakably soldiers. Nor did they seem to be men who had beat their swords into plowshares with the intention of converting their military skills to some idyllic use. If the Aluf operation was in fact about to begin—if Israeli forces were at this moment poised to invade the Arabian Peninsula, it was vital that they know that a military force of what must be experienced mercenaries was already in place at EQ Station.

The thought of what might lay ahead of her made her shiver with an apprehension she had not felt in all the years she had worked as an agent of Mossad. The unvarnished truth was that she was acting for the first time as a penetration agent and each hour that passed moved her more deeply—and alone—into unknown and very dangerous territory. No arrangements had been made, so far as she knew, to get her out once she had the information Mossad required. 'A spy,' Shimon had once told her, 'must always be ready to improvise.' That was small comfort to Amira now as she rode in brooding silence through the darkening desert night.

She considered the American beside her. Conversation was impossible with Colonel Hadfield so near. But since her instinct had suggested that the man Hayden, of all the group in the convoy, was not exactly what he seemed to be, she began to consider how she might cultivate him and turn him to her purposes.

Men were attracted to her. This was a simple fact of Amira's life. In some cases (and she thought about young Cecil Sawyer at Kalabishah) her mere proximity constituted a kind of subtle seduction. She disliked taking advantage of this biological accident, but she resolved that if it became necessary to seduce the American (or anyone else) to complete her mission, she would do it.

25 Long Island

Through the windows of the library where he sat at his Louis Quinze desk, Calder Smith Davis could look across the broad lawns and through a stand of ancient elms to where the ConEn helicopter waited on the pad to take him to La Guardia.

Atalanta, the family estate of the Davis clan for three generations, consisted of the main house, immense and half-timbered, the stables (no longer in use), a dozen outbuildings housing the staff and the large security force, a communications center, and an office wing. All were sited on twenty acres of manicured gardens and carefully tended forest land surrounded by a twenty-foot stone wall spiked on top to discourage intruders.

In the old days Davises had gone forth from here to the burgeoning industrial and financial centers of America to add to the family fortune, and in more recent times Calder's own brothers had gone to Albany and Washington to seek the political power for which they had been prepared since boyhood. It would have been a different country, the old financier reflected, if they had succeeded as they should have in the political wars. They had tried nobly. But because they were uncommon men, they had failed miserably to win the support of the common people. America was not the pastoral republic of solid yeomen envisioned by the nation's founders. Perhaps, Davis thought, it had never been. From the beginning the country had strayed from the Jeffersonian ideal. Somehow the Davises (all but Calder himself) had never truly understood this.

Calder, the most pragmatic of all the Davises, had always understood that America was a harlot. This had never made him love his country less. But the knowledge had shaped his life. Like Rome in her time, America, for all her depravity, was the repository and guardian of all the values of Western civilization. He knew that she could be wooed only with gifts, and he had lavished costly baubles on her. Now in the twilight of his life he intended to give her the greatest gift of all: command of her own destiny.

He regarded the austere young man seated across the desk, pad in hand. He was one of an army of young assistants and secretaries who lived in the Atalanta compound, totally loyal and discreet.

'*To the President of the United States,*' Davis dictated, '*the White House.*'

He pursed his lips thoughtfully. He tried to imagine the President's reaction when this message reached him. Poor Vincent—he was in for a terrible shock, but he was a man who needed to be shocked from time to time. Davis had often wished that the men who occupied the White House could be chosen for their qualities of leadership and intellect, but the system precluded this.

'*Dear Vincent,*' he said. '*It is time that I share with you my secret hopes for our country and for all the Western world. It is my hope that you will understand not only what I and my associates have done, but why.*'

The pen in the secretary's hand waited, poised for the next line. Davis studied the young-old face. It was composed, incurious. The best of them become machines, Davis thought. It is the nature of the world to do that to human beings now. For a moment he allowed himself the luxury of knowing that it was not a world he would have to inhabit for very much longer.

'*Many years ago, Vincent, we were all convinced that the greatest threat to the West was Marxism and the power of the Soviet Union. Those were the times of the Cold War we all remember so unhappily. But history plays tricks on us, and sometimes we plan for futures that never come. We, in the West, have done just this. And so have the Marxists.*'

He paused and then went on, selecting his words with great care.

'*What we did not foresee was that the civilized world would so soon become totally dependent on irresponsible nations of the Third World for survival. Nor could we have guessed that our courage would fail to the point that we would see our future collapse and still refuse to take the action needed to avert global disaster.*

'*There are, of course, many things that a technological*

society requires for survival, and at least half of them are to be found only in the underdeveloped nations around the world. But the most important of all these resources is, of course, oil.'

He paused again, waiting until the secretary stopped writing.

'I have used the word survival *several times, Vincent, because it is thut, and nothing less, that is at risk now.'*

He closed his eyes and touched them lightly with his delicate, pale fingers. He was unbelievably tired. He hoped that he could rest on the airplane, but he had no such expectation. He seldom slept while flying.

'If we had done what needed to be done in 1973,' he went on quietly, 'if we and our allies had had the courage to act the first time the Arab nations shut off the flow of oil, all that has followed would not have been necessary. But we did nothing, Vincent, except to proclaim to all the world our terrible dependency on the nations of the Gulf. It was then that I and my associates began to plan for what is now to take place.

'We recognized at once, Vincent, that despite our vast resources we could not take and hold the oil-producing states of the Persian Gulf. It would have taken concerted action by the governments *and* military forces *of all the Western nations to accomplish such a task. We also came to understand that even if such force were available, the governments involved now lacked the determination to act on behalf of the Western world's future. It is the curse of our time, Vincent, that we no longer seem to believe in our right to survive.'*

A light flashed on an intercom and Davis said, 'Yes?'

'Mr. Isaac Holt is at the main gate, Mr. Davis.'

'Yes. I rather thought he might come here,' Davis said. 'Bring him in and have him wait.'

'Yes, sir.'

Davis said, 'What did I say last, Charles?'

' "It is the curse of our time, Vincent, that we no longer seem to believe in our right to survive," sir.'

'Yes. All right.' He thought for a time and then continued dictating. *'Since 1973 my associates and I have spent heavily in the development of a synthetic fuels industry. If you read the report I had sent to you four days ago, you will see that we already have such an industry in being here and in*

Europe. Unfortunately the cost of our synthetic oil remains high, substantially higher than the crude obtained from the oil fields of the Persian Gulf. As long as the members of OPEC are able to manipulate the market price of oil, our synthetic industry cannot grow.

'The members of OPEC have not been all-wise, Vincent. The Gulf war between Iraq and Iran destroyed most of those countries' oil facilities. They have not yet been repaired, and given the political climate in the Middle East, may never be put back on line. Nigeria has reduced its oil exports to a trickle as a result of the refusal of most of the Western nations to sanction black Africa's war against South Africa.

'I do not need to dwell on these matters. Your own Secretary of Energy, George Rossmore, will be able to present you with the distressing facts about the availability of foreign oil.

'But the hard truth is that we can become energy-independent only if our infant synfuels industry is nurtured . . . and protected.

'Since we did not seize the oil of the Gulf when we might have done so, we are faced with a bitter choice. I did not expect the government of the United States to make this unhappy decision. I know it to be politically impossible.

'Therefore I—and my associates—have made the decision for all of us. I made it long ago, Vincent, when we established the New Peace Corps and more recently, the International Strategic Studies Group.

'The revolution in Arabia did not influence our decision. It merely supported it. The act of taking American and European hostages, in a repetition of the Iranian illegality, has provided us with a fortuitous means of diverting attention from an act that some will consider, I fear, inhumane.

'It is now my duty to inform you of the existence of a substantial military force that has been privately formed, trained, and equipped. This force is committed to taking the actions—the necessary actions, Vincent—that no Western government or combination of governments dare take in these timid times. Though it is a force commanded by an American (you were right to question me about General Collingwood and I regret having had to deceive you), it is international in makeup and organization. It was never intended that the United States should bear any responsibi-

lity for the actions taken by General Collingwood and his men.

'This international force will, within hours now, attack and occupy as much of Riyadh as is necessary for the rescue of the diplomats held hostage there. But it will also, simultaneously, take action to put the oil fields of the Persian Gulf states out of production for at least five years.

'This will make the United States, Western Europe, and Japan dependent on such oil as may be available from Alaskan, South American, British, and Mexican sources. And it will assure the survival and expansion of American synfuel production. No longer will the Gulf states be able to raise production whenever it appears that the West is becoming energy-independent.

'These are hard, commercial realities. As long as OPEC exists in its present form, America will never support its own synfuels industry. With the Gulf no longer producing, America—and the West—must.

'I pray, Vincent, that all this may be accomplished with a minimum loss of life. But whatever the cost, it will be done. The responsibility is mine, and I shall be there, on the contested ground, to accept it. I am an old man and my life is a small thing to risk in this great endeavor.

'Do not take this to be the blustering of a senile fool who has outlived his time. The military capabilities of General Collingwood's force are ample for the task. Ask Andrew Traynor to explain it to you. Andrew has been part of the ISSG from the start. Many others in your administration have been, as well, Vincent. But there is no need for a witch-hunt. When the plan succeeds—and it will—they will announce themselves to you proudly.

'I have not, despite what you may feel at this moment, precipitated the Apocalypse. It is sad but true, Vincent, that it is weakness and compliance that put great nations at risk. I have done what I have had to do—what Western leaders should have done long ago when our survival could have been assured by less extreme measures. There will be difficult times ahead. There will be some deprivation for our people until our industry can meet all our needs. But I have broken the oil weapon in OPEC's hands, thus assuring that our industry will survive and grow.' A dry, bitter smile hovered about the thin, gray mouth. *'My ghost will not demand it, Mr. President, but in times to come Americans*

will thank me for bringing them back to the path of discipline and greatness.'

Davis thought carefully for a moment and then decided that he had said all that needed to be said to Vincent Loomis. It now remained to see whether he had hidden inside him the leadership an American President should have.

'Type that for my signature, Charles,' he said. 'Then I will want you to carry it personally to Washington and deliver it into the President's hands.'

After the young man had withdrawn, Davis sat for a time looking about the vast library. Like all libraries, he thought, it was a repository for all that was great in Western culture. Perhaps in future times, when his will had been read and the nation owned this house and all that it contained, members of the public would stand in this very room as in a shrine and say to one another, 'It was here that Calder Smith Davis made his greatest gift.'

He touched the intercom and said, 'Have the helicopter crew stand by. We will leave in ten minutes.'

The disembodied voice of still another secretary said, 'Yes, Mr. Davis.'

'And send in Mr. Holt. I will see him now.'

Isaac Holt had never before visited Atalanta. He had, in fact, been specifically forbidden to do so by Calder Davis himself—a restriction that Holt suspected was not entirely dictated by caution. The prohibition, which had been in force since the day of Holt's initiation into the group that was eventually to become the ISSG, had been stated with such vehemence that he had come to believe that it was social as well as in the interests of security.

The Deputy DCI was not an easily intimidated man. Intelligence officers of his quality seldom were. But Calder Davis *did* intimidate Isaac Holt. Though he had done his best never to show that this was so, Isaac Holt held the old financier in some awe, and his secret sense of social inferiority was not, he suspected, a secret from Calder Davis.

The old man regarded Holt evenly and said, 'Ah, Isaac. You come to Atalanta at last.'

There was nothing he could have said, Holt thought, more calculated to make his—obviously unwelcome—guest feel disadvantaged.

Under ordinary circumstances Holt managed to submerge the feelings Calder Davis aroused in him. Ambition and a hunger for power could be called upon to cloak psychological uncertainties. And because it could be said that Calder Davis had compromised himself and his group by using Holt as he had during the buildup of the NPC and its clandestine paramilitary arm, the spymaster had very nearly convinced himself that in terms of real power he was Calder Davis's equal.

But at this moment, seated in this opulent room in this house set in this fortified park, Holt could feel his pretensions crumbling like sandcastles in a rainstorm.

'I know why you've come, Isaac,' Davis said. 'It was on the morning news.'

Holt reviewed in his mind all the services he had rendered to Calder Davis and considered how best to present the bill. The morning's work had gone so badly awry that since leaving the city he had been wracking his brains for some logical excuse for his sudden appearance at Atalanta. He could see the waiting helicopter and he knew that he had very nearly arrived too late to see Davis. What he desperately needed now from the old man was corroboration of the story he would tell the President on his return to Washington. He would claim—and Calder would confirm—that he had come to Atalanta to give Davis a special briefing on the latest intelligence to come out of Riyadh. If he had been with Davis, he could not be implicated in the death of Sam Abbott. What was needed, in the best intelligence operational terms, was a 'legend.' It was not possible for him to exclude from his thoughts the *criminal* term that defined his need: an alibi for murder. Since he had, in effect, committed murder for Calder Davis before, he believed that Davis must of necessity do as he asked.

But Davis's next words were not encouraging. The washed-out old eyes were unfeeling and the tone of voice was cold as he said, 'Why on earth was it necessary to kill him?'

'The bloody fool jumped from the window, Calder. It was an accident.'

'Was it that he wouldn't tell you what you thought you needed to know?' Davis seemed to have ignored Holt's previous statement.

'I tell you, he jumped. He took me by surprise. There was nothing I could do.' Holt heard with dismay the note of desperation that had come into his voice.

Calder Davis pressed his delicate fingertips together in an oddly prayerful gesture. 'You are a thug, Isaac,' he said quietly.

Holt stared at the older man, shocked into momentary silence.

'You are, you know,' Davis said, still in that cold, quiet voice. 'You dislike participating in personal violence. I find that peculiar, because you are a thug who loves violence as long as it is at one remove.'

'Now, wait a moment, Calder—' Holt protested.

The old man silenced him with a gesture. 'There was no need for you to question Abbott. None at all. You did that on your own because you enjoy the smell of fear. Was he very afraid of you, Isaac?'

Holt said harshly, 'I don't think you understand—'

'I understand perfectly. You frightened him but you didn't dominate him. You pressed him too hard and he went out the window. Were you alone at the time, Isaac?'

Holt, staring hollowly at the frail, gray man behind the desk, nodded. He was speechless.

'Then he probably did jump. You couldn't have pushed him. Defenestration is not your style, Isaac. But you could drive a man to suicide. That *is* your style.'

'Calder, I don't like this,' Holt said loudly. He could feel the pulse beating in his temples. For the first time in a long while he felt genuine fear. This incredible old fascist was going to *shop* him. It wasn't possible. Didn't Davis realize what he could testify to? Was the man losing his mind?

'What did you do, Isaac? Did you leave Martin to clean up the mess with the police while you came here to me? What did you expect me to do for you?'

The intercom made a muted sound. Davis touched the bar and said, 'Yes, Charles?'

'May I bring in the letter for your signature, sir?'

'Yes.'

Holt waited in agitated silence while one of Calder's young men came in, laid several pages of typescript before Davis, and waited in composed silence. Composure, Holt thought, was the hallmark of this place.

Davis read the pages with deliberate care and then

appended his neat, precise signature. He looked at the secretary and said, 'Take it straight there. Leave at once.'

'Yes, sir.'

Holt waited until the library door closed before he said explosively, 'I don't deserve what you have been saying, Calder. You have no right to speak to me this way.'

The watery eyes were unblinking. 'I have every right,' Davis said. 'Who has a better?' The voice was thin, aged, and yet edged with a steely contempt that cut into Holt's very fiber. 'You sold your Service to me, Isaac. In our positions we may not moralize about such things. But I had a right to expect competence, at least.'

'I came here for your *help*,' Holt said.

'No,' Davis said. 'Not this time.'

Fear and anger crowded into Holt's throat. When he spoke, the words came thick and tumbling. 'Aren't you forgetting Cole Norris? And that girl?'

'I am far from forgetting them,' Davis said softly. 'The Norris affair was necessary. But there was no need to kill that young woman. Your assassin was a brute, Isaac.'

'Calder—you know why it had to be done that way.'

'I know why you believe it had to be done that way. But then we have agreed that you are a thug at heart, haven't we, Isaac?'

'Damn you, Calder. *I can bury you.*'

'Perhaps, Isaac. But I think not.'

'*I can and I will.*'

Davis sighed and shook his head slowly. 'I do not often misjudge people's characters, but I have done so in your case. I have had to make explanations to my associates, and I dislike doing so.' The old eyes took on a glitter. 'You have made a great slaughter, Isaac. You killed that girl and Abbott—whom you had no need to kill—and that poor innocent taxi driver. And yet Cole Norris's brother—a *journalist*, Isaac—is still alive and a danger to us. Yes, I misjudged you, Isaac. I thought you were cleverer than you are.'

'Rivas won't get out of Arabia alive,' Holt said furiously.

'Great things are seldom accomplished cheaply,' Calder said. 'And death comes to all of us eventually. It is your clumsiness I object to, Isaac.' He shrugged his narrow shoulders. 'Well, this is no time for recriminations. It may well be that not many of us will get out of Arabia alive. A few reputations, a few lives, are a small price to pay for making a new world.'

Holt stared in astonishment. ' "Not many of *us*—"? What does that mean exactly?'

'*I* created the International Studies Group, Isaac. *I* built the NPC. *I* armed the men at Tokar. *I* formed the consortium that planned and funded our liberation from OPEC. Did you really think I would shirk now?'

'*You* are going to EQ Station?'

'Of course,' Calder Davis said calmly.

Holt sat slack-jawed. It has finally happened, he thought, stunned. The old men is senile. He has slipped into the abyss. He said very carefully, 'What possible good can you do there, Calder?'

'Probably very little. I am not a soldier or a scientist.' Davis touched his delicate fingertips together again in that praying gesture. 'It is a matter of noblesse oblige, Isaac. I do not expect you to fully understand that.'

'But that was never part of the plan, Calder . . .'

'It was *always* a part of the plan. Someone must be there to accept the ultimate blame. You did not imagine that anyone else would do it, did you? For the next few years we can't expect members of the ISSG to be stepping forward to say openly that what we are doing *needed* doing. For at least five years and possibly longer there are going to be many . . . inconveniences . . . for our people to face. They are going to be angry. They will sit in gasoline lines and in cold houses and damn the ISSG and the New Peace Corps. Their temper won't change until the plants in Wyoming and Montana and in the Ruhr are producing enough oil to replace what they will be temporarily sacrificing. Someone has to be willing to face their anger. I wouldn't have it fall on the country, Isaac. I will accept it. And I must be *seen* to accept it. Duty, Isaac. Simple duty.'

'Oh my *God*,' Holt murmured. He saw a black pit of personal disaster opening at this feet. Without Calder Davis to speak for them, those members of the government who had chosen to become involved in the coup stood in deadly danger. A thousand threats swirled ready to coalesce and strike them down. If Calder were not at the President's side to deflect the whirlwind, they were lost. '*God*,' he said again, shocked by the thought of what would come.

'I would hesitate to invoke the Deity if I were you,' Calder

Davis said dryly. 'It really does not become you.' He stood, slowly and with ancient dignity. 'There is really nothing more to discuss.'

'There is *everything* to discuss,' Holt said desperately. 'There's Rivas—'

'Time, Isaac. Young Rivas has managed to penetrate the plan, but he hasn't the time to prevent it. It would be a kindness if you could call off your assassin.' He closed the open folders on his desk tidily. 'But I will have to leave that in your hands. I must go now. I have a long journey ahead of me and you know how I dislike flying.'

Holt dragged himself erect, his face white.

Davis regarded him with an expression that was almost one of pity. 'I can offer you one escape, Isaac,' he said. 'You can come with me if you choose.'

'With *you*?' Go with this crazy old man? To face what? Holt considered it for only a moment.

Davis's thin, nearly lipless, mouth formed a smile. To Holt it seemed that the financier's head had transformed itself into a death mask. The old man was ready to die. He was *hoping* for death.

'No? I thought not,' Davis said. 'Then I bid you good-bye, Isaac. And I leave you with this last suggestion. Why not go to the Russians? A man like you will be quite at home with them. It really no longer matters. What you and people like you have never understood is that there is a reason neither we nor the Russians can deal effectively with the Third World. It is because they are the future, Isaac. They will inherit the earth. All I can hope to do is to give us a little more time to build our dams against the flood. It may not work, but it has to be tried.' He shook his head pityingly at Holt. 'Tell them, Isaac. They won't believe you, but tell them anyway. They have a right to know.' He turned away and walked slowly down the length of the long room, swaying slightly with his old man's gait.

Holt stood, his mind racing, searching for options. He was still standing in the silent library when the sound of the helicopter taking off prodded him into motion. Then he walked to the door like a man leaving a funeral.

26 The Arabian Sea

On the wing of the bridge of the aircraft carrier *Novgorod*, Vitse Admiral Semyon Semyonevich Prokushkin, Commander of the Battle Group Red Banner, leaned his spare frame against the splinter shield and thoughtfully studied the dark sea to the north.

Though the battle group was blacked out (more a tradition than a precaution in this time of 'smart' weapons, Prokushkin thought), he could still make out the sleek silhouette of the *Dostoyny* and the turbulent phosphorescence of her wake as she kept station four hundred meters abeam the *Novgorod. Dostoyny* was one of two Krivak Class destroyers which, with the *Nikolayev*, a Kara Class guided-missile cruiser, and the submarine depot and supply ship *Borodino*, formed the Red Banner group.

The combat ships had left the *Borodino* behind at sunset to rendezvous with the flagship of the Arabian Sea Submarine Flotilla while the rest of the battle group closed the Arabian coast at flank speed.

Admiral Prokushkin disliked the break in his patrolling program and he disliked even more leaving the *Borodino* behind to perform the routine, but essential, task of supplying the three diesel-powered submarines with the fuel they required to maintain a watch on the shipping lanes between the Strait of Hormuz and the Cape of Good Hope. Prokushkin had, on several occasions, asked Moscow to provide him with nuclear boats to patrol these waters, but he had never received them. The nukes, he was told, had other, more vital, duties to perform nearer the Soviet Motherland.

It annoyed, but did not surprise, Prokushkin that Soviet naval doctrine—even after almost a generation of hard work by advanced naval thinkers like the late Gorshkov—had still not progressed too far beyond the defensive concepts in force since before the Great Patriotic War.

The Americans (whose own Arabian Sea battle group lay not far away, under the southern horizon) might worry constantly about the growth of Soviet sea power, the vice-admiral thought. But in his opinion, the Soviet Navy was still far from the long-range striking force it should be.

Above his head in the darkness, Admiral Prokushkin could hear the snapping of his own fleet commander's flag: the red star, hammer and sickle in a white quarter, and the three white stars in the red field of the ensign. He was proud of that flag. It had taken him a lifetime to earn it. Now, all that he secretly wished for was a chance to fight the Americans, whose aging ships he encountered almost every day in the far-flung waters of his patrol area.

What the admiral dreamed of was a pure ship-to-ship encounter, a clean fiery battle of men and vessels, missiles and aircraft. He did not allow himself to think of the chaos such a wished-for battle would trigger. He was a sailor and a Soviet Man and he wished for a sailor's war. It was the Americans he had studied all of his naval life. It was their doctrine and methods he had followed and improved upon. The ship on which he stood and which carried his flag was the result of years of work and argument by Gorshkov and himself, men who understood the worth of sea power—the *true* inheritors of the American Mahan.

But despite his hunger for one great sea battle before the end of his time as Commander, and despite the fact that Battle Group Red Banner was a force of greater power than any single Soviet warrior had ever yet commanded—the *Novgorod*'s air group and the nuclear missiles of the *Nikolayev* and the Krivaks could deliver more destruction than the massed armies commanded by Zhukov in the Great Patriotic War—Admiral Prokushkin was uneasy about his present assignment.

The message, relayed by an ocean-surveillance Cosmos, had come directly from President Suslov himself. At the earliest possible moment the *Novgorod* was to launch recce flights over the northeastern sector of Arabia's Empty Quarter. If military operations appeared to be in progress there, the *Novgorod*'s air group was to hold itself ready to interdict them.

The orders were straightforward and unequivocal, but they were the last orders Vitse Admiral Prokushkin had been prepared to receive. They implied an operation not suited to the capabilities of Battle Group Red Banner. Prokushkin's force had been assembled to dog and harass the Americans *at sea*. It was swift and mobile and potentially deadly against ship targets. Its armament was largely nuclear, designed to vaporize, if necessary, the old U.S.S. *Nimitz* and her accompanying escorts.

But the Red Banner group was ill prepared to conduct any sort of air operations six hundred or more kilometers inland from an unfriendly coast. And the coast of the Kingdom of Oman, which the *Novgorod* was closing at thirty knots, was still unfriendly to ships of the Soviet Navy. Almost anywhere else in the Arab world, ships flying the star, hammer, and sickle ensign of the fleet would be welcomed as the providers of the munitions and Kalashnikovs with which Muslims had been killing one another for twenty years. But not Oman. The West had stubbornly maintained a presence there. And it was this coast the *Novgorod*'s Yaks and Antonovs would have to penetrate to carry out the mission ordered by the Comrade President.

Kapitan Pervogo Ranga Ivan Kutusev, Prokushkin's flagship commander and an old friend, appeared on the bridge wing beside the admiral. In the reflected glow of the red battle-lights shining through the windows of the bridge, his bearded face looked as if it had been painted with blood.

Kutusev saluted easily and said, 'No contact with the Americans.'

'I didn't expect any,' Prokushkin said. 'But they will get very curious the moment we launch aircraft. Signal *Dostoyny* and *Silny* to maintain a full sonar schedule. There is at least one American missile boat between us and the coast.'

Captain Kutusev accepted the implied reprimand in silence. An American submarine was known to have entered the Arabian Sea from the Gulf of Aden, but *Novgorod*'s air patrols had failed so far to locate it.

'Land,' the admiral said. 'I can smell it.'

'We are still three hundred kilometers from the Omani coast,' Kutusev said.

'I can smell it nonetheless. It stinks of sand and dust.'

Kutusev made an apologetic noise but did not speak immediately. Friendship implied certain privileges, but criticizing orders was not necessarily one of them. Kutusev preferred to remain silent until invited to speak his mind.

Presently Prokushkin, familiar with his flag captain's ways, said, 'All right, Ivan Yurievich. What's troubling you?'

'I am wondering why this recce could not be done better and with less risk by a Cosmos.'

'It has been done by a Cosmos,' Prokushkin said. 'But the miracle men of Star City are not quite perfect, after all. The sandstorms have been a problem. Moscow wants a closer look.'

'There is more to it than that,' Kutusev said. 'But if I am not to know, then very well.'

'Don't get moody, Ivan Yurievich,' the admiral said. 'I wasn't told either. But we can guess, can't we, old friend? There is something there and Moscow wants to take a close look. And maybe to rattle a saber just a bit.'

The flag captain leaned on the splinter shield and looked down at the phosphorescence in the water rushing along the ship's flank. The metal hummed with the power of the turbines. The vessel felt alive as it drove eagerly northward. 'It is not the sort of thing we should be doing,' he said. 'Splitting the air group could tempt the Americans.'

'Surely not,' Prokushkin said. 'Moscow wants to put a finger in their eye, that's all.'

'I will wager the order originated in Dzerzhinsky Square,' Kutusev said.

Prokushkin gave a short, hard laugh. 'That's a wager I won't take, Ivan Yurievich.' He was silent for a thoughtful moment and then asked, 'What is the latest met report?'

'The weather is clearing. By first light the Cosmos could count the hairs on their heads.'

'Worried about your aviators?' Prokushkin asked. He knew exactly what was troubling the flag captain. The pilots and navigators of the *Novgorod*'s air group were dedicated, but they were inexperienced. Nor did he, as senior naval officer of the Arabian Sea front appreciate being so limited in his tactical options. The American Navy might be sliding into eclipse, but it was still formidable. Knowing well the timidity of the ruling clique in Washington, Prokushkin thought it unlikely that the *Nimitz* and her battle group would suddenly appear to challenge the violation of Omani and Arabian air space. The Americans had not behaved with such courage as that for many years. Their record of protecting allies was not impressive. But even if the possibility of challenge was slight, it existed. The key to success in battle was always the application of superior forces at a time of your own choosing. Acting as a foil for the bastards of Moscow Center was not a way to begin any engagement. If things were to go wrong, Prokushkin thought, he might have the sea battle he dreamed of. But not on his own terms.

'The men of my air group are ready for any assignment, Comrade *Vitse Admiral*,' Kutusev said, somewhat stiffly.

Prokushkin uttered that short, barking laugh again and squeezed his subordinate's arm. 'Don't be so touchy, Ivan Yurievich. The *Novgorod* is *always* ready. I know that.' He lifted his gold-braided cap to allow the hot wind to dry the sweat on his bald scalp. 'Join me in my quarters,' he said. 'We will break out a bottle.'

'I'll come directly, Semyon Semyonevich,' Kutusev said.

'See that you do,' the admiral said and squeezed the flag captain's arm again in friendship.

Prokushkin walked through the red-lighted bridge, noting with professional satisfaction the attentive stance of the quartermaster at the helm, the alertness of the ratings at the radars and the computer terminals, the respectful attention of the navigating officer on duty. Kutusev ran a tight ship and Prokushkin approved of that.

As he stepped over the scuttle into the companionway he encountered his flag secretary, Starshiy Leytenant Barsov.

The young man was pale, blond, and angular to the point of cadaverousness. It was fitting, Admiral Prokushkin thought (and not for the first time), that Piotr Aleksandrevich Barsov should so resemble an embalmed corpse. It was an open secret in the ship that the admiral's flag secretary was a political surveillance officer assigned to the commander of Battle Group Red Banner by the KGB's General Batrayev. Prokushkin despised young Barsov and had taken enormous pleasure in refusing to promote him to a rank suitable to a vice-admiral's flag secretary. Barsov would remain a senior lieutenant, Prokushkin thought, until he retired, died, or until his masters at Moscow Center reassigned him to a more easily intimidated flag officer.

'Get some ice and open a tin of caviar,' Prokushkin ordered. 'Have my steward serve it in my day cabin.'

'At once, Comrade Admiral. For one?' The sere young man, despite his unsavory calling of police spy—or perhaps because of it—always affected a servile manner as he attempted to ingratiate himself with his commander. An impossible task, Prokushkin thought.

'For two,' he said brusquely.

'The captain will be joining the *vitse admiral*?'

'Yes.'

'Will the *vitse admiral* wish me to take notes at the conference?'

Irritated, Prokushkin said, 'Kutusev and I are going to discuss seamanship, not politics, *Leytenant*.'

As he made his way toward his day cabin, Prokushkin cursed himself for a bad-tempered fool. It was never wise to be too sharp with the men the KGB planted on the fleet. But what could one do? Building a navy was not a task that could be carried out using Lenin's theories as a handbook. The plain fact was that though the ships of the Soviet Navy were the finest in the world, the men were mostly conscripts. Even the officers who flew the *Novgorod*'s aircraft were, compared to the American carrier pilots of vessels like the *Nimitz*, inexperienced. It worried the admiral that he was being asked to risk these men in a snooping expedition hundreds of kilometers inland. And what would happen if one of the eager youngsters decided to do something rash? Or if one were lost, or shot down by the Arabians?

Risky, he thought, risky business. We could be starting a war out here, a war no one could win, and without ever knowing why we were doing it.

But Moscow must know what it's about, he told himself. One has to believe that.

27 Ramat Gan, Israel

Gershon Agron, sales manager of the Tel Aviv distributorship for Coca-Cola and quondam Lieutenant Colonel and Commander of the Fourth Reserve Infantry Battalion of the Israel Defense Force, gave a final tug to the webbing straps of his duffel bag and stood breathless in the living room of the flat he shared with his wife and two teen-age daughters.

The three women—Aviva, his wife, and the two girls, Malkah and Deborah—sat in a line on the leatherette-upholstered couch and regarded him tearily. The girls, he thought (not for the first time), were not great beauties. It was unfortunate that they resembled him rather than their mother, who had been quite good-looking before she began putting on weight. He often remembered with pleasure his meeting Aviva: that meeting had been the only good thing to have come to young Lieutenant Agron out of the Six-Day War. Aviva had been assigned as a communications clerk to his battalion of paras and theirs had been what the old folk liked to call 'a whirlwind courtship.' Everything had been whirlwind quick in those days, Agron thought. Quick and terrifying and at first thrilling. But in the end the war had been a disappointment. Nothing really had changed. Agron had fought in four wars and he, like the whole country, felt weary of the endless battle.

He drew a deep breath, as much to indicate that the time had come again for him to leave as to ease the tight fit of his uniform. His gesture brought forth another flurry of sniffles and tears from his women. He checked his watch again, ignoring the imported Swiss-moderne clock on the end table which he had bought as an eighteenth-anniversary gift for Aviva and which had never kept proper time. He hated these late-night departures. There had been too many of them: flurries of national stress and partial mobilizations and endless practice exercises and, of course, four departures for war, real war. At that, he thought, he was luckier than some. There were still men liable for service who had fought in the 1956 war, men older than himself, with more important civilian careers.

He stood at the window and parted the blackout curtain enough to see the street below. The transport, a military truck belonging to the battalion headquarters company, had not yet appeared. No other traffic moved in the quiet suburb. There was, he reflected bitterly, no gasoline for civilian vehicles. There had been less and less ever since the trouble in Arabia and though Israel certainly did not receive its petroleum products direct from the Arab world, it had always managed to draw on the world pool, buying where it could. But now there was none at all except for the army and air force and Agron wondered if the government had not waited too long to act. That, he thought sourly, was what came of relying on American promises.

The radio was on, the volume turned down. The whole family had lived by the radio this day, listening to the coded mobilization orders which everyone, including any Arab spies within earshot, had learned to interpret. The set was on now because Aviva insisted that they keep listening. There was always a chance, she said, that the mobilization would be called off. 'The Americans *have* to give us oil,' she declared. 'They *promised*.' Aviva Agron had relations in the United States, well-off people who visited Israel every two years. It was inconceivable to her that the Americans would fail their only real friend in the Middle East.

But Agron knew better. The Americans had their own problems. It no longer concerned them that Israel's economy, long staggering under the burden of defense expenditures, was finally near a shuddering halt without oil to power the country's industries or run the tractors in the orange groves or even fuel the glittering blue-and-white toys of the national airline.

'Well,' Agron said with forced cheerfulness. 'It seems my transport is late. How about a glass of tea?' His parents had come to Israel from Russia in the Second Aliyah and drinking tea in a glass, straining it through a sugar cube, had remained an Agron (née Agronsky) tradition.

The suggestion set Aviva into bustling action. Aviva was

one of those Jewish wives who face every possible tribulation with something to eat or drink. There were, after all, Agron thought, ethnic stereotypes that were dead on target.

'Help your mother, girls,' Agron said distractedly. What could be holding up the transport? He hated prolonging these awkward farewells. One did not get better at them as one grew older. Quite the reverse.

He thought about Plan Aluf and suppressed a shiver of apprehension. The staging in Beersheba would be held to an irreducible minimum to protect the element of surprise. But no precautions seemed to Agron likely to catch the Arab radicals napping. And did the staff really imagine the IDF could attack and seize—and *hold*—any substantial proportion of the Saudi oil fields? Destroy, yes, perhaps, almost certainly. Though what good *that* would bring to a fuel-starved Israel was difficult to imagine. And then there was the question of how the rest of the world would regard still another Israeli preemptive attack. Over and over again the army and air force had struck first and devastatingly at the Arabs. And each time outside pressure had forced Israel to return what it had won. So in the end, we won nothing, Agron thought.

He caught a glimpse of himself in the pier glass near the doorway. (Another anniversary gift, he remembered.) The vision was not a reassuring one. The lean, suntanned *sabra* of earlier times was simply not present in the room. Who was it staring back at him from the glass, anyway? A middle-aged salesman of foreign soft drinks, that was who. A civilian in a uniform that was too tight for him, balding, with a very frightened look deep in his eyes that everyone, even his daughters, could read.

Aviva brought him his tea and he sat on the edge of a chair, once again like a stranger in his own house, drinking it. Farewells among Jews were supposed to be emotional to the point of hysteria, he thought. Another racial stereotype. But somehow he had never been willing to allow himself that sort of unseemly display. So spoke the *sabra*, the Second Aliyah aristocrat. Lord God, he thought, I do feel like weeping. I am so tired of running off to war. The whole country is tired of it. When will it end?

The door buzzer sounded and Aviva and the girls jumped at the noise. Agron went to the window again and this time the truck was there. He stood, shrugging and half smiling helplessly, and then his wife and his daughters were hugging and holding him and he felt the tears hot but still unshed in his eyes. It was time to leave for still another war.

28 Washington, D.C.

Raymond Scofield Turner settled into his chair at the long table and regarded the men present with interest. The Crisis Room in the west wing of the White House was crowded with members of the National Security Council and their staffers. Across the broad expanse of polished mahogany, the Joint Chiefs of Staff lent a touch of color to the otherwise conservatively, even drably, dressed civilian members. General Stanley Lescher, the chairman, was new to the NSC, having only recently been appointed. He was a portly Air Force officer, a trained scientist as well as a former combat pilot of Korean War vintage. Turner did not know him well. In Washington social circles Lescher was known to be a brilliant negotiator, a fairly lax disciplinarian (a hangover from his days as a fighter pilot), and a lover of good food and drink. That was the sum of Washington's knowledge about the nation's top military man. Politically he was regarded as something of a 'right-winger,' though, thought Turner, that was a label that was almost automatically assigned in the capital to any officer who expressed dissatisfaction with the balance of Soviet-American power.

The Army Chief of Staff, General Carlton Osgood, was a black man, a product of one of the Military Academy's first desegregated classes. He had come to the Pentagon after a distinguished tour as commander of NATO. The word *distinguished* was not one Osgood himself would have used. Turner knew that the general had been moved from his post in Brussels at the secret request of the European allies, who resented his continuing demand that they keep their forces at a level of readiness they regarded as unnecessary. The President had been disturbed by the controversy, but, because Osgood was both black and highly competent, had resolved matters by promoting him to the JCS.

The solution had not been completely satisfactory for

either the President or for Secretary of Defense Andy Traynor. Searching for ways to reduce both the military budget and the balance of payments, Traynor had put forth the notion of removing the Rapid Deployment Force from its bases in Egypt and reducing the force itself to a headquarters. Osgood's reaction to this move had been furious argument, which had been stopped only by a direct order from the Commander in Chief.

Turner, studying the expression on the handsome ebony face, had the strong feeling that General Osgood remained angrily unconvinced of the wisdom of the decision.

The Chief of Naval Operations was Admiral Aaron Thesiger, a man nearly as old as Turner and long overdue for retirement. Thesiger was worn out, the Secretary of State thought, by his long, losing fight to keep the Navy battleworthy. His face was gray with illness and frustration.

Next to the admiral sat General Harmer, the Marine Commandant, whose nickname 'Beachhead' was said to express not only his military fixation but his intellectual limitations. Under Harmer's reign the Marine Corps had once again become what it had been before World War II, a force to storm enemy coastlines in landing craft and rubber boats. One of Harmer's most quoted pronouncements was: 'Computers? Aircraft? Shit, hold the beaches and let the Army and Air Force take care of the rest of that crap.' Both Lescher and Osgood considered General Harmer a dinosaur, but Secretary Traynor regarded him highly.

The Air Force Chief of Staff, General Aldo Biaggi, was not present, being at the moment occupied with an inspection tour of the SAC bases and their aged force of B-52s—an airplane Biaggi had flown as a twenty-one-year-old second lieutenant.

Around the head of the long table sat some (but not all, Turner noted) of the civilian members of the NSC. Andrew Traynor was present, as was Secretary of Energy George Rossmore. There was no representation from Treasury and Interior, nor from Education or Human Resources—all of whom had been given official status in the council by Vincent Loomis.

A representative of the National Security Agency with whom Secretary Turner had only a nodding acquaintance, a young man named Burton Welch, sat quietly next to Quinn Dawson, the CIA's Director of Operations. Isaac Holt, the

Deputy DCI and heir apparent to the late Cole Norris, was conspicuously absent.

Raymond Turner silently chided himself for thinking of Norris in such bland terms. Less than a week ago Norris had been the subject of fevered speculation in the government and among the members of the Washington press corps. Yet in a matter of days the horror and bafflement surrounding his death had faded, pushed aside by the pressure of events, trivial and vital, that seemed always to engulf Washington. This , of course, was not to be blamed on Vincent Loomis and his administration, Raymond Turner thought. The tremendous growth of the media since the 1950s had reduced Washington's attention span to a matter of days. Was it, Turner wondered, his age that made him feel that this was so? Or was it simply a dreary fact of life in the last years of a century that had blanketed the world with technological changes—not all of them benign?

The air conditioning held the temperature of the Crisis Room to a chilly sixty degrees. Turner's thin blood required more warmth than that and he shivered slightly. Young Harold Ellis, the State Department Intelligence Case Officer he had brought with him to act as aide, leaned forward and asked if he wanted his coat. The Secretary of State was always mildly annoyed by the way in which his own subordinates treated him like a frail old man. Which is exactly what I am, he thought. Frail and ill-tempered, a creature to be regarded with mingled astonishment and concern by the young Ivy League gentlemen of State. A thin smile crossed his wrinkled lips. There was sad humor in his situation—the ancient molting hawk among the sleek, compliant doves of Foggy Bottom. It was the act of a true diplomat, Turner thought, for young Ellis to have carried a coat for his chief through the suffocating heat of the Washington summer because he knew an old man would grow chilled in this air-conditioned basement lair. As an act of grudging politeness, the Secretary stood and allowed Ellis to drape the coat over his shoulders before sitting down again.

He looked at the bank of clocks on the wall above the steel map cases. It was three minutes before the hour. At the stroke of two, the President would arrive. Vincent Loomis had his faults, but tardiness was not one of them.

Turner now noted with some distaste that Chief of Staff

Charlie McKay had appeared with Press Secretary Elmer Harper, pollster and general dogsbody. They settled into chairs near the President's place at the head of the long table. Turner bridled at Harper's presence. He had nothing against the man personally, but if this meeting concerned the national security (and that was, at least theoretically, the purview of the NSC), it was not fitting to include the Press Secretary among the conferees. But it had grown increasingly de rigueur in recent administrations to consider at the highest level the 'public relations' and 'image' problems of any crisis.

This administration, Turner thought, regarded the electorate and the press as some sort of composite being that resembled nothing more than a shark: a body constantly hungering for news, and a set of sharp jaws intent on capturing that news in savaged and undigested chunks. Small wonder there was so little thoughtful consideration of problems out in the country. That huge stomach was choked with reportage delivered by the jagged mouth of the media in Washington, and there was never time to digest anything before a new chunk of bloody meat was dispatched along the gullet of newsprint and television signals. The whole being was driven by a blind compulsion to know everything *now, immediately*, so that it could be forgotten, mentally excreted barely in time to make room for the next day's forage.

One could almost feel sorry for men in Elmer Harper's position. They had to brave the jaws and file down the teeth and attempt to limit the damage to their principals.

And though it went against his inclinations, Turner could even feel some sympathy for the members of the Washington press corps, whose careers and sustenance depended on producing fodder—spiced, when possible, with hints of graft and incompetence—for the American beast of their own creation.

At two minutes before the hour, Carl Shepherd and his deputy, Paul Chancellor, came breathlessly into the Crisis Room. Shepherd's face was flushed with suppressed agitation and Turner, remembering his last conversation with the FBI Director, wondered what new information had come into his possession that so unsettled him.

Shepherd took a chair next to Turner and accepted a locked briefcase from Chancellor, who settled into one of the chairs reserved for NSC members' staff assistants.

The FBI Director leaned close to Turner and would have spoken, but at that moment President Loomis came into the room closely followed by Peter Gilmartin.

'Sit, sit—' Vincent Loomis's heavy face mirrored his own agitation and impatience. He took his place at the head of the table and swept the room with hooded, angry eyes. Without preamble, he said, 'Early this morning we received a hot-line communication from the Soviets. Peter will read it to you. There will be copies for all of you to study. No copies will be taken from this room.' His expression became stonier—and somehow more commanding—than Raymond Turner had ever seen it. '*There will be no leaks*. I want that to be crystal-clear to everyone present.' He fixed the aides and assistants sitting behind their chiefs. 'I address myself particularly to the staffs. If there is a whisper about this meeting in the press, or if Elmer hears so much as a rumor of a story outside this room, there will be a wholesale housecleaning. Is that understood?'

The staff members, unaccustomed to being addressed in such unequivocal terms, murmured resentfully.

'*I asked if that was understood*,' Loomis said in an angry voice.

The younger staff men and assistants began to look concerned. Apparently, Raymond Turner thought, the Cole Norris affair had not been forgotten by the President yet. It was obvious that Vincent Loomis was deeply concerned that there should not be still another wave of crisis stories sweeping the country out of Washington. Interesting, Turner mused. Was it possible that Vincent Todd Loomis had, since the last meeting here in the White House, decided to become more *presidential*? Lord knew it was time—and past time for such a metamorphosis in the Chief Magistrate of the Republic.

'All right,' Loomis said. 'Get on with it, Peter.'

Peter Gilmartin, his handsome face somber, took a sheaf of pages bearing the blue Olympus classification band and began to read Comrade Ivan Kirilovich Suslov's brusque message to the President of the United States.

When Gilmartin had finished and settled once again in his chair, the silence in the room was electric. Vincent Loomis waited for someone to speak.

When no one did, he said, 'Let's begin with you, General Lescher.'

The Chairman of the Joint Chiefs pursed his lips thoughtfully before speaking. 'I can't make an immediate recommendation on a reply, Mr. President. The Department of Defense has been going on the assumption that the New Peace Corps Station in the Empty Quarter is simply another one of their research establishments.' He turned to Andrew Traynor. 'You will recall, Mr. Secretary, that we had a request from Cole Norris for a special shuttle flight that was refused by higher authority.'

Peter Gilmartin frowned nervously, remembering his own part in refusing Norris's plea.

Traynor said, 'There was no reason to spy on the NPC, Mr. President. If we began that sort of thing, the cost could run into tens of millions. Those people are everywhere.'

'Let's limit this discussion to the station in south Arabia,' the President said.

'Very well, sir. We did a cost-effectiveness study on Cole's request and estimated that a special flight would be far too expensive to consider. After all, at best it would have been a fishing expedition,' the Secretary of Defense said. 'A much simpler approach was decided upon. I merely took it upon myself to ask Calder Davis if there was anything unusual happening at EQ Station.' A nervous smile hovered about his lips as though he were secretly amused that so trivial a matter would even interest this high-level group.

Raymond Turner, whose years of experience in diplomatic negotiating had made him highly sensitive to the signals of tone and body language, felt a coldness in the pit of his stomach. The Secretary of Defense, he thought suddenly, was badly frightened and hiding his fear behind a shield of facetiousness. Traynor was lying. But why? Turner looked at each man present. George Rossmore's expression was rigid, his cheeks drawn and bloodless. Turner wondered, Rossmore, too?

Andrew Traynor paused, seeming to consult the notes he had before him. But Raymond Turner was certain he was organizing his thoughts for a defense. Of what?

'Ever since Calder and his associates took over the structure of the old Peace Corps and turned it into the NPC we have made it a point to maintain a separation from their activities, Mr. President,' he said. 'Of course, no one knows that better than you—being so personally close to Davis.'

That, Turner thought, was a shrewd thrust. But why was

it necessary to remind the President of his own, almost worshipful, relationship with Calder Davis?

'Even before this administration took office, Mr. President,' Traynor said, 'it was policy to stay at arm's length from the NPC. The organization could not function at all in the Third World if the host countries thought that there was any connection at all between the United States government and the people working out of NPC stations.' He looked across the table at Dawson, the man from the Central Intelligence Agency. 'I think you, Quinn, can confirm that.'

Dawson frowned and said, 'Yes, Mr. Secretary, but—'

The President spoke up immediately, 'But what?'

Traynor interrupted at once. 'What I mean to say is that even the intelligence community has made every effort to stay clear of the NPC. And properly so, I think. We have enemies enough without spying on our friends. I don't think a rude note from the Soviets justifies a change in that policy, Mr. President.'

Raymond Turner watched the President intently. He was being offered an out, an easy way to ignore the fact that Calder Davis's vast enterprise was under some suspicion of wrongdoing. Would he take it, Turner wondered? Vincent Loomis was not a rock of integrity. At least he had never given any indication that he was. Was there some bit of statesman in that mass of politician?

Loomis said, 'You were about to say something, Dawson. What was it?' Turner felt a flutter of hope.

'Yes, Mr. President,' the Director of Operations said. 'I am sorry that Isaac Holt isn't here because this should more suitably come from him—'

'Skip the protocol. Speak up,' the President said harshly.

Dawson said, 'I have no documentation for this, Mr. President. Please bear that in mind. But there was Company talk. There always is. Not much in this case, actually. But still—' He paused as though searching his mind for exactly the proper way to continue. 'Director Norris had some sort of personal project under way, sir. The rumor is that it concerned the whole NPC setup. That's all I know about it. As I say, it was something he was handling personally. He did that sometimes.' Apologetically he said, 'Director Norris was a very idiosyncratic man. He sometimes undertook projects on his own. Not often, but sometimes. It was the way he operated when he was in the field in Southeast Asia and he never completely abandoned the practice, even as DCI.'

Turner watched the President carefully. He had grown paler, the lines in his face seemed more deeply etched.

'I don't think this is adding anything to the discussion of the problem at hand, Mr. President,' Andrew Traynor said. 'The Cole Norris business is something else entirely. We shouldn't be straying so far afield.'

Raymond Turner spoke for the first time. 'I don't agree, Andrew. It appears that anything connected to the NPC is germane at this moment.' To Dawson he said, 'Is there anything you can add to what you have already told us? Was there any sort, any sort at all, of operation being conducted by the Agency against the NPC?'

'Absolutely not, Mr. Secretary,' Dawson said heatedly. 'Our charter does not permit domestic operations of any kind.'

'But the NPC is not a domestic organization, Mr. Dawson,' Turner said in a mild tone.

'Technically that is so, Mr. Secretary,' Dawson said carefully. 'But much of the NPC's financial infrastructure is—how shall I put it?—embedded in the American corporations that are part of the worldwide network of multinationals which support it. Please understand that I am not an expert on the subject of the NPC, but almost any intelligence officer in any service in the world could tell you that there is no country outside the Soviet bloc where some part of the NPC does not operate. And, of couse, the prime mover in all of this has been Mr. Davis. We simply could not conduct any sort of—well, operation—with the NPC as target. It would be a violation of the law.'

'I really think we are getting sidetracked, Mr. President,' Andrew Traynor said.

'A moment, please, Andrew,' said the Secretary of State. 'Let's pursue this for a bit longer.' To Dawson he said, 'Yet in spite of what you tell us, you believe that Cole Norris was conducting some sort of investigation of the NPC?'

Dawson, by now thoroughly sorry he had ventured the information, said, 'I did preface my remarks by saying that I had no hard evidence, Mr. Secretary.'

'Surely Director Norris was as aware as you are that any domestic operations by the Central Intelligence Agency would be in violation of its directive from the Congress,' Turner pursued.

'Of course, Mr. Secretary. But as I said, sometimes Director Norris chose to develop his own operations without involving the Agency.'

'I appreciate your wish to protect the intelligence community, Mr. Dawson,' Turner said. 'And the legality or lack of legality of the Director's investigation—'

'*Alleged* investigation,' Andrew Traynor said quickly.

'Point taken, Andrew,' Turner said and still again addressed himself directly to Dawson. 'Surely there have been some in-house questions asked, Mr. Dawson?'

'Questions, sir?'

'Certainly. Questions, Mr. Dawson. It seems inevitable to me that the Agency would be disturbed by the fact that Director Norris was conducting some sort of operation—' he nodded at Andrew Traynor as if to indicate that his objections were being considered '—*rumored* to be concerned with the NPC. And, one may suppose, the International Strategic Studies Group has become a sort of braintrust for the New Peace Corps—'

George Rossmore broke in with what seemed to Raymond Turner an agitated objection. 'Really, Raymond. Surely no one can believe the ISSG is a threat to anyone. Some of the most prominent men and women in the United States and Europe are members of the ISSG. I am myself, and so is Andy. And there are literally hundreds of people of influence, both in and out of government, who have joined. You were asked to join, yourself.'

'What are you getting at, Raymond?' the President asked impatiently.

'I am merely wondering why it has not occurred to anyone within the intelligence community that Cole Norris was brutally murdered at a time when he was conducting a project concerning the New Peace Corps.'

For a moment the room was silent, filled with tension. The only sound was the humming of the bank of timepieces on the wall. Then George Rossmore erupted into anger. 'Raymond, that's *obscene*.'

Andrew Traynor rushed to add his support. 'I can't believe a man of your reputation would allow himself to have such thoughts, Turner. It is absolutely absurd.'

The Secretary of State's eyes remained fixed on Dawson. 'Is it absurd, Mr. Dawson?'

Dawson spoke with extreme reluctance. 'There has been some speculation at McLean, Mr. Secretary. I would be less than truthful if I denied it.'

The President moved in, his voice edged. 'And?'

'The Agency believes the Director was murdered by terrorists, Mr. President,' Dawson said flatly, without expression.

'That sounds like an official pronouncement, Mr. Dawson,' Raymond Turner said.

'It is, sir. There was, of course, an in-house examination of the few available facts at the top level. The consensus was that Director Norris's murder was an act of terrorism by a group or groups unknown,' Dawson said.

'I recall, Mr. President,' said Turner, 'that that was Isaac Holt's first conclusion at the meeting we held the morning Cole Norris's body was found.'

The President looked at Carl Shepherd. 'Have you anything to add to this, Carl?'

The FBI Director's face was moist despite the chilly air. 'You will remember, sir, that I was informed that the investigation would be conducted outside the Bureau.'

Vincent Loomis flushed angrily. 'I also remember that you argued the law with me. I ask you again, have you anything to add to this discussion?'

Shepherd took a deep breath and said, 'The Bureau thinks it likely the attempt to kill Cole's brother has a direct connection.'

'Connection with what, Carl? With Cole's death or with the NPC?'

'Mr. President,' Andrew Traynor said. 'I must protest all of this. We are here to discuss President Suslov's threat. I don't see how any of this relates—'

'I will decide what we discuss here, Andrew,' the President said brusquely. 'Well, Carl?'

'Of course it *is* possible that the attempt on Michael Rivas was a follow-up act of simple terrorism. He had just returned from a Muslim country. He had been some weeks with the Afghan rebels. It is conceivable that some Marxist-oriented splinter group or other might have killed Cole Norris and then tried to kill Rivas.' Shepherd's voice grew stronger, more positive, as he spoke. 'But somehow I find that answer too pat, too simple.'

George Rossmore said, 'You mean it offends your vastly

experienced policeman's intuition, Carl?'

'I don't pretend to be a policeman, George,' Shepherd said evenly. 'But I *am* the Director of the FBI. I ask you to remember that.'

'Oh, my *deepest* apologies, Carl,' Rossmore said. Turner noted that the Secretary of Energy's face was glistening with sweat.

There was a momentary interruption at the door and a whispered conversation among the members of Charlie McKay's staff. McKay listened and then murmured to Peter Gilmartin, who said, 'That can wait.'

The President glared at the interruption and then said, 'All right, Carl. What else has the Bureau to offer?'

'I don't know whether or not this is the place to speak of it, Mr. President,' Shepherd said.

'You heard what I said at the beginning of this meeting. Whatever is said here is secure.' Loomis once again swept the room with his hooded, imperial gaze. 'Or else. Speak on, Carl.'

'When Rivas left New York—against police instructions, I should say—he came here to Washington. He met briefly with Isaac Holt—'

'That is hardly surprising,' Traynor said. 'Holt was his brother's deputy, after all.'

'Yes, that's true enough,' Shepherd said. 'But he was followed from the Lincoln Memorial, where he spoke to Holt, to Dulles. Whoever tried to kill him in New York was still trailing him. That doesn't sound like normal terrorist procedure to me.'

'And, of course, you identified the man following Rivas,' Rossmore suggested.

Shepherd shook his head, 'No, we did not.'

'You are certain he was being followed, then?' Turner asked, knowing the answer in advance.

'Beyond question,' Shepherd said. 'Rivas took a Concorde to London. From there he went immediately south to Dartmouth, where he met with a man called Wyndham, whom Interpol knows as a soldier of fortune—a mercenary—'

Andrew Traynor sighed theatrically and sat back in his chair. 'Really, Mr. President. Have we *time* for all this cloak-and-dagger silliness? Where is all this supposed to lead?'

Shepherd plowed ahead determinedly. 'He was followed there and back to London by a man fitting the description of the one seen by our agents here in Washington. Both Rivas and this man left London that same afternoon. They went on separate flights. The man who was trailing Rivas lost some time because the Brits were following *him*—at my request. But Rivas's destination, Andrew, was Salalah in Oman. And Salalah is EQ Station's port on the Arabian Sea.'

'So,' Traynor said, 'at long last we come to it. Rivas is trying to get to EQ Station. Well, good luck to him. He undoubtedly could have gone there as a guest of the NPC if he had troubled to ask. I suppose he felt he couldn't do that. Journalistic integrity, no doubt. But what we have here is a long rigamarole that amounts to nothing at all. With all due apologies to you, Harper—' he waved at the Press Secretary '—what we now know is that Rivas is like any other damned scribbler. He's after a story. He is managing to contain his grief about his brother and he's off to play at investigative reporting. Good Lord, Carl. Is that what all this is about?'

'The man Rivas saw in Dartmouth is dead, Andrew,' Shepherd said evenly. 'His boat was run down in the Channel early this morning.'

'Where are you getting your information, Carl?' the President asked, his hand raised to silence Andrew Traynor's objection.

'I'm sorry, Mr. President,' Shepherd said miserably. 'I couldn't just back away from this matter. I spoke to Sir Allan Sawkins of Special Branch. He put a man on Rivas and whoever it was who followed him down to Dartmouth.'

'Good God,' Rossmore said. 'Now we have the Brits in an uproar. I should think we'd want to clean our own Augean stables.'

Shepherd said, 'Sawkins told me that Wyndham was under suspicion of tax fraud. The British tax people were certain he had been collecting large sums of money from somewhere for the last year or more. They were going to pay him a surprise visit. But when they arrived in Dartmouth, his boat was gone. The British Coast Guard, or whatever they call it, fished wreckage out of the Channel a few hours later. The weather was clear and the sea light. They are certain he was trying to make a rendezvous with someone out there and got himself run down.' He addressed himself directly to Traynor. 'Yes, damn it, Andy. I think all of this adds up to something.' He turned back to the President. 'There is just one thing more, sir. The man with whom Rivas spent the night after he was attacked, his publisher, a man named Abbott—he is also dead. He fell from a window early this morning.' Shepherd breathed deeply as though he had just completed a long run.

'Mr. President.' The young man from the National Security Agency, the organization entrusted to monitor sensitive communications in and out of the United States, was licking his dry lips.

'Yes, what is it,' the President said sharply. 'Who are you?'

'Burton Welch, sir. NSA.'

'All right, go on.'

'It may not be pertinent in any way,' Welch said in a prim, engineer's didactic tone. 'But we intercepted a telephone call to Washington from Kingswear in England yesterday. Ordinarily in such a routine intercept the computer would break off surveillance the moment the parties began to speak. We have to be very careful not to commit any act that a court would regard as an infringement of civil rights. . . .'

'Yes, yes,' Loomis said, 'very commendable.'

'But this particular call was made from a public telephone in Kingswear—'

'Where the hell is Kingswear?' General Lescher demanded.

'At the mouth of the Dart River, General. Or as near as makes no difference,' Admiral Thesiger said. 'The Royal Naval College is near there.'

The NSA man waited politely until the admiral had finished and then said, 'As I was explaining, Mr. President—I have yesterday's log with me if you care to see it—the call was made from a pay phone to a Washington number. The reason the computer chose to record it was that the call was received by a *scrambler* phone.'

Shepherd sucked in his breath and said softly to Turner, 'I'll bet whatever you like that that call was made at the same time that Rivas was in Dartmouth. I feel it in my gut.'

The President glared at him for the interruption. 'A scrambler phone, you say. Did you *un*scramble the message?'

'Ah, no, Mr. President,' Welch said.

'Why not, since you took the trouble to intercept and record it,' Loomis said, exasperated.

Young Burton Welch looked almost apologetically at Quinn Dawson across the polished table. 'Well, sir, it was a scramble program flagged to Central Intelligence. We never decrypt such conversations unless specifically authorized to do so.'

President Loomis looked in amazement from Welch to Dawson and back again. 'Let me understand you. NSA intercepted and recorded a scramble call from Dartmouth—Kingswear—whatever—to a CIA telephone yesterday?'

'Yes, sir. I have the logs here.'

'Never mind the logs, damn it,' Loomis said. 'Dawson, what do you know about this?'

'Nothing, sir. Absolutely nothing,' the Director of Operations said vehemently. 'We have no operation running of any kind in south England.'

'I want a transcript of that call immediately. Get on it *now*.'

'*Yes*, Mr. President,' Dawson and Welch said almost together.

'Go now. Both of you. I want that transcript in thirty minutes. Welch—'

'Sir?' The young man was already on his feet and gathering his notes.

'Can you tell from the recording who made the call and who received it?'

'I'm afraid not, sir. It isn't possible to take voiceprints from scrambled recordings. They are too badly doctored by the scrambler program.'

'Then a transcript will have to do. Get on with it.'

The others sat silent while the CIA and NSA men left. At the door there was another whispered conversation between the Secret Service man on duty outside and one of Peter Gilmartin's staff assistants.

The President ignored it and spoke to General Lescher. 'I think it is time to take a look at EQ Station, General. How soon can we get an SR-71 over southern Arabia?'

George Rossmore said swiftly, 'Mr. President. Please, I ask you to consider how this will appear to Calder Davis and his associates. Calder is your *friend*, sir. If you want to know anything about any part of the NPC, all you have to do is ask him.'

Loomis looked bleakly at his Secretary of Energy. 'But Calder isn't here, is he, George? He's on the way to Europe and out of touch.'

'Still, sir. Just a matter of a few hours' wait. Surely that is the best way to handle this?'

Once again, Raymond Turner thought, Vincent Loomis was being tested. Perhaps *tempted* was the more nearly proper word.

The President shook his head slowly, with an almost pitiable weariness. 'No, George. Not this time. General? What about the SR-71?'

General Lescher's look was level and coldly unsympathetic. 'It will take twenty-four hours, Mr. President. We are down to a single squadron of Blackbirds and they are at Beale Air Force Base in California.' He frowned and went on doubtfully. 'If an airplane is immediately operational—and that may be difficult because of problems we have had holding on to qualified maintenance personnel—but if one is operational, we can get it as far as Germany tonight. We will have to have permission from Bonn for that, by the way, Mr. Secretary.' He addressed that comment directly to Raymond Turner, who nodded agreement. 'We can send a KC-10 tanker to Bir Jifjafah in Egypt. Permission again, Secretary Turner. And the tanker can meet the Blackbird somewhere over the Med for refueling. Then we can make the overflight and have some hope of getting the aircraft and its data back to Germany for evaluation. Yes, I think twenty-four hours will just about do it.'

Loomis met the Chairman's steady gaze and nodded. 'Very well, General. See to it.'

'Yes, Mr. President.'

Loomis turned toward the door in a sudden rush of irritation. 'What the *hell* is going on there?'

Peter Gilmartin said, 'There is one of Calder Davis's secretaries outside, Mr. President. He has a letter from Calder for you.'

'Well, get it and bring it in,' the President said angrily.

'He won't surrender it, sir,' Gilmartin said. 'He was ordered by Calder to deliver it into your hands only.'

'All right, all *right*. Send him in here, then.'

Closely escorted by a Secret Service man who viewed the letter in his hand suspiciously, Calder Davis's secretary approached the President.

'All right,' Loomis said, 'give me the letter, boy.'

The young man surrendered the letter and was quickly hurried out of the room.

'I suppose, gentleman,' the President said, 'I had better read this at once. I can't imagine what Calder was thinking about to insist on such damned dramatics. It's not like him. But excuse me for a moment.'

He opened the heavy envelope and extracted the three typed pages inside. From long habit, he verified the signature before returning to the salutation and then the body of the letter.

Turner watched curiously as the President's knuckles whitened and suddenly the pages in his hand began to tremble, so that he was forced to spread them on the tabletop to continue reading them.

When he had finished he sat for a moment in absolute silence, his eyes staring at some unseen thing in the middle distance. Raymond Turner felt a painful apprehension as he studied the President's face. It had gone livid, bloodless, like a mask carved from veined stone.

The men in the room stirred uneasily, but Vincent Loomis ignored them and slowly read the letter still again, from the beginning.

'My God,' he said in a hushed and strangled voice. '*My God—What have you done—?*'

The level of agitated conversation rose suddenly to a confused babble. Men who had spent years with Vincent Loomis did not recognize the man who sat at the head of the table in some kind of living paralysis of rising horror and fury.

When his eyes focused once again, they fixed directly onto George Rossmore and Andrew Traynor. They stared back at him, frozen by what they saw in his face.

'*Get the Secret Service in here,*' the President whispered.

Peter Gilmartin reacted with characteristic bewilderment. Charlie McKay was much swifter, though he was as confused as anyone in the Crisis Room.

Two Secret Service men, galvanized into action by the expression on McKay's face as he called them, burst into the room with revolvers drawn.

'*You—*' Loomis said in a strangled voice. He had pushed himself to his feet and was pointing at Andrew Traynor. '*Get up—get on your feet—!*' He gestured to Rossmore as well, his hand closing into a fist as though he would attack him at any moment.

To the Secret Service men he said, '*Arrest those men—I*

want them held in close confinement—'

The men of the presidential bodyguard were picked for their loyalty and courage, but they were nonplussed by the order they had been given. Were they actually being told by the President of the United States to arrest and hold two members of the Cabinet? Visions of reprimands and dismissals raced through their minds. To their credit and that of the government they served, the thought of 'coup' did not enter their heads until much later. But they hesitated, looking about the table for some sort of confirmation.

Raymond Turner, the oldest man present, still reacted most swiftly. When the Secret Service men looked to him, he snapped at them: *'Do what the President orders!'*

The guards closed in on a stunned Rossmore and a terrified Traynor and quickly hustled them out and the Crisis Room erupted into argument and questions.

President Loomis brought his palm down on the table with a sound like the crack of a pistol. 'Sit *down, all of you!*'

When the baffled confusion was under some control, he said in a hollow voice, 'Thank you, gentlemen.' For the first time that he could remember, Raymond Turner felt a glimmer of admiration for Vincent Loomis.

The President drew a deep breath and then spoke more firmly. 'Before we decide on a reply to President Suslov's message, you had better hear what Calder Davis has to say.' Then he picked up the letter and began deliberately to read aloud.

Six
July 17, the sixth day

There is nothing more difficult to take in hand, more perilous to conduct, or more uncertain in its success, than to take the lead in the introduction of a new order of things.

—Niccolò Machiavelli, *Il Principe*

29 Ar Rub' al Khali

Under a sky that resembled an infected wound, the small convoy drove northeast. The desert dawn, lingering just below the horizon, was streaking the dust clouds with veins of red and orange. The wind had diminished, leaving an oppressive stillness. The plumes of sand thrown up by the wheels of the vehicles seemed to hang suspended in air and the slitted combat lamps cast odd, flat fans of light into the emptiness ahead. When he raised his eyes to the zenith, Rivas could see the suggestion of stars behind the dusty overcast, vague points of brightness like diamonds seen through muddy water.

Rivas, in all his wanderings, had never before seen a desert like this one. Since leaving the pebbled, alkali plains of the Qara ridges, the vehicles had been traversing a dark immensity of rolling sand dunes, many of them thirty feet high. Colonel Hadfield's driver, the mute tribesman, steered the command car by the tiny compass light, but Rivas had the impression that had the compass failed, he would have continued to lead the convoy northeast, guided by some inner lodestone quite beyond the understanding of anyone not native to this wasteland.

Now, as the light along the eastern horizon grew stronger, Rivas could begin to see the dimensions of the desert through which the three vehicles crawled like insects, prodding the twilight with antennae of dim illumination.

Each time the command car topped a dune, the meaning of the words *Empty Quarter* became more apparent. In the gradually increasing light, Rivas could see, each time the crest of a dune was reached, an endless procession of similar dunes stretching to the horizon. In the dawn it was impossible to guess whether that horizon lay a mile away or a thousand, but to the limit of vision lay only a dark, frozen sand sea. This, thought Rivas, was a desert to rival the Sahara.

The woman was asleep, her head resting against the unpadded steel side of the vehicle. The scarf with which she had veiled herself had fallen away and in the glow of the compass light Rivas could see the soft, curving lines of her face, the sleep-slackened shape of her mouth and dark line of her brows. Not for the first time in the last few hours, Rivas wondered what she was seeking in this company and in this place. He was intensely conscious of the occasional pressure of her thigh against his as the command car lurched on the uneven terrain.

Like Cole, Rivas was a man of strong sexuality. But unlike his dead half brother, Rivas had disciplined himself against the use of sex as an anodyne for real or imagined failure. His Mexican paternity with its double-standard value system made it difficult for Rivas ever to accept completely the sexual license of his generation. Unwilling to be celibate, Rivas had made the only possible accommodation with his time: he had limited his affairs to women with whom he could be friends and upon whom he could not in conscience place the burden of fidelity. It was this restraint, rather than (as he had by this time permitted himself to believe) his uncertain and dangerous profession, that had kept him a bachelor. One of the concomitants of this basically sterile life-style had come to be the unease with which he regarded any strong attachment to any woman he did not know well.

Amira Shallai, in the few hours he had been near her, had disturbed Michael Rivas considerably. Physically she was more voluptuous and overtly *female* than the women who shared his beds. But beyond this, he was disturbed by an element of innocence, of vulnerability, that he sensed in her—and which reason told him simply could not exist. Not here. Not under these conditions.

He shifted his grip on the M-16 between his knees and looked away from the sleeping woman. Good God, he told himself, this is no time or place to be mooning like a child in his first attack of puberty over a woman he had known for fewer than twenty-four hours. He owed it to Cole to keep his wits about him, and Dr. Shallai was a distraction he did not need.

The inflamed ugliness of the predawn sky was changing into a growing daylight. The streaks of dusty dark caused by the high layer of sand still in the air were blending into a mottled blaze of brilliance from the sun, which still lay below the horizon. The dunes had begun to take on a roseate glow of reflected morning.

Colonel Hadfield said quietly, 'The sandstorms are done for a few days.' The Briton had not spoken for hours, but the advancing brightness seemed to have thawed his cold reserve somewhat.

'How much farther to the station, Colonel?' Rivas asked.

'Thirty miles,' Hadfield said. 'Another hour.'

Rivas looked up at the sky. 'Could we have flown in after all?'

'Possibly,' Hadfield said. 'It doesn't matter. Sometimes it is better to know this country from down here. A man should get the taste of it.'

It was obvious that the old Trucial Scout officer loved the desert with a passion. 'The Rub' al Khali is larger than your state of Texas, Hayden. We are only nicking the edge of it. A million square miles of this.' His voice took on an edge. 'There's more oil under us than ever came out of Arabia. More than ever *will* come out, thank God.'

'Are they looking for oil at EQ Station?' Rivas asked.

Hadfield turned to stare and Rivas knew that he had made a blunder. Of course, any man signed on with 'the Brigade' would know that whatever was being done at EQ Station did not directly concern a search for oil. Rivas, silent, cursed his own weary carelessness.

'When did you say Wyndham found you?' Colonel Hadfield asked.

'I didn't say, Colonel,' Rivas said cautiously. 'Actually, I didn't spend much time with Ian. I was late, remember?'

Hadfield looked long at Rivas, his expression unreadable in the half-darkness. 'I have been meaning to ask you,' he said. 'Why, exactly, were you late? The others managed to get to Salalah on schedule.'

Rivas met his glance and said deliberately, 'I was in jail, Colonel. I was on my way to Kingswear in plenty of time, but I was picked up for driving with liquor on my breath. Your countrymen are touchy about that. I spent two nights in Canterbury jail. All right?' He let the defiance in his voice grow as he imagined Captain Hayden would have done.

Colin Hadfield, accustomed by a lifetime of military service to accept alcoholism as the source of endless troubles among soldiers, was deflected onto familiar ground. 'There is no liquor at EQ Station, Hayden. Not for the guard force. You had better understand that.'

'Wyndham explained that,' Rivas said, letting his tone go sullen. 'You don't have to go into it again.'

The grizzled brows descended, almost masking the narrowed eyes. 'Colonel,' Hadfield said.

'Colonel,' Rivas said, 'Sir.'

'You are part of a military unit, Hayden. Don't let the lack of a flag confuse you. Discipline is the heart of the Brigade.'

There it was again, Rivas thought: the almost mystical emphasis on 'the Brigade.'

The woman's eyes were open, fixed on the two men with intense, silent interest. She had been listening to the exchange, that was plain. What did 'the Brigade' mean to her?

Hadfield turned away from Rivas and murmured a few words of dialect to the driver, who pointed briefly at the brightening horizon. Rivas followed the gesture and saw a low structure darkly etched against the growing light. It was a concrete block not more than three by six feet, too low for any human habitation. Atop the block stood a stubby antenna. The whole was surrounded by a wire-mesh fence half submerged in drifted sand.

Colonel Hadfield reached into a compartment and extracted a black metal box. He pressed the single button on the box and returned it to its place.

'IFF, Colonel?' Rivas asked.

'Yes,' Hadfield said shortly.

It came suddenly to Rivas that the convoy was passing through some kind of defensive zone. The sand dunes must conceal mines, only that would explain Hadfield's action with the transponder. EQ Station, Rivas thought with a chill, did not depend simply on mercenaries dragooned out of Africa and Europe for protection of its southern flank.

Rivas wondered what would happen if—or when—errant nomads passed this way to raid their neighbors. But perhaps they no longer did. One sudden death would be more than enough to make this place taboo to the Raschid.

From the automatic sensor station, the convoy took a bearing of 015° and continued through the rolling dunes at reduced speed. The sky was now swiftly turning red-orange, the streaks of darkness vanishing in the growing blaze of light. The limb of the rising sun touched the edge of the desert and suddenly all semblance of the fetid dawn had changed into a brilliance that was like a shower of diamond spears. Even Amira Shallai, who must certainly have been no stranger to desert sunrises, drew in her breath at the splendid sight.

Hadfield's face was ruddy in the light. His expression was rapt. Once again, Rivas was struck by the way in which the old soldier regarded the wilderness through which they moved: possessively, with protective concern. Rivas would not have been totally surprised to hear him quote Omar: *Wake! For the Sun who scattered into flight/The Stars before him from the Field of Night. . . .*

Rivas looked again at Amira Shallai and was surprised to find that she was smiling at him. It was a strange and moving moment as the three intruders and the mute Arab shared the dawn.

The sun pushed higher on the horizon and as it did they were given one last display of wonder. The level rays danced and glittered from the silicates in the sand, so that it seemed that the dunes had been transformed into a rolling sea of tiny diamonds.

'It's going,' Amira said with quiet regret. In seconds the shimmering sand had become sand again and the touch of the sun a furnace's breath. The sky faded into a colorless glare streaked with the last mare's tails of dust from the dying storms. To the north the air seemed clearer, but still without color. Rivas felt the sweat start on his neck and arms. By the time the sun's limb had cleared the horizon completely, the woman and the two men had hidden their eyes behind dark sand goggles and reerected the barriers that had momentarily fallen.

It was almost exactly one hour after dawn when the command car, laboring in the deep sand, crested a dune higher than the others, turned sharply right, and came to a stop. The vehicles behind closed up and the three machines paused, the sound of their engines an alien rumble in the desert stillness.

A mile ahead Rivas could see EQ Station. He was stunned by the size of the place. He knew that it had been built on an abandoned Saudi air base, but he was not prepared for the size and complexity of what he saw rising out of the desert.

The old buildings had fallen into disrepair, savaged by the winds and blowing sand of the Empty Quarter. But new raw concrete-block structures appeared to have mushroomed from the dunes. Rivas could see at the far edge of the station, fully a mile and a half from where the convoy had paused, what appeared to be a cooling tower for a nuclear power station. Grouped around it were a number of blocky structures whose roofs were a jumble of antennae and communications dishes. On what had once been the parking ramp near the wide runway—a vast plain of ferroconcrete whose outline was blurred by the thin dusting of thousands of tiny sand dunes—a long, low building had been erected, at the northern end of which stood a five-hundred-foot spire that could be nothing but a television transmitter's antenna. This was flanked by two large parabolic radars whose angles indicated to Rivas that they were, even at this moment, tracking satellites—or some other object far above the featureless sky.

In addition to the buildings Rivas could see from his vantage point on the dune, there were concrete entrances let into what appeared to be mounds and sand dunes, but which, on closer scrutiny, were not sand structures at all, but solid hillocks made of poured concrete.

The cost of erecting all of these buildings in this remote spot, Rivas thought, had to be enormous. He had seen active military air bases that did not have one-half the scale of EQ Station.

Revetments and hangars had been built into the sand along the main runway, all of them constructed so as to be invisible from the air. A number of helicopters stood on the concrete hardstands, though the overwhelming impression of the place was of a base awaiting a large, very large, contingent of aircraft. Bomber bases in England during the war must have looked like this, Rivas thought, while the squadrons who lived on them were away bombing Germany. The place was far larger than any old bomber field Rivas had ever visited, but the *feel* of the place was the same.

On the hardstand before the low building housing the television equipment stood a Lockheed TriStar. Even at this distance Rivas could see that its paint had been scarred and stripped from flying through a sandstorm. Whoever had arrived aboard that airplane, Rivas thought, had had a miserable ride.

Most of the roads that had once connected the various sections of the old Saudi base lay under drifts of sand and had an abandoned look. But the perimeter fencing was new, and to judge from the insulators along the top of it, electrified. Despite its isolation, EQ Station was not a hospitable oasis. Quite the contrary. It was a fortress.

Then Rivas realized what it was that was lacking. People. From the top of the dune he could see a single file of what appeared to be men in NPC uniform patrolling the fence. But on the ramp, on the roads, and around the buildings, hardly a living being could be seen. A pair of technicians seemed to be making adjustments to one of the radar dishes on the rooftop, but that was all.

'Welcome to EQ Station,' Hadfield said.

Amira Shallai said, 'It is larger than I expected it to be.'

'And emptier,' Rivas said.

The file of armed men had reached a gate and were opening it, shoving against the drifted sand. Colonel Hadfield gave a signal and the convoy left the dune and descended toward the fence-line.

Rivas noted as they approached that the men carried Uzis and were commanded by what appeared to be an officer. There was certainly no question whatever that this base was a military establishment. Rivas glanced at Amira to judge her reaction. After all, she had some experience of NPC stations, though he doubted she had ever seen one quite like this.

At the gate, the officer signaled the command car to stop. When he spoke, there was a heavy German accent mingled with his English. Germans, Britons, South Africans, Americans, Rivas considered. A multinational force—part of 'the Brigade'?

'Welcome home, Colin,' the officer said. 'Good journey?'

'Uneventful,' Hadfield said.

The young German studied Amira carefully, and then gave his attention to Rivas. Hadfield had descended from the command car and the German walked a short distance away toward the gate with him, speaking urgently.

Hadfield turned and stared at Rivas. Amira Shallai watched the proceedings with interest. Rivas felt a cold and spreading chill as the German raised his Uzi, seemingly as if by inadvertence, so that the muzzle pointed directly at him.

The two men returned to the car and Colonel Hadfield said coldly, 'Get down here.'

Rivas alighted, stretching his legs.

Hadfield put his hand on the M-16. 'You won't need that any longer.'

The young German, his face sunburned and peeling, stepped between Rivas and the car and spoke formally. 'Mr. Rivas,' he said. 'Michael Rivas.'

For a moment Rivas was tempted to argue, to attempt to deny. But it was obvious that the young German knew exactly to whom he was speaking.

'Mr. Rivas, you will please come with me. I regret the necessity, but you are being detained.'

30 Moscow

In the fifth sub-basement of the GRU computer center under Arbatskaya Square, Academician Yelena Markarova bent diligently over her computer terminal.

Yelena was a product of the Party schools and of Leningrad University, a computer specialist who had spent more than ten years in the service of the Military Intelligence Directorate of the Soviet General Staff. She was a tall, colorless woman without great ambitions, but gifted with a mind capable of deriving much pleasure from the collection of old and obscure facts. Her personal hobby was writing computer programs based on the great chess games of history: programs that would never be run and which would serve no purpose if they were. But it pleased Yelena to know that in the fifth game of the famous Korchnoi-Karpov match in the Philippines, Korchnoi achieved his first mate with a move of N4 x P. Hers was a mind that relished detail.

Her official task in the fifth sub-basement at Arbatskaya Square was the preparation of the African section of the daily intelligence précis circulated among the officers of the General Staff. This document was usually fifty or more pages long and Yelena sometimes suspected it was not read very carefully by the busy men for whom it was intended. But her Party training had conditioned Yelena not to question the habits of persons in authority. Her job was to produce the African section of the précis. If it was not studied carefully, that was regrettable but not her concern. Meticulously and with an almost religious diligence she sifted the reports pouring into the computer center. She selected those within her purview, fed them into the computer, and then digested the output into the daily précis.

The raw intelligence data were gleaned by the thousands of informers and agents comprising the Glavoyne Razvedyvatelnoye Upravleniye networks set up by Soviet military attachés all over the world. These networks differed from the ordinary KGB operations in the specialized character of the information they sought. While KGB's Moscow Center scooped in information with a broad shovel, the Military Intelligence Directorate used a trowel, daintily selecting all those scattered facts that could conceivably be of specific interest to the military.

Yelena's selections were made exclusively on a geographical basis. She was not called upon to evaluate the information. That was the task of others more qualified.

She was now halfway through her shift at the computer console and she had collected all the day's material with her customary diligence. Now the digested précis was appearing on the display and Yelena prepared to type the final product.

In Africa it had been a quiet twenty-four hours. The attachés in the black People's Republics of the dark continent had found little they would consider of interest to the men and women of Arbatskaya Square. A change of defense ministers seemed imminent in Angola, but the new man shared the approved Moscow line and no substantive changes in military policy were expected.

In the Sudan, where Russians were not yet dominant, a member of the attaché's staff had been refused permission to visit the west coast. The attaché had made a formal protest and would renew the application for permission at a later time.

The new Soviet naval facilities being built at Mesewa in the People's Republic of Ethiopia were now eight months behind schedule and would not be prepared to service the fleet's nuclear submarines until next March.

The next item aroused Yelena's interest slightly more than the preceding ones simply because it originated in Zimbabwe, with whom the Soviet Union had official diplomatic relations, but concerned South Africa, with whom the USSR had none.

The air attaché of the Soviet embassy in Salisbury received information from South Africa by a circuitous route, but his information was generally accurate, if rather dull. He reported that thirty old Hercules transport aircraft had filed a flight plan to fly to Karachi from Johannesburg. These airplanes, the attaché in Salisbury reported, had been converted to spray aerosols at a plant in Germiston, where much conversion work was performed on airplanes purchased by the NPC. A point of technical interest to the attaché, a young Soviet Air Force colonel, was that these Hercules were the largest aircraft ever converted for use as spray planes. He believed that the craft would be used to spray insecticides in the Indus Valley, where, it was rumored, an epidemic of malaria was raging. The government of Pakistan, however, denied this.

The Hercules, Yelena noted in her copy of *Jane's*, was the C-130 troop carrier of the United States Air Force, long since replaced by the larger and swifter C-5A. The aircraft, declared surplus by the Americans, had been purchased in great numbers by Third World governments for military use and by the NPC, to whom these particular Hercules belonged, as cargo carriers and general-purpose transports.

With that bit of information put into the computer, Yelena made some corrections and emendations on the screen with a light-pencil, and waited for the end of the run.

When the computer signaled, she fed a sheaf of GRU classified intelligence forms into the hopper and began swiftly to type the day's précis.

31 Ar Rub' al Khali

Through the glare-bright day the helicopters, ninety of them, all painted the color of desert sand and bearing no markings, flew west. The interior of the lead machine was laden with military stores and weapons. The door gunners manned their mini-guns and the other occupants sat hunched over their gear, each man lost in his own thoughts.

The sun, hazed by a high layer of dust in the air from the recent *khamseen*, burned through the Plexiglas panels with a searing intensity. The aircraft flew low, less than a thousand feet above the sea in a salty haze that softened the light but seemed to magnify the heat. Ahead could be seen the thin brown line of the Arabian coast, the guardian range of bare hills etched hard against the white of the eastern sky.

In any military operation, General Collingwood thought, there is a time of maximum risk. This was not always the moment of commitment to battle. That particular moment's risk was balanced by the possible successes to be achieved. The greatest risk came when the force entered the time frame in which it could be surprised and destroyed while engaged in a necessary action not directly related to an assault on the objective.

For the ninety helicopters of the Brigade's forward echelon, the moment began now, as the aircraft entered Arabian air space. It would continue throughout the remainder of this day while the force assembled at a desert salt pan called Al Mubarraz, where the helicopters would have to be refueled from previously dispatched tanker aircraft.

Nightfall would decrease the danger marginally, but the helicopters would remain on the ground and vulnerable until 3.00 A.M. local time, at which time the final approach to Riyadh would begin, timed to arrive thirty minutes before dawn.

Collingwood's plan was committed to memory by every officer and soldier in the assault force: the helicopters would approach the city from the south, the force would divide into two sections, one of which would take possession of the international airport north of the city and secure it for the arrival of the remainder of the Brigade in Hercules transports. The smaller section of the assault force would land directly in the American embassy compound, in the grounds and on the roof of the main embassy building, to secure the hostages. This section, with Collingwood in personal command, would hold the embassy compound until troops from the airport could clear the route between the embassy and the airfield. The entire force would then withdraw by air, supported by a squadron of Kfir and Panavia Tornado fighters flying directly to Riyadh from the base at Tokar.

Collingwood and the staff had pondered for some time the advisability of making this first move across the Red Sea in daylight. But it was absolutely necessary to stage the assault force at the Al Mubarraz salt pan, since it was the only natural lake bed that would support the landing weight of the KC-10 tanker needed to refuel the helicopters. Collingwood, Stuart, and Cory Conant, who was the Brigade's expert on air operations at forward bases, had finally agreed that the salt pan would be too difficult to find in darkness without the use of radio. The fiasco of Desert One was in their memories; no unconventional-warfare specialist had ever forgotten it. It had become famous as a horrible example of bad planning and worse execution—an operation almost designed to fail tragically, as it had.

So the risks were weighed and the decision made. The helicopter-borne assault force would cross the Red Sea and hide in the wilderness until the morning of July 18, the day selected for the attack on Riyadh. Collingwood was well aware that though the remnants of the once formidable Royal Saudi Air Force lay in neglected bits and pieces on hangar floors at the northern air bases, it was remotely possible that there were still enough flyable aircraft available to Pan-Arabian radical converts to raise the risk factor from none to negligible. But the true threat came from satellite surveillance. The end of the *khamseen,* which had made it possible to begin the operation, had also stripped the cover from it. Collingwood's intelligence sources informed him that no United States satellite currently watched the Arabian

Peninsula. But the Soviets surely did. In fact, at this moment, Collingwood thought, the movement of his ninety helicopters was probably being photographed by a Cosmos.

But Collingwood had spent enough years in the Army to know that the information would first have to be recorded by the satellite in space. It would then be recalled by a ground station in the Soviet Union. Next it would have to be reconstituted from its digital form into analog—photographs and heat-sensor readings. These data would then have to be examined and evaluated by photo-intelligence officers. These officers would then buck the information up to their superiors, who would do the same with theirs, until it reached the Soviet General Staff level, at least—possibly higher. Then, and only then, could the Soviets begin to decide what, exactly, they intended to do—if anything—about an attempt—albeit a belated one—by some Western government to take the hostages from the radicals in Riyadh.

All of this bureaucratic, military, and political paper-shuffling could not take less than twelve hours; perhaps it would take considerably more when one included the time necessary for accusatory diplomatic exchanges between Moscow and the capitals of the West.

And if, at the end of that tangled trail, the Russians decided to interfere with the Brigade's operation, Collingwood thought grimly, they had better be prepared for a fight. He doubted that the Russian squadron now operating in the Arabian Sea had naval landing-force troops aboard. The main purpose of the Soviet naval presence was to harass the American task force in the area and worry the owners of the tankers that had, until recently, sailed in a steady stream out of the Strait of Hormuz for the Cape.

The American units in the Arabian Sea, however, included the nuclear carrier *Nimitz*. And she carried two battalions of Marines as part of her normal complement. It *was* conceivable that these troops could be used to interfere with the rescue operation and Collingwood did not relish the possibility that his men might find themselves shooting at American Marines. But this possibility was remote, he had concluded. Not only would it be militarily unwise, politically it would be suicidal. And, as Collingwood well knew, President Vincent Todd Loomis did nothing, ever, that might put his image at risk.

It was characteristic of Jeb Collingwood that he gave almost no thought whatever to the political repercussions in Europe of what the Brigade was about to do. His instinct told him that the people of the West, and this included the American people as well, would probably applaud the Brigade if the operation was a success. They would be unaware, or uncaring, of the fact that a new force had suddenly appeared on the world scene. They would simply agree that the Brigade—and by extension the NPC—had done only what their own governments should have done and were afraid to do.

All of these considerations faded swiftly as the leading elements of the assault group cleared the low hills and struck out into the desert.

The formation flew in two stepped files, one destined for each of the assigned targets. In practice operations the pilots had become accustomed to this formation and it was being used on the flight in to Al Mubarraz to add a final polish to the operational plan.

Collingwood moved from his seat beside the pilot into the rear with the gunners. The helicopters were nearly new Bell H-120s, each carrying ten soldiers in addition to the necessary light weaponry and ammunition.

Collingwood knelt in the door with the wind tearing at his flak jacket. The door gunner, a young Australian with a fringe of sandy curls spilling out from under his helmet, grinned nervously at his commander. Collingwood smiled back and squeezed the boy's shoulder. The hot wind felt as though it were scouring his face but he knew that there was nowhere on earth he would rather be at this moment than here, on his way to war with his troops.

The ground below was mottled brown and dun, the color of a buckskin horse. The rocky earth was giving way to the frozen waves of the sand sea and the shadows of the low-flying helicopters rose and dipped, in silent flight across the dunes.

A dozen yards from the open door, across the howling emptiness, hung Peter Stuart's command chopper. Collingwood could see Stuart grinning at him from his place beside the pilot. The door gunner was a black man and he, too, was grinning, his teeth white against the blackness of his skin.

Stuart's file was the group that would take and hold the

airport for the arrival of the Hercules transports with the remainder of the Brigade. There had actually been trading going on in the huts at Tokar, Collingwood knew, men bargaining for places in the helicopter assault teams. It filled him with a soldier's pride and confirmed something he had always secretly believed: that true professional soldiers fought for the unit, the squad, the regiment far more willingly than they did for some fantasy of patriotism. Perhaps, he thought, it was a product of the time into which these men had been born. The great ideals had all been proven to be dross. The fine-sounding words the politicians liked to use had turned out to be wind and not substance. When Jack Kennedy had said that Americans would bear any burden, confront any enemy, in the defense of liberty he may well have meant it. But if he had, Collingwood thought, he had been almost alone. When it became apparent that his words meant being bloodied in the jungles of Vietnam, the heart had gone out of a generation. Except, Collingwood thought, for some few of those who had done the actual fighting. They had kept the faith—if not with some vague ideal of patriotism, at least with one another. Those who had done that and survived had become soldiers, by God. And some of them were here, ready to do what professional soldiers always did. Pull the bloody chestnuts out of the fire. Collingwood felt the air in his lungs and sucked in the smells of war: wool and sweat, oil and cordite and high-test gasoline and the dusty tang of a strange land flowing past the open door. He was filled with such joy that he felt like crying out in triumph.

He looked up and out at the white emptiness of the sky and then down at the sandy emptiness of the sand sea. For the first time in months he relaxed totally and allowed himself to savor the moment.

32 EQ Station

The room in which Rivas found himself confined was one of a block that had been originally built to house the instructor pilots when Ibrahimah had been used by the Royal Saudi Air Force. It was a long, low structure made of concrete bricks now much weathered by blowing sand. It contained some twenty individual rooms opening into a narrow hallway. The floors were of cement dusted with the ever-present sand. As Rivas was escorted through the barracks he could see that most of the rooms stood empty and abandoned.

The West German Corpsman who guarded him was uncommunicative and refused to answer any of Rivas's questions about the base, about the authorities' intentions, or about the reason for Rivas's confinement.

Now a single Corpsman stood outside Rivas's door, an Uzi machine pistol slung over his shoulder, and Rivas prowled the small room, sand gritting under his desert boots.

The cubicle had been furnished—hastily, it appeared—with a cot, a table, and a television set which was either broken or connected only to some cable system presently inoperative.

A bank of clerestory windows set high in the back wall let in the light and from time to time a speaker grille above the door—part of the air base's public-address system, Rivas surmised—crackled but emitted no intelligible sound.

He lay down on the cot, aching with weariness and a desire to sleep. Failure lay like a foul taste on his tongue. He had done again exactly what Cole had accused him of doing all those long years ago in the Laotian highlands. He had made emotional judgments and rash decisions.

At this bleak moment the memory of that time seemed so clear that it might have been yesterday. Rivas had been living with the Meo far up-country, building a part of the secret native army the Agency supported. He had grown too close to the tribesmen and their families. He had done what Cole, his Case Officer down in Bangkok, called 'gone gook.'

When the collapse was imminent, the Agency had begun to cut its losses, pulling the advisers out and leaving the tribesmen to face the North Vietnamese invaders alone. That was when Rivas had mutinied, refusing to leave his people. And Cole had arrived on one of the black Air America airplanes with two Company hoods from Bangkok. 'Brother or not,' he had said, 'you'll come out now or we grease you on the spot. I am not leaving any Agency people behind to get themselves captured and put on display by the NVA.' And Rivas had known beyond doubting that Cole had meant exactly what he said.

A week later, Rivas had found himself in Washington and out of the Agency. He had never again seen his brother alive.

And for fifteen years, Rivas thought, he had liked it that way. Yet here he was, in the middle of one of the world's last wildernesses, because Cole had written him a letter. *Hermano,* he thought, even with one of us dead we are still a sorry combination.

He awoke with a start, conscious of a change in his surroundings. The angle of the light was different, the yellow sun of afternoon slanting now into the tiny room through the clerestory windows to form a bar of light on the opposite wall.

Through the concrete brick walls came the sound of aircraft engines. Not jets—propeller-driven airplanes. They were landing and there were many of them.

He dragged the table to the wall and stood on it. He could just see over the high windowsill through the thick, wired glass that was dulled and pitted by the wind-driven sand.

The building in which he was confined backed onto the neglected taxiways of the airfield. Beyond them lay the main runway and beyond that a row of the underground bunkers he had glimpsed from outside the perimeter fence.

But the airfield that had been all but deserted that morning was now swarming with sudden activity. A line of old Hercules C-130 transports was forming before the mouths of the underground bunkers. Other Hercules were landing on the main runway at close intervals. As each aircraft turned off the runway it was taxied to the end of the line at the bunkers.

Suddenly an iron voice spoke from the grille above the door, startling him and seizing his attention.

The announcement was first made in French, then in Italian, then in Arabic, and finally in English.

'All newly arrived medical personnel will report to Dr. Clevenger's laboratory for briefing. At once.'

There was a pause and then the announcement was repeated, again in four languages. Rivas waited for more, but the grille fell silent. Frowning, Rivas returned to his view from the sand-scarred window.

As the aircraft joined the line at the bunkers, the flight crews—three to an airplane—were collected in personnel carriers and driven off, leaving the Hercules in the hands of other persons, all of whom wore yellow radiation suits. Rivas watched with increasing apprehension.

The yellow-suited crews, looking like spacemen, opened the cargo bays of the aircraft and entered the cavernous interiors dragging thick, cable-reinforced hoses that led back into the bunkers. Rivas rubbed at the dirty glass, trying for a clearer view. Each bunker, which must have once been an underground hangar for a Saudi fighter but was now obviously being used for some other purpose, was marked with a sign that Rivas could not read at this distance. But he could recognize the radiation-warning trefoil easily enough. His mouth felt dry.

The sun lay close to the horizon and the men working on the aircraft cast long, ominous shadows. From time to time a spear of reflected light would glint from the faceplates of the protective suits. Rivas shivered. Whatever was being loaded into the Hercules must be highly radioactive.

The aircraft themselves looked strange, unlike any others of the type Rivas had seen over the years. But there *was* something familiar about their appearance. The undersides of the broad wings were latticed with plumbing and Rivas recognized it in a flash of memory. The airplanes used to spray Agent Orange onto the jungles of Vietnam had carried similar equipment thinner and less complex, but very like what he was looking at now.

These airplanes had been modified to spray some heavier compound. Something, Rivas thought with a shudder, far deadlier.

He dropped to the floor from the table and stood breathless for a moment as the adrenaline pumped through his system. Cole had been right about the New Peace Corps—but he had not gone nearly far enough. What was happening here was more ominous than even he could have imagined.

Rivas moved to the door and listened. He tried the knob and it turned. He drew a deep breath and slowly opened the door to look directly into the muzzle of an Uzi. His guard had been changed, but the swarthy face that regarded him over the sight of the machine pistol was no friendlier.

Rivas said, 'Why am I being held?'

There was no response, only a slight gesture with the weapon. The man was lean, clean-shaven except for a drooping mustache. The eyes were small and dark brown, expressionless as the eyes of a basilisk.

'¿ Porqué me han hecho preso?' Rivas demanded.

Again the gesture to retreat, nothing more. Rivas tried Italian and then limping German and French. The muzzle of the Uzi touched Rivas's chest and pushed him back into the room. Rivas surrendered and sat down on the cot, his mind racing desperately. When the door closed Rivas went to one knee examining the table on which he had been standing. It was of metal, the legs secured by rusted bolts that he could not move.

He turned back the thin mattress on the cot and examined the springs. They were of tempered steel that could never be twisted free with bare fingers.

He sat frustrated and filled with dread. His reflection stared back at him from the blank face of the television set.

Suddenly he heard activity in the hallway. Voices and the footsteps of many men. He came to his feet as the door burst open and two new men in the uniform of the NPC came into the room. They, like all the guards, carried Uzis.

A third man appeared in the doorway: a thin, aged man with skin as fine and transparent as parchment, and pallid blue eyes. He, too, wore the familiar desert twill bush jacket with the rainbow flash at the shoulders. It hung loosely on his spare, stooped frame.

'Mr. Rivas? I am Calder Davis. I have something to say to you.'

33 EQ Station

Huddled in the cargo bay of the NPC Nomad, Dr. Cecil Sawyer felt the change in pressure and altitude as the airplane started its descent into EQ Station. The Nomad was an Australian-built turbofan light-cargo carrier and few concessions had been made for the comfort of the occasional passengers. It was piloted by two Sikhs in NPC uniform, taciturn men who had not thought it worthwhile to carry on even a cursory conversation with either of the occupants of the rear cabin.

Cecil Sawyer was grateful for being ignored. He was accustomed to being regarded lightly and though he had convinced himself that he should resent such treatment, he would have been agitated by any special attention from strangers now.

Ever since his talk with Helmuth Reich at Naziat, his nerves had been stretched to the breaking point. What was worse, his eidetic memory made each and every incident since that time impossible to forget or even to put into perspective.

His traveling companion, apparently American, had boarded the NPC airplane, as he himself had done, at Bahrain. The name stenciled on the navy-blue military-style canvas suitcase he carried was H. GRANT. He was a large man, heavily muscled, with cropped sandy-gray hair and a face that looked as though the skin had been stretched over rock. His eyes were almost colorless and were never still. Coming as he did from the industrial Midlands of England, Cecil Sawyer had no personal acquaintance with hunters, but H. Grant's unblinking stare was a look Sawyer associated with policemen of a peculiarly vicious sort—the black-uniformed constables who kept order in the industrial slums of the cities where he had spent his youth.

What set Sawyer's nerves to jangling, and what he could

not induce his flypaper mind to forget, was that as H. Grant climbed aboard the Nomad, Cecil had caught a glimpse of a slim commando knife strapped to the large man's massive leg.

It was possible, indeed even probable, Sawyer thought, that travelers in the wild parts of the world—and the Rub' al Khali certainly qualified as one of these—habitually went armed. Still the combination of the terrible knife and the unblinking eyes made Mr. Grant an unpleasant traveling companion.

Plagued by a neurotic fear that the flight to EQ Station might depart without him, Sawyer had climbed aboard the Nomad a full hour before the announced takeoff time. He had sat sweltering amid the bundles of strapped-down cargo. Grant had come aboard with the pilots, had taken his place across from Sawyer, and had not uttered a sound during the six-hundred-kilometer flight. Worried as he was about Amira's peril and frightened for his own safety, Cecil Sawyer decided he would be very glad to see the back of H. Grant the moment the airplane deposited them on the ground at EQ Station. The company of sinister fellow travelers was certainly company he could do without, even though he faced arrival at the infamous desert station with lonely apprehension.

How quickly, he wondered, could he find Amira? EQ Station, the NPC people in Bahrain had told him, was on an immense half-abandoned air base. The hospital staff outnumbered all the other units there—and that had set him to wondering why such a thing should be so and whether or not it would be possible to locate Amira at all within the twenty-four-hour limit set by Reich.

How great was her danger, really? And finally, would she *listen* to him, take him seriously enough to abandon whatever dark work she had been sent into the Rub' al Khali to do?

He stole a glance at the man across the aisle. Could he be a Black Septembrist? It didn't seem likely, but just because he appeared to be an American didn't absolutely make him one. There was just no way of knowing. Not for the first time in the last forty-eight hours, Dr. Cecil Sawyer felt like a man out of his depth and in danger of drowning.

When, after a long time circling, the Nomad touched down and came to a stop on the ramp of the old air base, Cecil Sawyer waited until his companion had walked down the steps to the ground before moving himself. He lifted his totally unsuitable plastic traveling case and stood in the door of the aircraft blinking into the hot glare of the westering sun.

An open vehicle was waiting, H. Grant already sitting beside the driver and staring at Sawyer with an expression that had changed from frigid disinterest while aboard the airplane to equally frigid impatience now.

Sawyer hurried down to the concrete and threw his case into the rear of the vehicle. He climbed in with haste enough to bark his shin painfully on the sun-hot metal. The driver was a black man wearing a uniform similar to Cecil Sawyer's own. And Sawyer noted with a shock that he was armed. He had never before seen a New Peace Corpsman carrying a weapon and the sight left him open mouthed.

The car started and drove across the broad expanse of concrete toward what had once been an administration building. Painted across the face of the building in fading letters was the legend *Ibrahimah*, and the elevation, *860 meters*. The name and elevation were repeated in Arabic cursive.

He looked around him and noted an American Lockheed parked nearby. It was painted in the colors of the ConEn Corporation, though the paint appeared to have been scoured away in a number of places and the pilot's cockpit windscreens were missing. No work was being done on the large, three-engined jet. It had a curiously abandoned look.

But behind him, and on the far side of the huge runway, Sawyer could see a great deal of activity. A long line of dun-colored aircraft bearing no markings at all were being swarmed over by large crews wearing yellow overalls and glassine-faced helmets. Sawyer frowned in perplexity. As a radiologist he was perfectly familiar with antiradiation suits. They were seldom used in ordinary medical operation, but researchers working in nuclear medicine sometimes needed such protection. He had heard through the NPC grapevine that there were nuclear power experiments going on at EQ Station, but he could not imagine how some thirty aircraft could possibly have become contaminated enough to require that their crews wear antirad clothing.

As the car drew up before the administration building, Sawyer heard someone call his name. It was so unexpected that it took him a moment to respond. Around the open door of a hutlike building of the ubiquitous concrete brick stood a group of men, some in NPC uniform, others wearing various bits of flying gear. Apparently they were being fed inside the building, though it seemed unlikely that it had originally served as a messhall.

One of the men left the group and approached Sawyer. It took the doctor a moment to put the man in context, but once that had been accomplished, he recalled his name at once. It was Clark. He was an Australian and it had been he who had flown the Nomad that had carried Sawyer from Marseilles to Cairo when he had been first assigned to Kalabishah Station. Jock Clark. Now Sawyer remembered him perfectly: one of the hundreds of pilots in NPC service, men who flew personnel and cargo to all the out-of-the-way places where New Peace Corpsmen worked.

'Let me out, please,' Sawyer said. 'There's a chap I know.'

The driver said shortly, 'You've already missed the medical briefing, doctor. My instructions are to take you directly to Dr. Clevenger.'

Reinforced by the obviously friendly greeting from the pilot, Sawyer said what he would never have said in other circumstances. 'I will find the administrator directly myself. Just drop me off here.' He did not think to wonder if his action was, subconsciously, an escape from the silent company of the intimidating H. Grant. He got out of the vehicle and waved it off with what he hoped was a commanding gesture. He was, after all, a professional man and the driver must certainly be no more than some sort of policeman—why else would he be carrying a weapon?

'Sawyer, isn't it?' the pilot asked. 'What are you doing here, doc?' Red-faced under a baseball cap with the NPC rainbow on it, Clark was carrying a sandwich in one hand and a can of Coca-Cola in the other. He lifted the Coke and said, 'Would you believe no beer?'

'Hello, Jock,' Sawyer said. 'How nice to see a familiar face.'

'And you, doc. Haven't seen you since Cairo.'

'Are you stationed here?' Sawyer asked.

'Not bloody likely, mate,' Clark said. 'We just flew those

old crocks in from Joburg.' He gestured at the queue of aircraft across the field.

Sawyer turned to look again at the airplanes and their yellow-armored attendants. He was a trifle alarmed by Clark's airy comment. 'You aren't going to fly them out, surely?'

Clark shook his head emphatically. 'The minute the yellow jackets took them over we were told to keep our bloody distance. Now we're just waiting for them to unload that Nomad you came in on and it's out of this armpit and off to Salalah, then everyone scatters for home leave. One glorious month in Perth for me, doc.'

Sawyer frowned, sensing that he had come upon something quite out of the ordinary. Did this have some bearing on the reason Amira was sent to this place? He asked, 'Are there pilots enough left here to fly those aircraft?'

'If there are, better them than me, mate. Those are bloody strange kites.' He stepped closer to Sawyer and said confidentially, 'I've been flying for ten years, doc. The last four for the NP bloody C. And I've never seen Hercs set up like those are. Television cameras built into the nose, black boxes everywhere, and then all the tanks and spraying equipment—heavy stuff, doc. We were within fifteen percent of maximum gross when we took off from Joburg this morning. And the tanks inside were bloody empty. Before we took off there were boffins crawling all over the kites. Now that lot—' He nodded at the rad-suited crews. 'No thanks, doc. Not for me. I'm for Perth and all the beer I can drink in a month. . . .'

A voice behind Sawyer spoke in clipped British tones. 'Dr. Sawyer?'

Cecil Sawyer turned to face a grizzled man wearing an Arab headdress and a worn NPC tunic decorated with faded military ribbons.

'My name is Hadfield, doctor. You are due for a special briefing now. Come with me.'

At that moment Sawyer was startled by a sudden hissing roar from somewhere beyond the low dunes to the west of the base. He looked up to see what appeared to be an aircraft approaching on a course that would have taken it low across the airfield. But that was only a swift impression, because a dark sliver of metal streaming fire and white smoke lanced up out of the desert to meet the oncoming jet.

There was a sullen crumping sound and where the aircraft had been there was now an expanding ball of oily flame and crazily spinning metal shards raining down. The fireball struck the ground near the base perimeter, crashed through the fence in a bounding confusion of fire and dust, and finally came to rest against an old and empty revetment, where it lay burning and crackling and sending a column of greasy smoke high into the still desert air.

34 Washington, D.C.

A deeply perturbed Raymond Turner stood at the window of his office in the Department of State and watched the Soviet Ambassador alighting from his car in the carriage entrance to the building. He had arrived in an immense Mercedes with CD plates and Turner wondered why it was that the diplomats of almost every nation represented in Washington, excepting, perhaps, the British, used the German machines instead of cars built in their own countries. Was there a message in that, he wondered, or was the sleepless night simply catching up with him and allowing his mind to dwell on absolutely inconsequential matters? He was well aware that deeply troubled people tend to avoid thinking of their problems by cluttering their thoughts with trivia.

Beyond the heavy plate glass, Washington sweltered in the summer midday. The air seemed to be thickened with the humidity rising from the Potomac. He thought, as he often had, that it would probably increase the quality of administration done if the nation were to leave Washington as a ceremonial capital and move the business of government to some other place, perhaps a site in the Rockies, where the air was bracing and there were fewer traditions.

Trivia again, he thought, rubbing his tired eyes. This was hardly a time to be thinking about Mercedes and broader horizons. Until three in the morning he had stayed by the President's side, examining intelligence reports and weighing options. The administration's position was now grotesque, with two members of the Cabinet under secret house arrest, the acting head of the CIA missing, and God only knew what explosion about to take place in Arabia. Little wonder that after a flurry of furious action the President had fallen into a paralysis of indecision. He was meeting at this minute with Carl Shepherd and his close aides in the administration.

It was a meeting at which Turner himself should have been present. He would certainly have attended; this was not the time to leave Vincent Loomis's side. But Turner had been urgently called back to the State Department when the Soviet Ambassador had demanded an emergency meeting.

Yevgeny Baturin was a typical high-level Soviet diplomat: aged, dedicated, capable of great charm or arrogant bad manners—depending on his instructions. He had been in Washington for almost seven years and probably knew the Americans as well as any Soviet *apparatchik* had ever known them. There were times when Turner even suspected Baturin of liking Americans, though this aberration had never softened the Russian's conviction that America was the Soviet Union's *glavni vrag*—the main enemy.

When Baturin was shown into the Secretary of State's office, Turner regarded his agitation with dread. Given the events of the past six days, he had been anticipating an angry visit from the Ambassador. It would have been too much to expect the Soviets not to follow up their peremptory hot-line message of the day before. Plainly, the soothing and totally ambiguous reply had not satisfied the men in the Kremlin.

Baturin's face was damp from the exertion of the short dash through the heat from car to air-conditioned building. He carried his customary attaché case—a prop which he had never opened in Secretary Turner's presence, his memory being sharp and precise.

'Mr. Ambassador,' Turner said. 'Please sit down.'

Baturin dropped his portly, well-tailored body into a chair and said, 'Mr. Secretary, I have matters of great seriousness to discuss.'

Turner favored him with a diplomatic smile and replied, 'I always regard my talks with you seriously, Yevgeny.'

Baturin made an excited gesture that indicated he was not interested in amenities this day. 'I have been instructed by my government to say first that the message received by President Suslov from President Loomis was totally unresponsive and unsatisfactory.'

'I am sure the President will be sorry to hear that,' Turner said. 'But if you will recall the subject of President Suslov's inquiry was the New Peace Corps. This government does not control the NPC, nor is it privy to that organization's plans. President Suslov's questions might better have been addressed to others.'

Baturin looked genuinely pained and worried. He mopped his wet face with a handkerchief and said, 'Raymond, let us not start fencing, please. We both know that what happens in the Arabian Peninsula is of vital importance to the Soviet Union and the United States equally. In the interests of détente I ask you to conduct this discussion on a realistic basis.'

What would you say, Turner wondered, if I were to tell you that Calder Davis has decided, alone and in his infinite wisdom, somehow to stop the flow of oil out of that unhappy place? For years the bureaucrats in your country have planned to take that oil when they needed it. If we gave you the straight answer to your question, would you go to war? The thought moved a cold knot into the pit of the Secretary's stomach.

'Yevgeny,' Turner said. 'You and I are always realistic with one another. Nations who own twenty thousand nuclear warheads are never frivolous.' He rose from behind the broad antique desk and moved to the window, looking toward the White House. The midday traffic on the streets was heavy despite the tightening shortage of gasoline. Government workers and tourists mingled on the sidewalks. Heat shimmered from the pavements. The city looked the same, with its crowd of visitors and natives going about their business. But it was not the same. Events of the last week had stretched nerves, spread more than the customary number of rumors. The press corps was too experienced in the ways of Washington not to know that something unusual was happening. And in Washington, the unusual was cause for concern. Television crews loitered on the White House grounds waiting for the news—whatever it might be—to break. Or to leak. As it certainly must, soon.

Baturin said, 'I have been instructed to tell you, Raymond, that we are aware—and deeply concerned—about what is happening in the Empty Quarter of the Pan-Arabian People's Republic. . . .'

Turner's eyes hardened. 'You are a trifle premature, Ambassador. The United States recognizes no "People's Republic" in Arabia. We can hardly be expected to do so while a hundred Western diplomats are illegally held hostage there.'

Baturin drove on, determined. 'Raymond, let's not fall to

quarreling about the form of Arabia's government-to-be. All that will be settled in due course. I am instructed to show you some photographs.' He lifted his attaché case to his lap and opened it. Turner's eyebrows rose at the historic breach of Baturin's personal tradition. He extracted a sheaf of large prints. Turner instantly recognized them as prints from the new Svoboda series Cosmos satellites. Similar material had been pirated from the new satellites by the electronics whizzes of the National Security Agency. Baturin spread the prints on the bare desk. 'These pictures were taken from three hundred kilometers in space, Raymond. These—' he tapped the first series '—were taken while there was still a sandstorm blowing and there is very little detail. These were taken yesterday, and there is somewhat more . . .'

Turner, suddenly dreading what he might see, inspected the photographs. The quality was excellent, despite the fact that the material had been computer-transmitted from, probably, Tyuratam in the Soviet Union. The prints showed an air base, largely abandoned. Ibrahimah in the Empty Quarter. A single large aircraft, a triple-engined jet, stood on the ramp at some distance from the buildings which housed the experimental works of the NPC Station. Turner could see the communications dishes, the workshops and laboratories, the empty ramps leading down into the underground hangars that had housed Saudi fighters before the outbreak of the Gulf war.

He looked up at Baturin and shrugged. 'Well, Yevgeny?'

'We went to a great deal of trouble to get these, Raymond,' Baturin said, bristling slightly. 'I may be breaching security, but I shall tell you anyway that the satellite which obtained this material was originally programmed to watch Riyadh. We set the parameters when the hostages were taken. . . .'

Turner said icily, 'How considerate of you, Yevgeny.'

'To watch, nothing more,' Baturin said hastily. 'We have the right.'

'And that, of course, is how you have managed to be so helpful,' Turner said ironically.

Baturin brought the discussion back on course swiftly. 'To obtain these photographs, we had to reprogram the satellite. Now, if you please, Raymond. Look at these.' He offered the last set of prints.

Turner felt a dryness in his mouth. The air base was no

longer empty. A line of what appeared to be C-130s was being worked on near the underground hangars. Heavy cables—no, they were too large to be electrical connections—hoses of some sort ran from some of the cargo bays of the aircraft into the hangars. Crews in substantial numbers were at work. There was something odd about the way the crews appeared to be dressed, but since the photographs were taken from directly above, it was impossible to see enough detail. The color reproduction was excellent and from that Turner could see that the ground personnel around the old transports were all dressed in yellow. He knew beyond a doubt that he was looking at the means Calder Davis intended to use to achieve his purpose—that purpose so openly and yet so cryptically stated in his letter to President Loomis.

'Well, Raymond?' Baturin demanded. 'Do you see?'

Turner was reminded, not happily, of an Adlai Stevenson righteously displaying to the U.N. Security Council photographs of Soviet missiles in Cuba and offering to wait until hell froze over for the Russian delegate's explanation.

'I see a couple of dozen obsolete transports being serviced at an NPC station, Yevgeny,' he said with more calm than he felt. 'Transports, by the way, probably belonging to an international organization—*not* an American one—which is known throughout the Third World for its charity and good works,' he added, despising the note of smugness he deliberately injected into his statement.

'I see,' Baturin said angrily. 'That is all I am to be told?' He began to return the photographs to the attaché case.

'There is very little more I *can* tell you, Yevgeny,' Turner said. 'We are conducting our own investigation, of course, in response to President Suslov's hot-line message of yesterday. In due course, you will be notified of the results.' He could feel his heart thudding dully in his chest and was amazed at the cool confidence of his tone. The first qualification of the diplomat is the ability to lie well. Niccolö Machiavelli probably said that, Turner thought.

Baturin stood. 'One more thing, Raymond,' he said. The diplomatic anger had gone from his voice and he simply sounded concerned. 'I tell you this so that you may tell it to the President. If it becomes public knowledge, we will deny it. Our military people are so edgy about what is happening in the Empty Quarter that an overflight by one of the aircraft from the *Novgorod* was ordered—'

'That would be a violation of Arabian air space, Yevgeny,' Turner said.

'Of course.' Baturin shrugged. 'That gives you some idea of how nervous my government is about all this activity by the NPC.' He looked worriedly at the Secretary of State. 'The aircraft has not returned to the ship. It is long overdue and must be considered lost.' He moved toward the door, his shoulders slumping, the very picture, thought Raymond Turner, of the failed diplomat.

'I tell you about the aircraft, Raymond,' Baturin said, 'so that you can convince the President that we mean business when we say that if he does not take action—we will.'

When he had gone, Turner walked to his desk and pressed the intercom bar.

'Yes, Mr. Secretary?'

'Have my car brought round. And call the White House. Tell Peter Gilmartin I am on my way. I must see the President without delay.'

For a moment Raymond Turner slumped in his chair. Then he raised his eyes to the framed quotation on the paneled wall. *Our country! In her intercourse with foreign nations may she always be in the right; but our country, right or wrong.*

There are times, Decatur, Raymond Turner thought, when I could wish you sat in this chair rather than I.

Then the Secretary of State rose and hurried out of the room.

When Raymond Turner's limousine entered the White House grounds and approached the porte cochere it had become necessary to drive through a throng of reporters and television technicians. The number of media people had trebled since this morning, and as Turner walked swiftly from his car into the Executive wing he was assailed by shouted questions and surrounded by photographers holding their cameras high to snap over the heads of the crowd. Turner, who was aware that a simple 'no comment' could often be expanded into three minutes of supposition on the evening news, complete with gloomy wrap-up, remained silent until he was inside. In the hallway outside the Oval Office he found Carl Shepherd sitting on a chair opposite the warrant officer who carried the 'football'—the case containing the nuclear codes of the day. This individual, or one like him, remained—by law—within call of the President's person at all times. His presence was customarily ignored by the men who worked in the White House, but the Secretary of State never encountered him without feeling a cold chill brush his spine.

Carl Shepherd, his face grim and gray with fatigue, carried a bulging briefcase. 'Thank God you're back, Raymond,' he said.

Turner indicated the closed door of the Oval Office. 'Who is with him?' he asked.

'General Lescher and General Weyland.'

That had an ominous sound to Raymond Turner. Weyland was the Commander of the Strategic Air Command. What, he wondered, had happened in the two hours since he had left the White House for his meeting with Ambassador Baturin?

'Raymond,' Shepherd said, moving closer. 'Knowland, the agent in charge of the New York office, flew in—'

'Later, Carl,' Turner said softly. 'Not here.'

Shepherd nodded. 'Sorry.' He ran his fingers through his thinning hair and said, 'That circus outside is getting bigger. How do they always know when things go wrong?'

'The Washington press corps has a nose for trouble, Carl.'

'Jesus,' Shepherd muttered. 'It's going to get worse before it gets better.'

The Oval Office door opened and a haggard-looking Peter Gilmartin came out with the two Air Force officers who had been meeting with the President. To General Lescher, he said, 'You'll stand by in the Military Office, then, General. The moment you have anything, call my switchboard. My secretary has orders to put you through immediately.'

Lescher and Weyland, their blue uniforms glittering with stars and ribbons, hurried down the hallway toward the elevator to the lower levels. Gilmartin said, 'All right, Raymond. It's you and Carl now.'

The two men followed Gilmartin into the Oval Office. Vincent Loomis sat at his desk, telephone in hand. He signaled Shepherd and Turner to take chairs. He looked tired. The lines in his face seemed to have grown deeper, the pouches under his eyes darker. Yet, thought Turner, as Loomis sat there at the rosewood desk, the flag standards behind him bearing the national colors and the presidential flag, he looked more—how did the news media put it?—more *presidential* than ever before. Was it true in Vincent Loomis's case, as it had been true of many other ordinary men before him, that crisis and the office itself made the politician into the President?

When Turner had returned to the State Department for his meeting with the Soviet Ambassador, the President had seemed to have worn out his angry energy and appeared about to sink again into indecision. He was more in command of himself now. But whether he could command the situation remained to be seen. Still, Raymond Turner felt the beginnings of hope.

Loomis said into the telephone, 'I don't care what the Majority Leader wants, Charlie. Tell him that I will brief the leaders of the Congress tomorrow and I want *both* parties represented. Now get on with it.' He hung up the telephone and looked across the desk at Turner with a wan, humorless smile. 'If we get through this, Mr. Secretary, remind me that you are entitled to at least one "I told you so." ' The smile quickly vanished and he said, 'General Weyland tells me we should have the SR-71 in position soon now. He doesn't want to land it in Egypt because there are no facilities there to handle its data. It will have to fly to Rota in Spain. Fortunately that won't take more than forty minutes at the speed the Blackbird flies.' He glanced at the world clock on his desk. 'It is eight o'clock in Arabia—getting dark. So what we'll get will be radar photography and some other technical stuff. Say another hour for printout and transmission. Then maybe we'll know something.'

'I don't suppose there is anything from Calder?' Turner asked, knowing the answer.

'Nothing. I have every communications system we possess trying to get through to him,' Loomis said, frowning. 'But that goddamned letter makes it plain enough he's said all he is going to say to us. No—to *me*. I can't dodge *this* bullet. It's mine.' His mood grew even darker as he said, 'I'm looking at impeachment, Raymond.' His large fists appeared from behind the desk and for a moment Turner thought he might smash something in his angry frustration. But he brought himself under control and said, 'Well, Raymond. What did Baturin have to add to all of this?'

'The Soviets are jumpy, Mr. President. They flew a

reconnaissance from their carrier in the Arabian Sea—the *Novgorod*. The airplane failed to return.'

'Shit,' Loomis said angrily. 'Why the hell did they do that? Aren't their goddamned spy satellites good enough?' He shoved himself away from the desk and began to pace. He stopped before the fireplace and stood for a long moment staring at the Gilbert Stuart portrait of Washington above the mantel. Turner could guess at his thoughts as he looked at the man who had warned Americans against 'foreign entanglements.' But that was a long time ago, Mr. President, Turner thought, in a different sort of world. And for a time Turner felt that both he and the President were longing for that different, slower, *safer* world.

Loomis turned and said, 'I have ordered the Arabian Sea Task Force to close the Omani coast, Raymond, and to begin flying enough patrols to keep track of the Russians. I want Oman protected, at least. I don't know what Suslov is likely to do, but we have to be prepared.' The hooded eyes grew even more somber. 'I have ordered a Defcon Two alert as well. I didn't want to, damn it. But we have to show we still have some teeth just in case the Russians decide Calder is our agent.'

A Defcon Two alert, Turner knew, meant that the Trident submarines, the few which had been completed, would put to sea and the Strategic Air Command bombers would increase the number of aircraft on airborne alert. It was a gesture, but not a very convincing one. None of the MX missiles were yet deployed, the Minuteman force was vulnerable to a first strike, and the ancient Titans which comprised a fifth of the ICBM force had all been deactivated and scrapped but not replaced with anything of comparable power. The Rapid Deployment Force, the only American military unit which might conceivably have been of value in this particular crisis, now consisted of a brass-heavy headquarters rusting into impotence at Fort Bragg in North Carolina.

Considering the beleaguered and gloomy President standing under the Stuart portrait, Raymond Turner knew how bitterly he must now be regretting many of his own decisions—decisions which had come too easily, or which had been made to appease others.

Vincent Loomis was the picture of a man caught in a circumstantial net of his own making. To his credit, Turner thought, he was not casting about for scapegoats.

'The point is, Raymond,' Loomis said heavily, 'that we have dozens—*hundreds* of systems producing information—and not one of them is telling me what I want to know. Calder made his intention clear enough. But *how* is he going to accomplish what he's set out to do? I just don't know, and no one has been able to tell me.'

'Baturin showed me some of their Cosmos satellite pictures,' Turner said. 'I saw some thirty old Hercules transports on the ground at EQ Station, Mr. President. They were being worked on or modified in some way, but I am not technically competent enough to say how or why.'

'We can have a battalion of Marines at EQ Station by noon tomorrow. I don't want to order something like that, but I will if I must. We can face the diplomatic fallout later,' the President said.

'Good, Mr. President. I suggest you order the fleet Marines in at once,' Turner said.

The President nodded bleakly. 'The *Nimitz* is out of helicopter range now, but they should be close enough by dawn tomorrow.' He returned to his desk and sank into the soft leather chair. He pressed an intercom button and said, 'Ask General Williamson to come here right away.'

Williamson was the President's physician and Turner felt a stab of concern. 'Are you unwell, Mr. President?'

'I'm going to need something to keep me functioning for the next twelve or thirteen hours.' He once again essayed that sour smile. 'Think what the voters would say, Raymond, if they knew the President was on speed.'

He suddenly gave his attention to Carl Shepherd. 'You've been sitting there as if your pants are on fire, Carl. Have you something to say?'

'Yes, sir. I do.' Shepherd opened his briefcase and extracted a tape cassette. 'The agent in charge of the New York office brought this by hand, Mr. President. There is a transcript, but I think you had better hear it.'

'Another goddamned tape, Carl? I listened to the NSA's tape of that conversation they intercepted a half-dozen times today. They say there is no way they can identify the speakers. All it did was make my blood run cold. Someone here in Washington used a CIA scrambler phone to give someone in England instructions about Cole's brother, Rivas. I'm no prosecuting attorney, but it sounded to me like instructions to kill him. We've broadcast a warning, hoping that someone at EQ Station is listening and cares enough to let him know. He's there—somewhere. But if he's snooping undercover for a story, all we've accomplished is to blow his cover. So no more goddamned tapes, Carl.'

'This one is different, Mr. President. It was taken from a recorder that was in the pocket of a man who jumped—or was pushed—from a third-story window,' Carl Shepherd said. 'The man was Sam Abbott, Rivas's publisher.'

'Oh, my God,' the President said, his face graying.

'May I, Mr. President?' Shepherd walked to the communications console near the President's desk and inserted the cassette in the tape player. Almost at once the voices on the tape were heard in the Oval Office.

'You saw Cole's brother. He was here.'

'I make no secret of it. Why sould I?'

'Don't be hostile. We're both on the same side.'

Shepherd said, 'We can pick most of this up in the transcript, Mr. President. Let me go forward a way.' He used the fast-forward control and the voices chirped and squealed like the cries of small animals. The tape slowed to a normal speed and a familiar voice came from the speakers.

'Tell me what you told Rivas, Sam. That's really all I want to know.'

The reply seemed thicker, less distinct than before. *'I told him what I told Cole.'*

'The coroner found sodium amobarbital in the dead man's blood, Mr. President,' Carl Shepherd whispered.

'. . . what was that?'

'All that I could find out about the ISSG people in the government.'

The President winced at the mention of the ISSG and its penetration of his administration.

'Cole spoke to you about Calder Davis, didn't he, Sam?'

'Cole was afraid the NPC was recruiting soldiers.' The words were rapidly becoming slurred, as though enunciation was an effort of the will. *'He said that if it were so, it was an act of treason.'*

'And so you told him he was mistaken, naturally.'

'He wasn't mistaken. He was right.' A long pause, and then: *'And—so—you—had—him—killed. . . .'*

Regretfully, calmly: *'It was necessary. You can see that it was necessary, Sam.'*

'Rivas—' The effort to speak was agonizing. The listening men could feel it in the sympathetic tightening of their own throats. *'—will put it together eventually. . . .'*

'Rivas will never get out of Arabia alive, Sam.'

'Assassin . . . '

The tape played on now, unheeded. President Loomis, his face suddenly shrunken on the bones like a death mask, said, 'How . . .?'

Shepherd said, 'Abbott was once a CIA man. He never really forgot what the Company men call "tradecraft." He kept a recorder hidden in the pocket of his dressing gown. When he thought he might die, he used it.'

Abbott's voice cried from the speaker. *'Stay away—Judas.'* There followed the sound of breaking glass—and then silence.

The President looked at his companions. 'It was Ike Holt on that tape, wasn't it?'

'Yes, Mr. President,' Shepherd said. 'I'm sorry.'

The President's voice was made hoarse by his rage and inner pain. 'Find him. *You find him, Carl.'* Then he asked: 'Just how deeply do you think the Agency is involved in this?'

'As far as we can tell right now, Mr. President, it is only Ike Holt. He made free use of Company facilities, but there is nothing to suggest that the Agency itself is involved.'

'Thank God for that,' Raymond Turner breathed.

The President's eyes were like chips of agate, his lips white with anger and humiliation. 'Well, Carl—*you—find—him*. I don't care what it means to me or to the administration, I want him found and arrested and tried in open court—for murder and treason against the United States of America, goddamn his rotten soul. I'll see him in hell!'

Shepherd said quietly, 'As soon as I saw the transcript and heard the tape, sir, I put out a bulletin on him.'

'Where would he go if he were running?'

Shepherd said, 'There's only one place I can think of, Mr. President.'

'The Russians?'

Carl Shepherd shrugged slightly. 'Or some of their surrogates, sir. But I think the Soviets. He has a good deal to offer them. He has been an Agency supergrade for more than ten years. Just for that alone they would probably give him asylum and a new identity. But he knows *everything* about Calder and the NPC and EQ Station. No, sir, the Russians wouldn't hesitate a second before opening their arms to him. He's worth his weight in gold.'

'Then stop him,' the President said. 'I don't care how, but find him and stop him. I am not a man of really great hatreds, gentlemen,' he said in a low, now suddenly dangerously quiet, voice. 'But this is something different. I want Isaac Holt to get every bit of due process to which he is entitled. And then, damn him to hell, I want him to be strapped into an electric chair and executed for being exactly what that man Abbott called him—a *Judas*.'

35 EQ Station

Michael Rivas had never before met Calder Smith Davis, even though the financier had been a part of the national life of the United States—and the world—for longer than Rivas had been alive. Up close to the legend, Rivas was almost touched by the aged frailty of the man.

Davis signaled his armed escorts to step out of the room. The Corpsmen were plainly reluctant to obey. Rivas had the strong impression that the men—Middle Easterners of some kind, he guessed—regarded the old man with a reverence usually reserved for *mullahs* and holy men. When he considered it, he realized that the attitude was consistent with the ethnic reverence for old age that was very much a fact of life in this part of the world.

'Please,' Calder Davis said. 'I am quite safe here. Mr. Rivas would not do violence to an old man.'

The Corpsmen inclined their heads respectfully and stepped into the corridor. Davis walked to the door and closed it. 'They are Raschid tribesmen, Mr. Rivas. Educated abroad, of course. But brave, simple men nonetheless. Colonel Hadfield selected them a long time ago to serve as my personal protectors.' He regarded Rivas with a slightly ironic smile. 'I don't think I need protectors here, of all places.' He shrugged. 'But the colonel feels he knows best. You came here with Colonel Hadfield, Mr. Rivas. A competent man, wouldn't you say?'

Rivas could not shake off the growing sense of unreality that lay at the core of this interview. Ever since reading Cole's letter in Lugano he had been following a trail that led inexorably to this place and to this man. Yet there was something dreamlike here: the frail old man, the barely habitable barracks, the vast empty desert surrounding all.

'May I be seated?' Calder Davis asked, sitting himself on the edge of the cot. 'I had a frightening journey here and I must admit it tired me.' He gestured vaguely with a slender, almost transparent hand. 'I dislike flying intensely, Mr. Rivas, and my airplane had to fly through a sandstorm to get here.' Again, the slight, ironic smile appeared. 'I don't fear death, Mr. Rivas. A man of my age would be foolish to dread the act of dying. But flying frightens me nevertheless. It must be that I belong in a less hurried time. Fewer machines, perhaps. Fewer noises and sudden displacements. I was born when the century was very young, Mr. Rivas.'

Rivas found himself almost mesmerized by the thin, gentle voice and the faded, weary eyes. Calder Davis was near eighty, he knew. But here in these circumstances he seemed far, far older—a man from another age preserved by some miraculous process that could function only in this desiccated air.

Davis said, 'You have gone to a great deal of trouble and come a very long way. You are entitled to some explanations, Mr. Rivas, and you shall have them. You are, I believe, a journalist.'

Rivas nodded.

'And Cole Norris's brother.'

The mention of Cole broke the spell for Rivas. This was not some frail reincarnation of Pharaoh. This was Calder Davis, a banker, a man of money and power, a man whose financial—and political—interests spanned the world. He was real, of flesh and blood. And somehow he had brought about Cole's murder.

'You killed my brother, Davis,' Rivas said tightly.

'With infinite regret, Mr. Rivas,' Davis said.

Rivas felt a flush of quick fury. He could snap this old man's neck with his hands. He could snuff him out like a candle flame. Then why, he wondered, don't I *do* it?

Davis said, 'You show great restraint, Mr. Rivas. The ability to remain reasonable in the face of strong provocation is a mark of civilized behavior. Of *Western* behavior, Mr. Rivas. If you were an Arab, or a Persian, or an African, or any one of a thousand other nationalities, you would try to take revenge on me, even though my protectors might kill you for it.'

Rivas recognized a glint of madness in the old watery eyes, but perhaps he imagined it, he told himself. Besides, how did one define madness in these circumstances? The immense structure of power this man had built, the monumental philanthropies he had performed—these might be the product of a giant ego, but hardly the life's work of an unstable mind.

'We are both products of a culture that has worshiped reason since the Middle Ages, Mr. Rivas. Reason, tolerance —but there is danger in too much tolerance, my young friend. The Christian ethic can eventually lead to impotence in the face of a threat of extinction. I do not expect you to agree with that, Mr. Rivas, though in the depths of your soul—oh, yes, I believe in the existence of an immortal soul in man—you *feel* I am right.' Davis lifted a slender hand again in what Rivas suspected was a characteristic gesture of command. 'I have lived most of my life according to the teachings of the great minds of Western culture, Mr. Rivas. And I have, after many years, learned a simple truth.'

'Is this all part of that simple truth?' Rivas said. 'A private army? Paid killers—'

'I told you I regret your brother's death. I regret *all* the lives that have been lost and *will be* lost. I am happy that yours was not one of them.'

'Does that mean I'm not to be shot at again? What the hell is different now, Davis? I know more now than I did a week ago—'

'You are *here*, Mr. Rivas. And because you are here you are going to be offered a unique opportunity to write history. Someone should do it. Let us simply say that you have earned the right. Or, if you prefer, that fortune has brought you here at the right time.'

'I don't know what you're talking about, Davis,' Rivas said. 'I came here because I want to know *why* my brother had to die, and because people have a right to know what you're doing behind all your bloody good works and self-righteous talk.'

'Not self-righteous, I assure you, Mr. Rivas. I am not a truly religious man, but I know better than anyone that I am committing a very great sin. Yes, Mr. Rivas, there is such a thing as sin, just as there is evil. But you shouldn't have to listen to *my* personal dilemma or concern yourself about how I have solved it and what it must cost me. Consider only this. What future do you see for us, Mr. Rivas?'

'For us?'

'Not for you and me. We are unimportant in the balance of history. Banality is not called for here, Mr. Rivas. I mean for us as products of a thousand or more years of Western civilization.'

'I'm a reporter, Davis, not a historian or a philosopher.'

'You may become a historian, if you allow yourself to be.'

Calder Davis paused and Rivas was suddenly aware that the old man was trembling with fatigue and some overpowering inner tension.

'Hear me out, young man,' Davis said, essaying that same thin smile. 'You may be getting the last interview I will ever grant.' He studied Rivas with an almost pleading expression. He wanted, Rivas realized, desperately to be *understood*.

'Our world—the *Western* world—is crumbling,' Davis said. 'Our reason, our tolerance, our Christian belief in returning good for evil—all of the things that differentiate Western man from the people of any other culture the world has known—are destroying us.' He raised a hand again. 'Wait, *please* hear me out. Since these are the very characteristics that define our culture, the nations of the West *cannot* abandon them. Yet if things remain as they are, we will not survive into the next century. Yes, I know—and far better than you do—that we have sinned. We have been colonialists, we have exploited others, we have been racists—all of that. But now—and I mean now, this very moment in time—the nations of the West are overcome with such guilt that they will not defend themselves against the future every man knows is coming. We need time, Mr. Rivas. Time to gather ourselves again, to find a new strength—even to find the courage to sacrifice.'

'And you took it on yourself,' Rivas said bitterly, 'to sacrifice my brother—and a poor Puerto Rican cabby—and God knows how many others for this philosophic mish-mash you're spouting?'

'*I* know how many others, Mr. Rivas, and I bear the weight on my heart. I know that I will be brought to judgment for it, believe me, I do. But won't you hear me out? I will stop philosophizing, since you are not yet of an age to share my view of history. Let us speak of practical things. Let us speak of oil.'

'Oh, my God, so now we come to it. All this is about oil? Is that what the famous "Brigade" is intended to do? Steal the Arabs' oil?'

'We shall steal nothing, Mr. Rivas. For the last ten years my associates and I have been building facilities for the production of synthetic petroleum from coal and oil shale and tar sands. Do you know what *in situ* retorting is?'

'Yes, I think so. A section of an underground deposit is broken into small fragments and then heated to extract the oil. It takes millions of tons of raw material to get a few barrels of oil. Is that the way you plan to save Western civilization? I think you've gone round the bend, Mr. Davis.'

'Not a few barrels, Mr. Rivas. The process is more efficient than that. Today—right now—we are capable of producing a million barrels a day at our retorts in Wyoming and Utah. Our plants in the Ruhr can produce half that. Within five years we could produce all the petroleum the United States and Western Europe need. In ten years we would have a surplus, even exporting all that the Japanese might require at that time.'

'Then why don't you simply *do* it, Davis?'

'If we produce a barrel of oil today for fifty dollars—which is what it costs—with *no* margin of profit except for plant maintenance and capital improvements—the OPEC countries will sell a barrel of oil for forty dollars. If we bring the price down to forty dollars, they will sell for thirty. If we can make twenty-dollar-a-barrel oil, they will sell theirs for ten. *Until* the program collapses. Then they will raise their prices again and resume their systematic destruction of the Western world's economy. No combination of multinational corporations, Mr. Rivas, can actually engage in a price war with OPEC.'

'So you will use the Brigade to steal the damned oil fields, just as I said. Only the Russians won't let you, Davis. And even if they would, you can't have one-tenth the number of mercenaries needed to *hold* the Gulf coast. I don't care how good Collingwood is, or how beautifully you've managed to build yourself a private army. It won't work, Davis. Do you hear me? *It won't work*.' Rivas heard the shrill anger—and the fear—in his own voice.

'Of course it won't work, Mr. Rivas,' Davis said quietly.

Rivas stared at him.

'Not the way you imagine it, Mr. Rivas. I have never intended to try to take the oil fields from the Arabians. That would mean a bloodbath, and very likely the destruction of the fields for many, many years to come.'

Davis's voice seemed to grow progressively stronger now, as though he derived some inner sustenance from the immensity of his daring.

'At this moment, Mr. Rivas, the Brigade that so worries you is making ready to assault the American embassy in Riyadh. General Collingwood has more than ten thousand trained soldiers under his command. By noon tomorrow the hostages will be safely in Jeb Collingwood's hands. He will hold the embassy and the international airport in Riyadh. The entire world—the *Western* world, Mr. Rivas—will have something, at last, to cheer about. They will know that there is a force in being willing to protect their interests and their citizens. Rely on it. The United Nations will accept the Brigade as its own.'

'Never, Davis. Never in a thousand years,' Rivas said.

'You forget the ISSG, Mr. Rivas. Have you any idea how many U.N. delegations now have ISSG members in strategic positions? Hundreds. That is what the ISSG is *for*, Mr. Rivas. To put some teeth into a plan to establish world order. How long did you imagine the international anarchy of the last twenty years could go on? Think, Mr. Rivas. Do you know that seven out of every ten persons in the world today have no access to television, radio, newspapers, or even a telephone? Most of the planet lives in the dark ages, young man. How long can civilized nations allow their destinies to be ruled by such people?'

Rivas's mind began at last to encompass the scope—the vast scale—of Calder Davis's plan. Even as he listened to what could only be described as a paranoid personality's blueprint for remaking the world, he could not completely suppress an instinctive surrender to its appeal. The very *idea* of the Brigade, a kind of international vigilante band, repelled him. But the thought of some *action* being taken at last, some protest from the civilized nations, against the bullying outlawry of angry Third World nations, had a deadly appeal. In one sense, Davis was right. The world would learn at once that the Brigade existed and that it had performed a desperately needed action. Opinion might be divided, but on balance any force that said to the radicals and the terrorists: *Enough!* would be welcomed.

But what of the rest of Calder Davis's plan? The Brigade, the ISSG in the U.N., public approval of a rescue of the hostages were one thing—but it was obvious that Davis planned to go much further than that.

The old man seemed to have read his mind. 'The Arabians, Mr. Rivas, are the richest members of the Third

World. And because they are, it is they who must be subdued. They have no culture meaningful to our time. They were a great people once, but they have never advanced beyond the twelfth century in any of the concerns that denote modern nationhood. In our time, Mr. Rivas, we have seen the West grow slack and timid. Our experiments with permissiveness and luxurious consumption have made us lazy and fearful. I hope with all my heart that this is only a temporary illness, and not the symptoms of a fatal disease. But whether or not our civilization will live is not for you or me to guess. Like a physician who must bleed his patient, I have done what I think best. Only history will prove me right or wrong. That is why I want all this recorded, Mr. Rivas. I want someone to observe and record the moment when Western man is shocked back into reality. Will you be that someone, Mr. Rivas?'

The journalist in Rivas stirred. *Was* this history—or a great and terrible insanity, the crumbling of a once great man's dreams? One could look at Calder Davis and hear him speak with such earnestness and conviction and feel the ground shift beneath one's feet.

'I intend to stop the production of Arabian oil, Mr. Rivas, for the next five to seven years. I shall not *destroy* the fields, because very soon they will be needed by the Soviets and I would not have my actions be the cause of a war. But after tomorrow the oil fields of the Gulf coast will produce not one barrel of oil for some years to come. Believe me, Mr. Rivas, I have the means and I intend to use them. From tomorrow on, the West will be on its own in matters of energy production. The industry I and my associates have started will have to grow at a tremendous rate and there will be great sacrifices required.' Davis was very tired. Rivas could see the fatigue in his pallid face. 'This is not for profit, Mr. Rivas. Every cent that the new synfuels facilities earn will be placed in a trust to be disbursed by a commission to help the people whose lives are disrupted by the change. In fact, Mr. Rivas, all that I own will eventually find its way into that trust.' His expression grew more stern than it had been; the philanthropist metamorphosed into the world-planner. 'One other beneficiary will be the Brigade, and, of course, the ordinary echelons of the NPC. There will still be much work to do in the Third World.'

For a moment Rivas had an insane desire to laugh.

Somehow the Arabs were to be stripped of their beloved 'oil weapon,' the Arabians in Riyadh were to be stripped of their hostages, and the rest of the Third World was to be stripped of any power over the nations of the West. The lesson would be administered by the mailed fist of the NPC's Brigade. And then, as Davis saw it, the fist would become once again the open hand of friendship with NPC teams carrying on their work among the people of the Third World as though nothing had changed. But everything would have changed. No Third World nation or combination of nations would ever again dare to form a cartel to control a strategic material. It was all mad enough to work exactly as Calder Davis thought it would.

Rivas was about to speak when he heard a distant, muffled, sound. Almost at once he saw through the clerestory windows a column of oily black smoke against the darkening evening sky. Calder Davis did not react. Rivas wondered if he had failed to hear the sound. Somewhere on or near the station, Rivas knew, there had been an explosion.

Immediately the door to the room opened and one of Davis's personal guards entered and whispered in the old man's ear. An expression of rueful sadness came over the drawn, tired face.

'I must leave you now, Mr. Rivas,' he said, getting to his feet. 'Please think about what I have told you. . . .'

'The oil fields, Davis,' Rivas said. 'Tell me how—'

The thin hand rose authoritatively. 'All in the proper time. Consider what we have talked about. Think about the opportunity you are being given. I propose to send you to Riyadh tomorrow, as soon as we know that the hostages are safe. You may join the Brigade and write the most important story of your career. I most earnestly hope that you will do this, Mr. Rivas. Not only is it a task that you can do well and should accept—but you will be far safer with General Collingwood and his men than you are here.'

With that he went to the door, where he paused and turned back for a moment. 'Believe me, Mr. Rivas,' he said with melancholy gentleness, 'I am truly sorry about your brother and all the others who may die. No great thing is ever done cheaply.'

Then he was gone, and Michael Rivas stood looking at the closed door of his temporary prison.

36 Washington, D.C.

With its anticollision strobes making tiny, brilliant flashes, the Air Force helicopter descended through the summer twilight to the south lawn of the White House. On the Pennsylvania Avenue side of the mansion, the news people who had gathered there during the long, hot day heard the aircraft and rushed through the grounds to investigate, only to be halted by barriers and a phalanx of U.S. marshals.

As the helicopter settled on its landing gear, an Air Force major wearing a sidearm and carrying a locked metal case dropped to the grass and sprinted toward the basement entrance under the south portico.

In the Oval Office a telephone rang and Charlie McKay snatched it from its cradle. General Lescher, speaking from the Military Office, said, 'It's here.'

'Thank Christ, at last,' McKay said. 'Bring it in right away.' To the President, seated coatless with Raymond Turner and Carl Shepherd on the sofas flanking the dark fireplace, he said, 'We have the SR-71 prints, Mr. President.'

Vincent Loomis was gray with fatigue, with the lines framing his sensual mouth deeply etched and his cheeks showing a darkening growth of beard. The remains of a half-eaten meal lay on the low table between the two sofas. Stacks of papers overflowed the same table onto the maroon carpet.

The door opened and Peter Gilmartin hurried in, his seersucker suit rumpled, his collar damp. 'All stations on the hot line are ready to go, Vinnie,' he said. 'Everything is ready on Suslov's end.'

Loomis said, 'I want to use the new video setup, Peter. I want to see his face and I want him to see mine.'

'It's on line,' Gilmartin said. 'The interpreters are standing by.'

'Have someone bring down some fresh clothes for me. I

don't want the bastard to see me looking mussed,' Loomis said. For a moment his expression softened. 'Did you get through to the First Lady at Camp David?'

'Yes, Vinnie. She's all right. The children are fine. She's been a little worried about all the speculation on the evening newscasts, but she says you aren't to concern yourself about them.'

Loomis smiled briefly at Raymond Turner. 'Marie's a real politician's wife, Raymond. One vote I can always count on.' The smile faded and he said to Carl Shepherd, who had just returned to the White House from the Hoover Building, 'Anything on Ike Holt yet, Carl?'

'Nothing, Mr. President. I'm sorry,' Shepherd replied. He had taken the time to shower and change at his office, but he already felt as wilted and disheveled as he had before. This had been an incredibly long and difficult day for the FBI Director, and he realized that it was far from over.

There was a peremptory sound on the intercom and Charlie McKay hurried to the President's desk. A secretary's voice said, 'General Lescher is here, Mr. McKay.'

'Send him in.'

General Lescher marched into the room and laid the red-banded file of photographs and printouts before the President.

'I'm afraid these confirm the Russian reports, Mr. President. There are at least thirty aircraft on the old Ibrahimah base.' He separated one print from the others. It was a radar photograph, and it had been enhanced by computer so that details stood out starkly. 'Something is being loaded on those aircraft,' he said. 'You can see the crews working on them in this queue.'

Carl Shepherd leaned over the print. 'Troops, General?'

'No, Mr. Shepherd,' Lescher said. 'Not troops.' He extracted a sheet of computer paper from the case and handed it to the President. 'Those are readings from the Blackbird's electromagnetic spectrum-analysis sensors. Nothing untoward there. But this—' he produced another sheet '—is something else again. Now if you note the rem count—'

'I'm not a scientist, General,' Loomis said irritably. 'Explain. In words of one syllable, please.'

'I'm sorry, Mr. President. What you have there are the readings from the Blackbird's *radiation* sensors. The aircraft overflew the target area once at a hundred and thirty thousand feet and then came down to seventy thousand for a double check. Something down there is *hot*, Mr. President. Hot as hell.'

Charlie McKay turned pale. 'You don't mean there are nuclear bombs at EQ Station, General?'

'No, Mr. McKay. Nuclear warheads would not leak radiation that way. There is always a trace, of course, from any nuclear device. But nothing like this.' He looked grimly at the President. 'If you'll study the photographs carefully, sir, you'll see that what appear to be conduits of some sort are being used to put something aboard those old C-130s. Whatever it is is spewing particles everywhere. We ran a spectrum analysis on the air samples the Blackbird picked up at seventy thousand feet. Unfortunately the sample is inconclusive. But on the basis of the preliminary analysis, we're guessing that we're dealing here with one of the isotopes of ruthenium.'

'What, exactly, is ruthenium, General?' Carl Shepherd asked.

'One of the rare, heavy elements. Highly radioactive,' Lescher said.

The President regarded the suddenly silent general. 'Well, General Lescher? Go on.'

'Some of this information is classified, sir.'

'For God's sake, General. This is the Secretary of State and that is the Director of the FBI. Get on with it.'

'Well, sir. There have been biowar studies done on the isotopes of ruthenium. Our scientific people regard it as a prime material for use as a weapon.'

Raymond Turner said, 'I thought you said it was rare, General.'

'Yes, sir. In nature it is extremely rare. Almost nonexistent. But . . . '

'But *what*, General?' the President demanded.

'As a by-product of nuclear power production, sir, it is not rare at all.'

'I don't think I understand you, General. Are you telling us that this rare metal is found in nuclear waste?'

'Something like that, Mr. President. Spent fuel rods from nuclear power plants contain a quite reasonable percentage of ruthenium 106.'

'Is it lethal, General?'

'Any radioactive material is lethal, Mr. President. It

depends entirely on the concentration. In microscopic amounts it is relatively harmless. Of course, animal studies have suggested that it would result in a significantly increased cancer rate. . . .'

'And we have been considering this as a possible weapon?' Raymond Turner asked, his voice tinged with disgust.

The Chairman of the JCS returned the Secretary of State's look coldly. 'The Soviets, sir, have a very well developed radiological warfare capability.'

'To hell with the Soviets,' the President said. 'Get back to what's on the ground at Calder's EQ Station, General.'

General Lescher referred carefully to another classified file he had taken from the metal case. Then he said, 'Ruthenium—or for that matter any one of a number of heavy elements—can be used in a reasonably flexible way. As a weapon, sir, it would be minutely pulverized and mixed with any one of a number of liquids. Water would do. Or if you want the material to cling to objects, you could use a light oil. It can then be delivered onto a target as a simple aerosol. Of course the spray mechanisms and the vehicle used to carry them would become too lethal to be operated by humans—even if they were protected by antirad clothing.'

He paused for a moment, as though reluctant to continue this discussion.

'As for the ruthenium, itself, Mr. President, I am afraid it is easily obtained—now.'

'Why *now*, General?' Loomis demanded.

'I am not a physicist, Mr. President, but we do have specialists who study the literature carefully. Some time ago, sir, a paper was published on the extraction of rare metals from nuclear waste. The idea was to reduce the radioactivity of the waste and make disposal simpler. The Nuclear Regulatory Commission showed very little interest in the process, sir, because there seemed at the time so little likelihood that many more nuclear plants would be built. But the process was patented, Mr. President.' Lescher looked at the Commander in Chief without expression. 'By the NPC.'

He went on relentlessly. 'The patent was issued over a year ago. The process is called the Clevenger Method.'

The President half crumpled the papers in his hand.

'If this material were to be used as a weapon, General,'

Loomis said in a voice that had almost become a whisper, 'how effective would it be?'

Back on solid, military ground, General Lescher responded crisply. 'Ruthenium 106 has a half-life of three hundred and sixty-eight days, Mr. President. This makes it almost ideal for use in a military aerosol. One could vary the concentration according to the effect desired. If, for example, one were to distribute one curie per square meter on a chosen target, there would be a lethal concentration in place for approximately five years. That does not mean instant lethality, sir. If one were unprotected, one could remain in the target area for—say—one hour. Anything more would be lethal, of course. And even if one were exposed for that one hour and escaped to a clean area, one could not return. The effects of exposure are cumulative, you see.'

'Yes,' Vincent Loomis breathed, 'I do indeed see.' He looked bleakly at Raymond Turner and then at Carl Shepherd. 'I understand Calder's letter now, don't you, gentlemen?'

Turner asked, 'General, you said there would be a lethal concentration in a target area for five years. Please explain that.'

'Certainly, Mr. Secretary,' the Chairman of the JCS said. 'One curie per square meter would produce sixty-five rems per hour. This is clearly lethal. But after five years the material would have decayed by a factor of thirty-two. There is no clear dividing line for this sort of scenario. One hour after the attack by aerosol, the target area would be highly unsafe even for exposures under an hour. But the material begins to decay immediately and so the safe exposure time gradually increases. After, say, four years, it would be possible to remain inside the target area for a considerable time—if, of course, one were well protected by antirad clothing and had an ample supply of breathing air. That would be important if one were dealing with a water-based aerosol, since desiccation would mean that the radioactive agent would simply be resting on exposed surfaces and could be spread about easily by the wind.'

The President's heavy shoulders were slumped with weariness. 'One more thing, General. How large an area could be—ah, neutralized—by the method you describe?'

'There is no limit, Mr. President. As I explained, the

Clevenger Method had made it extremely simple to separate the components of nuclear wastes. The Environmental Protection Agency had been requiring that even old nuclear wastes be dug up and disposed of safely. The supply of ruthenium is therefore substantial. I can only make an estimate, sir. But I believe some three to five hundred grams, properly mixed into an aerosol, would neutralize one square kilometer. As to availability—well, our biowar people estimate that it would only take a year to a year and a half to accumulate two-and-a-half to three metric tons. With that amount of material to distribute, one could easily neutralize six or seven thousand square kilometers. Depending on the nature of the terrain.'

'Sweet Jesus,' Charlie McKay groaned.

The intercom began to ping urgently and McKay picked it up. He listened and then said, 'It's Dawson, Mr. President. Director of Operations at McLean.'

'Tell him to wait,' Loomis said. To General Lescher, he said, 'Thank you, General. That's all for now. Please tell Admiral Thesiger that I want that battalion of fleet Marines on the ground at Ibrahimah as fast as they can get there. It is vital that those C-130s don't leave the ground. Where is the *Nimitz* now?'

'Steaming north at forty knots, Mr. President. They should be able to launch their helicopters within two hours.'

Vincent Loomis said grimly, 'Get them airborne at the absolute limit of their range, General. We'll worry about retrieving them later.'

'Yes, sir.' Lescher began to gather his materials.

'Leave all that,' Loomis said.

General Lescher hesitated and then said, 'Mr. President—may I ask about the Secretary of Defense . . .?'

'No, General, you may not.'

'Very well, sir.' Lescher retrieved his silver-bullioned cap and hurried out of the Oval Office. Loomis heaved himself wearily to his feet and took the telephone. 'Yes, Dawson?'

'Mr. President, we have just received a report that the Israelis have begun massing armor on the Jordanian border near 'Aqaba. We don't know yet in what strength, but we believe the report is accurate.'

The President closed his eyes.

'Sir?'

'Yes, Dawson. I'm still on the line.'

'I'm sorry, Mr. President. Things are pretty tense here.'

'Yes, I can understand that,' Loomis said, trying to reorganize his thoughts to include this latest piece of disturbing news. 'What is the source of your information?'

'We have a man in the Knesset, sir. Premier Abrahams has called an extraordinary session. He told them Israel's oil situation is critical and that unless it improves immediately the army will move to secure an Arabian source of supply. Our man gave us a few hours' notice, but their U.N. delegate will tell the General Assembly tomorrow that they have no choice. Their national security is at stake. They feel the risk is minimal because the Saudi military no longer exists.'

'I see,' the President said wearily.

'There is quite a bit of confusion in the Middle East section here, sir. We are getting another report that we don't quite understand. At 0215 hours local time Riyadh seems to have come under some sort of attack.'

The President signaled Raymond Turner to pick up an extension telephone. 'The Secretary of State is here, Dawson. I have put him on the line. Go on with what you were saying.'

'Our informant in Jerusalem is very reliable, Mr. President. If the Israelis had actually begun military operations, he would have said so. But we still have good assets in Riyadh, sir. And their report is that the city is being attacked right now—by helicopter-borne forces, strength and nationality unknown, sir.'

Calder Davis, Loomis thought with a sudden cold and clear vision. The taped voice of the dead Sam Abbott came back to the President with a sharp and terrible clarity: *'Cole was afraid the NPC was recruiting soldiers.'*

And that was exactly what Calder's NPC had done. To Vincent Loomis the bitter knowledge was doubly galling because he knew he had avoided the responsibility of his office and allowed it to happen. The fault was not his alone—no member of any Western government had shown the courage to put an end to anarchy and terrorism. No Western leader had been willing to demand that emerging nations accept the rules of civilized behavior. Years of provocation had gone unanswered. Oh, yes, Loomis thought, there is guilt enough for all of us: We presented Calder Davis with the excuse, and now there is a new and unpredictable force in the world. . . .

'Give the Secretary of State all the information you have available,' he said as Peter Gilmartin came back into the room.

Loomis placed the telephone gently on its cradle and said, 'We will speak to Suslov in fifteen minutes, Peter.'

'The valet is in the dressing room with your things, Mr. President,' Gilmartin said.

It struck the President as a macabre joke that before he spoke to the old men in the Kremlin it was necessary that he make himself presentable so that he might appear untouched by the wreckage of a collapsing world. As a man who had lived by images, he, better than most, could appreciate the graveyard irony of his situation.

Seven
July 18, the seventh day

He sendeth down the rain from Heaven: then flow the torrents in their due measure, and the flood beareth along a swelling foam. And from the metals which are molten in the fire for the sake of ornaments, a like scum ariseth. In this way doth God depict truth and falsehood. As to the foam, it is quickly gone: as to what is useful to man, it remaineth on earth. Thus doth God set forth comparisons! To those who respond to their Lord shall be an excellent reward; but those who respond not to his call, had they all that the earth containeth twice over, they would surely give it for their ransom. Evil their reckoning! and Hell their home!

—Holy Qur'ân, thirteenth sura

37 EQ Station

The figure on the television screen began again. For several hours now, Rivas had watched the performance with uneasy perplexity. It was obviously a videotape and it was being run repeatedly. Rivas realized that it was being broadcast from the television facilities he had seen as Hadfield's convoy approached the base, and though his understanding of Arabic was imperfect, he understood enough to surmise that the telecast was intended for the workers in the oil fields to the north. They were being exhorted to leave and to seek refuge away from the coast.

The message was being delivered by a bearded, turbaned ancient who reminded Rivas of the Imam Khomeini in bearing and authority, but whose features were strongly Bedouin. Though no specific claim to religious authority was being made—at least Rivas's limping Arabic could detect none—the *image* being projected was plainly that of an ascetic holy man. From time to time he seemed to refer to a book, rather obviously the Qu'rân.

There was no way for Rivas to shut the set off and he was reluctant to pull the power cord from the wall. It was always possible that some useful information might be forthcoming if the tape of the anonymous holy man were ever stopped. Rivas estimated that the telecast had begun before midnight, but since it had appeared on the television set in his room in midcourse, it was quite possible that the exhortations had begun much earlier and had only been piped into his place of detention as an afterthought. Perhaps Calder Davis's afterthought.

The grating, guttural tones and the constant repetition were rasping Rivas's nerves badly. There was no avoiding them in the tiny barracks room.

He desperately wanted to escape from his confinement, but the high windows were unbreakable and the Corpsman with his Uzi still stood stolidly outside the door.

Rivas's mind repeatedly returned to his conversation with Calder Davis. How, he wondered, did a man like that come to this? Perhaps the veneer of civilization, even of one such as Davis, was thinner than most men realized. Enough provocation could eventually break through that veneer and cause catastrophic reactions. At least when the person in question commanded the powers Davis commanded, the results could be enormous.

The worst of it was that much of what Calder Davis had said was undeniable. It was madness for the developed nations to allow themselves to be bullied and blackmailed by societies whose ethics were those of a distant past.

Rivas had some personal experience of the Third World ethos and long before finding himself here it had troubled him. He remembered the Rivas hacienda in Mexico, where life was led in an ancient tradition of class distinctions, *machismo*, and a deep distrust of change. The day-by-day life of his father's family had been one of privilege, and it remained so to this day. The Rivas family land had been granted by the Spanish King, and their notion of democracy was to build adobe shacks with tin roofs for the *peón* families who lived on the estate. Of popular democracy in Mexico, there was very little. The forms were adhered to, but Mexico—like all the Third World—had a deep distrust of any idea more recent than the sixteenth century. To placate the intrusive giant of the north, Latin-Americans gave lip service to popular rule, but no more than that. Only violence by an ideologically fanatical minority ever changed the course of Latin-American politics, and it was the same everywhere in the Third World.

So in one sense, Calder Davis was right. Though he had not said so, implicit in his actions was the belief that it was fruitless to hope that Western-style democracy could ever take root in the soil of the Third World. Miguel Rivas's Mexican cousins—like any South Africans or Rhodesians (it was impossible to think of them in this context as 'Zimbabweans')—regarded the notion of one man, one vote an exercise in political insanity.

And what was true of Latin-Americans and Africans was doubly true of the Arabs. Theirs was a culture based on principles laid down by Mohammed in the seventh century. Giving them jet airplanes and high-rise buildings could not change that. It could only cause them cultural shock. The Iranian Shah's greatest error had been the attempt to wrench his society five hundred years forward in time. The same had been true of the Saudi princes. Change, Western values, and Western freedoms were to the devout Sunnis of the Arabian Peninsula nothing less than the keys for opening the yawning gates of Gehenna.

The Communists, ever opportunistic, had sought to capitalize on this clash of cultures. But all they had succeeded in doing was speeding up the dissolution at the interface between East and West. The paradox of Marxist-trained and -armed radicals regarding themselves as Islamic fundamentalists had become inevitable the moment the Soviets had made the decision to inject themselves into a conflict they could resolve no better than could the timid democracies of the West.

Rivas, fresh from covering the long guerrilla war in Afghanistan, knew at first hand how badly the Russians had mishandled matters.

But what about the West? Rivas wondered. As a man with a foot in both the West and the Third World, he had seen his own country fail just as badly. The last real effort to protect the small, admittedly imperfect, beginnings of democracy in Southeast Asia had been brought down by dissent and fear at home. It was useless to blame the politicians for being timid. Democracies did, indeed, get the governments they deserved. Rivas had spent the years since Vietnam roaming the world and he had become accustomed to seeing the West, with the United States as the prime whipping boy, retreat from confrontation after confrontation. The Cold War that Cole had loved so was still going on, and probably would for decades. But the unnamed war, between the oil-dependent West and the Third World, was being lost. . . .

Or so thought Calder Davis.

So he has done something about it, Rivas thought.

Is he really so wrong?

It shocked him as he realized that he was uncertain. There would always be questions about ends and means. That was the philosophical destiny of man. A Muslim would laugh at his crisis of conscience. *The spilling of blood was not the crime,* he would say, *that Western man has made it. You fight wars and are shamed by them. We fight the* jihad *and know that we will enter Paradise.*

So was Calder Davis wrong?

Rivas shut his eyes and tried to block out the sound of the haranguing *mullah* that filled the tiny room.

Cole, he thought, was far more the warrior than I. Would he have thought Calder Davis wrong if he had known the entire plan? Cole hated what he called 'drift'—the tendency of men to watch dangers coalesce and develop because when there was still time, no action was taken. So had Cole actually been killed to protect an idea he would have eventually embraced?

One more paradox, Rivas thought, that can never now be resolved. But of one thing he was certain: there was just enough of the Third World in Michael Rivas to make it impossible for him supinely to accept Calder Davis's prescription for a brave new world.

The fire out on the perimeter had burned for several hours. Apparently no effort had been made to extinguish it and even now, in the small hours of the morning, Rivas was aware of an occasional flare of bloody light sputtering in the darkness. When he stood on the table and tried to see the source, he could not, because his view was blocked by the silhouette of some low buildings beyond the air-base runway.

Outside his door he heard voices speaking in Arabic: one voice a woman's. He dropped to the floor and placed himself near the door to listen. The woman—and he was almost certain it was Dr. Shallai speaking—seemed to be arguing with the Corpsman standing guard. Her voice rose in anger, grew peremptory. The reply was argumentative and plainly colored by the tribesman's contempt for women.

The heated discussion continued for several minutes before Rivas could begin to detect a reluctant acquiescence in the Corpsman's tone.

Presently the door was opened and Dr. Shallai stepped into the room. She carried her medical bag. The armed Corpsman followed her closely. Her eyes were wide with unspoken warning and she silenced Rivas with an almost imperceptible shake of the head.

'Mr. Davis has sent me to treat your head wound, Mr. Rivas,' she said crisply. 'He wants you to be ready to travel this morning.'

Rivas accepted her statement without comment. Calder Davis had taken no notice at all of the half-healed injury and he doubted that he would have sent a doctor at this hour of the night.

During the journey from Salalah he had become intensely aware of this woman, and sensitive to her personality. It was a rare rapport that he had felt only seldom in his life. He knew almost certainly that she was lying now, and that she had come to him not to give help, but to ask it.

Amira turned to the Corpsman and spoke to him in Arabic. The man shook his head brusquely. He stood firmly, the Uzi slung over his shoulder on its webbing, but the muzzle pointed steadily at Rivas.

With an anger that Rivas felt was more feigned than genuine, Amira opened the medical kit and took out a stoppered bottle of disinfectant, a gauze pad, and some cotton swabs and a scalpel.

'Please sit here under the light,' she said.

Rivas sat on the edge of the cot, his legs gathered beneath him. The woman's tension was so great her slender hands were trembling. She spoke again to the tribesman and he stared insolently at her and then reluctantly moved so that his shadow did not fall on Rivas. This placed him to the left of Amira Shallai. The hand resting on the trigger of the Uzi was on a level with Rivas's eyes.

Amira looked directly at Rivas. 'I am sorry,' she said carefully. 'I shall have to use the knife.' Her hand closed over the scalpel and she brought it toward Rivas's head. She paused and the blade shook slightly. Her knuckles were white.

'Are you ready, Mr. Rivas?'

Rivas flexed his right hand, remembering. It would have to be right the first time. There would probably be no second chance. 'Go ahead, doctor,' he said softly.

The Corpsman leaned forward for a better view of the operation.

Amira half turned and brought the blade down, slashing across the back of the man's hand on the weapon. Rivas had a flashing impression of blood spurting and he heard the man's grunting suck of pain, but he was already in motion, bringing the edge of his hand across the man's throat in a blow that paralyzed his larynx and dropped him to his knees, gasping for breath.

Rivas was on his feet, and as the man dropped he struck a second blow, this one across the temple. The Corpsman sprawled facedown on the floor, his hand spattering blood on the gritty cement and smearing his weapon with red.

Amira stared at Rivas with wide, glowing eyes. She looked revolted by what they had combined to do to the tribesman. But almost at once she was in action. She knelt and felt the man's carotid pulse. 'He's still alive,' she said, and reached swiftly for her medical kit. She took from it a syringe and an ampoule of phenobarbital. She filled the syringe, stripped back the man's bloody sleeve, and injected him with the drug.

'Help me lift him,' she ordered.

Rivas lifted the man and laid him on the cot.

Amira immediately began to treat and bind the man's wounded hand. She worked quickly and Rivas appropriated the Uzi, checking the magazine and wiping the blood from the stock with the cuff of the man's desert twill trousers. Behind him, the videotaped *mullah* continued his endless admonitions to the faithful.

Amira straightened, replaced the syringe and scalpel in the medical kit, and said in a hushed voice, 'You did that very efficiently.'

Rivas detected a note of revulsion in her voice. He did not resent it. Nor did he question any of what had happened. It had been obvious, almost from the first time he had seen Amira Shallai, that she was far from an ordinary woman. At the moment he did not know why she had come to set him free, but it was enough that she had done so. Everything else would fall into its proper order. But they had to get out of this place instantly. It was evident that EQ Station was not a part of the NPC's military establishment. Rivas had seen only a few armed Corpsmen. It was implicit in what Calder Davis had told him about the coming assault on the embassy in Riyadh that almost all of the NPC's soldiers were with Jeb Collingwood's Brigade. They were hardly needed here. The desert and a few perimeter patrols were enough to keep intruders out and anyone Davis chose to detain in.

Rivas said, 'I want his jacket.'

Silently, she helped him strip the NPC uniform off the unconscious tribesman. Rivas's skin crawled a bit as he slipped his arm into the bloody sleeve, but he needed the coat with its peaceful rainbow flashes in case they should be seen.

Amira said, 'They shot down a Russian airplane.'

Calder Davis can't go back now, Rivas thought. Not that there was ever a chance that he would even consider retreating. He had too much invested in his plan: too much time, too much money, and too much absolute conviction.

'Let's get out of here,' he said. The base was studded with abandoned buildings. One of them would do for a place to hide and plan.

He took Amira's arm. Suddenly she was shaking as if with a fever. 'Don't fall apart now,' he said harshly.

'You don't know—' she breathed. 'You have no idea what is being done here.'

'I know what,' he said. 'I don't know *how*.'

'I do know,' she said. 'We must stop it.'

'That may take some doing,' Rivas said. 'Is there a communications center? They must be able to broadcast more than that.' He glanced back at the television set.

'Yes. It is near the hospital.'

'That's a start,' he said. 'Let's move.' He looked down into those incredible, dark eyes and essayed a brief smile. She was frightened and repelled by what she had seen and done. But she had *done* it, by God. This was a brave woman who could be counted on to do what must be done. In his lifetime he had known plenty of women, but never one like this one. 'We don't run,' he said quietly. 'We walk. Slowly.'

With the machine-pistol slung over his shoulder in the manner of the few Corpsmen he had seen, and with Amira Shallai at his side, Michael Rivas left the empty barracks and struck out across the drifted sand toward the perimeter of EQ Station.

38 Washington, D.C./Moscow

On the large screen of the hot line's new television link, the face of Ivan Kirilovich Suslov, President of the USSR, looked pallid and puffed with unhealthy fat. He had been in poor health for years. His eyes were small and suspicious, half hidden under brows that grew together over the short, thick nose.

President Loomis, who sat flanked by Raymond Turner and General Lescher, hoped that the camera did not do to his appearance what it was doing to Suslov's. Loomis had become accustomed to projecting a favorable image on television: it was this that had caused him to call for the new link's activation. But looking now at Suslov, Loomis wondered if he had not made a mistake. There was nothing in the Soviet politician's appearance that elicited trust. Quite the contrary. Let the impression at the Moscow end of the link be more reassuring, he thought fervently.

Behind Suslov he could see two men in uniform. One was Marshal Antonin Gerstman, the Minister of Defense. The other was unknown to him. Loomis spoke quietly to Raymond Turner. 'Who is the man sitting with Gerstman?'

'That is General Pavel Kazin, Mr. President. Chief of the Military Intelligence Directorate—the GRU,' Turner said, referring to the file supplied him by State's Department of Research.

Not a reassuring presence, Loomis thought, wondering how many other military advisers sat out of camera range to coach—or to supervise?—the conduct of this conversation.

The President spoke into the microphone under the television screen. In a soundproof room off the tiny television studio two interpreters, one instantaneous and the other more deliberate, heard his voice and watched his expressions on one of the two small screens in their enclosure. The instantaneous translator finished speaking to his opposite number in the Kremlin only seconds after the President fell silent.

'Good morning, Comrade President Suslov. I am sorry that it has been necessary to make this call so early in the morning. I hope it has not inconvenienced you.'

Suslov spoke abruptly and at length. The interpreter's voice issued from the speader grid above his image.

'I am a worker, Mr. President. A worker does not count a morning's sleep of great value. I am ready to sacrifice much more than that in the interests of détente. I use the word, Mr. President, even though it is apparently out of fashion in your country. And I am pleased that you reply to my message of yesterday face-to-face. There is a Russian proverb that says: "Mouths lie, but eyes do not." '

Damn the man, Loomis thought. Perhaps it was the translation process that made him seem ponderous and opaque, but one had to suspect any salutation that carried an accusation of duplicity couched in some obscure Russian proverb. And that absurd reference to being a worker had a Stalinist overtone that hadn't been popular among Soviet rulers since the 1950s. Whenever Suslov was going to be difficult, Loomis had been warned by Sovietologists, he fell into the habit of using outmoded clichés and cuzz words.

Apparently Suslov was going to take the position that this call, originated by Loomis, was the answer to his, Suslov's, first, and threatening, message. He was ignoring the evasive reply he had received by teletype. In this way he could assume a certain dominance, as though the President of the United States were replying to an indictment.

'Mr. Suslov,' Loomis said, 'I am speaking to you now because we have confirmed the information about Ibrahimah given us by your ambassador, Mr. Baturin. I want you to know at the outset that we are as concerned as you about the NPC activity—' he had been going to say 'at Ibrahimah,' but he amended it to '—in Arabia.' It was very possible that either Soviet satellites or the KGB had uncovered evidence of the attack on Riyadh. 'I must now tell you that we have taken your report so seriously that we are dispatching a force of Marines from the U.S.S. *Nimitz* to investigate.' Chew on that, you bastard, Loomis thought.

The scene in the Kremlin erupted immediately into angry and agitated discussion, none of which could be heard by the translators. More uniforms appeared and Raymond Turner identified Admiral Rodion Surovy, the Commander of the Soviet Navy, and General Boris Batrayev, the newly appointed Chairman of the KGB.

Suslov faced the television monitor. The bushy brows were lowered furiously over the small, hard eyes. 'It appears, Mr. President, that you have unilaterally chosen to use our warning—which we offered in good faith—as an excuse to use your troops to intimidate our Pan-Arabian Socialist brothers. That is not the action of a friendly nation, Mr. President. You are risking the peace.'

'I am sorry you feel that way, Comrade President,' Loomis said neutrally. 'It is not our intention to act in a provocative manner. But our decision to dispatch the Marines to EQ Station is not negotiable. We will, of course, present both our findings and our recommendations to the United Nations. We are calling for an immediate meeting of the Security Council.'

There were more consultations among the men with Suslov, and this time—Loomis thought—it was possible to overhear some of the discussions. The translators' voices came through the speakers: 'Comrade Suslov has asked Marshal Gerstman if, in his opinion, the Red Banner Battle Group requires reinforcement. Marshal Kazin says that Red Banner is capable of inflicting annihilating losses on any force intending to attack it. We are unable to hear Comrade Suslov's next question. It is addressed to General Batrayev. Batrayev states that in his opinion the New Peace Corps in Arabia is not, as claimed, an independent international organization, but a clandestine arm of the CIA. Admiral Surovy suggests that Naval Landing Force troops be flown immediately to the Red Banner Battle Group. Marshal Gerstman states that in the opinion of the General Staff it would be better to mobilize a strike force of Red Army airborne troops from the occupation forces in Afghanistan.'

Suslov turned and said, 'This matter is far too important to be the subject of futile argument in the Security Council, Mr. President. We both understand how impotent that organization has become. If you and I cannot come to some mutually agreed solution, I fear matters may swiftly escalate beyond our power to retrieve the situation.'

'I agree, Comrade Suslov,' the President said. 'That is why we have chosen to take quick action. The New Peace Corps is *not*—and has never been—an arm of the United States government, clandestine or otherwise. But if any action taken or proposed by that organization should become a threat to the peace, we feel we have a special responsibility to correct it. That is why we have—regretfully, Comrade President, but firmly—concluded that we should act on your warning and investigate the activities at EQ Station.'

Suslov's frown grew deeper and more suspicious. 'It is not in the national interest of the Soviet Union that American troops establish a foothold on the Arabian Peninsula, Mr. President. We do not accept the imperialist contention that the region is closed to us and that the Persian Gulf is an American lake.'

Loomis remained silent for a moment, weighing Suslov's words. Behind them, as behind all of this and similar disputes, lay the specter of a cutoff of oil. Always *oil*. He thought of the last view he had had of a smiling Calder Davis telling him how swiftly American and European synfuels facilities could expand '*. . . if, Mr. President,*' he had said, '*there were no Arabian production. . . .*' The old man was really intending to make the West bite the bullet if he could. And from what Loomis had learned, there was a better-than-even chance that Davis could do exactly what he said he could do.

The problem was that the Russians now felt they had an interest in the subterranean treasure in Arabia. They had carefully schooled and equipped the revolutionaries who had driven out the Saudi princes. They must believe, Loomis warned himself, that the oil of Arabia was within their grasp. No wonder they were reacting like spurred mules at the thought of American Marines in the peninsula. God, Loomis thought, if they only knew what Calder intended— Or *did* they know? No, it was impossible. If they knew, they would act.

Suslov's next statement, however, did not ease President Loomis's anxiety. The Russian laid a thick, clenched fist on the table before him. The body language was plain. 'We have reliable reports, Mr. President, that the Israelis are mobilizing. Troops are concentrating in the Negev, threatening both the Jordanian border and the Arabian Peninsula. Have you any similar information?'

'Unconfirmed reports only, Comrade President,' Loomis said heavily. It had been too much to hope for that the Soviet intelligence services would have missed the movements in Israel. Damn the Jews, Loomis thought. Why now? Why couldn't they have consulted with us? But he knew the answer only too well, and it did nothing to ease his feelings of guilt. The Loomis administration had never been anything but equivocal on matters touching Israel.

'The Soviet government remembers very well how Israel and the West entered into collusion at the time of the Suez Crisis. We cannot tolerate such a thing again.'

'I remind you, Comrade President,' said Loomis, 'that it was the refusal of the United States to countenance the attack on Egypt that ended it.' To add force to the thrust, he said pointedly: 'The Soviet Union was engaged in its own misadventure in Hungary at that time.'

Suslov flushed angrily as Loomis's words were translated. 'I do not need a history lesson, Mr. President. We are dealing with present realities. The government of the Soviet Union will not accept an American military presence in the Empty Quarter or anywhere else in Arabia. That is our final word on that problem.'

Loomis drew a deep breath and said coldly, 'The Marines will investigate EQ Station, Comrade President. You made that inevitable the moment you shared your spy-satellite information with us. We have, however, no intention of establishing a permanent military presence in Arabia. We did not do it when the Saudis ruled there, and it would have been far easier than now, and we will not do it in the future. I remind you that the Pan-Arabian terrorists you regard as the legitimate rulers of the country are holding one hundred Western hostages. In that matter the Soviet Union has not been forthcoming. You have refused to condemn their actions and there is every evidence that your government has not been unfriendly to the criminals. Therefore we reserve the right to act in accordance with our national interests.' Easy, Vinnie, he told himself. Don't let temper escalate this thing out of sight. There are nuclear forces out there. He deliberately forced himself to assume a more conciliatory tone. 'However, I can assure you that our Marines will remain in Arabia not one single hour longer than is necessary. And we will abide by any reasonable decision of the United Nations Security Council when the case is put to that body. We even undertake not to veto their decision if it is not exactly to our liking. That is as far as I am prepared to go, Comrade President.'

Suslov's expression momentarily betrayed his consternation at Loomis's statement. The Soviet leader was not accustomed to such firmness from Vincent Loomis.

'We must confer with the other members of our government,' Suslov said. 'I must leave you with the warning that we shall not accept any limitation on our freedom of action, Mr. President.'

The television screen went dark.

Loomis turned to Raymond Turner, who had listened to the conference in silence. 'You know the bastard better than I,' the President said. 'What will he do?'

Turner shrugged wearily. 'Something, Mr. President. He is an activist. When the Polish unions started up again with demands for more freedom of action, he moved in with troops. He is that sort of man and so are the people around him. He listens to the military, but he isn't ruled by them. All that business with Gerstman and Kazin and Admiral Surovy—that was deliberate window dressing. A hand on the six-gun to intimidate you. . . .'

'But will he shoot?'

'Maybe, Mr. President. It depends on the odds and what he has to gain or lose. One thing we must never forget. The Soviet Union needs Gulf oil. Not immediately, but soon. Within ten years they will have to import a third of their oil. And remember, too, that the Politburo is immortal. It plans far ahead.'

'That is hardly reassuring, Raymond,' the President said. 'What happens when their spy-birds pick up on the fighting in Riyadh?'

'If they think it is our Marines, maybe nothing at all. They won't like it and they'll make a terrible outcry about colonialism and American duplicity. But if they think the NPC is doing it—' The Secretary of State shook his head. 'I don't know, Mr. President. I just don't know. This is an entirely new thing Calder Davis has brought into the world. He has either been midwife to a new way of keeping the peace—or a new form of chaos.'

The President asked General Lescher, 'How soon can the Marines be at EQ Station, General?'

'The Marines will arrive there about thirty minutes after sunrise, at 0530.'

A light flashed on a blue telephone near the general's chair. He picked it up and said, 'Lescher.'

He listened, his face immobile. Presently he asked, 'What is the bearing?'

He replaced the handset in its cradle and looked first at the Secretary of State and then at the President. 'Give the bastards credit for good communications,' he said. '*Nimitz* has had an air patrol circling the Russians since nightfall, Mr. President. Admiral Marty now reports *Novgorod* is launching its entire air group for a strike.'

Loomis paled. 'Is the *Nimitz* in danger?'

'No, sir,' General Lescher said. 'The Russian strike force is heading northeast, toward EQ Station.'

39 Riyadh

David Kleinerman awoke abruptly from his nightmare. The foul blanket on which he lay was wet with his sweat and his heart thudded in his chest. He had been dreaming of death, a dream that he knew was compounded of the terrible fears he had forced himself to suppress in his waking hours. Like fragments of some dread-filled motion picture in dreary black-and-white, he saw himself in the littered embassy garden surrounded by burned-out vehicles and scattered records, while the masked demons herded an endless stream of people—all with pale European faces—out of the buildings whose walls were defaced by insulting graffiti, across the grass gone to sere weeds. In line after line they were shot by the demons, whose eyes gleamed like shining stones through the eyeholes of the masks, and as they fell, mouths gaping, bodies white and naked and streaked with black blood, Abou Moussa appeared beside Kleinerman with his mad, hateful expression twisted with triumph to ask Ambassador Jew: 'Where is your country now? Where?'

The dream had many variations and Kleinerman knew them all. Since sleep came these days only in fitful, restless intervals, the cruel subconscious mind began the images at once, so that there was little rest and no release at all for the Ambassador. He knew that part of his mental anguish was fueled by fury and frustration. When he had come to this country he had not imagined that there were, deep in his personality, such racial hatreds. He knew better now. The months of captivity and humiliation had liberated him from the restraints imposed on him by a civilized life. He remembered now his quiet reservations about some of the ideas he had heard discussed with such scholarly decorum at meetings of the ISSG. In that distant—or so it seemed—time he had been an ambitious foreign-service officer who believed that an association with Calder Smith Davis would benefit his career—as, indeed, it had. But he had secretly withheld his approval of the view of the Third World that dominated the ISSG.

All that was changed now. The veneer of civilization was thin on David Kleinerman, and it was growing thinner. The daily mistreatment and insult at the hands of his youthful Arab captors, and the hunger, humiliation, helplessness, and the slow dying of any hope that his country would act to rescue the hostages had taken a severe toll on the Ambassador. A cultured, liberal man had been, over time, turned into a near savage full of fear and hatred and a deep, racial fury.

The dreams were all compounded of these elements, and as he grew physically weaker the dreams grew steadily more vivid until it was difficult for him to separate them from reality.

Had he been taken out into the courtyard to witness brainless executions? Or was that particular dream built of threats and the smaller violence that had become commonplace in the embassy? Last night he had dreamed that his wife was raped and paraded through the building naked and shamed. Was *that* real, or was it only the dream image of his humiliation and defeat? He was certain he had seen the British *chargé* punched and beaten by a young thug wearing a ski mask. He knew that had happened because it was part of the terror of the first day, when the Marine guards had been overrun and the mob had poured into the embassy grounds.

He remembered the flag burnings and knew, almost certainly, that those had been no dreams. And the wanton destruction and defacing of the once proud building, *that* was real enough, even though it happened again and again in the nightmares.

This night's bad dreams had been devastating to Kleinerman, ripping away at his steadily diminishing hope. He awoke with tears on his stubbled face and a sick pounding in his chest. There had been a particularly loud crash of gunfire as the dream figures toppled in the name of Allah the Compassionate and the awakening had left him shaken and afraid.

He sat up and put his naked feet on the floor. The cellar where he had been confined for these months was dark; only the thinnest sliver of light leaked in under the locked door.

He came alert with a start. From outside came a cracking roar as an explosive charge burst somewhere in the embassy building. Immediately there followed the ripping sound of automatic-weapons fire.

He staggered to his feet and went quickly to the door, pressing his ear against it. There was shouting in the corridor and the sound of running men. He could hear faintly the whacking noise of helicopters.

By God, he thought, *they've come at last*! Who were they? Marines, most probably, or some special commando. It didn't matter now, the important thing was that the United States had tired of patience and had decided to act. For the first time in months, David Kleinerman felt a surge of pride and new hope.

There was more automatic-weapons fire in the building. Closer, now. The volley was followed by the stunning noise of concussion grenades.

He heard running steps and a scream of terrified fury as bullets whined, ricocheting from the concrete floor of the corridor just beyond the door.

Someone began rattling the lock on his door and he stepped back, searching the darkness for some object with which to defend himself.

There was no such thing in the rancid cellar. And his hands were still tied, as they had been almost from the first day of his captivity. With the breath rasping in his throat as if from some great exertion, Kleinerman crouched, his eyes fixed on the door. When it opened with a crash, he saw a silhouetted figure backed by a smoky light. The air reeked of cordite.

It was Abou Moussa standing there, as Kleinerman had known it would be. A hundred times in the last months he had been warned that the first act of the terrorists, in the event of an attack on the embassy building, would be to kill the hostages—himself first of all.

The young Arab screamed at him, '*Jew*!' and raised his AK assault rifle.

Kleinerman felt a great and angry regret that there was no time to torture the man, to repay him for the endless days and nights of humiliation and degradation. I will never see him dead, Kleinerman thought savagely, and that is the bitterest insult of all. . . .

The image was burned into the Ambassador's lurching

mind: the robed Arab with his raised weapon, the smoke billowing through the open doorway. Far off there was more gunfire and the shouting of orders and the noise of still more helicopters landing in the embassy compound.

A ripping sound deafened Kleinerman. He vaguely remembered the noises of battle from his experience of combat in Korea, but all that he heard now was strange. The rate of fire of the new weapons transformed battle into a continuous roar. The human ear was unable to distinguish the individual shots being discharged. The Arab appeared to fly into shreds, his robe disintegrating into tatters. The Kalashnikov he carried came spinning into the room to clatter at Kleinerman's feet, its stock splintered and its mechanism gouged and pitted by bullets.

Then another figure replaced the exploded man, who seemed to have melted into the concrete floor. This was a taller man wearing a beret and a uniform that Kleinerman could not recognize in the uncertain light.

'Ambassador Kleinerman?' The young soldier spoke English with the flat, harsh cadences of the northeastern United States, and to David Kleinerman it was the most beautiful sound he had ever heard. 'Ambassador Kleinerman? We've come to take you and the people out of here, sir.'

On the ground-floor level of the embassy building, where Jeb Collingwood had set up his command post, Cory Conant stood amid the ordered confusion of his headquarters communications section.

The soldier at one of the field radios pushed his headset up onto his temple and reported, 'Sir, they're still broadcasting that warning from EQ Station. They've been repeating it every six minutes.'

'Let me hear it,' Conant said. He slung his automatic weapon over his shoulder and squatted by the radio, a headset held to one ear.

'—all foreign workers are advised to evacuate coastal areas at once. Move now and do not stop until you are at least twenty-five kilometers from the coast. Workers in the Ras Tanura Peninsula must close down operations before 0600 hours today. All personnel in Al Qatif, Al Zahran, Al Kubar, and in the Mina al Ahmadi district of Kuwait are

warned to depart for safer areas immediately—'

Conant listened, perplexed and frowning.

'They are covering all the civilian broadcast channels with that, sir,' the communications clerk said. 'In English on this one, in Arabic on the others. They've had a *mullah* on the bloody telly since before midnight. He's saying about the same thing, only in fancier language. Why is EQ doing it, sir? The Brigade isn't going to hit the oil fields.'

Conant said, 'Take it down, I'll show it to the general.' He stood looking at the ordered military confusion that permeated the embassy.

It was still dark outside, but there was a hint of dawn in the sky to the east. Some of the windows were boarded over, repaired carelessly by the radicals who had occupied the building all those months ago. But others remained intact, and through them Conant could see the grounded helicopters clustered everywhere on the embassy grounds.

Outside, on the concrete plaza in front of the main building, an assembly point for rescued hostages had been set up and medical teams were at work on the bewildered and frightened civilians who were being found and herded toward the aircraft in small groups.

Earlier, Conant had spoken briefly to one of the embassy Marine guards, an eighteen-year-old private who had kept sobbing and insisting that he had tried to protect the grounds when the mob overran the walls. It was as though that moment had been yesterday and not almost two hundred days ago.

So far, Conant thought, the operation had gone exactly as planned, swiftly and smoothly. Three of the hostages, one of them the West German Ambassador's assistant, had been wounded. They had been rushed into one of the helicopters and flown immediately to the airport north of the city, which was now firmly under Brigade control with Peter Stuart in command of the troops there. Other hostages were being collected from the upper stories of the embassy and almost all firing had stopped. The Brigade had taken a dozen minor casualties, and four soldiers were dead. Their bodies lay in a row in the plaza outside with a single trooper standing guard over them.

The Pan-Arabians—or the terrorists, as the hostages called them—had been shot to pieces. They had been given no opportunity to surrender and they had taken very nearly one-hundred-percent casualties.

The communicator at the radio handed Conant a message form with the puzzling broadcast from EQ Station. Conant said, 'Tell Stuart we will be loaded and on the way to him in ten minutes. The general wants us out of here right now.'

'Yes, sir,' the soldier said and turned back to his radio.

Conant moved through the teams of demolitions experts who were now carrying their heavy charges into the building and down the stairs toward the basement levels. Collingwood intended to level the embassy once all the hostages were out. He did not intend to leave the building to the enemy.

Conant found the general with his intelligence officer, a Frenchman from the Foreign Legion named de Lattre, a middle-aged officer from a family with a long military tradition. De Lattre was saying: 'Very little activity in the streets, *Général*. A few street gangs with weapons. We've surprised them, filthy bastards. The National Guard have kept to their barracks.'

Conant was not surprised to hear it. The National Guard consisted exclusively of Bedouin troops whose loyalty had been to the House of Saud. Since the revolution they had been persecuted and harassed and confined to their living areas near the royal palace. Many had deserted, melting back into the desert. Others had been killed trying to escape the country, seeking vainly to follow their princes into exile. Conant was reminded sadly of what had happened a decade earlier in Iran, where the Shah's guards, the Immortals, had been abandoned by their royals and left to face the revolutionary mobs leaderless. Soldier's pay, Conant thought with a touch of bitterness. Those who most fiercely demanded loyalty seldom gave it.

Collingwood looked up and said, 'What do you have, Cory?'

Conant handed over the message form. 'EQS has been broadcasting that since before midnight, General.'

Collingwood read the penciled lines and frowned, 'I don't understand this. Jean-Claude?' He passed the form to the intelligence officer.

'I know nothing of this, *Général*,' the Frenchman said. 'Perhaps they are producing a little disinformation to confuse any response to us here.'

'Maybe. But let's find out.' He led the way through the

crowded, littered space to the men at the radios.

With that unfailing ability to remember the names and faces of his men, Collingwood touched the radio operator on the shoulder and said, 'It's Samson, isn't it? See if you can raise EQ Station for me, son.'

'Yes, sir, General.' The young soldier spoke into his headset, waited, and spoke again. 'I don't get anything in reply, General.'

'Are they still broadcasting the same message?'

'Yes, sir. Every six minutes, regular as clockwork. It must be on a closed-loop tape.'

There was a momentary flurry among the soldiers in the embassy rotunda. A young Corpsman trotted up to Collingwood, his battle-painted face wreathed in a smile. 'I found the Ambassador, General. The medics have him.'

'Good man,' Collingwood said. To Conant and de Lattre he said, 'Keep trying to get through to EQS.' He glanced at his watch. 'I want to be out of here in five minutes.' He turned and followed the man who had rescued the Ambassador.

David Kleinerman drank the hot brew hungrily. He was surrounded by soldiers in what could only be New Peace Corps uniforms, and he was at a loss to know what to make of it. They were as laden with weapons and baggy pockets filled with ammunition as any field soldiers he had ever seen, but their battle dress bore the familiar rainbow flashes on the sleeves. He could hear a half-dozen Western languages and accents and even a few Eastern ones. The medic who was examining him was plainly a Pakistani.

'Ambassador Kleinerman?'

Kleinerman looked up from where he sat on a canvas equipment bag to see a man as burdened as any of the others with weapons but wearing a Silver Star on his red beret.

'I'm Collingwood,' the soldier said. 'Thank God you're all right, sir.'

For a moment Kleinerman surrendered to his confusion. The only soldier named Collingwood of whom he had heard was the general who had commanded the RDF in Egypt and who had been retired by the President after public criticism of the Loomis administration's reduction of his command.

The general smiled briefly. His teeth shone white in the

flash-painted face. 'Yes, Ambassador. I'm *that* Collingwood.'

'Forgive me, General. I don't think I understand all this. I'm grateful for it, believe me. But I don't understand it. I thought you had been retired from the Army.'

'So I was, Ambassador,' Collingwood said evenly. 'This unit isn't a part of the army with which you are familiar. This is a special field force of the NPC.'

Kleinerman stared, first at the general and then at the intense military activity around him. This was no tiny band of soldiers. It was a military organization of considerable size and obvious battle efficiency. He still could see in his mind the tatters of bloody rag and flesh and bone that were all that remained of the arrogant Mohammed Musayid ibn Sulayil, who had been taught his radicalism in America, his Marxism in France, his terrorism in Libya, and his final sad lesson in the cellar of this building. These men might be members of the New Peace Corps, but they killed as mercilessly as any soldiers he had ever known. Still unnerved by his rescue and by the apparent confusion all around him, he wondered if that hateful young man were, in fact, now in Paradise with all the others who had been given their deaths by infidels. In the Name of Allah the Merciful, the Compassionate.

'Ambassador?'

'I'm sorry, General. I'm not myself yet. All this . . .' He gestured vaguely. 'When did the President finally order. . .?'

'The President, sir, had nothing to do with this. Nor, I am sorry to say, did the United States,' Collingwood said abruptly. To the Pakistani medic, he said, 'Can he travel?'

'Yes, General. He's weak, but otherwise in good health.'

'Then get him aboard a chopper,' Collingwood said, and turned away, leaving David Kleinerman staring after him. The Ambassador realized that his talk of the President and the Army had not been well received.

The soldiers were withdrawing now and Kleinerman was hustled along with them out into the plaza. Now he could see the grounds in the gray dawn, and they were as littered and defaced as they had been in his dreams. He saw the corpses of four soldiers in NPC dress and the others, the dead terrorists, many of whom still sprawled where they had been cut down by NPC gunfire. It was as dreadful a scene as he had imagined it might be.

He saw a group of soldiers trailing wires out of the building and fixing electric detonators to them. For a moment he thought of protesting the destruction of the embassy and all that it still contained, but he swiftly realized that all the records he might wish to save had long ago been stolen and displayed by the Pan-Arabian revolutionaries and that nothing remained here of an American presence but the vandalized building. Yes, he thought, blow the damned thing to rubble and be done with it.

He was lifted into one of the helicopters and found himself between a British embassy clerk and one of the women from the American secretarial pool. She looked half starved. Her face was bruised. Her hair hung lank and unwashed. She sat dazed. He felt a surge of bitterness against the men in Washington who had made the foolish decisions that had left this woman and so many others, himself included, to fall to the mercy of the mobs and terrorists. For nearly two hundred days he—and this woman—had been prisoners, hostages, subject to every whim of cruelty occurring to their captors. The woman was in a state of shock. So must all the others be. So must he himself be. He thought about Vincent Loomis and hated him.

The last of the soldiers were running out of the building. He could see General Collingwood standing near one of the helicopters, the timing mechanism in his hand. The helicopter in which the Ambassador sat started with a whine, the blades accelerating smoothly. The wind of their downdraft set the dry grasses and bits of paper littering the grounds to flying.

Out of the east came a whining roar of sound. An Arabian F-16 appeared like an arrowhead against the brightening sky. Behind it flew another jet of a silhouette unfamiliar to Kleinerman, but obviously a part of this NPC force because even as Kleinerman watched, a missile was fired and the Arabian aircraft dissolved into a fireball, spewing fragments and sheets of burning fuel down into the heart of the city.

Collingwood signaled and the helicopters began to lift off, swinging north as they climbed. Through the open door, Kleinerman watched the aircraft take to the air. Nothing had been left behind but the broken bodies of the young revolutionaries, who had quite probably been surprised when death fell on them out of the early morning sky. . . .

Kleinerman braced himself as his own helicopter lifted off. Only one remained on the ground in the embassy compound. He looked down at the city, a jumble of mingled mud-brick buildings and glass highrises reflecting the brightening sky. Wide avenues and twisted alleys made the earth into a complex pattern that mingled new order with old chaos.

He saw the flashes spearing like searchlights along the streets and then the tall embassy building leaned and crumbled into a mountain of rubble. A dust cloud rose into the still air. Against its dun-colored column of dust, Kleinerman could see General Collingwood's aircraft rising toward the light and falling into line as the machines, in line astern, moved north across the city toward the international airport, where lights flickered like watch fires on the still-dark earth.

40 The Arabian Sea

Kapitan Leytenant Nikolai Andreyev, Flight Commander of the First Naval Air Strike Regiment of the carrier *Novgorod*, looked down at the dark empty sea and then back at the instrument panel of his Yak 56 strike fighter. The navigational aids were all functioning properly and soon he would see the jagged coastline of the Arabian Peninsula. The sky overhead was showing the first blue-gray streaking that announced the coming of dawn. Behind and to the right of Andreyev's aircraft, the strike force flew in a widely staggered echelon.

Andreyev, a young man in his late twenties, felt a dryness in his mouth that was not caused by the pure oxygen he was breathing. In five years as a naval aviator Andreyev had never fired a shot or dropped a bomb in anger. Others had served with the occupation forces in Afghanistan, still others had actually fought the imperialist enemies of the Soviet Motherland in the air forces of the client states. But this was Andreyev's first flight into actual combat and he suppressed his excitement with difficulty.

The briefing officer aboard the *Novgorod* had made dire predictions about what might await the strike force at this mysterious place called EQ Station. 'We have reason to believe,' he had said darkly, 'that the entire base is ringed with ground-to-air missiles. Very probably American Hawks. Therefore it is of the greatest importance that all radar and communications installations be rocketed and destroyed in the first strike. Your next targets will be any aircraft discovered on the ground.'

The pilots of the strike force were all shown the latest satellite photographs of the target, and the line of transport aircraft parked beside the long runway were marked for special attention. Shipboard rumors, which had begun even before the word had come from Moscow to neutralize the

NPC base, were spreading through the fleet. It was said that the transports at EQ Station were intended to carry Israeli parachute troops in a surprise attack on the oil fields of the Gulf coast.

Andreyev raised the polarizing shield on his helmet and craned to see the aircraft on his wing. In the uncertain light the blue-camouflaged Yak was a barrel-shaped shadow outlined against the nascent morning. The two Kuznetzov vectored-jet engines made glowing fans of light under the VSTOL aircraft's high tail.

The weather had turned sharp and clear. The dust from the recent sandstorms in the desert peninsula had been swept from the sky by the cold winds aloft, and Andreyev raised his eyes to look up through the plastic canopy at the last stars of morning. Venus burned like a diamond in the west. At the zenith, the constellations of summer faded in the slowly brightening sky. Andreyev loved flying at this time of morning over the empty sea. The lonely beauty touched some chord of Slavic melancholy deep within him that neither a Party education nor a military career had ever been able to suppress.

For a moment he allowed himself to wonder if he and his fellow pilots were not at this moment the instruments of fate, the cutting edge of a fiery doom that might soon engulf the whole earth.

He shivered and lowered his eyes to the instruments again. The Arabian coast would slip under his wings in less than ten minutes now. This was not the time for fainthearted soul-searching. He was a Soviet Man, he told himself, and he would do what he must do. But he could not restrain himself from one last glance at the fading glory of the night sky, and he allowed himself to hope that he would be alive tomorrow to see it once again.

One hundred and fifty nautical miles south and east of the *Novgorod*'s strike force, the twenty helicopters of the U.S.S. *Nimitz*'s Marine battalion flew toward the same target. Their speed was 180 knots slower than the Yaks from the *Novgorod*, so that as their tracks converged, their actual separation increased.

Captain Richard Mead, Commander of Bravo Company, sat in the rear of the big Sikorsky at the head of a file of his men. Mead was a large, ruddy man of twenty-seven, made even larger by the battle dress, flak vest, and bandoliers of ammunition that hung from his thick, sloping shoulders.

He studied the faces of his men in the red-battle-lighted interior of the vibrating aircraft. They were very young. Their average age was less than twenty. Half of them were blacks—ghetto youngsters who had found a home of sorts in the Corps. None of them had ever been in battle, but Mead was convinced that if it came to that, these men would acquit themselves with honor. Mead was a man who could use such words without self-consciousness. The problem that troubled him was that they were so few. The battalion was seriously understrength and so, Mead suspected, were all the units of the Corps and the fleet. The distaste of the average American for the military life was quite beyond Dick Mead's understanding.

Mead shifted the weight of his flak vest on his shoulders and shoved the steel helmet off his forehead. Through the tiny window in the fuselage directly across from where he sat on the canvas webbing, he could see the brilliant eye of Venus sinking toward the western horizon. The fucking thing was bright as a rock star's diamond ring. He had seen a stone like that on a long-haired guitar-playing doper at a rock concert in Dago once. It must have cost what a Marine colonel might earn in three years.

He glanced down the double line of faces under the pot helmets. He smothered an impulse to smile. Some of the troops were actually dozing. Only one or two of the greenest men looked anxious.

There was nothing to be anxious about, he thought. All the battalion was expected to do was to police up an abandoned air base occupied by a corporal's guard of do-gooders. The idea that the NPC or any of its members might offer resistance to a force of trained United States Marines was ludicrous.

'Captain?'

One of the helicopter's enlisted crewmen had come back from the flight deck.

'The pilot would like to talk to you, sir. Would you come forward?'

Mead shrugged out of his webbing and followed the sailor up the narrow aisle to the flight deck. The pilot, a Navy lieutenant commander, twisted in his chair and said, 'Captain, we just got the word from *Nimitz* that we might run into a Soviet strike force. They're sending us some F-15s for air cover. I'll keep you informed.'

As Mead returned to his seat he felt the helicopter descending. The formation would probably stay right on the water now, at least until the Omani coast came into view.

Russians, by God! The pilot's information had stoked the fires of combativeness in the captain and filled him with a growing excitement. He had missed all the country's recent wars. Korea, the Pacific, Vietnam. Too young for Nam, not even born when the others were fought. All his life he had wanted to be a Marine, and when he became one he found that Marines did nothing but storm ashore at Pendleton in endless invasions of southern California. But this might be something else again. He had heard that the Russians who served in the naval infantry—their equivalent of the Marine Corps—thought mighty well of themselves. Not that anyone actually wanted war, he thought, but what were Marines *for* if not to fight?

He signaled his men to gather around him as he squatted in the aisle. Raising his voice so that all could hear him, he said, 'Now hear this, you grunts. The swabbies say we may run into some Russians.' He grinned at his men. 'I want all of you people to stay cool. But if it turns out they're looking for World War Three, we're just the outfit to give it to them.'

The pilot twisted in his seat to look back into the belly of the aircraft. You didn't have to be crazy to be a Marine, but it helped. He had just told the captain he might run into a fight, and the damned jarheads were cheering.

41 EQ Station

'The first thing she told us was that Dr. Kristof was dead,' Amira whispered. 'There was an accident in one of the underground bunkers ten days ago and four people received a massive overdose of radiation. Dr. Kristof was one of them.'

She shivered in the darkness and moved a bit closer to Rivas, not for warmth, but for human companionship and contact. For almost an hour, ever since they had taken temporary refuge in the abandoned storage building, she had been talking compulsively about the things she had discovered since arriving at the station.

'I had never met Dr. Clevenger before,' she said. 'She is a terrifying woman. Big, nearly six feet tall, with short gray hair and the coldest, cruelest eyes I have ever seen. It was she who told all the medical staff why we had been brought here. They expect thousands of casualties in the oil fields. They have been warning the workers to leave, but not many of them will go. There are still more than thirty-five thousand people in the fields. Maybe a third of them will get out in time and the rest will get huge doses. We medics are supposed to organize treatment for them—afterward. My God, it's horrible—a kind of genocide. . . .'

Rivas put an arm around the shuddering woman. She was exhausted and so was he. He wished more than anything that time would stop long enough for the two of them to rest. There was no hope of that. By now they were both known to be missing, he was certain of that. The military arm of the NPC was represented here by Hadfield and no more than a hundred mercenaries, even counting the South Africans with whom he and Amira had arrived. But that number was more than enough to conduct a search successfully in so empty a place as Ibrahimah air base.

He forced himself to think more practically about what

the Egyptian woman had told him. When it was added to the lecture he had received from Davis, it became clear that the old banker had the means to do exactly what he had resolved was necessary.

The old C-130s Rivas had seen lined up along the main runway were the means. Dr. Clevenger, whom Rivas knew by reputation as the icy scientist and exponent of unlimited nuclear power, had explained the method to the medical staff with cruel clarity. The bunkers contained an isotope of ruthenium which had been suspended in light oil to form an aerosol. The specially equipped C-130s would carry this poison to the north and release it in a corridor twenty kilometers wide from Bahrain to Kuwait. By midmorning today, Rivas guessed, not one barrel of oil would be pumped from the fields of the Gulf coast. At a stroke, Calder Davis would have put the production of half the world's natural crude on hold for five years or more. It would take that long for the fields to be safe again.

'I asked Dr. Clevenger who would fly those airplanes,' Amira said in a thin voice. 'She told me they would fly themselves.' In the darkness Rivas could see faintly the weary confusion in her eyes. 'I don't understand that. How can airplanes fly themselves, Michael?'

'My guess is that they have had inertial guidance systems installed,' he said. 'They may even be the same systems that guide cruise missiles. Calder Davis controls companies that have defense contracts. He could get the hardware necessary without any trouble at all. If the aircraft have been fitted with that kind of system, they would just follow a computer map of the terrain automatically. When the first cruise missiles were tested for accuracy, Amira, they delivered warheads to targets four thousand miles away with a circular error of two hundred yards.'

'They can't be stopped?'

'They could be shot down,' Rivas said. 'But my guess would be that anyone who engineered a hellish scheme like this one would take some precautions against the payloads being wasted. Pressure-activated destruct mechanisms probably. To scatter the material if the aircraft were hit.'

'Are you saying there is no way this horror can be prevented?' Rivas was aware of the outrage in her tone. She was a brave and capable woman—braver and more capable than any he had ever known before. And she was a physician. People tended to forget, in this age of medicine as science, that physicians were healers, dedicated to the saving of human life, not the taking of it.

'There must be a safety system,' he said.

'What does that mean?'

'It means that somewhere on this base there must be a way of communicating with the aircraft—of overriding their guidance programming. There would have to be, Amira. They couldn't risk something going wrong with the program and allowing the airplanes to wander off course and put the aerosol in the wrong place. There must be a range-safety officer somewhere who could take over manual guidance—'

'Listen!' she said.

Rivas got to his feet and went to a broken window of the storage shed. He could hear aircraft engines running. 'They're getting ready to take off,' he said. 'They're really going to do it.'

Against the eastern horizon he could make out the distinctive silhouette of a ground-to-air missile emplacement. Calder Davis had no intention of allowing his plan to be interfered with by any Arabian pilot who might stumble onto it. Or by any Russian, for that matter. Dr. Clevenger had told the medical team that the aircraft that had been shot down had, in fact, been a Soviet recce plane. What the consequences of *that* piece of insanity might be, Rivas could only surmise. The unauthorized presence of Soviet aircraft in Arabian air space surely indicated that the Kremlin was suddenly very concerned about the activities of the New Peace Corps in the Empty Quarter.

Amira came to stand beside him. He could feel her touching him and he was grateful for her presence and her support. It was more than just possible that he alone could do nothing whatever to prevent Calder Davis from carrying out his intention. But with Amira Shallai with him he was not quite ready to accept the inevitable without some protest. After all, Cole Norris had given his life—or had it taken from him—in an attempt to prevent this thing. But the aircraft were already being run up, and even as he stood listening, the first C-130 began its take-off. Time had suddenly begun to run out very rapidly.

Cecil Sawyer, pressed into immediate service at the station

hospital, was in a state of shock. Not only had he actually seen a Russian aircraft shot down and destroyed before his eyes, but he had then been rushed through a briefing by one of the junior medical-team physicians, who raised the hair on the back of Cecil's neck with a swift description of what would soon be required of all the medical personnel at EQ Station.

He had discovered that there were ninety physicians at Ibrahimah, and that each would command a traveling medical unit specializing in the treatment of radiation injuries. His briefing officer, a Vietnamese radiologist named Tran, explained that each team would be provided with a helicopter and a pilot, and that all casualties would eventually be brought back to EQ Station for such treatment as might be necessary but impossible to give in the field.

Sawyer, who had spent his unsupervised moments in a frantic search for Amira Shallai, was staggering with lack of sleep and fright. He had not found her; he was stunned by the information he had been given, and terrified by the knowledge that the NPC—to which he had given his trust and loyalty—was now to be responsible for an act of savagery that would make it—and all who served in it—infamous in every country in the Third World.

Sawyer found himself enlisted in a war, one that he could never have imagined possible even twenty-four hours earlier. Now he understood with a terrible clarity what had passed between himself and Helmuth Reich in Egypt. If Amira was spying on these madmen, she was surely in great danger and it was imperative that he locate her. But it seemed impossible to slip away for even so much as a moment now. The hospital—an immense concrete block building filled with few patients and nearly a thousand empty beds waiting for casualties—was the most heavily staffed unit on the station.

Through the night he had been processed, equipped, briefed, and herded from place to place by the tireless Vietnamese. At about midnight he had received still another shock when he passed swiftly through the single ward that was presently occupied. A few of the technicians, Dr. Tran explained, had been injured in an accident on the airfield. A valve had been inadvertently opened on one of the ruthenium canisters and they had taken lethal doses of radiation. 'Unfortunately,' Tran said, 'Dr. Kristof was overseeing the operation at the time and took the brunt of the discharge. He died last week.'

Sawyer knew Kristof only by reputation as a Nobel laureate for his work in nuclear medicine. The notion that such a man could have been involved in a scheme such as this one was in itself shocking. And to learn that he was dead. . . .

'There is a rumor,' the Vietnamese said, 'that Kristof disapproved of Mr. Davis's plan and that the accident was not what it seemed but a suicide. That is only a rumor, of course.'

Sawyer, despite his distraught state, was perceptive enough to notice that all of the Easterners and Third World nationals working at EQ Station were men and women who had been educated in the West and whose loyalties were to their adopted countries. In almost every case they seemed to feel a genuine aversion—if not outright hatred—for the regions of their births. The NPC had selected them with great care, he realized. Even in his own limited experience of Third World people lay the explanation. The men and women of the undeveloped world had an inbred attitude, difficult to find in the West, about the cheapness of human life. They tended to believe in draconian solutions to difficult problems, and Tran and the others he encountered here were totally committed to Calder Davis's view, which had been explained in the simplest possible terms to Sawyer at his briefing: The undeveloped nations could not be allowed to dominate the West. Even at the cost of great sacrifices, their power must be reduced drastically. It wasn't the oil the NPC intended to neutralize. It was the wealth and power it gave the Arabs that must be reduced. A simple solution to a complicated problem.

The horror, as Kafka had once written, was that there was no horror among these true believers. Even Sawyer, who had never been a racist or a chauvinist for the ways of the West, could discern a certain terrible logic in it. At Kalabishah Station there had been many discussions among the staff members on the dangers of introducing unrestricted wealth and technology into the Third World. They had lived and worked beside a lake caused by an enormous dam that had brought terrible problems to Egypt. Dr. Sforza-Barzani, who had worked in Pakistan, warned repeatedly about the folly of the Western world in permitting nuclear development in any Islamic country. He had seen at close range the efforts of the Pakistanis to combine Libyan money and French technology to build an Islamic nuclear bomb. 'A weapon,' Sforza-Barzani said often, 'that will be used malevolently, heedless of consequences.' He believed the work should be stopped, by force, if necessary. How, Sawyer wondered, was that different from what was being done here?

But it had been one thing to speak hypothetically, among one's peers, about using force to curb Third World power—and quite another thing to see it happening, and to become part of the action.

Cecil Sawyer saw no way of stopping what had already begun here. His vision was limited to finding the woman he loved and saving her from the furious retribution that must surely come. Helmuth Reich had been right. The numerous terrorist organizations would explode in rage against the NPC. Amira might be working for the Americans and so be a special target of Arab revenge. But so would every living man and woman on this base. In his mind he envisioned hordes of Arab terrorists advancing across the desert, green banners waving and swords flashing in the sun.

Sawyer could hear aircraft taking off in the predawn darkness. He moved to a window and strained to see what was happening, but the dark bulk of the communications center blocked his view of the airfield. In the east, the sky was growing lighter. He felt dizzy with fatigue. He said to Dr. Tran: 'I'm out on my feet, doctor. Can we take a break?'

For the last hour Tran had been guiding him through long lists of the hospital supplies, explaining how and where he could obtain what he would need to equip his medical team.

'There is very little time, Dr. Sawyer,' the Vietnamese said reproachfully.

'Five minutes,' Sawyer said pleadingly.

'Very well. Five minutes.'

Tran guided him through the outside doors and into the momentary freshness of the morning. A gray light gave everything a false look of coolness. There were lights on in the block of buildings between the hospital and the airfield. On the roof, a forest of antennas and electronic gear made a tracery against the brightening sky. Sawyer leaned on the concrete-block wall and closed his eyes and tried to calm the inner trembling that threatened to turn his knees to jelly. Amira, he thought, where in hell *are* you? Where, in this vast half-empty complex of mute and confusing buildings, roads, track, and runways, could she be? He was terrified of asking for assistance, helpless without it.

The speaker in the hospital entryway came to life and requested the presence of Dr. Tran inside. The Vietnamese grew agitated and tried to draw Sawyer inside with him. 'The medical teams meet in less than two hours, Dr. Sawyer.'

Cecil Sawyer, not always the quickest of thinkers, realized that he was being presented with what might be his only chance to escape the industrious Dr. Tran.

'Five minutes, doctor,' Sawyer said.

Reluctantly, his companion went to the door. 'Very well, doctor. No more than that.'

As the slender figure vanished inside the station hospital, Sawyer bolted across the empty grounds toward the airfield, not knowing where to look for Amira, but desperately anxious to begin.

Rivas and Amira Shallai stood in the shadow of an abandoned workshop near the airport runway and watched another C-130 turn into position and begin its take-off run.

'You think those aircraft are unmanned, Michael?' Amira asked.

'If they're carrying what we think they're carrying, Amira, they would almost have to be. But they're probably under control for the first part of their flight from over there where you can see the radar antennas. The safety operator would fly them off using on-board television and then lock in the inertial guidance,' Rivas said. 'If they can be stopped, that's where it will have to be done.'

'They must have found the Corpsman in your room,' Amira said. 'Why aren't they searching for us?'

'Maybe we're not first priority targets,' he said dryly. 'Davis offered me a chance to write history, but I suspect the offer has been withdrawn.'

The C-130 lifted off ponderously and began a gentle climbing turn toward the northeast. Another moved to the head of the runway and began to roll. Rivas counted only eight of the clumsy aircraft left on the ground.

'I wonder how a man like Hadfield could get himself involved in something like this,' he said. It was in his mind that the old Trucial Scout officer might somehow be persuaded to offer them assistance. But Amira killed that hope swiftly.

'He is an Arabist, Michael. He loves the Arabs, but he despises the oil and what it has done to this country. He wants it gone and everything the way it was, simple and pure.'

Another aircraft climbed toward the growing dawn and Rivas felt the minutes slipping away. It was six hundred miles to Ras Tanura, in the heartland of the oil fields, half that to the fields of Bahrain and Qatar, which surely would not escape the attention of the deadly programmers. The heavily laden Hercules were slow, but even so they would appear in the sky over the fields in an hour, possibly less if there were southerly winds aloft.

'Amira,' he said. 'Shall we try to stop this? I mean, really try?' He knew that her courage matched—and perhaps overmatched—his own. But it filled him with fear to think of Amira Shallai in a fight. And there would almost certainly be a fight before he could penetrate that building where the safety operator must be working at his console. There was no way it would be unguarded. 'We can try it,' he said, 'but . . . '

'But what, Michael?'

'I don't want anything to happen to you,' he said abruptly. 'Suddenly that is very important to me.'

She looked at him steadily and, it seemed to him, almost tenderly. 'Michael,' she said, touching his cheek with her fingertips. 'I am not what I seem to be. You had better understand that.'

'You can be anything you want to be,' he said. 'If we ever get away from this place alive, I plan to spend a great deal of time convincing you of that.'

'All right,' she said with a ghost of a smile. 'But until we do, think of me as a man.'

'I don't think I can quite manage that,' he said. 'But I'll try not to think of you as a woman I seem to have fallen in love with. Just take very good care that you don't do anything foolish.'

'There is a thing I must tell you. Now or later. You choose.'

'Tell me now. I don't want any more surprises.'
'Is there a radio in there?' She looked across the drifted sand toward the building topped by the radar dishes.
'There must be.'
'I must send a message to Tel Aviv.'
Rivas looked at her for a long moment. 'Well,' he said. 'No more surprises after this one, then.'
'Israel is planning to try and take the oil fields, Michael. I have to stop them—if I can. They must stay out of this *thing*.'
Rivas said, 'I rather think the President of the United States will see to that. But if there's a radio there, we'll find it for you.'
Mossad, he thought. Of course, there must be many Christian Arabs working for Israeli intelligence.
'All right,' he said. On impulse he kissed her lips softly. 'But start composing your letter of resignation.'
He stepped out of the shadow of the building and studied the apparently empty terrain between them and the communications center. Amira watched him, her emotions buffeted with conflicts and a strange sort of joy. He was a good man, a brave man. Possibly even a foolish man. Or were these the mental tremors of a thirty-five-year-old spy who had come nearly to the end of her endurance? she wondered. And then she thought that if things went badly and they did not survive the next hour, it was a good thing to know that this quixotic man loved her.
'Ready?' Rivas asked.
'Yes,' she said. 'Let's go.'

Cecil Sawyer stopped running and told himself harshly that he must try to organize himself. Simply running aimlessly was going to accomplish nothing. Twice in his wandering about among the buildings he had encountered men in NPC uniform carrying weapons, but they seemed intent on their own concerns and paid no attention whatever to him. Even when he heard the public-address system calling all medical personnel to report to the airfield, no one interfered with him. The last of the aircraft had lifted from the runway and a heavy silence had descended over the station. It felt more abandoned and understaffed than ever, though he could see men and women moving about between the supply depots.

The limb of the sun touched the eastern horizon and the sky brightened swiftly. Everything began to cast long, black shadows and the jewel-point of brilliance in the east expanded into a white glare as the sun rose above the dunes.

Ahead of Sawyer stood the large building with all the electronic gear on the flat roof. He did not think he should go there. Too much activity seemed to center on it. But if not there, he wondered desperately, then where?

Two people walked purposefully across his line of vision toward the building he had thought to avoid. In the flat, bright light of the new day, he could not make the pair out clearly. They walked between him and the rising sun. But there was something familiar about the smaller figure, something his subconscious recognized long before he could organize his thoughts. He had watched that figure a hundred times, twice a hundred, on the shores of Lake Nasser. It was unmistakably and gloriously Amira Shallai.

His first impulse was to shout and run after her, but he quickly curbed that wish. If she was in danger in this place, it would not do to call out her name. If she came to harm through his carelessness, his world might well collapse.

Instead, he followed her at a distance. There was a man with her. Now that they had moved out of the direct glare of the sun path, he could see that the man was slender, dark-haired, and armed. He carried one of those hateful machine-pistols that were so popular here—and no wonder, considering what was being done at this station. Was Amira being guarded? Was she under some sort of arrest? He followed, watching, until they paused at the entrance to the building before them.

A Corpsman, also armed, stood at the door. And as Sawyer watched, the man with Amira appeared to have quite carelessly changed the position of his weapon until it was pointing directly at the Corpsman's midsection. Surely, Sawyer thought, I am mistaken. But as he watched, all three—Amira and the two men—vanished inside the building.

Sawyer felt an explosion of alarm. He did not understand what had happened, but he knew that Amira was somehow in great danger. He broke into a run for the building, all of his carefully gathered caution dissolving in fear for the woman he had come to save.

Standing near one of the supply buildings, his Uzi slung over his shoulder, the man called Grant watched first Rivas and the unknown woman and then Cecil Sawyer disappear into the communications center. He had been using small field glasses and he had recognized Rivas earlier. He had considered simply gunning him down with the Uzi he had been issued by the British colonel who had assigned him to interior guard duty, but that would have made escape difficult.

Grant had not become a skilled professional assassin by taking targets in situations where the line of retreat was awkward. He thought briefly and sourly about the attempt he had botched on the Van Wyck Expressway. If it hadn't been for the target suddenly and inexplicably throwing himself to the floor of the taxicab, all this traveling would not have been necessary. But Rivas had just come out of a guerrilla-war situation. Grant understood better than most how preternaturally sharpened one's perceptions become in such an environment.

Well, it didn't matter now. Rivas had gone inside the building and Grant could not have planned a better killing ground himself. There was a helicopter on the ramp, a Loach, that he had spotted on his arrival. It was used for perimeter patrols, but it would serve to carry Grant out of this place as soon as his contract was fulfilled. He had been afraid that he would have to steal a vehicle and go overland, and from what he had heard of the Raschid from the other mercenaries, he had not been looking forward to the journey. Knowing the little Loach was available raised Grant's spirits considerably.

He closed the field glasses, put them into the pocket of his NPC jacket, and began to walk across the open ground toward the communications center. He did not unsling the Uzi. It was not his preferred weapon. Instead he reached down and removed the commando knife from the sheath strapped to his calf and slipped the blade up into his right sleeve.

Then he strolled casually up the sandy walk to the door of the building, opened it, and stepped inside.

42 Mexico, D.F.

'It is nine o'clock, Mr. Holt,' the Russian said in precise English. 'I suggest you remain here overnight and we will continue our discussions in the morning. I would stay with you, but there is an embassy reception and the trade attaché must put in an appearance. These Mexicans expect it.'

Isaac Holt regarded the elegantly dressed man coldly. Dmitri Ulanov was not known to Holt personally, but he was familiar with his dossier. He had been the KGB *rezident* in Toronto for five full years before being posted to the Soviet embassy in the Mexican capital. The day's bargaining had been trying, but Ulanov looked as fresh as the moment he had stepped into the safe house.

Holt moved to the window and looked out across the walled garden to the lights on the Avenida Insurgentes. The traffic was heavy, the headlamps of a thousand or more cars turning the street into a river of light that stretched away to the north and the even brighter blaze of the central city. No fuel problems here, he thought, no matter what Calder Davis manages to do. Mexico had more oil than it could use in a dozen decades. Would the government in Washington swallow the bitter brew Davis had mixed and plunge ahead with the vast synfuels plan he had envisioned? Or would the politicians scramble about and beg their way into dependency elsewhere? Well, what did it matter now? That was no longer Holt's problem.

The long day's bargaining had elicited offers of Soviet protection, meaningful work (and as career intelligence officers both he and Ulanov knew exactly what that meant), and finally—after more haggling and argument—Soviet citizenship. In return for these benefits Holt would be expected to spend the better part of a full year being thoroughly debriefed by the KGB and the GRU. He did not fancy that, but as a professional he would have been surprised if Ulanov had not insisted on it.

The *rezident* had been as agile in his bargaining as any bazaar rug-merchant, but both men knew exactly what was expected. As a high-ranking defector-elect, Isaac Holt had ample wares to deal into the negotiations. And as a functionary of the only acceptable sanctuary for Isaac Holt (a deputy director of Central Intelligence would hardly deal with Cubans or Czechs), Ulanov had equally valuable benefits to dangle before an obviously desperate man.

They had all but closed their deal, Holt knew. But there would be any number of meetings and talks here in this safe house on the peculiarly aptly named *avenida*. The KGB was, after all, a bureaucracy—one of the largest in the world. Bureaucracies produced many things: fiats, studies, regulations, intelligence. But a very large percentage of any bureaucracy's product was meetings, endless meetings. If I get away from here by fall, thought Holt, I'll be surprised. But eventually, it would happen, and Isaac Holt would find himself in the Soviet Union, safe from the fury of the President of the United States and from the tenacious ill will of the New Bloody Peace Corps and its brand-new field army. Perhaps, Holt thought, I had better give this man to understand right at the outset that he is not dealing with one of his own rank. Ulanov was a colonel in the KGB. Holt, as an Agency supergrade, had the authority of a general.

'I do not intend to be confined in any way, Colonel Ulanov,' he said.

'That was never our intention, Comrade Holt,' Ulanov said politely. 'You are under no restrictions here. I merely suggested that it might be better for your own safety if you remained here for the night. You are perfectly free to do otherwise. Though frankly, I would not advise it. You better than most should know that the CIA maintains a reasonably efficient station here.'

Holt, of course, knew that Ulanov was quite correct. He imagined that the Company was suffering from shock just now, with the Director killed and the Deputy Director vanished—and probably defecting (they would, of course, suspect that almost at once)—within the space of one week. But the station chief here in Mexico City was an old hand who remembered other, freer times. To Holt's certain knowledge, the Mexico City Station was better fixed for hoods than almost any other. Killing came naturally to many Mexicans. There were few Harry Grants, of course, but the quality of the local recruits was quite good. It would be wise to be careful and not chance being recognized. Shocked or not, the Agency must be turning every trick in the book to locate him.

For a moment Ike Holt allowed himself the luxury of despising Calder Davis. The old man had used him, subverted his loyalty, encouraged him to betray his trust—all in the expectation of a position of power in the lofty regions of that tangled complex of directorships and corporate presidencies he and his friends commanded. Instead of that, Calder had left him twisting and turning in the wind. Die, you old bastard, he thought bitterly. Die soon.

The memory of his last meeting with Calder Davis made Holt uncharacteristically quarrelsome. 'I've been cooped up here all day,' he said. 'And the place smells of cabbage.'

'Well, yes,' Ulanov said fastidiously. 'That is so. The troops tend to like coarse food. I can arrange for you to be taken to a restaurant, if that suits you. I would advise against it, of course. But it is for you to say, Mr. Holt.'

Tradecraft demanded that a potential defector stay immobile under cover until it was possible to move him with heavy protection. But Holt's rank and the American's manner made Ulanov both respectful and angry.

And as a onetime field agent Holt knew perfectly well that it was both unnecessary and rash to leave the safe house. He had gone to a great deal of trouble to reach it and he knew that he should remain in place. But there were many suppressed angers at work under the frigid surface he showed to the world. He said, 'Arrange it, Colonel.'

'As you wish, Mr. Holt,' Ulanov said, and left the room.

Holt returned to the window and stood for a time feeling the thin breeze on his face. He congratulated himself on his success thus far. I'm not done yet, Calder, he thought. And I shall have a long story to tell when I reach Moscow.

At fifteen minutes before ten Isaac Holt climbed into the rear seat of a black Cadillac with civilian plates. Beside him sat a burly, blond brute whose coat bulged obviously over a large-caliber pistol. Holt's professionalism was offended by the easily spotted weaponry. He said in English, 'Do you have to advertise that cannon under your arm?'

'I understand English little,' the blond agent said.

Holt raised his eyes to heaven in silent protest. He tapped a finger on the coat over the pistol.

'Ah,' the man said, and drew it out proudly. It was an enormous Skoda revolver, manufactured in Czechoslovakia. Holt regarded it with distaste. His own preference in weapons ran to silenced small-caliber Colts or PPKs. But it had been years since Holt had actually carried a handgun. 'Put the thing away,' he said as the Cadillac started down the drive through the garden to the gate opening onto the Avenida Insurgentes.

The car joined the traffic flow rolling toward Coyoacán and University City. The night was dark and the city lights seemed to cling to the earth, leaving the sky brilliant with stars. The air was crisp and cool with the smell of pines.

The driver, a slightly built Mexican, drove smoothly and skillfully. The avenue was four lanes wide and the traffic moved swiftly and noisily. The Mexicans were uninhibited in their use of automobile horns. Ahead, beyond the confluence of the Insurgentes and the Avenida Universidad, Holt could see the gaily illuminated mass of the Estadio Olímpico, where some athletic contest was in progress. He eased back onto the deep leather of the seat and began to relax.

Quite suddenly a car appeared beside them, red and blue lights flashing on its roof. Holt sat up abruptly. The white lettering of the *Policía* gleamed on the door. A hooter made his ears ring, even through the tightly sealed windows.

Holt's Russian companion leaned forward, frowning. He shouted something to the driver in Spanish. The driver shook his head violently and began to slow down.

The police car pulled ahead and another, unmarked, car took its place. Inside, Holt could see men in uniform and two civilians in the rear seat. He twisted around to look behind the Cadillac and found another police car there.

The Russian shouted again at the driver and was given a torrent of protest in return. The Cadillac veered toward the curb and stopped abruptly, hemmed in by the two police cars and the car with the civilians.

Two smartly uniformed troopers sprang from the car ahead. They were carrying automatic weapons. From the car alongside, the civilians had alighted. Behind them were two more troopers.

Holt's Russian escort lowered a window and started shouting angrily, protesting his diplomatic status. But the Mexicans were plainly not impressed. One of the civilians thrust his face into the rear of the limousine and said, 'Señor Isaac Holt?'

The Russian shouted for the man to back away. He did not. Instead he reached into his pocket and produced a police identification badge in a black leather folder. Holt never knew whether or not his Russian bodyguard mistook the folder for a weapon, but he saw the blond man pull the great Skoda from its shoulder holster. Ike Holt screamed, '*Noooooo*!' But his protest was drowned by the crashing roar of the large-caliber pistol. The policeman's face disintegrated into bloody meat as the impact threw him back against his companions. In the next instant the uniformed policemen had opened up with their automatic weapons, shattering the glass of the limousine into glittering dust in the light of the police strobes and the men in the rear seat into nothing human.

43 Washington, D.C.

The group of men gathered in the Crisis Room of the White House was somber. It seemed to Peter Gilmartin and some of the others that they had been in this windowless burrow for days instead of merely hours.

The electronic displays lining the walls had all been activated and computer maps of Europe, Russia, and the Arabian Peninsula flickered and shifted as intelligence information flowed into the White House with each change of status.

A bell on the communications console beside the President's chair ping-ed and a voice said, 'We have your call to Tel Aviv, Mr. President.'

Vincent Loomis exchanged glances with Raymond Turner and lifted the telephone. Turner touched a switch on a small speaker and nodded. The Chairman of the Joint Chiefs passed a sheaf of radio intercepts to the President.

'Mr. Abrahams,' the President said. 'I think you must know why I am calling you.'

The Israeli Premier, a *sabra* educated in England, at Cambridge, spoke in beautifully enunciated English reminiscent of Abba Eban's perfect diction. 'Please tell me, Mr. President,' he said.

Loomis's mouth tightened into a frown. Abrahams was not going to make this easy. 'Our intelligence reports that you have massed troops in the Negev near the Jordanian border, Mr. Premier. We further understand that it is your intention to invade the Arabian Peninsula. This operation must not take place, sir.'

Abrahams's cultured voice betrayed no emotion whatever, though every man in the Crisis Room knew that he must be raging at what could only be a leak from a secret session of the Knesset.

'May I inquire how you came by such information, Mr. President?'

Loomis, worn with fatigue and made edgy by the amphetamines he had used to keep himself awake and alert, snapped, 'It hardly matters where the information was generated, Mr. Abrahams. It is enough that it is accurate information and that we intend to act on it if necessary.'

Abrahams said icily, 'I cannot believe that you are threatening us, Mr. President. That would be too grotesque.'

'The situation in the Arabian Peninsula is chaotic, sir,' Loomis said, reining his anger. 'Riyadh is under attack at this moment by troops of the NPC. I know you will find that hard to accept, but it is true. There is no other explanation—'

That statement jarred Abrahams from his composure. '*Troops*—of the *New Peace Corps*?'

Loomis said wearily, 'Yes, Mr. Premier. I must take responsibility for that. . . .' Peter Gilmartin frowned and shook his head at the President, but Vincent Loomis went on grimly. '. . . I have been remiss in my duties and I have been too influenced by the respect and friendship I have had for Calder Davis. Somehow, under our very noses, the NPC has created a formidable military force to do what I and others like me have been unwilling to do for too long. It is our considered opinion that this military force has attacked the revolutionaries in Riyadh in an attempt to liberate our hostages. We do not know yet whether or not they have been successful. But plainly, the forces you have massed in the Negev must not become involved in what could become a general war in the peninsula.'

A button lighted in the telephone before General Lescher and he picked up the instrument, listened, and hung up. He scribbled a note on a pad and passed it to the President: *SR-71 reports the Soviet air group has reached Ibrahimah.*

The President glanced at the pad and nodded. To Abrahams, he said, 'We are sympathetic to your problems, Mr. Premier, and we are prepared to help you meet them. But your troops must stand down immediately. The situation is explosive.'

'I find what you have told me about the NPC shocking, Mr. President,' Abrahams said. 'But it does not alter the fact that Israel's economy is at a standstill and near collapse for lack of petroleum. The radicals in Arabia and elsewhere have decided on their own Final Solution. We cannot stand idly by and allow this to happen.'

'You have my word, Mr. Premier, that the United States will undertake to share with Israel all of our own supplies of energy, from whatever source.' His voice grew steely. 'But if your troops cross Jordan into Arabia, sir, I must tell you that I have given orders to the Sixth Fleet to fly its aircraft against them.'

General Lescher looked expressively at Admiral Thesiger. Both men knew that such an action was beyond the capability of the depleted and aging Sixth Fleet. Loomis was playing poker with Abrahams and the sailor and airman held their breaths for fear that the Israeli would call his bluff.

There was silence on the line. Never before, not even during the hours of the U.S.S. *Liberty* incident during the 'sixty-seven war, had any American threatened to use military force against the State of Israel.

'Avrom,' the President said, using Abrahams's given name for the first time, 'there are Russian air forces in Arabian air space at this moment. You know the intent of the Brezhnev Doctrine as well as I do. If you attack the Arabians, the Soviets will invoke the doctrine and move to protect what they now choose to call a socialist people's republic. It is a no-win situation for all of us. You *must* order your troops to hold in position.'

'I see,' Abrahams said in a bitter voice. 'We are threatened with the Sixth Fleet *and* the Russians.'

'I must have your answer,' Loomis said, inexorably. 'There is very little time.'

'Mr. President,' Abrahams said slowly. 'In recent years there has been a loosening of the ties that once bound our countries together. Now it has come to this.' He paused for several seconds before going on, his voice sad and angry. 'Now you promise us that you will share your resources with us and tell me I must accept that promise and rely upon it for our national survival.'

'The promise will be honored, Avrom. At whatever cost in effort or treasure. I pledge this government to share without stint.'

The reply came thinly and edged with doubt. 'Very well, Vincent. Our troops will stand down for now. That is all I am prepared to say at this time.'

The President replaced the telephone in its cradle and rubbed thick fingers across his eyes.

The button on General Lescher's telephone lighted once

more and he listened, and replaced the instrument. 'Mr. President,' he said. 'The C-130s we saw in the first SR-71 series have left Ibrahimah. They are approaching the coastal oil fields. The Arabians have been confused by the attack on Riyadh. They have made no attempt to intercept the C-130s and the Marines will arrive at EQ Station too late. I'm sorry, Mr. President. There is nothing more we can do.'

44 EQ Station

Calder Davis turned from the bank of television receivers and consoles as Dr. Clevenger, standing beside him, spoke to the three technicians recording the telemetry from the strike airplanes. The inside of the communications complex was one of the few crowded places on the huge reclaimed air base. Three flight engineers split the duty of acting as safety officers for the thirty C-130s which were now more than one hundred miles northeast of Ibrahimah flying at ten thousand feet. The television pictures they were sending back showed the desert terrain below, each landmark coming up onto the gridded screens exactly on schedule. At the moment the men at the consoles had nothing to do but watch. The programs long ago written for the on-board computers of the inertial guidance systems were holding the aircraft on a precisely calculated track and schedule. Helen Clevenger had been concerned lest the high rate of particle emissions from the ruthenium canisters in the aircraft cargo holds cook the delicate innards of the computers in the cockpits. But it was now apparent that this was not going to happen and Dr. Clevenger was relaxed and interested in the drama unfolding before her on the multiple television monitors.

The guidance telemetry unit was located in the center of a concreteblock room adjacent to the chamber containing the station's radio and television facilities. In each of these rooms a looped tape continued to be fed into the transmitters, sending out Davis's warnings to the workers in the oil fields. No one at EQ Station knew whether or not these warnings were having any effect and Davis regretfully considered the possibility that poor Dr. Kristof's original estimate of the casualties to be expected from radiation exposure might be pitifully inadequate. Davis sincerely hoped that this would not be the case, that the oil workers would do as they were being exhorted to do, and put some miles between themselves and the deadly rain of oil and radioactive dust that would begin falling within minutes now.

Besides Davis and Dr. Clevenger and the six technicians at the consoles, there were three armed Corpsmen in the telemetry center and two more, under the supervision of Colonel Hadfield (the only man in the Brigade, Calder Davis mused, besides the general himself, who was habitually addressed by his old military title).

A radio technician hurried into the telemetry center with a message. 'It's from Riyadh, Mr. Davis,' he said excitedly. 'The general's got them all out. They are loading everybody on the transport aircraft now. They'll be back in Tokar by 1500.'

Davis asked, 'Were there many people killed?'

The Corpsman said, 'We lost four men. A few of the hostages were hurt, but none seriously. They are already on the way out in the hospital airplane.' The young face showed a fierce pride. 'It's beautiful, sir. Just beautiful. They taught the ragheads a lesson they won't soon forget.'

'What were the casualties among the militants? Did General Collingwood say?'

'About one hundred percent, sir,' the young man said with ferocity. 'They never had a chance against our people.'

Calder Davis closed his eyes for a moment. Well, Collingwood had warned him months ago that one did not attempt an operation like the liberation of the embassy without overwhelming firepower and a willingness to use it. God have mercy on us all, Davis thought. They were our people and the Arabs should never have taken them hostage. *Would* never have, if we had stood up to our responsibilities long ago. But then one had to concede that this was *their* country, and we should never have come here to loot it. Well, all that was history now and soon this would be the Arabs' country again, and only theirs. . . .

Helen Clevenger, large and homely, moved busily from one console to the next, studying the telemetered rad-counts from each of the airplanes. Nothing she read seemed to disturb her, Davis thought. This was all one grand experiment to her. She was an expert on nuclear waste disposal, but her first—and strongest—love was weaponry. Now she was in her chosen element.

Colonel Hadfield trotted into the room frowning. 'Mr.

Davis, radar shows three dozen aircraft closing on us from the southwest.'

'Whose aircraft, Colonel?'

'No identification yet, sir. They could be Soviets from their carrier in the Arabian Sea. Or they could be part of the *Nimitz* task force. Shall I alert the SAMs?'

Calder Davis drew a deep, slow breath. 'No, Colonel. Tell the crews to take shelter. There is no need for more bloodshed now. We have done our job.'

Colonel Hadfield studied the old man for a long moment. What he was ordering was a lowering of EQ Station's defenses and that distressed the soldier in Colin Hadfield. But he was right. The job was done and Davis saw no need to kill American—or even Russian—pilots. In any case, there were too few surface-to-air missiles around EQ Station to turn back a determined attack. The few batteries spotted about the perimeter had been intended to destroy the lone snooper or an uncoordinated strike by the ragged remnants of the Saudi air force.

'Then I suggest you take shelter, sir,' Hadfield said. 'They will be here very soon.'

Michael Rivas prodded the outside guard before him into the building. Once inside the doors, he stripped the man's weapon and thrust it at Amira. 'Can you shoot?'

'I know how to use an Uzi,' Amira said.

Rivas prodded the Corpsman again. 'Move. Keep your hands at your sides.'

They walked swiftly down the corridor toward the heart of the building and stepped through a door opening into a room filled with electronic consoles. The occupants of the telemetry center heard them enter and turned to stare.

Rivas recognized Calder Davis standing in conversation with Colonel Hadfield. A large, muscular woman stood with the technicians at the consoles. Dr. Clevenger, Rivas thought. He searched the room swiftly for more armed men, but there were none. To Colonel Hadfield he said, 'Remove your sidearm, Colonel. Drop it on the floor and kick it over here.' To the Corpsman whose weapon Amira now carried, he said, 'Down flat on the floor. Facedown, arms and legs spread. *Move*.'

Colonel Hadfield snapped, 'What do you think you're about, you bloody fool?'

Rivas said coldly, 'I gave you an order, Colonel. Your weapon. Now.' He emphasized his words with an upward movement of the Uzi's muzzle. Hadfield unfastened his webbing and lowered his British Army revolver to the concrete floor. He slid it toward Rivas with his foot. 'This isn't going to get you anything, Hayden—Rivas—whatever your bloody name is.'

Calder Davis regarded Rivas calmly. 'You could have been in Riyadh by now, Mr. Rivas. General Collingwood has freed the hostages. You could have seen it happen.'

Rivas returned the old man's pale stare. 'History is where you find it, Mr. Davis.'

Amira said, 'A radio, Michael.'

'First things first,' Rivas said. He pointed the Uzi at the technicians standing with Dr. Clevenger. 'Which one of you is acting as range-safety officer?'

The technicians looked frightened but did not speak.

'Damn you,' Rivas said angrily. 'Who has those C-130s on a string? Answer me now or I'll blow you away where you stand.'

Helen Clevenger spoke harshly but with assurance. 'The spray planes cannot be diverted.'

'You're lying, doctor. Even you would never fly them off without being able to turn them if they go wrong.' He looked at the technicians. 'Well? What's it to be?' He raised the muzzle and fired a burst of four shots at the roof. The noise was deafening in the hard-walled room.

Two technicians ran for their consoles and the third swiftly joined them. Rivas stepped closer to where he could see the banked monitors and the images being transmitted by the cameras in the aircraft. On a computer map he could see the blips moving steadily north along the coast.

'Turn them out to sea,' he said.

Dr. Clevenger moved, but Amira covered her with her weapon.

'Stop there,' she said. 'He might not shoot you, doctor, but I most certainly will. Do not move again.'

'Turn them,' Rivas said. 'And crank in at least five-hundred-feet-per-minute rate of descent.' That course and rate would put all the hot aircraft into the Gulf fifteen to twenty miles from the coast. It was not a perfect solution, but it was the only one. Rivas watched the blips change course deliberately and he felt a loosening of the tightness in his chest. 'Now get away from the consoles,' he said.

One of the technicians, a bearded young man whose face had gone white with fear, turned desperately, 'We can't. If we don't hold them on course, they'll return to their original programming.'

Rivas looked across the room at Calder Davis. The old man seemed to have slipped into a dream state as his complicated plan had begun to unravel. Dr. Clevenger said angrily, 'What he says is true. If they leave the consoles the original programming in the inertial guidance will take over again. You'll have to stand there and guard them. How long can you do that before someone comes in and finds you here meddling?'

At this moment there was a clatter at the door and a young man ran into the room. He stopped, wide-eyed at the sight of Amira holding a weapon on the other occupants of the telemetry center. 'Amira,' he gasped confusedly. '*Dr. Shallai—what—*'

Rivas saw Amira turn to stare at the young man in astonishment. Whoever he was, clearly Amira had not expected to see him here. But before she could speak there was a sound from outside, the unmistakable crumping noise of high explosives. A string of blasts followed, each nearer than the last. Rivas, old memories of battle suddenly awakened, recognized the sound of a stick of bombs falling. He cast away the Uzi, caught Amira about the waist, and rolled to the floor and under a console as the last bomb in the stick struck the building and disintegrated it.

He held her tightly against him, protecting her as best he could against the flash of heat and the crash of breaking masonry. The roof beams bent and collapsed, spilling gravel and dust into the ruined telemetry room. One wall vanished, and with it Colonel Hadfield and Dr. Clevenger. A technician's body, dusty and bloodied, tumbled across the littered floor to end up against a still-standing wall, where it stopped, head curiously cocked to one side by a shattered neck.

A large television console toppled, pinning Calder Davis beneath it, but leaving his head and upper body free, so that he could open his eyes and stare dazedly into the empty sky through the rolling dust of the explosion.

Rivas heard other explosions, farther away, and then the

sound of jet engines as the aircraft that had delivered destruction so swiftly onto EQ Station climbed high into the sky to the north.

In the sudden, stunning silence, Rivas, Amira, and Cecil Sawyer staggered to their feet and looked about them. The building had been eviscerated. From somewhere nearby they could hear the keening scream of a mortally wounded Corpsman. Calder Davis lay on his back, his body crushed beneath the heavy console. Dr. Clevenger had vanished, as had Colonel Hadfield. Rivas, his ears still ringing with the noise of the explosion, stared at Amira, whose cheek was scraped and smeared with blood and dust. Her hair had fallen out of its severe arrangement and hung in long tangles to her breasts.

There was a movement beyond her and Rivas raised his eyes to see the figure of a large man, made ghostly by the white dust that covered him. He crouched in a doorway whose frame had held together. He was dazed as he pulled himself erect, but in his hand was a black shard. Rivas rubbed at his eyes and looked again. The man carried a commando's throwing knife.

Cecil Sawyer was the first to recover his voice and he said something plaintive, almost petulant, as though he did not understand why this should be happening and resented it. He started across the room toward Amira, and as he did so he stumbled on a large piece of nameless debris and fell hard against Rivas.

Rivas felt him stiffen and suddenly sag. As he loosened his hold on him and let him slip gently to the floor, he saw the black hilt of the commando knife, now, by some ugly miracle, protruding from the young man's back. Rivas gave a cry of stunned, animal rage and went to his knees to pull one of the Uzis from under an overturned desk. The man in the doorway stood empty-handed, hunched and swaying, his eyes dark holes in the powdery white that covered him. Rivas jerked the weapon free, leveled it, and pulled the trigger. Nothing happened. The weapon was useless. He slammed the Uzi against the broken wall in frustration.

Like everyone remaining alive inside the ruined telemetry center, the man known as Grant was stunned. But he was determined. From inside his torn NPC jacket he took an automatic pistol. Unsteadily he assumed a spread-legged stance, holding the weapon with both hands. Rivas watched the muzzle waver, then steady. It pointed straight at him across the twenty feet of littered space. Rivas knew with a sick certainty that he could never reach the man in time to prevent the shot that would kill him. He felt a great anger and an even greater sorrow. *The third time's the charm*, he thought. *It all ends here*. . . .

There was a rattle of gunfire. Four bullets struck the wall to the right of Grant, blowing dust and fragments from the concrete blocks. Three more struck the wall to his left. The pistol he held flew from his hands and he slammed back against the wall, the cloth of his jacket welling red. He slid to the floor and sat there, arms extended, hands empty and open, the once menacing mask of his face devoid of expression or purpose.

Rivas watched Amira lower the Uzi machine-pistol to the floor. It clattered at her feet. She was looking at the man who had taken the knife-throw. She went to him, knelt at his head, took his face tenderly between her hands. He was dying swiftly. He was trying to speak and Amira bent her head to listen. Rivas could see that she was weeping. Her hair brushed the dying man's face as she strained to hear what he was whispering. Then presently she kissed him gently on the lips and closed his eyes. She sat back on her heels and looked at Rivas. Tears streaked the dust on her face. Her shoulders shook with a combination of grief and bitter laughter. 'He came to save me, Michael,' she said, her voice trembling.

Rivas looked at Amira and the unknown man. I owe them both a life, he thought dazedly. Then he looked around him at the shattered building and the ruined consoles. We had it stopped, he thought bitterly. We had it made. *Damn* them, whoever they were. . . .

He went to Amira then and lifted her gently. In all this death and destruction, at least there was this one thing to cling to: the warmth of a human touch. Amira pressed her face against his chest and held him with a desperate intensity.

Rivas began to take her out of the wrecked building. She looked at the dust-caked body by the door leaning against a blood-smeared wall. 'Who was he?' she asked, shuddering.

Rivas said, 'He was the man who killed my brother.' He knew he could never prove that, but he knew in his guts that it was so. The choice of the knife, the determination to kill even in this hopeless moment, were the stigmata of the professional, psychotic assassin.

Rivas heard the whine of an approaching jet and his composure shattered. He raised his face toward the white sky and gave vent to his grief and rage. *'That's enough! Aren't you satisfied? Goddamn you, enough—!'* He held Amira fiercely, pressing his face against her tangled hair.

The jet roared low overhead and banked sharply. Rivas waited for the bombs or rockets to strike, but there was nothing but the howling noise of another jet flying over. He looked up and saw the unmistakable silhouette of a U.S. Navy F-15 banking and following its companion away to the northeast. In the distance Rivas could hear the whack-whacking sound of many helicopters approaching.

He stood in the ruins and looked about him. Calder Davis's white face and open eyes stared into the empty sky. The dead seemed to be everywhere. And now, *now*, he thought—here come the machines of war filled with men anxious to help, to save the bloody world. God protect us from the world-savers, he thought bitterly.

A blue-painted Marine helicopter appeared in the jagged piece of sky Rivas could see. It hovered there while a team of Marine commandos began to *rappele* down from the aircraft in a dazzling show of military virtuosity that for some reason infuriated Rivas. 'You're too late!' he shouted at them. 'You're too goddamned *late*, you bastards!'

Then, still holding Amira close against him, he resumed his careful way out of the destroyed building. And away to the north, he knew, a gleaming rain by now was falling on the oil fields of Arabia.

45 Ras Tanura

Kapitan Leytenant Nikolai Andreyev twisted desperately in the cockpit of his strike fighter, trying to catch a glimpse of the American Navy jets that had driven him away from his formation and far to the north.

Andreyev had delivered his ordnance expertly on the targets his briefing officer on the *Novgorod* had specified, and had immediately laid in a course for his return to the ship. But the formation had suddenly been surprised by a squadron of Americans who had split the flights into individual aircraft by the most aggressive and provocative maneuvers. With all their ordnance expended and under orders to avoid contact with any American fighters, the men of Andreyev's force had scattered like geese. The Americans had not fired, but they had herded most of the Soviet airplanes back toward the south, intent on following them, no doubt, all the way to the *Novgorod*.

Andreyev had found this humiliating, and seething with anger he had sought to outfly the pair of F-15s that had taken him as their special target. He had been unable to do this. His tubby Yak VSTOL was no match for the F-15s and he had been forced to run to the north.

Now he had passed his point of no return and he was frightened. He had insufficient fuel to return to the ship and below him lay the Persian Gulf coast of the Arabian Peninsula, territory as unfamiliar to him as the surface of the moon.

The American jets appeared suddenly on his right wing, the two of them flying a tight formation and, insultingly, dawdling along with their speed brakes extended.

The pilot of the lead aircraft lifted his polarizing face shield and stared across the intervening space at Andreyev. The Russian could see that he was grinning arrogantly. He wondered if the Americans knew that he had exceeded his operational range and now could not return to his ship. He wished them dead, smashed to pieces, gone from here.

He looked down at the Arabian coast five thousand meters below. He could see that he was over a heavily industrialized finger of land jutting out into the cobalt-and-turquoise waters of the Gulf. He glanced quickly at the chart on his panel and identified the peninsula of Ras Tanura. It was the largest oil port on the coast and he could see a number of tankers at anchor or moored to the narrow pipeline piers. From this height it was impossible to see more than the ships, the pumping stations, and the buildings.

Several times in his unsuccessful flight from the Americans, he had seen slow-moving multi-engined aircraft flying north three thousand meters below his altitude. He had been too busy fending off the harassing maneuvers of the F-15s to pay close attention, but he thought the large airplanes might be Hercules transports.

The American pilot still watched him insolently. Then abruptly the speed brakes retracted on the F-15s and they sprang ahead of the slower Yak. In an instant, probably in response to a radioed recall from their own ship, the two blue-painted jets had gone to afterburners and vanished, flying straight up into the brassy, cloudless sky. Andreyev was alone.

He immediately began calculating the amount of his remaining fuel and estimating how far back toward the *Novgorod* it would carry him. The result of his computations was not encouraging. To return to the *Novgorod* was impossible. It lay more than fifteen hundred kilometers from his present position. He estimated he had just fuel enough, if he was careful, and if his instruments were accurate, to reach the airport at Riyadh. It was not a pleasant prospect, since he had heard rumors (as had all the men in the fleet) that the Islamic Pan-Arabian revolutionaries had *not* (as the official news from Moscow claimed) consolidated their hold on the country—or even the city. But Andreyev accepted his restricted choices with characteristic fatalism. It was give himself into the keeping of what he hoped was a Marxist government, or give himself to the sea. The desert of the Empty Quarter was not an option. He had seen enough of it on the approach to Ibrahimah to know that.

He turned to the west and began a low-power, fuel-saving

descent. At four thousand meters he could see that the only ships in motion below were outward-bound, at what appeared to be forced draft.

At three thousand meters he noted that the roads leading inland from the coast were black with traffic: cars and trucks and people on foot. In the open spaces between pumping facilities, loading docks, buildings, and oil wells on the small peninsula, nothing moved. He found it eerie.

He leveled off at two thousand meters, nervously searching the sky around him and dreading a reappearance of any American fighters.

A distant shape in the sky just above his level alerted Andreyev. But it was not a returning American jet. Instead it was one of the old transport aircraft he had seen lumbering north along the coast—a C-130 Hercules, an obsolete American troop and cargo transport that was now flown by the pilots of a dozen small countries across the world.

As he watched it approaching his own flight path, he could see a plume of glinting haze streaming from it. Torn between his need to conserve fuel and his curiosity, he watched it carefully. He was struck by the thought that this, and the others like it he had seen previously, was probably the aircraft his briefing officer had warned might be on the airfield at EQ Station. If it was, his duty demanded that he observe it closely and perhaps force it down. There had been talk of collusion between the Americans and the Israelis, and of the possibility that the aircraft that should have been found at Ibrahimah but were not, were to be used in an Israeli move into Arabia.

Andreyev was a conscientious officer, conscious of his duty to the Navy, the Party, and his country. He put the stick over and banked his Yak into a wide turn to come in behind the slow-flying transport.

It was, indeed, a Hercules. He could see that clearly now. But it bore no national markings of any kind, only its drab desert-camouflage paint. And as he circled to move into position behind it, he had the crazy impression that there was no one in the cockpit. The flight deck, or as much of it as he could glimpse in his quick fly-by, was empty.

From a position slightly below and behind it he could now see that there were intricately plumbed ladders of pipes and tubing under the broad wings. It appeared that the airplane had been modified and converted from its original use into a spray plane. A fine haze of oily fog was coming from the nozzles and vaporizing in the slipstream. The spraying gear had been designed for a maximum spread, and as he throttled back to overtake the strange machine more deliberately, his windscreen was suddenly smeared with a light but viscous oil in which minute particles of some grayish metallic substance had been suspended.

All Soviet aircraft were equipped as though for nuclear war. It was Soviet doctrine that any future combat for Soviet forces must inevitably go nuclear. On the instrument panel of Andreyev's Yak there was a dosimeter.

As the oily spray cut down his vision, Andreyev broke away to the west. Because he could not see well through the smeary glass of the windscreen, he went on instruments. And his eyes went wide with horror. The dosimeter needle had moved swiftly from zero into the dangerous-exposure range.

His heart leaping with sudden fear, he raced west, toward Riyadh. Every second that he spent now in the cockpit of his contaminated airplane brought him closer to a terrible death.

There was no understanding in Andreyev, only terror. To increase his speed, he nosed the fighter steeply down, careless of his severely restricted view through the streaked and smeared Plexiglas around him, conscious only of that fearsome needle standing solidly in the red zone.

He was flying even nearer the ground now, forcing himself to attend to the instruments which told him his height, heading, and attitude.

But Kapitan Leytenant Andreyev was a naval aviator, accustomed to flying from the deck of his familiar ship, and his altimeter was set to the level of the sea.

The mean altitude of the terrain between Ras Tanura and Riyadh is 461 meters. That was exactly how much safe altitude above the ground Nikolai Andreyev believed he had in hand when, terrified eyes fixed on his flight instruments, he flew his fighter into the ground on a rocky plateau a mere forty kilometers from the peninsula of Ras Tanura, where the ground, the buildings, the oil rigs, the pumping stations, and the abandoned tankers moored to the pipelines now glistened in the sun with a deadly, but oddly beautiful, sheen.

THE END

THE BALL BEARING RUN
by Walter Winward

As World War II raged savagely across Europe, two civil airlines—BOAC and Lufthansa continued to fly to Sweden along the hazardous route they nicknamed—The Ball Bearing Run. For without the vital supplies of ball bearings from the neutral factory of Lunstrom, both powers knew that their war machines would grind to a halt. Then Alfred Lunstrom and his beautiful niece, Natalie, were suddenly abducted by the Germans—held as the bait in a brilliant attempt to prevent the Allies from bombing the crucial factories of the town of Schweinfurt. . . .

SBN: 0 552 11940 7 £1.50

SEVEN MINUTES PAST MIDNIGHT
by Walter Winward

The compelling novel of a perilous plan to snatch one of the highest-ranking Nazis from Hitler's infamous Bunker. The Horsetraders—a small team of British and American crack-commandos. The Operation—a simple trade-in: life and liberty for double-agent 'Valkyrie' in exchange for vital information about Stalin's post-war ambitions and the location of Germany's hidden gold reserves.

But only when they were actually in Berlin would one of their team—a woman—be able to recognize 'Valkyrie'. And as Berlin crumbled and blazed all around them as the Russians moved in, the Horsetraders discovered that one of their own team was a fanatical Stalinist agent . . .

'Splendidly detailed war-time thriller . . . creates a most ingenious climax'.

British Book News

SBN: 0 552 11551 7 £1.25

THE DEVIL'S ALTERNATIVE
by Frederick Forsyth

"Whichever option I choose, men are going to die." This is the Devil's Alternative, the appalling choice facing the President of the USA and other statesmen throughout the world.

As the gripping story gathers momentum, the reader is transported from Moscow to London, from Rotterdam to Washington, from a country house in Ireland to the world's biggest oil tanker which threatens to pollute the whole of the North Sea. The climax is the most exciting that even this master storyteller has contrived, and the last-minute surprises in the concluding chapters take the breath away.

SBN: 0 552 11495 2 £1.95

THE DOGS OF WAR
by Frederick Forsyth

The discovery of the existence of a ten-billion-dollar mountain of platinum in the remote African republic of Zangaro, causes Sir James Manson—a smooth, ruthless City tycoon—to hire an army of trained mercenaries whose task it is to topple the government of Zangaro and replace its dictator with a puppet president.

But news of the discovery has leaked to Russia—and suddenly Manson finds he no longer makes the rules in a power game where the stakes have become terrifyingly high...

SBN: 0 552 11695 5 £1.75